the Inheritance

Center Point
Large Print

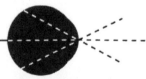

**This Large Print Book carries the
Seal of Approval of N.A.V.H.**

the Inheritance

SECRETS *of the* SHETLANDS
VOLUME 1

MICHAEL PHILLIPS

CENTER POINT LARGE PRINT
THORNDIKE, MAINE

This Center Point Large Print edition
is published in the year 2016 by arrangement with
Bethany House Publishers,
a division of Baker Publishing Group.

Copyright © 2016 by Michael Phillips.

Scripture quotations are from
the King James Version of the Bible.

The text of this Large Print edition is unabridged.
In other aspects, this book may vary
from the original edition.
Printed in the United States of America
on permanent paper.
Set in 16-point Times New Roman type.

ISBN: 978-1-62899-963-1

Library of Congress Cataloging-in-Publication Data

Names: Phillips, Michael R., 1946– author.
Title: The inheritance / Michael Phillips.
Description: Center Point Large Print edition. | Thorndike, Maine :
Center Point Large Print, 2016. | ©2016
Identifiers: LCCN 2016003497 | ISBN 9781628999631
    (hardcover : alk. paper)
Subjects: LCSH: Large type books. | GSAFD: Christian fiction.
Classification: LCC PS3566.H492 I54 2016b | DDC 813/.54—dc23
LC record available at http://lccn.loc.gov/2016003497

This is a series about generational legacies, those that extend in both directions. As I have written these stories, my thoughts have been filled with influences that have come down to me from my own parents and grandparents and ancestors even further back, including their Quaker heritage. And I am constantly reminded of those who have followed, namely Judy's and my sons and grandchildren, and whatever my life has been and will be capable of passing on to them.

More than two decades ago I dedicated books of a series to our three sons. They were young, and my father's heart was filled with visions of the years ahead we would share together. Now they are grown men. Whatever legacy a father is able to pass on to his sons looks much different to me at today's more mature vantage point from which to assess life's unfolding and progressive journey—both mine and theirs.

Therefore, to our three sons and the men of spiritual stature they have each become, I gratefully and lovingly dedicate the volumes of this series.

---

the Inheritance

to
Patrick Jeremy Phillips

CONTENTS

Part 3—November 2005

Part 4—Winter, 2005–2006

Part 7—October 1953

Part 8—July 2006

Whales Reef Tulloch Clan Family Tree
(Descended from Highland Clan Donald)

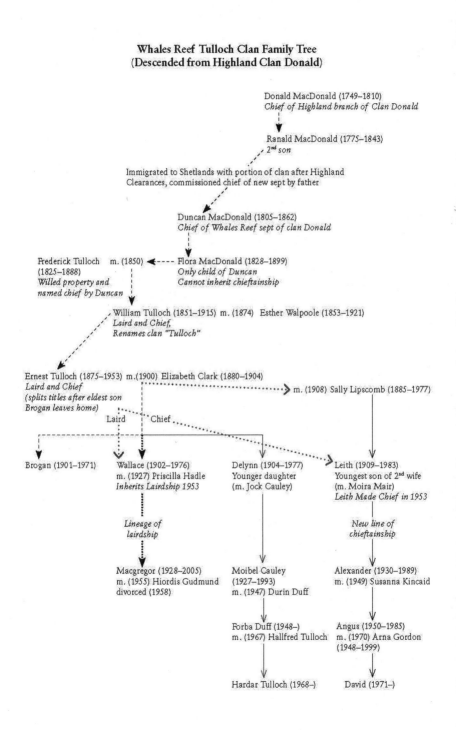

Donald MacDonald (1749–1810)
Chief of Highland branch of Clan Donald

Ranald MacDonald (1775–1843)
2ⁿᵈ son

Immigrated to Shetlands with portion of clan after Highland
Clearances, commissioned chief of new sept by father

Duncan MacDonald (1805–1862)
Chief of Whales Reef sept of clan Donald

Frederick Tulloch   m. (1850)   Flora MacDonald (1828–1899)
(1825–1888)   *Only child of Duncan*
Willed property and   *Cannot inherit chieftainship*
named chief by Duncan

William Tulloch (1851–1915) m. (1874) Esther Walpoole (1853–1921)
Laird and Chief,
Renames clan "Tulloch"

Ernest Tulloch (1875–1953) m.(1900) Elizabeth Clark (1880–1904)   m. (1908) Sally Lipscomb (1885–1977)
Laird and Chief
(splits titles after eldest son
Brogan leaves home)
                    Laird   Chief

Brogan (1901–1971)   Wallace (1902–1976)   Delynn (1904–1977)   Leith (1909–1983)
                     m. (1927) Priscilla Hadle *Younger daughter*   Youngest son of 2ⁿᵈ wife
                     Inherits Lairdship 1953 (m. Jock Cauley)   (m. Moira Mair)
                                                                          Leith Made Chief in 1953

                     Lineage of   *New line of*
                     lairdship   *chieftainship*

                     Macgregor (1928–2005)   Moibel Cauley   Alexander (1930–1989)
                     m. (1955) Hiordis Gudmund (1927–1993)   m. (1949) Susanna Kincaid
                     divorced (1958)   m. (1947) Durin Duff

                                               Forba Duff (1948–)   Angus (1950–1985)
                                               m. (1967) Hallfred Tulloch m. (1970) Arna Gordon
                                                                          (1948–1999)

                                               Hardar Tulloch (1968–)   David (1971–)

PART 1

JUNE 1924

1

A Boy and a Bird

Whales Reef, Shetland Islands

On a late afternoon of a surprisingly warm day, a small lad sat on a large stone with the blue of sky and water spreading out before him. The air was full of motion, but for this one of Shetland's minor islands the wind was relatively light. The chair-rock of his perch jutted out of the ground near a high bluff overlooking the sea.

The boy lifted his face to the fragrant breeze as he watched the birds soaring above. He loved the birds, and he loved the sea. But today that love was tinged with sadness.

He looked beside him. On a tuft of sea grass lay a tiny bird with a broken wing.

The boy was only seven, but the music of the angels stirred within him. He valued life in all its forms. From almost the moment he was born he possessed an uncanny connection to the animal kingdom. It was not merely that he loved animals. This boy *understood* them far beyond the usual capacity of humans to comprehend their winged and four-footed brethren of creation.

By the time he was three, his father and mother

avowed that he knew what every dog around him was thinking. With searching eyes he looked at the infinitely fascinating nonhuman faces of the creatures around him. By age four he walked among the sheep and cows and ponies his father tended for the laird as if he were one of them. He talked to them too. His strange communications, however, came in whispers, gestures, and other-worldly noises whose subtleties were known only to the animals. A word or sign from the boy brought instant obedience from any of the laird's half-dozen sheepdogs, as well as their own Shep, the boy's constant companion now resting at his feet.

A brief gust blew up from the cliff face in front of him, ruffling the tiny bird's feathers and sending the boy's carroty thatch into a momentary flurry. He steadied himself on the stone and breathed deeply.

Those living beings most at home here—who had been here the longest and doubtless the first to settle in this place—were those who had made peace with this land of wind. The continuous currents were sometimes their ally, often a stimulus, occasionally a friend . . . but never an enemy. Wind was necessary to their survival, whether generated by the earth spinning on its axis or by their own powerfully created musculature.

These wind-lovers were the birds.

The winged species of the Shetlands, at once exceptional yet commonplace, were majestic and colorful in their diversity. For sheer quantity they seemed numerous as the sands surrounding these isolated islands in the middle of the North Atlantic. If the ancient parable was true that two were once sold for less than a penny, no one would now pay a penny for even a thousand of the gulls, thrushes, swifts, swallows, sparrows, finches, and bramblings that swarmed these moors, inlets, and rocky coastlines.

But earthly eyes do not always perceive eternal merit. Even the tiniest of these had worth for those who saw them as creatures imagined into being out of God's fathering heart. The most insignificant of creatures—both birds and boys—had stories to tell.

Young Sandy Innes, son of the laird's game-keeper, had come upon the bird lying helpless and alone beside the rock. A pang seized his heart, for the tiny life was precious to him. That life, however, looked fragile and was ebbing away.

He knew the bird was dying.

With a single gesture to Shep behind him, he sat down on the rock. The dog had made no move since. The first impulse of Sandy's boyish love was to stroke the feathery back. But he knew that doing so would frighten the poor tiny thing. He did not want it to die in fear, but in peace.

So he sat.

And waited.

A tear crept into his eyes as he gazed on the tiny creature beside him.

When he heard footsteps moments later, the boy turned. A tall figure was walking toward him.

The man saw the bird on the ground. He sat down on the thick grass with the bird between himself and the boy, the black-and-white form of his gamekeeper's sheepdog motionless behind them.

No word was spoken for several minutes. Neither felt compelled to disturb the tranquility of the moor behind them and the sea before them.

"What are ye aboot, Sandy?" said the man at length.

"The wee birdie is dyin'," replied the boy. His high voice was soft, tender, and unsteady.

"Yes . . . I see."

"I wanted tae sit wi' him so he wouldna be alone. I didna want him tae die wi'oot a body wi' him."

The man pondered the words. The only sounds were the breeze, which rose into an occasional swirl about their faces, and the gently splashing waves against the rocky shoreline below.

2
A CELT IN THE MAKING

It has been said that the defining characteristics of the Celt are deep emotion and an intuitive bond with the natural creation. The man and boy shared a common link to that ancient heritage. In the brief moments they sat together, they were drawn into oneness by the birthright of their prehistoric pedigree. The very loneliness of this island they called home, the wind surrounding them, the breaking waves of the sea, the cries of the gulls in the distance, even the faint odor of peat smoke drifting on the island breezes from the village, combined with the poignant broken creature-life between them to resonate in their hearts with the unspoken mysteries of life. The fullness of the hour pervaded their mutual Celtic consciousness.

It was the most natural thing in the world for the approach of death to stir the Celtic temperament. From the unknown antiquity of its pagan roots to the symbolism of the gospel brought to Scotland's shores by Columba in the sixth century, the Celts were ever conscious that the everlasting cycle of life—a story affirmed by nature year after year—was always being renewed. And death was part of it.

The boy continued to stare at the bird. Though he intuitively sensed much truth hidden to those many times his years, death to him was yet a great unknown. Where did the *life* go?

He had not yet reached the age when clan lore would seize him with visions that had fired the imaginations of Scots boys for centuries. When that day came, he would dream of fighting as a tartan-clad warrior with his clan beside Robert the Bruce at Bannockburn or bonnie Prince Charlie on the fields of Culloden. Whether it meant victory as at Bannockburn or defeat as at Culloden, the honor of fighting for Scotland's freedom was the same. Centuries of failed history had taught Celtic Scots to revere the glory of its fallen as well as its triumphant heroes. Even in defeat, its legendary men and women represented the nobility of the Scottish character and the spirit of its nation.

On this day, however, the boy's heart was tender toward this tiny fallen creature. His was the grief of the Celt for whom death, whether in the field of battle or on a lonely moor, was honorable.

Again the man broke the silence. He sensed the high stirrings of the moment. He was one acquainted with the Eternal Now of inner quietude. He felt the lad's heart and shared his sorrow.

"Ye're often alone yersel', laddie," he said.

"Not a bit o' it, sir. I hae the wind an' the sea an' a' the animals for my frien's. There's yer sheep an' ponies an' my daddy's cows, an' a' the birds on the island. Hoo can a body be alone wi' such life aboot?"

The man smiled. *Spoken like a true Celt,* he thought to himself.

"Weel, wee Mannie," he said, "there's mair wisdom in that head under yer shock o' red hair than most has any idea. I'll bide wi' ye an' yer wee friend."

This time the silence remained for some time. No more words were needed. The hearts of this boy and this man had joined in care for the fallen creature between them.

They would remain special friends for the rest of their lives. Henceforth, whenever they met and a quiet smile passed between them, their thoughts would stir with reminders of this day.

3

SHARED PASSING OF LIFE

After some time, another figure approached.

Book in hand, a young woman came toward the man, boy, dog, and bird.

Observing the scene and drawing toward it with slowing step, she felt something momentous at hand. She did not speak, yet felt no reluctance to join the silent gathering. Though a stranger to the island, she sensed that her presence would be welcome.

The girl sat down a few feet away. At first glance, her age would have been difficult to determine. She was not tall, probably an inch or two above five feet, and of such a childlike countenance that a hasty observer might have taken her for fifteen. The expression of peace in her eyes, however, spoke of maturity beyond the teen years. She was, in fact, a few months into her twenty-second year.

The man turned and smiled. He did not know her, but he knew the look in her eyes.

"We are helping this little bird die in peace," he said serenely.

She smiled and nodded. This was no season

for words. Like him, she was acquainted with the Great Silence.

After perhaps twenty minutes a soft moan sounded from the dog. His dog-soul felt a change. The boy's attention was riveted on the tiny form on the grass. He saw a slight flutter. The next moment it was over.

The boy stared down for another few seconds. Liquid grief glistened in his eyes. He blinked hard, then at last stood.

The man reached into his pocket and dug out a small coin. He reached up and handed it to the boy.

"This is for ye tae remember the day, Sandy," he said. "Ye canna spend it for a sweetie in Mistress Macpherson's shop. 'Tis a wee token tae keep. I want ye tae tell me one day when ye ken what it means."

The boy took the coin, looked down at it a moment where it lay in his palm, then pocketed it. He turned and gazed into the man's eyes.

"Shall we bury the wee birdie, Sandy?" asked the man.

" 'Tis naethin' mair tae be done," the lad replied. "God will take care o' it noo."

The boy turned and walked away across the moor. The sheepdog jumped up and bounded away after him.

Man and girl were left alone. Neither wanted to spoil the mystical moment.

At length the young woman rose also and walked away toward the village. The man remained, a dead sparrow at his feet, staring out from the bluff over the sea, contemplating many things.

4
First Entry

The newcomer to the island was a young woman who courted solitude as the anchor for her soul. What further this adventure far from home might hold in the days to come, she could not foretell. She merely knew that the brief encounter just past had sent indescribable emotions plunging into her heart.

She had to be alone. She must write about it.

Book still in hand, she wandered aimlessly along the bluff overlooking the sea in the general direction of the village from which she had come earlier. After a short time she turned inland over the heathery turf of the moor. In the distance the terrain rose toward a hill of modest height in the center of the island. At its peak she saw what appeared to be a pillar of some kind. What it was made of she could not tell. It bore investigation. But the hill was too far away for a leisurely walk. At the moment her mind was not set on exploration.

She spied a flat boulder ahead, walked to it and seated herself comfortably on its surface, still reflecting on the boy and man. *What a curious pair.* She doubted they were father and son. The man was old enough to be the boy's grand-father.

And their colorful dialogue!

She knew they were speaking English, at least that's what the Shetland guidebooks called the language of these islands. But though the boy's words had been few, she had scarcely under-stood a syllable. The man could not possibly have known her an American, for, hearing them, a sudden shyness had come over her and she had said not a word. Yet he had obviously sensed that the Shetland dialect would be a mystery to her and thus modified his own speech for her benefit.

Who is he? she wondered. He bore himself as a man of dignity and no doubt education. But he was dressed in modest, almost shabby, attire. And what an enchanting boy, with such tender feelings for a fallen bird.

With a thoughtful sigh she placed the leather journal in her lap and traced with a finger the embossed design of a Celtic cross on its brown cover. Almost reverently she opened the volume. After her aborted attempt to draw a puffin near the cliff earlier that morning, this would be her first written entry since her arrival.

She took a fountain pen from her bag, removed its cap, thought for a moment, then methodically began to draw. Soon a remarkably lifelike sketch of the bird on the ground and the boy on the stone beside it began to emerge. After a quarter of an hour, when she was satisfied with the image, she paused and strained her mind to remember every word of the conversation she had heard, trying to make sense of the exchange.

Above the sketch, in an artistic script, she wrote, *A Boy and a Bird*. Below the drawing she began to record her experience. She did not want to omit a single detail of the memorable scene.

After several minutes she glanced up. The man still sat in the distance where she had left him, as if keeping watch out over the sea.

5

LIFE STORIES

Still seated beside the dead bird at the edge of the bluff, Ernest Tulloch, laird and chief of the small island clan of Whales Reef, watched the quiet maiden walk away from him in one direction while young Sandy Innes and Shep receded from view in the opposite. He smiled as the back of Sandy's head bobbed away like a small orange ball against the green of the moor and the blue of sky and sea.

The youngster gave the impression of being an urchin, to all appearance poor, raggedly dressed, his thick crop of bright hair shooting out in all directions. He could be seen roaming every inch of the island the whole of the day and half the long twilight of summer nights. Unusually small for his age, he had few playmates among the boys of the village, and behaved oddly, so it was thought, around animals. All contributed to the generally accepted notion that he was a little touched in the head.

The chief knew such perceptions were as false as most gossip. The lad was cared for, nurtured, and loved at home. He himself made sure that his parents were well provided for, and the elder

Innes was invaluable to him. The boy was small but hard, wiry, and in splendid health. Both eyes and brain were quick, sharp, roving, and possessed of more intelligence and insight, and in more important directions, than that of most adults in the village.

He was certainly a philosopher in the making, thought Tulloch. He might even be a genius. It would require time to reveal whether the latter was so. The fact that the general perception of him lay in precisely the opposite might have indicated the clearest evidence of the future possibility.

As if his thoughts were drawn in the same direction as the young woman's, the laird smiled to himself. He would have been proud to call the lad his grandson.

As yet, however, he had none of his own. What would his grandchildren be like, he wondered. Would they love this island and its heritage as he did? Would they carry on the Tulloch name with pride? What would become of the lairdship and chieftainship that now rested together on his shoulders? In this new century of progress, would a day come when the very words *laird* and *chief* had no more meaning and perhaps cease to exist at all?

Times were changing, thought Tulloch. He knew change was inevitable. But many of the modern trends taking place in the wider world did not bode well for small communities like Whales Reef with their traditional values and culture. Would his posterity share the love he felt for these people who were his to watch over?

It was already clear the modern century would not wait even two generations to infect his beloved island with the lure of self-gratification. Brogan, his eldest and heir, had left for university in England and had not been the same since. He certainly showed no inclination to carry on the family heritage. He was twenty-three and, to all appearances, hated every minute he had to spend on the island. For all Ernest could tell, Brogan despised his name and upbringing and everything they represented.

The very thought sent a knife into Ernest's heart. And the broader question was: What would become of the lairdship if Brogan left Whales Reef for good? A laird and chief must be intimately involved in the daily life and affairs of his people. He had to mix with the fishermen, visit with the shopkeepers, know every name on the island, and be aware of every concern of every family. None of that could happen if Brogan was living in London or Manchester or Glasgow.

In such a case Ernest would have no choice but to pass on the mantle to Brogan's brother, Wallace. As for their younger sister, Delynn, and stepbrother, Leith, much about the future would depend on how they grew, even on whom they married. The same could be said of Wallace. At twenty-two, he was a retiring young man. Passive of personality, a lifetime in Brogan's shadow had deepened the inborn reticence of his nature. Tulloch feared that his second born could be susceptible to an unwise alliance, a possibility that bore heavily on his decision about the lairdship. Would Wallace be capable of carrying the responsibility as custodian of the island's property and the fortunes of its people? Not if his future wife turned out to be anything like Ernest's own mother, who had possessed not the slightest affection for the island or its residents. It was probably her lack of interest that made Ernest more determined than ever to preserve the legacy of both lairdship and chieftainship. He realized, however, that not every man was fortunate enough to find a wife perfectly suited to such a life. He had loved his mother, but she had not cared about Whales Reef. He had indeed been the most blessed among men, thought Ernest, to have found two wonderful women—Elizabeth, the wife of his youth and mother of his first three children, and dear Sally, the wife of his maturing years.

The only one of his three sons whose heart seemed to beat with the same abiding love for their ancient pedigree was fifteen-year-old Leith, the only child of his second marriage. Yet he was still a teen. Much could change in a short time.

Ernest had not foreseen the alteration of outlook the university years would bring to Brogan. What wonderful times they had shared as father and son when Brogan was Leith's age. The reminder brought tears to Ernest's eyes. He had tried to be a good father. But whenever he detected the discontented look in Brogan's eyes, all he could think was that somehow he had failed.

It was with bittersweet memories that a father watched his sons and daughters grow into adulthood and leave the playfulness of youth behind. Yes, change was inevitable. One had to make the best of it. Yet not all change was accompanied by joy. Only a few short years after the happy days of their childhood, if things did not change, he was contemplating what circumstances might force him to the heartrending decision of divesting his eldest son of the lairdship and chieftainship.

The idea had even crossed Ernest's mind—he had not yet confided it even to Sally—that he might find it necessary to break with tradition altogether and pass the two titles on separately after he was gone. Hopefully it would not come to that. He was loath to break the practice of the double title endowed upon the same man.

Ernest turned his gaze once more to the young woman in the distance, sitting with book in her lap. From the looks of it she was writing.

Who is she? he wondered. He had been drawn

to her countenance the moment she had come walking toward them. He hoped to find out more about her. He had the feeling, young as she was, that her life had a story to tell.

His brow furrowed with a question that gnawed much closer to his own soul. *What story will Brogan's life tell?*

And what about his own?

Like every man, Ernest Tulloch wondered whether his life would have a lasting impact. Would anyone remember him two or three generations from now? What would they write on his tombstone? What permanent legacy would he pass on to his posterity, both his children and those who came after?

He did his best to shake away the pensive thoughts. But it was not easy. Melancholy had become his unwitting companion in recent years. The estrangement with Brogan had plunged like a thorn into his father's heart.

Legacies, however, were God's business. His own duty was to live every day as God's man and leave the rest to his heavenly Father. The only legacy he needed be concerned with was that *God* remembered his name, even if no one else did.

Ernest's eyes still rested on the young woman across the moor.

What is the story of her life? he asked himself again. Perhaps she was writing it even now.

PART 2

LATE SUMMER, 2005

6
BRIGHT FUTURE

Washington, D.C.

Pensive reflections can be dangerous to your health, especially for one trying to leave the past behind.

A smartly dressed woman of about thirty stood looking down on a corner of D.C.'s famous Mall. It was nothing like the view commanded by the corner office of her boss, who in her leisure moments gazed out on the Washington Monument, the Capitol Dome, and the White House in the distance.

But hey, she thought, at least she had a window. Not bad for a country girl.

And an office of her own!

She had never dreamed of occupying more than a cubicle in a dingy back room of some small business in Podunk, U.S.A. That was all a pencil pusher like her could hope for. People from her family didn't go to college, certainly not university. She knew she had been lucky just to get past junior college.

She remembered thinking in those days that maybe someday she might open an accounting office or even a small antique shop—in spite of the past, she still loved old furniture—though she had no idea where she would get the money to start a business of her own. If she could just earn a degree, land a job somewhere, and support herself, she would be happy.

So much for the vague dreams of a business major named Loni Ford entering her junior year at the university.

Everything changed when Madison Swift bounded with all her energy and dynamism into her life.

Now here she was looking out from a modern high-rise office complex in what was arguably the most important city in the world. At least in the political world.

Standing in an office of her own! Sometimes, thought Loni, she still had to pinch herself.

If she didn't yet have an office in the *financial* center of the world, that day might come eventually. An expansion of their firm to New York was rumored to be in the works for next year. If the suits upstairs picked her boss to head up the new division, who could tell where her own future might lead? A year or two from now she could be staring down on Central Park, the Hudson River, or the Statue of Liberty.

Why, then, did unwelcome waves of disquiet sweep over her at the most inconvenient times?

Loni never knew when they might strike. Uncomfortable memories out of the past.

Unbidden.

Uninvited.

Unwanted.

Rising without warning.

Until . . . suddenly a spiral of bittersweet nostalgia engulfed her.

This morning, on her way across the Mall, it was a tourist family gazing up at the Monument. She recognized them instantly. She didn't know them, but she *knew* them.

For one like her, the signs of religious conservatism were unmistakable.

The long dresses, the bonnets and beards and wide-brimmed hats, the flock of compliant children, exact replicas of their parents, trailing behind. Mennonite, Brethren, Pentecostal . . . it didn't matter.

They always sent her thoughts in the same direction. They were ubiquitous reminders of her grandparents' plain dress and antiquated ways.

Sight of the family had been enough. Her thoughts quickly tumbled back through the years . . .

To think that she might have become such a one herself.

Or . . . had she always been destined to go her own way, to forge a different path?

Such reminders and the questions they raised—

she could never put her finger on it—oddly almost made her homesick, but with a longing for a home she had never known. Sometimes the yearning in her heart became so strong she felt its ache inside.

But she couldn't go back. She had no desire to return to that life. The home she yearned for wasn't back there anyway.

It never had been.

Where was it? Maybe that was what part of her was still trying to figure out.

Loni shook her head and tried to dismiss the morose musings from her brain. Important developments were in the wind. This was no time to get maudlin and melancholy.

She needed to put all that out of her mind and focus on the business at hand.

The deal had been all but closed last week. She and Maddy had flown out to meet with the Board of Directors of Midwest Investment Group at their headquarters in Des Moines. Even if she did say so herself, their presentation had wowed them. She and Maddy had arrived back on the East Coast confident that Midwest's execs would sign on the dotted line. The phone call from the board's chairman ten minutes ago confirmed that their instincts were well-founded.

"Thank you, Mr. Stanley," Loni had said into her phone. "Express our appreciation to the rest of your board for their gracious hospitality during our visit as well. The moment Miss Swift is back in her office I will have her call you."

She listened a moment.

"Yes, I've been following that," she added, then paused and listened again. "It's so hot that livestock is actually threatened . . . yes, you're right, a hundred and five is certainly off the charts . . . well, we shall all have to pray for rain and a cold spell. We wouldn't want to start this new partnership with your clients having a disastrous year! No," she laughed, "that wouldn't make either of us look very good!"

Loni continued to listen to the man heading up the group of Iowa investors.

"That sounds fine," she said. "I'm sure Miss Swift will have me working on the final documents immediately. You will have them before the weekend for your signatures. Then all that will remain is to have the funds transferred to us so that Miss Swift can get it working even harder for you and get those dividends for your investors bumped up. . . . Good, that will be fine. I know you will be happy with the results. . . . Yes, and I won't forget about the rain! Miss Swift will be in touch within the hour. Good-bye, Mr. Stanley."

She set down the phone, walked to the window, and stood a moment. It was a great triumph and she had been part of it from the beginning.

Yet with the exciting phone call still resounding in her ear, from out of nowhere had come the reminder of the family she had seen that morning. Yes, too many reflections could be hazardous to your health, and this was no time for them!

With a final effort she shoved the images of her grandparents back into her subconscious, like she did with her journal when she wasn't traveling—out of the way, tightly shut. Out of sight, out of mind.

Alonnah "Loni" Ford turned and strode back to her desk. Listening carefully through her open door, forty minutes later she heard the latch from across the hall. She jumped up, hurried from the room, and followed her boss, investment analyst Madison Swift, into her expansive office.

Swift heard her steps and turned.

"You look like the cat that swallowed the canary!" she said.

"Congratulations, Maddy!" exclaimed Loni. "You got the Midwest account! I got off the phone with Stanley half an hour ago."

"That's fantastic."

"I said you would call him the moment you returned."

"I certainly will. This is one of my biggest catches yet. And I couldn't have done it without you, Loni."

"I am only your assistant," said Loni with a smile.

"Hardly! If I don't watch out, the men upstairs will start noticing *you* instead of me—if they haven't already."

"That will never happen, Maddy. I owe everything to you. You do know how grateful I am for all you've done, for the confidence you have in me."

"Plenty of time for all that later. Besides, you earn every penny I pay you. Your presentation to those folks in Iowa couldn't have been better. Midwesterners can be tough. Going into the thing, when I told you to research it, I suppose part of me was pessimistic we could pull it off."

"Hog and wheat farmers have money too. Midwest has been the safe investment for farms throughout six states for decades. Their assets are enormous. I knew you could increase their return and their dividend share to their investors."

"Well, I'm glad you kept prodding me," said Maddy. "And once we got there, you certainly spoke their language! All it took was to put a country girl with a straw hat and down-home twang in front of their board."

"You were the star, Maddy. I did nothing more than pave the way for you to close the deal. But maybe you're right that, as you say, I speak their language."

"I know you have a rural background, Loni. Are you from Iowa or Nebraska?"

"No, my roots are closer to home. Actually I grew up just a stone's throw from here."

"*Are* you a farm girl?"

"Not exactly. Rural and country, yes, but we raised no hogs or wheat. Just a few chickens for eggs, and several cows. Everybody has cows."

"What did your folks do then, Loni?"

"What is this, Maddy, twenty questions? I'm a city girl now."

"I doubt that. You can take the girl out of the country, but you can't take the country out of the girl. Isn't that how it goes?"

"Not true in my case. To answer your question, we made furniture. But those days are behind me."

"However you did it, I'm glad you were able to help me charm those Midwesterners into entrusting their money to us. And now we've got work to do. Sorry, Loni . . . this means a late one tonight. Hope that's okay."

"I was supposed to have dinner with Hugh. But he'll understand."

"Sorry, Loni—blame it on me."

"We both have unpredictable professions. Neither business nor politics run on nine-to-five schedules. We knew that when we began seeing each other."

"You're sure it's okay?"

"Promise."

"All right then. While I'm returning Stanley's

call, why don't you run down and get us a couple of double lattes, on me. Then maybe later we'll order in. We've got to get the documents prepared. This is huge—I want no delays."

"I'm on my way," said Loni, heading for the door.

"Oh," her boss added behind her, "I almost forgot. There's something else I want to talk to you about."

Loni paused and turned back.

"There's an event coming up in a few months I want to send you to—a training conference for relative newcomers in the investment world."

"You want to send *me?* I'm just your humble assistant."

"Are you kidding! Loni, you're my right-hand man—no sexism intended!—my protégé, my rising star. You practically put the Midwest deal together yourself. I shouldn't be getting the kudos for it, you should."

"You were the brains, Maddy. I'm the hired help."

"I told you I want you to stop thinking that way. I had plans for you the first time I set eyes on you, Loni Ford. I still do. I want you to think like an executive, not a flunky."

"I know, I'm sorry. I'll try . . . but it's hard. You're in a whole different league than me."

"Nonsense. The Midwest deal wouldn't have happened without you. Anyway, my mind is made up. I want you to go to this conference and learn everything you can. It will be a great experience."

"If you say so. Where is it?"

"At Gleneagles."

"Where's that?"

"You've never heard of Gleneagles? Golfing Mecca, political summits . . . Gleneagles. It's in Scotland."

"You want me to go to Scotland!"

"First week of November. Pack your bags, Loni."

"How would I get there?"

"Heathrow, then Edinburgh. Lots of financial gurus from Europe will be there."

"Why don't you go, then?"

"I haven't ruled that out. As much traveling as I've done, I've never been to Scotland. I'd like to visit there someday. My mother's maiden name is MacGregor. My roots are Scottish. We're related to the old Robin Hood of Scotland, Rob Roy MacGregor. But the thrust of the conference will be for the kind of thing you need to take the next step up in the investment world. Besides, I've got too much going on here."

"You're the boss!" laughed Loni. "Who am I to say no to an offer like this? It sounds fun—though I wish you would go too. I'll be intimidated without you."

"Nonsense. You'll do fine."

"What will the weather be like then?"

"I don't know. Late autumn, that's our nicest weather here. Indian summer, you know. As for the weather in Scotland at that time of year, I haven't a clue. Like I said, I've never been."

7

SHETLAND SHEPHERD

Whales Reef, Shetland Islands

These desolate moors were unlikely breeding grounds for philosophers.

The barren, isolated landscape of the Shetlands may have been home to innumerable gulls, guillemots, bramblings, finches, puffins, swifts, swallows, fulmars, and a hundred fifty other flying species. Sages and scholars, however, were few and far between.

Indeed, among the millions of winged creatures that inhabited the sixteen hundred miles of rocky shorelines of the Shetland archipelago, humans were the oddity. Sharing this region with the birds—neither so visible nor colorful—were diverse species of whale, otter, seal, dolphin, and porpoise, all of which found Shetland's deep tide pools and numerous bays and inlets lush feeding and breeding waters for their kind. The fish they consumed daily by the ton were even more plentiful than the birds.

After melting seas filled the valleys of earth's prehistoric continental masses, these northern-most outcroppings of the Scottish glacial range had somehow been thrust high enough off the ocean floor to grow living things. They produced more rain than snow, more boulders than trees, more peat than grass, and more birds and fish than anything else.

The walker out early this misty morning knew every inch of this particular one of Shetland's diverse islands like the back of his hand. He had been exploring the moors, coastlines, cliffs, and caves of Whales Reef almost since the moment he could walk. He now wore knee-high rubber boots over corduroy trousers, a thick woolen overcoat, leather gloves, and a wool cap with flaps over his ears.

He loved this tiny island. Yet he rarely traipsed the path between his home and the village without being reminded of that day more than twenty years before when he had sprinted out of the village as if the devil himself were after him. In his mind the woman *was* the devil. The image replayed itself in his brain yet again.

———

A boy of ten, known to every man, woman, and child on Whales Reef, darted through an irregular conglomeration of alleys, lanes, and pathways. A minute later he emerged from the last houses of the village.

Without slowing his step, and clutching a book as he ran, he flew across the rock-strewn ground. By the time he was climbing the hill toward the monument at the center of the island, his lungs were burning. Several minutes later he collapsed in a heap at the foot of the great pillar of stone.

At last the emotions prompting his rash act poured out. A great wail burst from his lips. He lay on the ground and sobbed.

The feel of the horrid woman's hands sent cold chills through his body. He could still hear her frightening words and feel her long, bony fingers probing his head and shoulders. The memory of her voice was as terrifying as the feel of her touch as she stood over him, crooning and chanting in a strange and hideous tongue.

———

The man whose boyhood was never far away smiled wryly at the memory. He had certainly not been a philosopher back then. He was viewed by some in the village as a troublemaker at best, and at worst a wicked boy beyond hope of redemption.

He chuckled to remember what some of the village women used to call him. Though a thoughtful man, David Tulloch was above all an optimist. His sense of humor and love of life were infectious, though not always visible at first glance. By nature his angular face wore a serious expression. A strong chin, wide mouth, well-formed Roman nose, and penetrating gray eyes tended to give a more somber impression than what he felt inside. His lips were always ready, however, for a friendly smile or mirthful grin, and an occasional outburst of laughter whose sound was known to everyone on the island.

Regarded by the redoubtable Miss Barton and her fearsome cousin as the mischievous village prankster, he was loved by most of the other children for his pluck and daring. And when he did land himself in trouble, their respect for the chief's son was heightened all the more as they watched him take his punishment without a word. Even when Miss Barton's rod brought tears to his eyes, young David could be counted on to be smiling and laughing again within minutes. His good humor annoyed the schoolmistress even more than his roguish behavior. She expected her charges to cower. His refusal to comply was a constant thorn in her very active old man.

David Tulloch's philosophical leanings had come later in life. But he knew their seeds had been sending down roots even on that fateful day. The small notebook he had taken to school that morning was the same as that under his arm today. In the years since, he had made a lifetime's study of the many native categories and genus of fowl that roosted among these islands. He still treasured this little book he had carried around as a child, sketching what birds he got close enough to see clearly, traipsing the length and breadth of the island to find their nests and hidden retreats. His research in the years since had advanced to considerably more sophisticated levels. He took the book with him these days as much for sentimental reasons as for the chance to fill in one of the blank pages that remained. A glance through it on this chilly morning reminded him, with some disappointment, that his artistic skills had not kept pace with his zoological expertise.

His eyes fell, as they often did, on the torn edge near the front where one of his first attempts to draw a puffin had been unceremoniously torn away. It was a simple incident from childhood. Yet in many ways that day still defined who he was.

———

"What is that ye're busy wi', David?" his teacher had asked, her tone more firm than the words.

The boy glanced up from the book in his lap. "Nothing, Miss Barton," he replied.

"Dinna fib tae me, David. It must be something tae keep ye from paying heed tae Sister Grace."

"It's nothing, ma'am—I was just drawing a wee birdie."

" 'Tis nae time for birdies. Gie it tae me.

Noo take yer place in the chair in front."

"Please, Miss Barton, I winna draw no more."

"Get up, David," said the teacher. She took two quick strides toward him and grabbed the book from his hands. She opened it hastily, found the offending drawing, and ripped the page from the book to crumple it in her hand.

Tears stung the ten-year-old's eyes.

"Stand up," commanded his teacher. "Gae tae the front."

"Please, ma'am, may I have my book?"

"No, ye may not hae yer book! I shall give it back tae ye when ye repent o' yer disobedience. Ye've a carnal mind an' a rebellious streak in ye, David. Now sit ye doon in front so that Sister Grace can drive the demon oot o' ye. You dinna want tae go tae hell, do ye?"

"No, ma'am."

"Then sit ye doon an' close yer eyes."

Having by now witnessed the incantations performed by the tall and imposing visitor over several of his classmates, including his best friend Armund, David trembled as he slowly walked forward. He eased onto the straight-back wooden chair reserved for those who must endure their appointed fate. The self-styled "Sister

Grace" laid her hands on his head, sang unintelligibly for a few moments in an eerily terrifying tone, then began a passionate outpouring for the divine fire to fall on the wayward youngster before her.

Suddenly the urge to flee seized young David with overpowering force. He leapt to his feet and wriggled out of the clutches of the sorceress. The flamboyant woman gasped at the effrontery of the young scalawag as he darted across the floor, grabbed his notebook from the outraged schoolteacher's hand, and made a mad dash for the door before she could stop him.

"Come back here, David!" shrieked the teacher as she hurried after him to the open door. "David . . . stop!" she cried.

But the lad was already across the street and making for the moor as fast as he could run.

"I dinna care who yer daddy is, David!" shouted Miss Barton. "Ye will . . ."

But her voice was lost in the wind as the young reprobate disappeared from sight.

———

The memory from his boyhood still stung, yet was not without humor as he remembered it. The incident was in many ways responsible for his personal life's journey to discover what was true and what was not. David was grateful for that journey, thus even for the youthful turmoil that had been part of it. He still blamed the woman for Armund's death and for the terrible aftermath of division she and her husband had wrought on the island. Whether or not he had forgiven them, he did not know. He still wasn't convinced they deserved forgiveness. It was a more difficult mental and emotional quandary to resolve the rift their visit to the island had caused in his own mind with his father.

A crisp whistle from David's lips brought a black-and-white sheepdog bounding toward him.

"Well, laddiepup!" he said, burying his hands in the furry mane of his companion. "Shall we see if the tammylories are gathering on the cliff this morning?"

The spongy peat turf beneath his feet as he and his dog continued on reminded him of the uniqueness of his island home. He dreamed of publishing the definitive work on Shetland wildlife that would provide a needed scientific counterpoint to certain of Darwin's assumptions. Though his thesis on the subject had been viewed with skepticism at Oxford, he knew the response was mostly due to the liberal leanings of academia. None could refute his research.

His writings to date—two published books on Shetland wildlife—had not ventured in the direction of evolutionary theory, but were more the field-manual type. Nor did he allow himself to drift into similar controversial regions when conducting wildlife seminars or serving as the "resident expert" for various tours that traveled about the islands. These activities provided an adequate living for a single man, though the market for such books as his was highly specialized. Sales numbered in the hundreds, not thousands.

His true love was trying to figure out what it all *meant*. Why were certain species here? Where had they originated? How had they come to exist in the first place? How did the Divine Hand actually *create?* Had God fashioned every creature species, from gnat to whale, fully formed by divine decree? Or had He set conditions in motion out of which the diversity of life in the animal kingdom evolved and developed over billions of years on its own? Or was a complex combination of both forms of "creation" at work throughout the universe? And most important, what were the implications for mankind, the highest of the species, and how he lived?

Maybe he was a philosopher as well as a naturalist, thought David with a smile.

He had no leisure at this moment to further contemplate his supreme act of childhood rebellion at school or his metaphysical role in the eternal scheme of the universe. As he came over a small rise, a sudden bleating of sheep erupted. Seeing its shepherd, the flock came scrambling and scurrying toward him in a *baa*-ing frenzy. Seconds later he was surrounded by a tempes-tuous noisy sea of white.

"Good morning, laddies and lassies!" he greeted them with a laugh, turning about and sinking his hands in a dozen woolly coats as their owners bumped and jostled to get close to him.

The morning ritual lasted but a minute. Having welcomed their master, the frenetic swarm gradually wandered away to continue the eternal quest of all living things. In the case of this particular breed of hearty Dunface sheep, the sustenance of life took the form of tiny green shoots that found their way to the surface through dense layers of peat. The demands of a sheep were not many. Whether such creatures needed love—or were even aware of the love a man such as their master had for them—was a ques-tion perhaps more for the philosopher than biologist or sheep breeder, though this Shetland shepherd was in fact all three.

The only thing all would agree on was that to survive, sheep needed little more than grass and water. The latter was to be found here in abundance. The sheep that made this island their home had to work a little harder to find sufficient quantities of the former.

8

FATHER AND SON

Thirty-four-year-old shepherd-author-philosopher-biologist David Tulloch, chief of his small clan, continued toward the center of the island, gradually climbing the steepening slope to its central high point. It could not truthfully be called a peak, only the highest of a random assortment of hills, this particular one some three hundred fifty feet above the sea.

It had rained heavily most of the night. The ground beneath his feet was saturated, the air cold and misty and laden with moisture. At least no more rain was expected for several hours, perhaps not until well into the afternoon.

On most mornings David struck out in the opposite direction, either through the village, often stopping in at the bakery, at other times directly across the island eastward to his uncle's. The dawn had lured him out early today, however. His uncle would still be asleep. He would check on him in another couple of hours.

Macgregor Tulloch, the enigmatic seventy-seven-year-old laird of the small island clan was to all appearances in good health for a man of his years. He had always lived alone—since his unfortunate marriage, that is. Assumed to be his nearest relative, though the connection was not in a direct line, his great-nephew David was the closest the old man had to a son of his own. More fittingly, a grandson. Nor could any young man have been more devoted to the eldest Tulloch of his clan. The two loved each other with more than could be accounted for by mere filial affection. David owed his education and career to his great-uncle. He could never hope to repay him if the old man lived to be a hundred and twenty. For as long as he did live, however, David would do his best for him. Together uncle and nephew represented laird and chief of this small island. Along with their links of blood and mutual affection, the two titles solidified yet deeper the binding ties between them.

David slowed as he reached the crest and turned to gaze about him. Three quarters of a mile southwest, his home spread out with its outbuildings, stables, paddocks, and pastures. Though architecturally plain and constructed of the same gray stone as every other structure on the island, the *Auld Hoose* was considerably larger than any home on the island except the laird's. Until several generations ago, it had served as the ancestral home of the laird and chief of Whales Reef.

The day's cloud cover was high enough that beyond his house, almost straight south, he could see every cottage and building of the village. From this place, on a clear day, the entire outline of the island—some four miles north to south by a mile and a half east to west—was visible, surrounded by the waters of the North Atlantic.

David brought his gaze back around to the immediate precincts where he now stood. His eyes came to rest on the gigantic pillar of stone in front of him, set deep into the earth and rising to a height of twenty feet. Of a single irregularly shaped chunk of granite of incomprehensible weight, how and when it had come here and by whom it had been erected was the great mystery of Whales Reef. The faintest of markings, whether Pictish or Viking no one knew, were mostly weathered away and hinted at prehistoric peoples of antiquity. Druids also came in for their share of the legends. The only thing everyone agreed on was that no one knew where the great "standing stone" came from or what it signified.

It had been known for generations simply as the *Muckle Stane*—the Great Stone. David's memories drifted once more back through the years.

————

The boy's father found his son asleep at the foot of the stone several hours after his flight from school. Miss Barton's cries after him had been heard by enough of the village wives, busy with their morning laundry, that soon the whole island knew what had happened. Miss Barton's walk out to the Auld Hoose during the school's dinner break was witnessed by most of them as well. Subtle divisions were already infiltrating the close-knit community over the strange teachings and weird conjurations—some of the more practically minded dared go so far as to call them occult enchantments—of the man and his wife, distant cousin to the schoolmistress, ensuring that sides would be joined over the affair. The gossip resulting from the commotion at the school had already begun fanning the flames of the heated controversy destined to tear the tiny hamlet apart with conflict, bitter feelings, and strife. The tragedy that would result would be felt for a generation.

The chief sat down on the ground. The boy felt his presence and woke from his tearful sleep. His emotion had been spent, but the explosive incident rushed back into his memory. He gazed up into his father's eyes where he found compassion mingled with sternness.

"What are you doing out here when you should be in school, laddie?"

"The tall lady was there, Papa. I canna

bide her. She's a witch lady. I didna want her touching me."

"Did she touch you, laddie?"

"Aye, Papa. Miss Barton made us all sit in a chair and close our eyes. Armund cried when she chanted over him, but Miss Barton gave him a whack on the side of his ear and told him to be respectful. I didn't want to cry. But I couldna bide the feel of the lady's fingers on my head."

"What did you do?"

"I ran away, Papa."

"She meant you no harm, laddie, nor Armund either."

"She said I was going to hell, Papa. She's taller than any woman ought to be. And her speech is queer. Just the sound set me trembling."

"That's because she's from another part of the world, Son."

"It's not that, Papa. She speaks in words no one can understand. She makes people do strange things. One of the girls fell off the chair and moaned and rolled on the floor. It's barmy. She's a witch, I know it."

"You mustn't call any woman such a thing, laddie."

"She's not a good woman. I'm not the only one afeared of her."

"Nevertheless, you were rude to run

away. Miss Barton demands that you be disciplined. You have to set example for the other children."

The boy was silent and dropped his eyes. "Yes, Papa," he said.

"If you will apologize to Miss Barton and Sister Grace, you and I will have no more words about it."

"But I'm not sorry, Papa. Miss Barton tore up my drawing, and I didn't want to sit in the chair or roll on the floor or say strange things."

"If you do not apologize to them, David, I will have to whip you myself."

"Yes, Papa."

"Which will it be, David?"

"I will not mind if you punish me, because I know you love me. I don't think Miss Barton or Sister Grace like me." He paused and drew in a halting but resolute breath. "I will take the whipping from you, Papa," he added softly.

————

Putting the memories of the past away again, David walked toward the monolith where he had taken refuge from Sister Grace, and what he was still convinced were her dark powers and contrivances.

He stretched out his right hand and laid his palm against the rough surface. He stood a moment, then breathed a quiet prayer in the ancient tongue of the Scottish Highlands.

A Dhe ar n-athraichean, cum agus dion do shluag anns an eilean seo le curam agus gradh. Gum biodh an aon eolas aca ort mar an Athair is a bha aig Criosda ort fhein. Agus gum biodh eolas agamsa oirbh, agus geill dhuibh, mar fhear-daimh umhail, fad mo re 'smo lo. Amen.*

It was from no bondage to ritual that the young clan chief thus prayed for the island people under his charge. His encounter with the so-called Sister Grace had forever exorcised the demons of ritual and formula from his heart. No less superstitious a man dwelt on the island than David Tulloch. He was merely a traditionalist who loved the old ways and revered his proud heritage. Not-withstanding the impact of North Sea oil, if modernity had not quite swept the Shetland Islands entirely into its wake, it had made more inroads than young chief David Tulloch was happy with. As the Muckle Stane was the oldest reminder of humanity on the island, possibly with circuitous spiritual links back to

---

*God of our Fathers, keep and protect your people of this isle in your care and your love. May they know you as their own Father as Jesus knew you. And may I, their humble kisman, know you, obey you, and be their faithful servant all my days. Amen. (Gaelic translation by John Angus Morrison)

St. Columba, or even St. Ninian himself, he would affirm the connection by the laying of hands on the memory of antiquity. Whatever symbols might have been carved into its surface, David drew from the stone the high import of the human quest to know the Almighty. He chose for it to mean *more,* perhaps, than had been intended.

A few years after their conversation about the incident at school and the discipline that had resulted, father and son had made a happier pilgrimage, though equally solemn, to the hill of the monument. There the chief had taught his son the Chief's Prayer he had just prayed.

David went out every morning in a different direction, unplanned and random, not merely for the exercise, to greet his sheep, and because he loved every inch of this island, but also to contemplate the needs of the several hundred inhabitants who made Whales Reef their home. He did not always think of Armund and Sister Grace as he walked, though on most days he thought of his father. It was a complex relationship, that between David and the former chief, even if one that now occupied only David's heart and mind since his father's untimely passing. His father's death and the haunting memory of Sister Grace and her husband more than anything had implanted into David's consciousness the kind of leader he was determined to be. If the function of chief to the tiny clan of Tullochs was a ceremonial title of tradition, it was one he took seriously. He would *serve* his people and do his best for them.

He continued on his way past the granite monument and down the northern slope of the Muckle Hill. The springy ground occasionally sank beneath his booted feet, squishing with brown peat water if he hit a low spot. Whether the waterlogged peat ever dried out, even in rare seasons of relative drought, until it was cut for fuel was doubtful.

Periodically he arrived at the remnants of a dry stone dyke, climbed over or walked through where it was broken, and kept on. As the only cattle on the island were at the Auld Hoose and in the village, and as his own and his uncle's sheep were free to meander where they pleased in search of grass, there had never been much need of fences on the island. The sheep paid no more heed to such boundaries than they did the rain.

9
HATS, BOOTS, AND WHISKEY

Aberdeen, Scotland

Stretch limousines weren't exactly the status symbol in Scotland that they were in Houston. They were also harder to find.

But the Texan who had flown into Aberdeen the night before was a man of fixed habits.

Big habits.

He did things *his* way. It didn't take long after his first gusher at a youthful twenty-two to get used to the good life. He had been living large ever since. Limousines, expensive food, flashy clothes, and the best whiskey money could buy were as entrenched in his appetites as his Texas twang. Neither, however, was as deeply ingrained as he led people to believe. It was imperative to the persona he showed to the world that it thought him older than he was. He had an outsized mustache that along with his sideburns he'd tinged with hints of gray to help sell the illusion, together with his boisterous Texas bravado. He wore the state's stereotype with calculated ease.

He wasn't about to change his routine because

of a trip overseas. When he traveled he always brought with him two hats, three pairs of boots, and four bottles of whiskey. The limos he had his advance people hire locally, whatever they had to do to find one. Today's was supposed to be in front of the hotel at five minutes before six.

For this trip, out of respect for Scottish excellence in the manufacture of what they called *whisky,* he'd left his own brand home. He had been to Scotland many times. It may have been a backward country in most respects, but in the distilling of spirits, the Scots were *almost* the equal of his stateside Tennessee brethren.

It wasn't just that a limo more comfortably fit his six-foot-four, two-hundred-forty-pound frame. It was the status of knowing that heads turned as he passed. He was never happier than when at the center of attention. The moment he walked into a room, he wanted eyes watching and ears listening to *him.*

Life was his stage. Though he was neither old nor a Lone Star native as he led his audiences to believe, he played his leading role with Texas flair and good ol' boy panache. He made people believe what he wanted them to believe about him. And mostly it worked. His money, as they say, *talked.*

Shortly after the limo pulled up in front of the Aberdeen Thistle, though it was too early for a standing-room-only crowd, he nevertheless treated the small audience milling about at that hour to a grand entrance. Exiting the elevator, he strode through the lobby like a galleon under sail. Doffing his white ten-gallon hat as he went, he was perfectly aware that every eye in the place was on him. His tan alligator-skin boots echoed sharply across the hardwood floor. He exited with a flourish, approached the limo, handed the young man holding its door a twenty-dollar bill—he always tipped in dollars—and was gone.

North Sea oil meant this city was well-accustomed to Texans. But Jimmy Joe McLeod cut a wider swath than most. His grand entrance into the most expensive restaurant on Union Street a short time later was equally flamboyant.

Three of the men who represented the top tier of the U.K. arm of his corporate conglomerate, and oversaw all his oil interests on this side of the Atlantic, were already waiting for him.

"Where's Thorburn?" asked Jimmy Joe, shaking hands with each of the men. Commandeering one of two available chairs, he settled his huge frame into it as if preparing to hold court.

"He's on his way, Mr. McLeod," replied one in clipped Scottish brogue. "He just telephoned."

"Good, good! You fellas'll have to excuse the early hour. Hope you don't mind—still on Texas time. Hardly slept an hour. Been up since three."

A young waitress in black approached the table.

"Hey, darling!" said the Texan, leaning back in his chair. "How 'bout a pot of the strongest black coffee you can get hold of. And rustle us up some steak an' eggs while you're at it."

"All we have is bacon and sausage, sir," she replied timidly.

"Bacon . . . ain't that what you folks call ham?" said the big man, glancing around the table with a grin.

"More or less, yes," answered the man beside him.

"Well, then, lots of that ham, and whatever else you got to go with them eggs. Just keep it coming, little lady! You boys ordered yet?"

Seeing from the girl's expression that she was overwhelmed and a little uncertain whether she had understood a fraction of the thick drawl, one of the other men motioned her toward him.

"We will have five full-cooked breakfasts," he explained. "Another man will be joining us shortly. Ask the cook for extra bacon on one of the plates, if you wouldn't mind, for our guest . . . and *coffee,*" he added.

"No bother," she replied, smiling. "Thank you, sir. I wasn't exactly sure—"

"I understand." He nodded with a reassuring smile.

10

THE NORTH CLIFFS

Whales Reef, Shetland Islands

Arriving at the North Cliffs, David slowed, walked toward the edge of the precipice, and gazed down the sheer drop of two hundred feet.

By now it was after six. A light breeze off the sea met his face. Below, the gulls were raising a din with their shrill cries.

He drew a deep breath of the tangy sea air. Whether it bore hints of rain to come, he couldn't quite tell. Most of the islanders possessed an uncanny predictive gift. Today, however, the forecast eluded him.

This was one of his favorite places on the island. He would never forget the first time he had come here. His knees nearly buckled as he clung to his father for dear life, inching closer to the edge until, with his father's hands securely holding him, he had ventured a peek as straight down as he dared.

That had been on his birthday walk at five or six, an annual practice, his father said, passed down from some grandfather or great-grandfather of former times. They came to the cliffs every year thereafter. His knees grew steadier, his gaze over the cliffs braver, his awareness keener of both the beauty and the danger of this northernmost extremity of the island.

It wasn't merely the high cliffs that were dangerous. In spite of today's relative calm, the sea spreading out before him was the most treacherous constant of life for Shetlanders. No one who called these islands home was immune. Everyone knew *someone* who had been claimed by these waters.

The reminder prompted yet one more image, intruding unbidden into his mind.

———

The storm had risen with such sudden fury, none expected it. His friend Armund was only twelve at the time. But two of his father's men had departed to follow the Fountain of Light, as the dubious movement of Sister Grace and her husband was called. If he was to bring in a catch this day, he needed his son at the nets along with the one faithful hand who remained. The strife that the movement had caused on the island was so poisonous that no man who was part of the Fountain would work on the boat of a man who was not. Among the fishermen, most had by now pledged their loyalty to the prophet and prophetess and boasted of the accompanying "signs." Those few like Armund's father who refused to do so were rudely ostracized from the rest of the fishing community.

The church, indeed all of Whales Reef, was in an uproar. Arguments were constant on every corner, in every shop, and dominated conversation at the pub. Neighbor refused to greet neighbor. Families no longer spoke to their relatives. Lifetime friendships were severed. Many traveled to the stores in Lerwick rather than patronize the shops of former friends on the other side of the conflict. None of the Fountainites, as they were called, would break bread with those on the outside who, by their obstinate spiritual blindness, refused the divine revelations.

David, also twelve, was too young to foresee the impact those few years would exercise on his future growth. He was old enough, however, to wonder why neither his father nor his uncle spoke out against the division tearing the community apart. The minister was the worst of the lot, fomenting resentments from the pulpit week after week and denouncing as agents of the devil those who did not acknowledge Brother Wisdom and Sister

Grace as God's chosen messengers. Why did neither chief nor laird speak out their opposition?

The day's storm erupted less than thirty minutes after the *Bountiful*, one of the smallest and oldest boats on the island, left the harbor with Armund and his father and eighteen-year-old Felix Kerr aboard. A morning meeting of the Fountain delayed all other departures. By the time the harbor filled with fishermen coming to their boats, the wind and seas had whipped into a frenzy. Most of the men clustered in small groups, a few remarking how providential the meeting had been in keeping them from the danger. A few clicks of the tongue and significant nods toward the angry sea, with the faint outline of the *Bountiful* at the horizon, said what most were thinking: that evil tidings befell those who denied the Light.

Word somehow spread through the village and infiltrated the school that the *Bountiful* was in trouble. Knowing that Armund was with his father, David jumped from his seat and sprinted through the streets toward the harbor. Miss Barton's cries after him were no more effectual on this day than they had been during Sister Grace's visit.

Arriving at the harbor, rain now falling in sheets, the outraged son of the chief looked about. Every boat was moored fast while their owners and crews stood peering into the spray and mist. A half dozen of them, including the father of his second cousin—owner of the largest craft on the island, the new, bright red boat he had recently purchased and christened in honor of his son—could easily have weathered the wind and waves and pulled the *Bountiful* to safety. But none made a move to help.

"You must go after them!" the boy cried, rushing into the group of fishermen.

"Take it easy, young David," said Noak Muir, one of the Fountain's new leaders. "Ye can see the weather's against us."

"Your boats are big enough," pleaded David. "Cousin Hallfred, please—you fished in worse than this with your new boat. My father told me you were in a terrible storm a month ago and didn't take on a gallon of water."

The stoic man stood staring as if he'd heard nothing. He had never liked David's father Angus and was not about to heed the pleadings of his son.

"'Tis only Providence working its mysteries, laddie," added Muir. "If they'd been at the meetin', they'd be here safe wi' the rest o' us. Ye wouldna expect us tae raise our hand against the will o' the Almighty, noo, would ye?"

"It's not God's will for them to die!"

"He takes His retribution on them that deny Him, laddie. Though he hasna yet joined us, surely yer daddy's taught ye that much."

"They'll sink if you don't help!" cried David.

"Mortal men such as us canna stand in the way o' awful Providence, David lad," put in Willie Gunn solemnly. " 'Tis the Almighty himsel' who's brought the tempest tae bear witness tae the power o' the Light an' the futility o' standing against it."

David twisted away and sprinted over the cement quay to the farthest reach of the harbor wall. The danger to himself was great, for giant waves were breaking over it. None of the men made a move to stop him.

Proceeding as far as he dared, David stopped and sent his gaze out to sea. By now the *Bountiful* was attempting to return. But the tide was against her, and the swell had risen dangerously. David watched, tears stinging his eyes. He could tell she was taking water.

Finally the brave but aging craft began to list. Huge waves slammed against her side as if she were a toy. One after another, great breakers crashed over the bow.

Slowly and inexorably the sea claimed its victim.

She sank lower and lower . . . until the *Bountiful* was lost to sight.

———

David filled his lungs again as if to shake away the memories that seemed determined to haunt his thoughts on this day. He turned and made his way along the well-worn sea path encircling the island, set back some eight feet from the edge of the cliff.

A few minutes later he turned again seaward, left the path, and crept over the side of the bluff. Though dangerous enough, it was not so treacherous here where the cliff face gave way to a slope blanketed in thick, tightly rooted sea grasses. After a steep descent around several great boulders, then stooping beneath the projecting overhang of a horizontal slab of granite, he entered the dark recess of a cave carved into the vertical north wall of the island by eons of time and the fabled Shetland winds and rains.

It was probable that the adventurous boys of the island, now as in generations past, knew of the cave and had secretly visited it. Technically, however, the cave was off-limits, not only because access was dangerous but because for as long as anyone alive could remember it was called the Chief's Cave. Right of entry could supposedly be granted only by the chief. By reason of its location, however, it was not an ordinance rigidly policed by chief or laird or anyone else.

How former chiefs may have used the cave, David didn't know. But after the two deaths that had stung his youth, it had become his secluded hideaway from the world. He came here to read, to think, later to write. He had shed tears here, too, especially for the two whom he had loved who had been lost to the waters of the deep.

He loved this place for a host of reasons, certainly among them the view it afforded of the sea. Its mouth also commanded an unsurpassed vista over the cliff faces extending to the right and left of the cave. Hundreds if not thousands of nests, rookeries, and roosts along the rocky and treacherous bluff's surface opened their secrets to him from here. Protected as he was by the shadow of the cave, he could sit for hours without being detected by the birds that made these north cliffs their home. He had handwritten drafts of his books and taken thousands of the photographs that filled his files while sitting in this very place.

Pleasant recollections flew through David's head as he entered the Chief's Cave.

His eyes gradually accustomed to the dim light, slowly coming to rest on the three small "standing stones" that had been set in a triangle into the dirt floor of the cave toward its back wall. They were obviously but tiny replicas of the great stone on Muckle Hill, only fifteen or eighteen inches in height. Still, getting them down the steep narrow grassy path from the plateau above and into the cave had been no small feat.

His father once told him a true story from their own generational past. It explained why different Tullochs now bore the duties of laird and chief, whereas in former times both titles had rested on a single head of the clan. He had been too young to remember the details. Being two generations closer to the events, his uncle surely knew them. But he rarely spoke of the past. David could remember little more than that *three* brothers were involved, not two, and that Chief, Laird, as well as a mysterious clan *Bard* all had something to do with it. During their time the roles of chief and laird had been split. How and under what circumstances, David could not remember.

David walked into the darkness of the cave's interior. He stood before the three stones, laden in his mind with heavy symbolism from antiquity. He was convinced they signified some truth from more recent times in the legacy of his own family as well. They had not been placed as they were without purpose.

"What is your tale, you three stones?" said David softly. "What mysteries do you have to reveal?"

The stones remained silent. Whatever their secrets, he would have to await another day for their revelation.

11
BIG OIL

Aberdeen, Scotland

In the Aberdeen restaurant, the last of the early morning coterie arrived and joined the Texan and his three Scottish colleagues.

The newcomer was a slight man, thin and not more than five-foot-nine. The walking stick in his left hand was sturdy and served more than a decorative purpose, for the man's gait was accentuated by a pronounced limp. Probably in his early forties, he was easily five or six years older than his thirty-seven-year-old employer, though an initial glance at the two gave precisely the opposite impression. In appearance and demeanor the two men were striking opposites. The Scotsman was soft-spoken and gentlemanly. His kindly manner, however, belied a ruthless streak known only to his closest intimates—one of his most valuable assets in the eyes of his American boss. The same fire of ambition drove them both, which explained why the diminutive Aberdonian had for the past five years been Jimmy Joe's right-hand man in the U.K.

"Hey, Thorburn!" exclaimed the Texan ebulliently, yanking a chair out from the table. "Park it here—take a load off them feet."

"Hello, Mr. McLeod," said the Scotsman, extending his hand. "I trust you had a satisfactory flight."

"Middlin' is about the best I can say. Even with my own personal jet, the altitude blows up my head. And jet lag always—"

Just then the coffee and tea arrived.

"This oughta help!" said the Texan enthusiastically.

McLeod stretched out his massive arm and took hold of the pot with his fist. "Anyone else for coffee?" he asked.

"I'll have some," said Thorburn.

The other three Scots opted for tea. Their breakfasts arrived shortly, one plate piled high with thinly cut ham to accompany several thick links of sausage. With three hastily gulped cups of weak coffee inside him, the Texan was anxious to get down to business.

"I want to know the status of our offer on that island," he said. "You got that ol' codger to sign on the dotted line yet?"

"Unfortunately, we have no progress to report," answered the man called Shaw.

"You took him my latest offer?"

"A month ago. I delivered it personally."

"And?"

"Same answer as he's given for six years. He refuses to sell a square foot of his land."

"Dad-blamed coot. I've been more than patient, but time's running out. If I don't get my hands on it, BP's gonna control the whole dang place. I'll have no choice but to fold my cards. That's not a thing I like to do. What's it gonna take?"

"Unfortunately, money means nothing to him."

"What does? What's the old boy's game? It's high time we called his bluff, put an end to this standoff."

"I am afraid the man is as old school as they come, Mr. McLeod," now said Alexander Crawford, their resident Shetland expert. "There's nothing he wants except to keep everything as it is. He wants to protect the village and its people."

"Protect his people? Dang, how better can he do that than selling? We'll fix the whole lot of 'em up for life."

"It's more about protecting the old ways and traditions. He sees the people as his clan. He insists he won't do anything that jeopardizes their way of life. He's old and set in his ways."

"Dad blame it—doesn't he know we can make him a millionaire?"

"He cares nothing about that," replied Crawford shaking his head. "I know his type. Shetlanders are a breed apart and only give lip service to being British. They're as independent as any people on the planet."

"I gotta have that real estate!" Jimmy Joe banged his fist on the table. "I'll fly up there myself and talk to the old boy."

"I'm afraid that would do more harm than good. I'm sorry to say it, and no offense, but the instant he set eyes on that hat and your alligator boots, he wouldn't give you the time of day. The only thing Shetlanders dislike more than the English is Americans who think they can buy anything they want."

"Did you tell him that we'd relocate his people, pay 'em top dollar? What can those shacks they live in be worth? I've seen the pictures. Couldn't be worth twenty thousand each. We'll pay 'em fifty. Heck, I might even go to sixty thousand. Make 'em rich. Why would they refuse an offer like that?"

"They don't care about being rich."

"Nobody doesn't want to be rich!"

"Maybe not in your world," rejoined Crawford. "Things are different up in the Shetlands. Sure, oil has changed the islands. Quite a few landowners did get rich and are loving every minute of it. But overall they're an independent breed. Some of those houses you're talking about are over a hundred years old."

"There, you see what I mean. That's exactly what I was saying—it's time they were leveled and the place put to better use."

"I'm afraid I didn't make my meaning clear.

What I mean is that they are so old that to the people who own them they're as valuable as a castle. The old man owns all of them anyway."

"A hundred-year-old shack of rocks is no castle."

"For the man or woman who calls it home it is."

"You're talking plumb nonsense—most ridiculous thing I ever heard."

The Texan leaned back in his chair and let out a sigh. "I'll go up and talk to the old boy myself," he reiterated. "Nobody says no to Jimmy Joe McLeod when there's a deal on the table. I tell you, I'm holding the cards to win this pot."

"If you don't mind my saying so, Mr. McLeod," put in Shaw, "in my opinion Mr. Crawford is right. The frontal approach is not likely to be appropriate with these people, going in, as I believe you Americans say, with all guns blazing—"

The Texan threw his head back and roared. "You got that right, boy!" he laughed. "I think you picked up my meaning exactly. That's how we do things in Texas!"

His laughter died away. A more serious expression than he had yet assumed came over the Texan's face. He turned to Thorburn, who had remained mostly silent thus far.

"Look, Ross," he said in an uncharacteristically soft tone, "I need that real estate. I don't care what it takes. There's always a way. I *want* that land."

"I will see what I can do," replied Thorburn. "There may be a possibility or two we have not yet exhausted. I'll explore some legal channels. There may be pressures we can exert, and . . . well, as you say, there are always ways."

"I assume you have people who can take care of it?"

"Yes, we have people," nodded the other.

"Then whatever it takes, Thorburn. You get me that island."

12
REMINDERS

Washington, D.C.

Neither two double-shot lattes nor the intense concentration needed to finalize the Midwestern Investments deal had been able to expunge from Loni Ford's mind the effects of her unsettled broodings from earlier in the morning.

She slept fitfully that night, awoke early, drank more coffee, and was back in her office by 7:30. Maddy had her working straight through till noon on the Midwestern paperwork.

"You look like you're ready for a break," said Maddy at her door about 12:15. "We're nearly there, and I have a lunch meeting with some of the execs. Why don't you take an hour or two and get out of the office?"

"That's thoughtful of you, Maddy," said Loni. "Are you sure?"

"Absolutely. We'll have it wrapped up this afternoon. We'll hit it again at two or two-thirty."

Loni leaned back in her chair and exhaled a long sigh. The thought crossed her mind to call Hugh and see if he could break away for an impromptu lunch. On second thought, she wasn't hungry. She was more in the mood to be alone. "I think I'll go out for a walk then," she said. "Fresh air is just what I need."

"Good. I'll see you in a couple hours."

"Thank you, Maddy."

Forty or fifty minutes later, returning from a walk along the Mall and munching the last of the apple in her hand, Loni found herself sharing the congested sidewalk in equal measure with tourists and political types on their way to and from the power lunches for which the city was famous.

These particular two or three blocks, known for their specialty boutiques, galleries, and antique shops, were so familiar by now she usually hurried past every window without a glance. Today her pace was more leisurely.

Amid the din of cars, taxis, buses, and pedestrians, an occasional shout and a dozen blaring conversations on every side, the faint strains of music caught Loni's ear. It was soft, eerily melodic, as if coming from some distant world. Hauntingly it drew her.

She walked toward it. Moments later she entered the open door of an antique furniture shop. The soft music coming from the back of the shop enveloped her with peace. The bustle of the city faded as if she had stepped through a Narnian portal into another century.

Loni stood and breathed deeply—the familiar aromas of old oak, wood stain, varnish, and leather instantly transported her back to her grandfather's workshop.

Mesmerized by the music and nostalgic reminders of childhood, she looked around to find herself surrounded by a great variety of antique pieces large and small. She recognized every design—armoires, dressers, mirrors, picture frames, plant stands, tables, chairs, travel escritoires, chiffoniers, desks, cabinets, benches, bookcases, secretaries, side-by-sides.

Slowly she wandered about, gazing at the various pieces with a more knowledgeable eye than a casual browser. She loved the smells, tools, implements, and supplies of the furniture-maker's craft. With a pang she recalled her grandmother's recent letter, explaining her grandfather's decision to retire from the work he loved. She could not escape the gnawing realization that his hope had been for her to marry within the Fellowship and carry on the business. She knew he was disappointed. But it was not a life in which she could ever have been happy.

Making her way to the back of the shop, she detected the strong aroma of Danish oil coming through the open door of a workshop. Rag in hand, the man inside stood and came toward her.

"Sorry," he said, "I didn't see you come in."

"That's fine," Loni said with a smile. "I was enjoying a look around. I can never resist vintage furniture, especially the wonderful smells."

"I know what you mean. I'm never happier than when my hands are brown with stain and oil."

"That is an exquisite Hepplewhite chiffonier you have over there."

"You know your antique furniture!"

"And from 1790, according to the date inside the drawer . . . when they were at their best. Did you refinish it yourself?"

"Yes, actually, I did. I stripped it down and refinished it, as far as I have been able to research it, with what I believe was its original lacquer. And how, if I may ask, do you know so much about eighteenth century furniture?"

"I come from a family of furniture makers," answered Loni. "I practically grew up in my grandfather's workroom. I've sanded and oiled and varnished more pieces than I can count."

"You're not looking for a job?"

Loni laughed. "I'm afraid I'm overextended as it is!"

"Might I have heard of your grandfather's products?"

"I doubt it. It was a relatively small family business. My grandfather is William Ford, from

Pennsylvania. He specialized in replicating classic designs from the past."

"I *do* know of your grandfather's work! He has a fine reputation. In fact . . ." The shopkeeper laid aside the rag and walked into the front showroom. Loni followed.

"I thought so," he said. "Look—here is one of your pieces."

Loni came alongside him. He was standing in front of a small writing table. She drew in a gasp of astonishment.

"That *is* my grandfather's!" she exclaimed. "I remember this very piece. Actually . . . you're not going to believe this, but I sold this table myself to a customer from Pittsburgh, if I'm remembering accurately. How did you come by it?"

"It was part of an estate sale," explained the shopkeeper. "Obviously, the recent crafting of your grandfather's pieces does not technically qualify them as antiques. But the design is classic, the quality impeccable. So on the few occasions when a Ford piece comes my way, I price it for its quality rather than antiquarian value."

"This is remarkable!" said Loni, stepping back to view the desk better. "I'll tell my grandfather what you say about his work. He will be very pleased."

"What about your father? Is he in the business as well?"

"No, my father is dead. I never knew him."

"Oh, I'm sorry."

"Thank you," said Loni. "Actually," she went on, "what drew me through your door was the music. What is that you have playing? It is very unusual."

"It is Celtic music," replied the shopkeeper. "I'll show you."

He led the way to his counter and a small CD player. He handed Loni the case.

"My wife and I love Celtic music," he said. "This particular piece is called 'Leaving Lerwick Harbor.' "

"Where is that?" asked Loni.

"Lerwick is the main city in the Shetland Islands."

"There is something about it so . . . I don't know what to call it," said Loni. "Haunting . . . melancholy . . . nostalgic. It gets inside you."

"My wife is of mixed Scottish and Irish extraction. She says that Celtic harmonies get deep into your soul in a way no other music can. It is music you *feel*. You want to *be* there."

"The moment I heard it, I felt as if I had entered another world."

"I couldn't have said it better myself," said the shopkeeper. "I find that Celtic music transports you to wild seashores and lonely moors and desolate mountains. Before you know it, you've left the stress and pace of the modern world behind."

"Strange words for a man with a shop in the middle of D.C.!" laughed Loni.

"If I could move my shop to the tiny Irish village of my wife's ancestors, I would do so in a heartbeat. Unfortunately, to make a living selling antiques, we have to be where there are customers. So my wife and I satisfy our love for the old country by visiting Ireland, Scotland, England, or Wales once a year to buy for the shop. That way we get the best of both worlds."

"I see what you mean. You are fortunate indeed."

Loni left the shop feeling strangely warmed by the serendipitous encounter.

13

RELINQUISHED DREAMS

Eastern Pennsylvania

An aging man of eighty-one, stooped slightly in the shoulders but still vigorous, beard and hair white as snow, the latter poking out from beneath the edges of a wide-brimmed hat, stood in front of a large, red, two-story wood farmhouse. He was watching four men half his age pull down the final straps onto a flatbed wagon piled high with a good portion of his most prized possessions.

He had helped them load every item on the wagon. His assistance lifting tables, bookcases, benches, sideboards, routers, jigsaws, chop saws, and a variety of ornate cabinets—some but half completed—was far from superfluous. He had shouldered more than his fair share of the load as they had hoisted up the heaviest of the tools and machinery. Some of the equipment beneath the ropes had been crafting fine furniture in his workshop for a dozen decades—far longer than his own years. The youngest of his nephews, even in this insular agrarian society where honor of one's elders was sacred, was astonished by the old man's vitality.

The hard work of the afternoon was behind them. All that remained now was to secure the load . . . and for him to come to terms with the passing of a legacy. Where he stood observing a lifetime of love and labor come to an end, he presented the image of a powerful man who had lost only a portion his manhood's strength. He pretended to supervise the ritual of ropes and knots, but his heart stung him afresh as he said a silent good-bye to the life he had known. But he would shed no tears until his nephews and their sons were gone.

His dreams had been dying a slow death for some time now. Many tears had already fallen. Today represented but the final nails driven into the invisible coffin of his hopes and expectations. It was time to bid farewell to them one last time and allow what fragments of those dreams might remain to follow new generations.

Perhaps the pursuit of dreams, then laying them to rest, were inevitably yoked seasons in the cycle of life. Every alpha had its omega. Beginning and end. Spring's planting was followed by autumn's freeze. The land must go fallow that it might bear fruit again.

The oldest of the four turned from the wagon and walked toward the house.

"I think that's about it, Uncle William," he said. "Looks like you've got it tight and secure."

"I think so. It's only three-quarters of a mile.

We'll take it slow." He allowed a tinge of sadness to express what he knew words could not.

"We'll make you proud of us, Uncle William," he said, extending his hand.

"I know you will, Jacob," said the older man as the two shook hands affectionately.

"The name and heritage will continue."

"I am certain you will do them both proud."

"Thank you, Uncle William." He stood a moment. "So," he said, "we'll be off then. We want to get everything inside before dark."

He turned to the tractor and climbed up into the seat. His uncle turned, walked up the steps toward the house, then sent his gaze back around again to observe their departure. He stood still watching from the porch five minutes later as the wagon clattered slowly along the narrow dirt lane into the distance behind the tractor, the sons of his nephew walking behind it. At length he turned one last time, opened the door behind him, and slowly walked inside. His wife was standing at the kitchen window. The two embraced.

"Well, Anabel," he said, forcing a smile, "there goes my life . . . and my father's and grandfather's before me."

"It's still in the family," said his wife, a graceful woman of seventy-nine whose stateliness still held in spite of a mane as white as her husband's. "That's something to be thankful for. The name will go on."

"Not exactly how I envisioned it," the man said.

Husband and wife left the kitchen and sat down in their two favorite chairs in the adjoining living room. Silence filled several long minutes.

"I never *really* expected it to come to this," sighed the man at length. "All those early years when my father was still alive, Chad running around in the shop making toys from scraps of wood, then as he grew going on occasional sales trips with me, and later when Dad was scaling back and I was assuming more of the workload . . . I assumed Chad would carry on after me, as I was taking over from my father, just as he had learned the trade from his father. It never entered my mind that it wouldn't go on, that Chad wouldn't value the family business like I did."

"He might have in time," said his wife. "There's no way to know what might have been. I don't think he lost his love for woodworking, even for the family business. It's just that he fell in love. But who can tell? He might have come back."

"We will never know," William said. "And even after what happened, I somehow still never expected this day. I suppose I was shortsighted, blind to the reality that we would get old and that this day had to come. I thought she would eventually embrace our life, carry it on with her own husband and family. I simply never . . ."

He turned away and brushed a gnarled hand across his face.

"I never expected for the two of us to be sitting here like this," he went on in a faltering voice, "old, alone, no youngsters around . . . the house quiet. How can I not help feeling that I somehow failed? Failed my ancestors, my family, even failed you."

"Oh, William, you haven't failed me. We have had a good life in spite of our loss, in spite of what people said about us. I wouldn't trade my life for any woman's in Pennsylvania."

"What about the criticism? Surely you haven't forgotten—"

"Of course not. Some of my closest friends were among them, God forgive them. I haven't forgotten how much their gossip hurt."

"But what if it was true—that somehow it *was* our fault?"

"You don't really believe that?"

"I don't know. Probably not. The fact is, two generations under our charge left the community. It is difficult not to blame myself."

"As I have said before, Chad didn't leave the *faith,* he left our Fellowship. But there are many others less strict. Ours is one of the rare exceptions in the wave of liberalism that has infected the Society."

"I should have seen it coming. It was my fault for allowing him to be exposed to the world. I should have seen that he wasn't strong enough to withstand its temptations."

The woman sighed. "I understand your grief, William. I harbor similar doubts myself. It's been so many years. Then a day like today comes, another letting go, and it seems like yesterday." She, too, blinked back tears and dabbed her eyes with a tissue.

"But we cannot look back," she went on in a tone of mingled determination and resignation. "The Book says that any man who sets his hands to the plow and looks back is not fit for the Kingdom. As you are haunted by whether you did right by our son, I am troubled by the same questions about his daughter. What might I have done differently?"

"She had more doubts at an earlier age than we realized. She may have been destined to leave the moment she arrived on our doorstep."

"How do you mean?"

"I have the feeling she was compelled by a past she knew nothing about. It was always pulling at her. She was never at peace here."

"I hope she is at peace now. Will she ever come back, William?"

"To stay, you mean . . . to live?"

His wife nodded.

"I cannot imagine it. This was never her home."

"I wonder where that home is," said the wife, her tone reflective.

"I doubt she even knows."

Neither attempted to find further answers to their questions. The house grew eerily quiet.

"Now that Frank's boys will be using most of your tools and equipment," said Anabel, at length breaking the silence, "what will become of the workshop and storeroom?"

"I kept enough tools to stay busy. They will still sell what I am able to make. I do not intend to sit and do nothing. When I can no longer even do that . . . well, who can say? We've crossed one bridge today. Let's save that next bridge for a later time."

"Whatever the future holds," she said, reaching for his hand, "we have each other, William. I am more thankful for that than you can imagine."

14

THE MUCKLE ROOM

Whales Reef, Shetland Islands

David Tulloch returned from his early ramble to the North Cliffs and the unbidden reminders of the past prompted by it. Walking into the home where he had spent his entire life, he made his way straight to the kitchen and poured water for the day's first pot of tea.

Sipping at the cup in his hand, he wandered into the Muckle Room, not so large or "great" as the great room of his uncle's house, so styled by his great-great-great grandmother. Esther Walpoole was an English lady of sufficient distinction to look with undisguised disdain on the traditional heritage of the family into which she had married. She had come north to marry Ernest's father, William, but had never forgotten—nor let anyone else forget—that she was first and foremost, born and bred, an *Englishwoman*.

One of the first orders of business after her union with the Shetlander was the construction of a grand new domicile for the laird and chief and his wife on the east side of the island. Fortunately for David, old William Tulloch's wife had been

101

so consumed with designing and furnishing their new quarters that she had neither remodeled nor dismantled the Old House, or *Auld Hoose* as it had been known ever since. His present home had come down through the generations, finally to him, looking much the same, David assumed, as it had years before she moved from it. Esther Walpoole Tulloch had her new "cottage," so to speak, and he now had her old one.

For one who loved tradition, loved all things old, loved his family legacy and its Scottish roots, every inch of the place was precious to him.

David's gaze strayed across the wall opposite. Exquisite nineteenth century oak bookcases were filled from floor to ceiling, mostly with volumes passed down through the decades—the family library had been divided about equally between the two houses—along with those he had added himself. Most of his own personal library used in his research, however, he kept in his office upstairs.

The room held two sideboards, several writing tables, and three glass cases full of china, silver, and pewter, vases, goblets, and glass-ware. Though old, none of the contents was of particularly high antiquarian value. The Chippendale furniture, Delft ware, and collection of Derby porcelain that had come north with Esther Walpoole's dowry was all still displayed in what had become her new home.

Between windows and above sideboards and cases, the three walls of the Muckle Room adjoining the books were colorfully accented with traditional Scottish memorabilia resembling a Highland hunting lodge more than a family home—faded tartans, a variety of swords, dirks and sgian-dubhs, a ram's head, two antlered stag heads, a coat of mail, a shield, and an ornately painted Tulloch family crest. From two large hooks hung an ancient set of decaying bagpipes that would never make music again. Few Norse-minded Shetlanders were enamored of such things. Nearly every item in the room had come from the Highlands of mainland Scotland with old Ranald MacDonald in the early 1800s.

David's eyes fell on the harp in the corner of the room reportedly belonging to his great-grandmother, Moira Tulloch. For decades it had stood where it sat on this day, serving no purpose other than lending one more element of subtle charm to the aura of Celtic tradition. No one to his knowledge had played it since her time. The poor thing was missing several strings and fully a third were broken.

With cup of tea in hand, he walked over to it and plucked one string, then another. The random sounds without melody were yet curiously peaceful. They filled the room with melancholy reminders of days gone by.

The solitary vibrations penetrated deep into

David's soul. The death of his best friend at twelve had shattered his innocence. Losing his father a short time later deepened the scar. It took time for his youthful laughter to return. When it did, what sounded from teenage David Tulloch's lips was no longer the laughter of childhood but of youth gradually growing wiser in the often painful ways of the world.

As the mantle of the chieftainship settled upon his own shoulders at his father's passing, and as manhood overtook him, David's buoyantly optimistic nature returned. His smile and humor were sufficient to charm most of the village mothers and grandmothers who, a dozen years before, had wondered if he would ever amount to anything. Once the emotional spiritualisms of the Fountain movement spent themselves, and the broken families and friendships left in its wake began the process of restoration, life on the island slowly returned to what it had been before. Except for his cousin Hardy, who inherited his father's disdain for David's side of the family, most of the fishermen and their wives took to their young chief.

Though he rarely spoke of it, David never forgot the divisions that had nearly destroyed their community and had indeed split the church. If schoolmistress Barton and parish minister Aedon had not been gone from Whales Reef by the time he became chief, he would have taken what steps lay in his power to oust them. As it turned out, such was not necessary. By David's twenty-first year the island was well on its way toward the healing of most former breaches. Though hard feelings remained in some quarters, at least the village was able to worship again as one.

Sunday services in the parish church, however, rarely included the new chief. In the aftermath of the Fountain's cultish influences, David found himself embarking on a spiritual quest he knew could never be satisfied with the teachings of a church . . . any church. He had to discover the truth on his own. Amid his quandaries and quest, David took refuge in the Gospels. There his aching soul found sustenance. The red letters of his New Testament sent down roots into every corner of his being. His resulting spiritual journey had been amply rewarded in the years since with strength of character and a depth of wisdom well beyond his years.

But his spiritual pilgrimage had been a quiet and inward one, occupying that region of his being where he kept the memories of Armund and his father, and the bitter reminders of the erstwhile prophetess and prophet. Even the class-mates who had watched him squirm away from the touch of Sister Grace, and who, like him, had suffered from the Fountain's mischief could not completely understand the inward quest those memories prompted in David's heart. They were not driven to discover what it all *meant*.

More than anything else, what set David Tulloch apart from his fellow islanders was his intense drive to know truth. He was a complex man with both a jovial, gregarious side seen by the world and an inner nature informed by the pain of loss. These two seemingly opposite sides of his psyche joined as one into a fierce determination to protect the people of the island from any outside influences that would once more disrupt their way of life.

Even as the tones from the harp strings slowly dissipated, the striking of the half hour turned David's glance toward a large grandfather clock standing in the opposite corner. Its reverberating chime subdued the fading tones of the instrument into silence.

David gulped down the remainder of his tea, returned the cup to the kitchen, then grabbed coat, hat, and walking stick from beside the door. Moments later he strode for a second time that day out into the chilly morning, this time to the village and a visit to his uncle at the Cottage.

15

A Tough Fisher Breed

Lerwick, Shetland Islands

As the chief walked through the quiet morning toward the village, twenty miles away in Lerwick on mainland Shetland, the city's wholesale fish-processing warehouses were noisy beehives of activity.

Mornings were always busy as fishing boats came in from a night on the water—or after several nights—to unload their catches. The holds and scales and ice machines could scarcely keep up.

Cod had been running especially well for the past several weeks. Warehouses were full and ships laden with the sea's bounty sailed daily for Aberdeen, Edinburgh, Glasgow, London, and the Continent. Freshness and supply determined price. A load of herring, salmon, haddock, sole, mackerel, or cod brought into Lerwick before eight had to be in an iced container on its way south by six that same evening, arriving in markets ready for a thousand vendors, from door-to-door fish vans to major supermarket chains. Nobody wanted old fish.

Fishing was a feast-or-famine enterprise. The Shetlands had been enjoying its abundance for several years. The hardened seafarers reminded themselves that it couldn't last forever. Notwithstanding continental complaints about the over-fishing of North Sea cod, however, Shetland's fishermen were enjoying it while they could. Those owning their own crafts were making out best of all.

David's third cousin Hardar Tulloch, one of Whales Reef's toughest, most outspoken but certainly skilled fishermen, had just unloaded his two boats after several days at sea. Most of his crew roomed in Lerwick and would soon be off to their showers and beds and a few days' rest before heading out again.

"Who will join me for a pint or two before we start back for the island?" said Hardy as the city-dwellers gathered their belongings and stepped onto the quay.

The men of Hardy Tulloch's crew knew their boss did not like to drink alone. Though strong beer before eight in the morning was not to everyone's taste, there were some who could think of nothing else after a hard night on the water. For those of more refined habits, tea and coffee and cooked breakfasts could also be had at the Puffin's Beak, Hardy's favorite haunt in the city.

There was a time when the Puffin's Beak had

been mentioned in one or two guidebooks as among Lerwick's most popular and colorful pubs, full of "local atmosphere," they called it. The place had fallen from that distinction since adopting a policy of keeping its doors open twenty-four hours a day and serving beer as happily at six in the morning as six at night. The move was intended to draw fishermen into the establishment and had succeeded admirably. It was now the preferred destination for fishermen throughout the Shetlands whenever their boats put in at Lerwick.

The steady influx of Shetland's tough fisher breed through its doors, however, had a distinct drawback. Every inch—floor, walls, tables, chairs, the bar, the ceiling, seemingly even glasses scrubbed as clean as detergent and water could get them—bore the unmistakable aroma of the sea.

From top to bottom and inside out, the place smelled of fish. It had long since been abandoned by the guidebooks. Neither its regulars nor its owners minded, certainly not the fishermen who considered it their second home in the city.

Money primarily flowed in the Shetlands from three sources—fish, wool, and oil. The men who made their living from the first two rarely crossed paths socially with the third. The oilmen took their leisure moments in the Craigsmont Lounge, sipping wine or cognac while seated in expensive leather chairs surrounded by tapestries and oil paintings, and enjoying Havana cigars in its subdued atmosphere of wealth. They would not have been caught dead in the Puffin's Beak. Nor was it likely that Hardy Tulloch would have received much more than rude stares with accompanying sniffs of noses held slightly aloft had he ventured into the oilmen's domain at the Craigsmont.

As for the shepherds who kept their sheep healthy and sheared, producing wool for the women who knit Shetland's woolen goods, they were too busy to drink much beer or cognac. Neither establishment saw much of them.

"What do you think, Hardy?" asked BillyBlack, a Whales Reef incoming resident from Glasgow—what Shetlanders called a "sooth-moother"—and skipper of Hardy's second craft. "Is Keith's home brew better than this as he claims?"

Five of the men who had accompanied Hardy from the fish market and now sat around his usual table in the Puffin's Beak were drinking from tall glasses containing the beer in question. Another held a cup of tea. A mug of steaming coffee sat on the table in front of the last member of the group.

"After seventy-two hours at sea," replied Hardy, waving his pint in the air, "any beer in a dry room suits me jist fine!"

"But what's your opinion of Keith's brew?" persisted Black.

" 'Tis good, like he says. Might be the best, who can say?"

"When you marry Audney, you'll be able to drink as much of it as you like!" called Gordo Ross from the end of the table.

"Ye think Keith'll give me the right o' the tap any time it suits me? I dinna think he's likely tae gae that far," Hardy replied jovially.

"Not for his own son-in-law?"

"I'm nae convinced Keith an' Evanna is altogether happy aboot the prospect o' callin' Hardy Tulloch their son-on-law!" laughed Hardy.

"But ye're goin' tae marry Audney, isna ye, Hardy?" asked young Ian Hay, one of Hardy's youthful protégés.

"Oh, aye! Ye can be sure o' that, Ian."

"When are ye goin' tae ask her, Hardy?"

"I'm bidin' my time . . . jist bidin' my time. Ye canna rush a bonnie woman the like's o' Audney, ye ken."

"When ye an' Audney's married an' ye inherit the pub, are ye plannin' tae do the same for the islanders as Keith does?"

"Shush, keep yer voice down, Ian," put in Rufus Wood. "Nae one's tae ken, ye mind."

"Not me," said Hardy with a firm shake of his head. "Let a'body pay like everyone else."

"But you'll keep the special brew?" pressed Black.

"If I dinna come up wi' better. Anythin' Keith Kerr can do, I can do him one better."

"Will you keep fishing?" now asked their coffee-drinking mate, the one Englishman among them.

"Depends. Good money in the fish jist noo."

"Hard work, though—and dangerous. You might fancy yourself a pub owner."

"Aye, no a bad life. Canna say what I might do. But wi' a woman like Audney tae call mine, might be all the mair reason tae keep close tae home—especially at night!"

Laughter and smiles went round the table.

"Audney's a beauty all right," commented Wood. "But I hear she fancies yer cousin David."

Hardy's eyes flashed. He spun toward Wood.

"David's no man enough for the likes o' Audney Kerr," he growled. "What ye speak o' was a long time ago. She was jist a lass. Noo she's a buxom beauty an' she deserves a real man. That's why she'll be the wife o' Hardy Tulloch an' none other. An' if David tries tae stand in my way, it will be the worse for him. I've put him on the ground in the past, an' I winna hesitate doin' it again."

"Ye're no feared o' hurtin' our chief?" asked Ian.

Hardy roared with derisive laughter. "Oor

so-called 'chief' is the last man on Shetland I'm feared o'! An' he'd be well advised tae stay oot o' my way in the matter o' Audney Kerr."

Hardy lifted his glass and downed what remained in a single gulp, slammed it down on the table as if visibly punctuating the warning, then shouted for a second pint.*

---

*The broken bits of dialect here and elsewhere are not true reflections of Shetland speech, which would be most unintelligible to readers. These fragments are more representative of mainland Scottish speech. They are included to flavor the narrative with hints of the "sound of Scotland," though the specifics of that sound varies widely from region to region. In actual fact, true Shetlandic and its predecessor, the more ancient Norn, derive from the Old Norse of the Vikings and Lowland Scottish English, also with reminders of Dutch and German. While Shetlanders will communicate with visitors in a heavily accented form of recognizable English, speech between native Shetlanders, especially outside of Lerwick, is extremely difficult for outsiders to make heads or tails of.

16

BAKER AND CHIEF

Whales Reef, Shetland Islands

Without an inkling that he was the object of such heated remarks from his cousin to his cohorts in Lerwick, David passed a few simple stone dwellings clustered in random disarray at the edge of the village. He continued into the small town, greeting the few who were out at this hour. Most, however, were still inside encouraging their peat fires into life for the day, evidenced by the wisps of smoke trailing up from the chimneys around him.

By the time the sun rose as high in the sky as it reached in the Shetlands, the women would be in their yards hanging out laundry. Today was expected to be warm—as warm as the mercury climbed in the Shetlands on a day in September, which was somewhere in the mid-fifties Fahrenheit. In July it might reach sixty. But in these northern climes, summer was well past. The weather had already begun to turn.

A minute or two later, David walked through

the door of Coira MacNeill's bakery. A shrill bell above the door announced his presence. As its echo died away, the proprietress walked into the main shop from her ovens in back, wiping her hands on the stained apron around her ample midsection, brow perspiring freely.

"Weel, yoong David," she said, "ye're oot early—fine day, is it?"

"Bit misty just now, Coira," he replied. "And chilly enough, though it's never cold of a morning in here."

"Nae in a baker's shop, that's the truth."

"If your butteries are out of the oven, I'd like a half dozen. I'm on my way to Uncle Macgregor's. He's especially fond of them."

"Aye, been on the rack these ten minutes."

"They're still warm then. He and I will enjoy them with our tea."

The plump woman disappeared again, returning a moment later with a small white bag. She laid it on the counter, and David set several coins beside it. She scooped them up and deposited the proceeds into the till.

"And you'll have that cake ready for Uncle Macgregor's birthday next week?"

"Aye, laddie. But he's a dour auld man. Hardly seems the like tae be havin' a party for his birthday."

David laughed and picked up the bag. "I'm planning no party, Coira. Just Dougal and me and

Saxe and Isobel and a few others. Not that you wouldn't be welcome yourself, as would anyone in the village—"

"Nae, nae . . . I wouldna set foot in the man's hoose."

"I know how you feel," rejoined David. "I'm afraid you and Aunt Rinda still bear him a grudge after all these years."

"Your aunt's a shrewd judge o' character, yoong David, ye mark my words."

"That may be, Coira. But I find her to be wrong in this case. The man's not what you think. He keeps up a gruff exterior to annoy people like you. But he's been good to me. That goodness has to come from somewhere."

"Weel, I'll grant ye that. But he never smiles when he comes in my shop."

"As why should he, the way you treat him? Do you smile at him, Coira?"

"I wouldna give him the satisfaction!"

"There—see what I mean? It seems to me you're to blame too. You ought to try flashing him one of your pretty smiles sometime and watch if he doesn't melt."

The woman flushed at the compliment. But she gave no indication that David's words would alter her opinion of the laird.

"I will allow that I'm aye indebted tae him for bein' more than fair wi' my rent," the widow MacNeill reluctantly acknowledged. "Hasna raised it in twenty years, an' if a body gets ahin', he's nae bothered aboot it."

"As I recall, he actually lowered yours when your husband died."

"Weel, 'tis true enouch, I'll grant ye that. Still, I dinna like the man. And ye shouldna call him Uncle when he's nae such thing."

"He's my grandfather's cousin," said David. "What would you have me call him, my cousin such-and-such removed? And whatever else he may be, he's a man deserving of my esteem. With my own daddy dead, 'Uncle' is the most respect I can give him, so that's what I call him, whatever the exact relation." David turned toward the door. "Good morning to you, Coira," he said cheerfully as he left.

As her bell tinkled behind him the woman watched the young chief leave her shop, thinking to herself that he was a fine lad in spite of his affinity for the aging Macgregor Tulloch.

Distant as the relation between the two men was, however, even on an island filled with second, third, and fourth cousins, the old man had no closer family to watch over him in his old age. Coira MacNeill was humanitarian enough to be grateful that David loved the man.

No one, she thought, should have to reach the end of his days alone.

17

UNCLE AND CHIEF

David continued through the village and past its small harbor, taking note of which fishing boats were readying for their day's labors on the waters of the North Sea.

Reminded again that somewhere out there the wreck of the *Bountiful* lay on the bottom, with the three bodies of its crew who had perished in it, he waved at several fishermen as he walked by. Most returned his greeting. Had Hardy Tulloch been present rather than at the Puffin's Beak in Lerwick, he would likely have ignored David altogether. The two young men may have shared family roots, but they had little else in common. The one exception was Audney Kerr. If the involvement between the three could not properly be called a "love triangle," it was certainly true that feelings ran high. Everyone on the island was watching developments.

Leaving the eastern precincts of Whales Reef, David followed the shoreline for another three-quarters of a mile before striking off inland. He crossed the road and continued toward the largest structure on Whales Reef save the wool factory, his uncle's home and ancestral seat of the laird of the island. Though in reality it was far more than could be done justice to by such an appellation, the spacious and, in its own way, magnificent dwelling had been known for four generations simply as the Cottage.

Ten minutes later David crested a slight rise and caught his initial glimpses of the gables and turrets of the home of the man for whom he felt such affection, seventy-seven-year-old Macgregor Tulloch.

Strange, thought David as he approached and glanced up at the chimney. No white trail of smoke rose from it. He now realized that the pleasurably familiar smell of peat had not met him as he walked toward the house. A fire was always burning in the hearth of the massive stone fireplace of the Cottage by this hour. His uncle Macgregor was always up by 6:30 or 7:00 to stoke the coals, add fresh peats, and put on the kettle for tea before heading out to his dogs and sheep.

Macgregor Tulloch had lived alone since the ill-fated marriage of his youth. Though he had two men and a woman who lived at the Cottage and worked for him, he did not want anyone stoking his fire or brewing his tea. He preferred to enjoy the first hours of the day either alone or with a visit from David. He would share the morning hours with no one else.

His butler-valet and housekeeper, therefore,

ate breakfast in their own apartment on the ground floor at the end of the south wing. His game-keeper, in his private lodgings adjoining the barn, did the same.

As he drew near the house, a commotion of barking interrupted David's thoughts. Three rambunctious white-and-black sheepdogs sprinted toward him with boisterous wagging, licking, sniffing greetings.

"Where's your master this morning, lads?" said David, stooping to give each of the three a tussle and affectionate pat.

David looked about. Everything seemed in order, other than the complete lack of evidence of human life. Leaving the dogs outside, he opened the great oak door of the Cottage and walked inside. A lifeless chill met him. Walking through to the kitchen, he found it cold and dark.

"Uncle Gregor!" he called. "Uncle Gregor . . . it's David. I've come with fresh butteries!" he called again as he set the bag on the table.

He made his way into the spacious great room where the huge fireplace sat stone-cold. The coals had been packed the previous night, but no sign of life was anywhere. Unconsciously David shivered.

Growing alarmed, David flipped on the lights and made for the stairs. He took them two at a time, hurried down the corridor, then slowed as he entered his uncle's bedroom.

The moment he saw the form lying motionless under the familiar blanket of MacDonald tartan, and the ghostly white face on the pillow, he feared the worst.

He hurried to the bedside, placed a tender hand on his uncle's shoulder. No response came from beneath the tartan. Hesitantly David laid a gentle hand on the pale face where it lay in apparent peaceful slumber.

The cheek was ice cold.

"Oh, Uncle Gregor . . . Uncle Gregor!" whispered David in a forlorn tone of grief-stricken affection.

He withdrew his hand and stood staring down at the bed as tears filled his eyes. Wiping at his eyes and blinking hard, at length he stooped and tenderly kissed the cheek whose owner had departed for warmer regions sometime in the night.

18

LIFE IN THE FAST LANE

Washington, D.C.

The days following the final Midwestern Investments signing were hectic for Madison Swift and her able assistant, Loni Ford. News of the deal was already circulating throughout the financial world.

Everyone wanted a piece of Madison Swift. Suddenly she was on Wall Street's radar screen as someone to watch.

Several days later Loni walked into her boss's office following Maddy's return from a luncheon meeting.

"Jackson from Fidelity called while you were out," she said, taking her customary seat opposite Maddy's desk. She passed across the phone message. "He's insistent on talking to you."

"Not interested," replied Maddy. "I'm happy where I am."

"I told him that. He wants to talk to you anyway."

"Nothing he says will make me jump ship."

"He insists . . . says they're preparing an offer you can't refuse."

"Just watch me!"

"You might as well get it over with and call him. Otherwise he'll keep hounding you. And I'll have to keep passing along his messages!"

"He's one of those guys who thinks if he can keep you on the phone long enough, eventually he'll sway you to his point of view. But okay," agreed Maddy, "I'll call him. Anything else come up in the last two hours?"

"Montgomery—in charge of Far East small cap upstairs—wants to pick your brain about some new directions they're considering for China."

"China!"

"That's what he said."

"I'm no expert on the Chinese economy."

"I told him that's what you'd say. But your reputation has people on tenth talking. At least that's the water-cooler scuttlebutt."

"Are you a water-cooler eavesdropper, Loni?" said Maddy with a smile. "Picking up the office gossip? I didn't know that about you."

"Just enough to keep you abreast of what you need to know."

"Good girl. Got my back, I like that."

"I try. Anyway, I think Montgomery simply wants to meet you and get your big-picture impressions."

Maddy nodded. "Fair enough, I suppose. Got to keep the suits on tenth happy."

"And the deadline on the Campbell acquisition

is looming," Loni went on, glancing through her notes. "It's next week—they want your final report by Monday."

"I'll have it ready."

"All right, changing directions," Loni said. "Here's a list I'd like you to look at." She handed Maddy a single sheet. "I'm trying to get you scheduled for fall. These are the speaking requests that have come in. I need to start prioritizing, let some of these folks know you won't be available. You'll see that a number of the dates conflict."

"Goodness, Loni!" exclaimed Maddy. "There must be ten or fifteen."

"Twenty-seven. Invitations have been pouring in. You're the rising star in the investment world, Maddy."

"I had no idea. When did they all come?"

"I've been saving them up. I thought it would be best for you to look at your calendar with everything in front of you. People are talking about you, Maddy. This is just the tip of the iceberg."

"Are you trying to flatter me?" said Maddy with an amused smile.

"You know I would never do that. Well, *almost* never. But just to give you an idea of what I'm talking about, there's a rumor floating around the building that Forbes is looking at doing a feature on you."

"Get out of here!"

"Really. The new face of investments and all that. True, it's only a rumor. But there are reasons why rumors get started."

"I'll believe it when I see it."

"Believe it, Maddy. Just look at that list—high schools, universities, investment groups, banks, senior groups. You've put a face on investing that everyone can identify with. Kids are interested, of all things! That Children's Mutual Fund you started—sheer genius. You've sparked something, Maddy. You've brought the stock market into ordinary folks' lives. They love it."

Maddy took in Loni's words thoughtfully. She was quiet for several seconds.

"You'll notice I've got the Gleneagles conference blocked out for early November," Loni added after a moment. "That's when I'll be gone—I assume you still want me to go to that thing?"

"Absolutely."

"And you're not planning to go?"

Maddy shook her head.

"That's what I assumed," laughed Loni. "I booked my flights this morning."

"Fantastic."

"But I wanted to talk to you before I scheduled anything for you during the week I'll be gone," Loni added. "Not that you couldn't handle everything without me, but—"

"Forget it, Loni," interrupted Maddy. "You were being thorough and thinking of me. I appreciate that. You didn't want my schedule to get overloaded when my able-and-talented right hand wasn't here to help keep the plates spinning."

A sheepish expression came over Loni's face. "I wouldn't say it *quite* like that," she said.

"Well, you done good, Loni Ford, as always," said Maddy. "All right, I'll look over your list."

19

PASSING OF A LEGACY

Whales Reef, Shetland Islands

The morning of Macgregor Tulloch's funeral dawned drizzly and cold. All along the coast, the wind tore the white tips of an endless succession of waves off into horizontal spray strong enough to reach halfway up the shore. Remnants of fog blew in vapory shreds from the sea until they disappeared inland in wind and rain. Miles of gray cloud separated the islanders from the great light above that brought warmth to the earth.

The man whose body lay in the coffin, however, borne in a buggy pulled by two of his own specially bred, sturdy half-Shetland ponies, cared no more for the weather. He was gone from the world of shadows, taking his secrets with him. He now resided either in the Land of Light or in the Pit of Death. Opinion among those he left behind on the island that had been his lifelong home was varied as to which of the two was his final, and deserved, destination.

Few of those following the makeshift hearse in the time-honored tradition could truly be said to be *mourning* on this bleak day, only in the sense that death of any kind reminded them of their own mortality. A pall of expected sadness had hung over the island since news of the laird's death. Those who would truly miss the man, however, could be counted on the fingers of one hand.

In truth, every one of them would miss him more than they realized before many months were out. For he had been to every man, woman, and child of them far more than a mere figurehead.

Dougal Erskine—tall for a Shetlander, though a good two inches shy of six feet and approaching sixty—appeared especially auspicious in top hat and tails. Walking ahead of them, he led the procession with reins in hand attached to two of his master's faithful equine friends pulling the carriage. The men who followed Erskine and the conveyance clattering over the rough cobble-stones were dressed dutifully in their Sunday blacks. Their presence was not so much out of reverence for the dead, but from superstitious fear of offending the Powers of the unknown. No doubt they were also paying their respects to David, already being referred to as "the young laird." Whatever their ambivalence toward Macgregor, his great-nephew was a favorite among young and old alike.

As for the women, they had their own reasons for trudging en masse after the men in spite of the gusty wind and slanting rain. There was nothing quite so delicious as stirring up a pot of old gossip. Though no new information would be gleaned on this day, the funeral and its aftermath presented ripe opportunity to dredge up all the business from fifty years before, brought fresh to their memories by the occasion. The wagging tongues would carry on about the same things they had discussed a thousand times before in those fifty years—the dreadful humiliation visited upon their beloved Odara Innes in the prime of her youth.

Few of them had ever forgiven Macgregor for marrying the Norwegian trollop, Hiordis Gudmund. What kind of name was that anyway? A princess she might have been in Norway, but on Whales Reef she was considered a hussy. Rinda Gunn and the bolder of the women didn't mind saying so. That the woman had disappeared and come to an untimely end herself, or so the rumor went, "twas nae mair nor she deserved," said Rinda. Offending Providence was the least of Rinda's worries. She was a woman who spoke her mind.

The procession out of the village and up the hill to the church also turned the minds of not a few toward the more recent controversy of twenty-four years ago. The effects still lingered in spite of the young chief's attempts to erase memory of the Fountain of Light from Whales

Reef. The mere sight of the church reminded them of the split and the bitter feelings that had resulted on both sides.

Rinda Gunn had been outspoken then too, declaring the secret signs boasted by the Fountainites "the wark o' the de'il, ye mark my words," a blast from her tongue that included her own brother in its withering rebuke. Her conclusion was perhaps validated in part by the group's judgmentalism, which was more in evidence following fresh outpourings than Spirit fruits. In spite of its enigmatic and evasive Christian jargon, whether the movement that had swept through their islands was truly a "cult" in the technical sense would be for the future history books to determine.

As they walked, a few cleavages could be observed that fell roughly along the old lines separating the Fountainites from the rest of the village. None, however, dared speak of it. All agreed that the young chief was an even-tempered and pleasant young man, and that only one thing was capable of arousing his fury— any hint of the Fountain of Light. In his opinion it had been an evil time in the life of Whales Reef. Any man or woman who stirred that pot again would have him to answer to.

Thus the black-clad villagers continued through the rain, silently pondering their now-dead laird, or Odara Innes and her Norwegian usurper, or those years when a "strange gospel" nearly destroyed their village.

Most of the women would not hear a word the Reverend Stirling Yates uttered in the church or at the graveside. Their attention would be riveted on Odara Innes, still in their eyes beautiful at sixty-nine. They would always see her in the flower of her youth—the Shetland beauty spurned by the youthful son of their laird now lying dead in front of them—destined to live the remainder of her life in loneliness.

What would she do? they wondered. Would she spit on the coffin of her youthful love? Many had wondered whether she would attend at all.

The carriage pulled up in front of the church. The two ponies came to a standstill as Dougal stopped and the reins relaxed. David Tulloch, chief and now presumptive laird of the small island clan, stepped to the back of the carriage, flanked by Noak Muir, Keith Kerr, and his uncle Fergus Gunn. Standing two on each side, the four slid the casket out and carried it into the church.

Curious as they filed into the church what the minister would say about the old curmudgeon, the villagers spent the next half hour mostly listening to passages of Scripture about eternal life, with appropriate reminders to live well before their own time came.

Forty minutes after they had carried it inside,

the four men bore the casket out the church doors, across the gravel, and through the cemetery's chipped and peeling black iron gates to where the burial site had been prepared.

The trailing assembly closed ranks, gathering slowly and stiffly around the open grave. Celtic superstition mingled with reverence for tradition, along with just enough Christian jargon to keep them all more afraid of hell than sin, and fearful of offending Him who held the keys to death and Hades.

Rinda Gunn stepped forward to join her husband Fergus on David's right. Behind them stood several of their oldest children with their husbands and wives, as well as their two unmarried daughters, all of whom had returned to the island for the funeral. Bakery widow Coira MacNeill stood beside Odara Innes and her father, retired Whales Reef veterinarian and local curiosity Alexander Innes, now approaching ninety and considered no less an oddity now than he had been all his life. Keith Kerr, the closest friend David's father had had in the village, stood beside him on the left, now joined by his wife, Evanna, and daughter Audney, the village beauty of the present generation.

The Kerrs, owners of Whales Fin Inn, had left eighteen-year-old Rob Munro at the inn, though at this hour no one was likely to require the services of the pub, not even Hardy Tulloch's men. The inn's only guests, two American bird-watching tourists, had eaten an early breakfast and were gone to Lerwick for the day.

Along with David and Dougal Erskine, two others in genuine mourning on this day were old Macgregor's self-styled butler, Saxe Matheson, and his sister, Isobel, the dead man's housekeeper, who stood stoically side by side. Both cherished a deep devotion to their now-deceased employer, an ancient loyalty that would be difficult for a modernist to understand. What was to become of them now, they did not know. But neither would lose a moment in transferring that same affection to Macgregor's young kinsman. They were of the old school. Loyalty to chief, bard, laird, and clan was bred deep into the marrow of their souls.

The wool factory's manager, David's cousin Murdoc MacBean, and his family stood behind the Gunns. Postman Sarff Fenris stood next to his sister, Grizel, and her husband, Tevis Gordon, with their son and two daughters.

In ever-widening circles the villagers and island fishermen, wives, crofters, and all those employed at the wool factory gathered round. Even village eccentric Armond Lamont was present among them, though to anyone's knowledge he and Macgregor Tulloch had never so much as exchanged a word. That assumption, in actual fact, was far from true. The two men were on closer terms than anyone, even David himself, who did know of their friendship, suspected.

The only village native and relative of the dead laird conspicuously absent was Hardy Tulloch. He and the half of his crew comprised of tough Glaswegians were at his boat on this day, more indifferent than all the rest. Even those locals who were dependent on Hardy for their livelihoods would not work, whatever they may have thought of him, on the day the laird was rejoined to the earth. Among them, Gordo Ross and Rufus Wood were sufficiently traditionalists to join the day's mourners. Even young Ian Hay, in whose eyes Hardy could do no wrong, had been pressured by his parents to attend.

While his second craft bobbed idly in the harbor, Hardy set out with the *Hardy Fire* into a sea far too rough for more prudent men.

At the graveside, Reverend Yates's brief comments and lengthy prayer were unmemorable. It was a bitterly cold day. Every one in the company was relieved when the final Amen was pro-nounced. All that remained was to lower the departed into his final resting place. The honors were carried out by Noak Muir and David Tulloch holding the ropes on one side, with assistance from Fergus Gunn and Keith Kerr on the other. The company then filed silently by, the men's heads uncovered, each with his or her own final thoughts about the man at rest at the bottom.

Last in the line—whether by intent or by the collective subconscious design of the company it would be difficult to say—came the spurned love of Macgregor Tulloch's youth, Odara Innes.

The eye of every woman peered from beneath their black bonnets, anxious to witness for themselves what she would do.

Even the heavens seemed to sense the dramatic tension of the moment. The rain let up. The wind eased.

Odara came forward behind her father, then paused beside the grave.

The shuffling of the many feet ceased. Silence descended.

Odara stared down into the hole. A tear crept down her cheek. Her lips moved almost imperceptibly.

Then one hand, trembling slightly, went inside her black coat and produced a single rose on its stalk. Its blossom was of a deeper red than blood itself, so deep that in this light it almost appeared black.

She held it several seconds, then tossed it into the hole where it came to rest atop the casket.

An audible gasp went round the churchyard. Those for whom the day represented an opportunity for revived gossip about Odara Innes and Macgregor Tulloch had certainly been provided ample fodder for their itching tongues.

But already Odara was gone from the grave.

She walked briskly through the iron gates of the cemetery back toward the church. Umbrella slanted against the resuming rain, she continued around the building, caught up with her father, slipped her hand through his arm, and the two continued on in the direction of the village. None hurried to accompany them.

A slow murmur crept through the crowd at what they had witnessed. Noak, Fergus, and Keith began filling the hole. A few of the men joined them.

The rest proceeded in slow procession back down the hill in the wake of the enigmatic Innes father and his daughter.

Once through the black gates and removed a safe distance from the silent listening stones of the dead, low whispers erupted into a dozen private conversations.

The men were unconcerned. The women were all asking the same question about what they had seen. *What did it mean?*

Had Odara actually *forgiven* the man? Or was the rose on the coffin a final act of spite, her chosen means to trample on his grave in triumph that at last he was gone to the hell he deserved?

Halfway to town, David fell into stride beside his aunt Rinda Gunn, whose husband Fergus had remained behind with Reverend Yates and a few others to see to the final interment. She was engaged in lively conversation with Evanna Kerr about the mysterious rose. Sensing David behind her, and knowing his hatred for gossip—today she was not inclined to provoke an argument—she swallowed what she had been about to say.

She turned toward her nephew. Though on this day his serious side predominated, David nevertheless flashed the two women a wide smile. Even to her critical eye, his aunt had to admit that he was a handsome young man dressed as he was in black suit and tie. His characteristic sandy-brown crop of hair blew about in the breeze. His rugged face, not so weather-beaten as those of the island fishermen, was filled with a kind, sincere, and honest expression.

"Hello, Auntie. And you, Evanna," he said as he joined them.

"Weel, young David," said Rinda, "ye're the laird noo."

"No laird yet, Auntie."

"What for no?" retorted Rinda.

"When a man dies, there is much to be done. It's only been a few days. Uncle Macgregor's solicitors have to sort through the papers to make sure all the laws and protocols are followed. Ownership of land is legally complicated, transferring deeds and titles—everything takes time."

"Tish tosh wi' all that!" rejoined David's aunt. "The man's deid, an' good riddance!"

"Auntie—dinna speak ill o' the deid!" exclaimed David, lapsing into Scots dialect. "I loved the man."

"Weel, I didna. He was an ill one."

"If Odara can forgive him at the end, surely ye can yersel'," said David.

"Oh, aye—forgive him, ye're thinkin'! Is that what ye think the floer in's grave was meanin'?"

"What else, Auntie?"

"Didna ye see it? Twas a *black* rose—a rose o' death. What was she doin' but layin' one last curse on the man as he lay in his grave?"

"Auntie!" exclaimed David. "She was doing no such thing. It was a gesture of forgiveness, you mark my words."

"What think ye, Evanna?" said Rinda.

Mrs. Kerr cast a quick glance in David's direction. No doubt aware that David was soon to become the most powerful man on the island, she was far less inclined to offend her chief than was his aunt. "I cudna rightly say, Rinda," she replied. "The rose looked to be mair red tae me."

"It was black, I tell ye! But, David," Rinda went on without pausing, "when will ye be movin' tae the Cottage?"

"I told you not to get ahead of yourself, Auntie," replied David. "There are titles and deeds to be sorted. I haven't exactly made up my mind what to do. I am fond of the Auld Hoose."

"'Tis no a place fit for the laird o' Whales Reef."

"It was the laird's home for generations, and it is fit for me."

"Not noo that ye're laird. Ye must bide fit tae yer station an' yer callin'. Ye want tae make yer mum prood."

"I hope to make her proud by the man I am, Auntie, not by where I live."

"That's as well as may be, but there's nae reason ye canna do both."

"Perhaps not, Auntie," David said with a chuckle. "We shall see. All things in good time."

PART 3

NOVEMBER 2005

20
SEASON OF CHANGE

Whales Reef, Shetland Islands

When David Tulloch drove off the last ferry onto Whales Reef, it was 4:45 in the afternoon and the sun was about to disappear into the sea. Already dusk was hurrying north. It had been a long day. He was tired and looking forward to a quiet evening with oatcakes and tea in front of his fireplace.

More than three months had gone by since his great-uncle's funeral. Life on Whales Reef had, to all appearances, continued on as normal, uninterrupted by a momentous passing of more import to the island's residents than they understood. David, who would be the most affected of all, had no idea what changes lay on the horizon. He had just completed a week serving as resident speaker and guide for a tour of Germans on the three big islands. This morning's final lecture had concluded before lunch. After the inevitable expressions of gratitude and farewells, he had driven south from Unst and Yell with three ferry crossings to make. How good it was at last to see his own wharf through the mist!

He had no more tours, lectures, or conferences until Christmas, and then nothing scheduled until February. By late spring tourists would be flocking north once more in hopes of observing the runs of orca or killer whale. At present, however, he was anticipating a quiet and uneventful winter to work on his current book. He enjoyed the personal interactions of tour groups, but it was wearying. He always found it good to get home.

Dusk was thickening as he drove from the landing to Coira MacNeill's bakery. A light shone through the front window. Luckily she was still in the shop and had not yet retired to her upstairs quarters. He walked inside to the familiar tinkling of the bell.

"Coira," he called. "It's David . . . are you here?"

"Aye" came the woman's voice, followed a few seconds later by her person. "But only just. I was aboot tae be turnin' oot the light."

"Have you more oatcakes?" asked David. "I'm just back from a week in the north. I need some for my tea."

"There's always oakcakes, though I'm oot o' bread, scones, an' the rest."

"That will suit me fine, Coira. I want to put my feet up to a warm fire and enjoy being home."

"Where were ye this time, David?" she asked

as she began filling a white paper bag from her glass case.

"Up on Unst."

"Ye been away a good while. I haena seen ye in days."

"A week. This was my last stint with the tourists for the year."

"Who was they this time?"

"Germans—a bird-watching group from Hanover. Pleasant folk, but I'm glad to be home."

Coira set the bag on the counter. David handed her a five-pound note.

"Yer cousin Murdoc's some anxious tae see ye, David. He's been in two or three times askin' if I kenned when ye'd be home. I told him I'm no yer mum, nor one who keeps an itinerary for a busy man like yersel'."

David laughed. "Still," he said, "he knows you're more likely to know the goings-on of Whales Reef than any other soul. I'll run by the factory on my way home."

"He seemed anxious, David, worried like, ye ken? What's it aboot?"

"I haven't an idea. But if I did, I would think twice before I told you, Coira!" he added, laughing again. "Whatever he has to talk to me about would be all over the village in less than an hour." He turned toward the door with his oatcakes.

"Are ye sayin' I'm a gossip, yoong David?" said Coira before he could get to the door.

"I said no such thing, Coira. It's just that you and the town wives keep such close council that the minute you know a thing, the whole place kens it."

"Can I help it if fowk come into my shop? I canna keep them fae talkin'."

"Maybe not, but you can help what *you* say in return. Sometimes I'm thinking you're a bit free with the dispatching of other folk's news."

"I can haud my tongue as weel as the next woman!"

"That you *can,* I have no doubt . . . whether you choose to hold it may be another matter. Thank you for the oatcakes, Coira," added David quickly. He turned for the door before she could reply further. Whatever tongue lashing was sent after him as he exited the shop was thankfully drowned out by the bell and its echo. The door banged shut and silenced the temporary annoyance of its owner.

David returned the half mile back along the coast, then inland up a wide, skillfully cobbled road, arriving at length in front of a surprisingly ornate two-story stone building now known simply as the Mill.

The double-lane driveway—where in this region even the main roads were wide enough only for a single automobile—spoke silently of better times. A century had passed since expensive carriages had clattered along this drive, bearing wealthy southern visitors from their yachts and ferries up the hill to spend a week or two in what was one of the Shetlands' most glamorous Edwardian hotels. Island walking tours and nature excursions were then all the rage among British aristocrats and the wealthy from the Continent.

But fads and airplanes, depressions and World Wars and automobiles bring change to out-of-the-way places, and the Whales Reef Hotel had suffered the consequences. In the middle years of the previous century, after being used as a wartime hospital, it sat empty for a decade. Abandoned and in disrepair so serious it threatened the building's survival, the villagers had disparagingly dubbed it "England's Folly."

Thankfully, the once proud edifice had been rescued, rehabilitated, reroofed, and progressively refurbished over the years by Macgregor Tulloch's father, as well as by Macgregor himself, and now served more utilitarian purposes. Electricity had been installed when it arrived on the island. Indoor plumbing came later. Finally oil boilers to heat the massive building in place of dirty and inefficient peat fireplaces were added some years after the discovery of North Sea oil in the 1960s. It was the largest structure on Whales Reef and represented the hub and source of the island's economic vigor.

Lights shone from the Mill's ground floor windows in the gathering darkness, as well as from his cousin's upstairs office, indicating the usual life and activity within. As David parked in front, however, his was the only vehicle to be seen. None of the thirty or more workers—mostly women, a good number fishing widows—who earned their livelihood at the Mill would have considered driving to or from work. The only concession afforded the weather, in the event of a snowy blizzard or a driving rain, was the rare occasion when Murdoc MacBean, the Mill's manager, ferried the less hardy—several older than seventy, two more than eighty—to and from their homes in the Mill's red van like a school bus making its rounds. Even on the most inclement of days, however, the majority of the workers buttoned their coats, slid their rubber boots over their stockings, and set out from their homes for the Mill under wide hats or umbrellas. They were Shetlanders, after all. What was a little rain to them?

As David walked toward the front door on this evening, the familiar red van was out of sight, safely stowed in the garage at the back of the building. There it usually remained unless deliveries were to be made to the mainland—as the largest island, officially Shetland, was known—or unless the weather took a nasty turn.

He walked inside to bright lights and a hubbub of activity throughout the huge single room, most of the ground floor's original hotel dining facility and ballroom. The varied conversations and machinery sounds combined with a colorful visual array, a symphonic spectacle of sight and sound unlike any other. David never tired of it.

The place bustled with the life of a human beehive. The whir of spinning wheels combined with the clatter of great looms at the far end fashioning iconic Shetland wool blankets. A few knitting machines were spread about, along with several clusters of women seated in circles whose blethering tongues were moving as fast as their fingers wielded their needles. Most of these were knitting Shetland lace or sweaters. David stood a moment and took in the sight with pleasure.

Shouts and greetings from all through the great room rose to meet him.

"It's the chief . . . Good day tae ye, laird . . . Hoo are ye, yoong David? . . . 'Tis aye the new laird!"

None paused in their work. But every eye turned toward him, accompanied by smiles and more words of welcome.

As was his custom, David proceeded about, greeting each woman by name, asking about their families and showing keen interest in what they were crafting and in the particular patterns forming from their needles. An occasional ripple of laughter from the chief's mouth was music to their ears. David's laugh had been one of his trademark characteristics since boyhood.

"An' hoo are ye this evening, Eldora, my dear?" said David, leaning down and planting an affectionate kiss on the wrinkled cheek of the Mill's oldest worker, eighty-eight-year-old Eldora Gordon. She was formerly Eldora Innes and aunt to Odara whose dark rose at the laird's graveside was still being talked about.

The elderly woman beamed. "Ye're a scamp, laddie!" A delighted cackle followed. "Ye canna go aboot kissin' the lassies sae freely. Folk'll git the wrong idea."

"I don't kiss all the lassies, Eldora," David said with a grin. "Only the bonniest ones!"

21
WHAT'S IN A NAME?

Above the Atlantic

Sitting in coach on a Boeing 747 heading west, Loni Ford leaned over a leather-bound journal on her lap, pen in hand.

Following a short hop between Edinburgh and London, and the first two hours of her transatlantic flight home from Heathrow, she had read, dozed, glanced through several magazines, and attempted to review her notes from the Gleneagles conference just concluded.

Then came the flight attendant's voice beside her. "Miss Ford," she said. "*Alonnah* Ford?"

Loni glanced up with a smile and nodded.

"I have your vegetarian meal."

"Oh . . . thank you," said Loni, pulling down the tray table.

As the attendant moved away, Loni's thoughts tumbled back to a time long before she had turned herself into *Loni* Ford.

She never knew when the mere mention of her given name would exert a hypnotic spell and set off a succession of contemplative reflections. That's why she always packed her journal when she traveled, the book whose story she was writing herself.

As soon as her meal was finished, she had taken the journal from her bag. She held it thoughtfully, then slipped her favorite Sailor fountain pen from its pocket inside the book's cover, removed its cap, and set nib to paper.

That was two hours ago. She'd been writing on and off with many pauses and faraway gazes out the window ever since.

Her pen stilled as she scanned the page in front of her.

At such times of pensive reflection, the rushed pace of life seemed to fade into slow motion. Somehow the disengagement forced by air travel often brought with it a mood of reflective quiet.

She could not truthfully say she *enjoyed* gazing back at her girlhood years and earliest memories. Confusion about one's self wasn't always *fun*. Yet seasons of self-examination were necessary to growth. Where better than in an airplane six miles above the earth to gain a bird's-eye view of life—present *and* past—just like the view of the earth floating by below.

The company shrink was always harping on the "integration" of what he called their "many conflicting selves." She put up with the yearly interview without allowing him to poke around in her psyche too deeply. Any poking around in those regions she would handle herself, thank you very much. Imagine the delight of gray-haired old Dr. Glossop if she let slip she was an orphan! He would be performing a psycho-analytical autopsy before her mandatory hour was out. With follow-up visits required!

Definitely not!

Suddenly another voice startled her out of her reverie. A girl of five or six was standing beside her in the aisle. The question from her lips was simplicity itself.

"Hi, what's your name?" she said innocently.

It was the entrée to every relationship, especially for the childlike, the most fundamental identification of personhood. Without knowing it, the tiny stranger had plunged her fellow traveler into a conundrum probing the very meaning of the universe.

"Who *am* I, do you mean?"

The girl nodded.

"Hmm . . . I think today maybe I am Alonnah," answered Loni with a wistful smile.

"I'm Sophie," said the girl before scampering away.

Loni stared down the aisle after her young visitor. Slowly the quizzical smile faded from her lips. As many times as she had been asked her name in recent years, she hadn't replied by saying Alonnah in longer than she could remember.

She flipped back to the front of her journal.

Inside its cover, in her own hand, she read *The Journal of Loni Ford.* She had intentionally become Loni after leaving home for college. The name symbolized an attempt to say good-bye to the past, maybe even leave the shadowy Alonnah behind as well.

When traveling, however, she could never escape the Alonnah Ford on her driver's license, and now, for this most recent trip, her passport. When officials asked her name, as little Sophie just had, she did not have the luxury of using a trendy self-styled nickname.

However she tried to avoid it, the question of identity always brought inner conflict. She had a pretty good idea who Loni was—or so she thought. But Alonnah remained a mystery.

She looked down again at the book in her lap. This wasn't Loni Ford's journal at all. It was Loni's reflections about Alonnah.

For years she had tried to forget Alonnah. Now that she was a seasoned veteran of life at thirty-one, she realized how impossible that was. Alonnah was intrinsic to her deepest self. There was no getting away from her. Alonnah was part of the package.

And yet . . . *who was Alonnah?* And where had she come from?

They were questions Loni was unable to answer. Her early memories of life with her grandparents only scratched the surface. But the roots, the heritage beyond them, were sketchy at best. She knew who Loni was. She had, in a sense, created her—fashioned her purposefully, almost as if inventing a new persona. She was comfortable in Loni's skin.

But what of the shadowy Alonnah?

Her different selves weren't in harmony. The Loni Ford of the investment world and the Alonnah Ford of her childhood were two different people.

Which was her *real* self?

Dr. Glossop would probably dredge up all kinds of terms to describe her. Then he would tell Maddy that she had a basket case for an assistant!

But how could she feel at home with her childhood self when she had no idea where that little girl had come from? When she knew nothing about her mother? When information about her father was doled out in such painstaking thimblefuls that she could not help wondering whether it was even true?

She had no illusions that writing down her thoughts in a journal would get her to the bottom of it. But at least it provided an outlet for the disarray of her fragmented self-image.

Dr. Glossop would no doubt approve of the journal. Psychologists were all about getting in touch with one's inner child of the past.

But she had no intention of letting a word about it slip in his hearing any more than she intended to divulge the fact that her parents were dead.

This was one book whose pages no one else in the world would ever lay eyes on!

22

THE MILL

Whales Reef, Shetland Islands

The Whales Reef woolen mill was a thriving tumult of creative enterprise involving every phase of wool production. Clumps of wet, dirty, matted wool came into the back of the building after the shearing. That same wool went out in the Mill's delivery van in boxes to be shipped as finished hand-knit sweaters and scarves, shawls and other items of lace, yarn, caps, mufflers, and a myriad of products, some machine-woven, though much of it produced by hand. The reputation and quality of its name-patented *Whales Weave* brand was spoken of by vendors and retail outlets as among the best the Scottish isles had to offer. Murdoc MacBean's reputation on Shetland, Unst, Yell, Fetlar, and Bressay, moreover, was as an imminently fair man who would pay the sheep ranchers of the Shetlands more for their shorn wool than any buyer on the mainland. If it turned out that he had an excess inventory of wool, it was shipped to other woolen mills throughout Britain or the Continent.

For a small island operation, the Mill's activity

was remarkably diverse. It had begun as a means to provide employment for the widows of fishermen lost at sea. Demand for its products was sufficient to engage anyone on the island who was willing to work.

Meanwhile, the fishing industry ebbed and flowed in its inevitable cycle. Though oil had brought prosperity to many parts of the Shetlands, not every fishing village found it to be so. Few were as fortunate as Whales Reef in having a second commercial enterprise able to take up the slack during lean times.

David continued about the floor, smiling and asking the villagers about their work. At the far end of the room, his kinsman Murdoc MacBean descended from his office. As he came down the stairs, gradually all eyes turned toward him. His face wore a serious expression.

"Hello, David," the man said, extending his hand as they met.

"Murdoc," replied David with a smile. "I stopped in at Coira's. She said you've been asking when I would be back. Here I am."

"I need to talk to you, David," said Murdoc in a low tone. He took a step closer and leaned toward David's ear. "In private."

The two men turned back to the staircase. Conversations around them slowly ceased. David glanced back from the bottom stair. Every eye rested upon them.

"What are they staring at?" David asked as they walked upward. "I've never known them to be so quiet."

"They're wondering what we're planning to talk about," replied Murdoc in a soft voice. "I've tried to keep it from them. A few have figured out that something's amiss. Word spreads, you know."

The moment they were inside the office with the door closed behind them, David turned to his cousin.

"Figured out what, Murdoc?" he asked. "What do you mean, something's amiss? Is someone hurt? Has there been an accident?"

"Nothing like that, David. It's about money." He sat down behind his desk and motioned David to a nearby chair.

"What about it?" asked David.

"The operating account—at the bank, you know. According to our bookkeeper, it's dwindling. I didn't want to worry you about it. I kept thinking it would take care of itself."

"What did the bookkeeper tell you?" asked David with a puzzled expression.

"When I went into Lerwick two months ago to sign checks, she said that since the laird's death, no money had been deposited into the account. She said there was enough of a cushion to cover expenses for a while. She seemed confident the problem wouldn't last much longer. I didn't think much more about it. But about a week ago she telephoned to let me know that still nothing has been deposited. This time I heard urgency in her tone. Obviously she doesn't want us to face a situation a few months from now where our working capital runs dry."

"I'm not sure I understand, Murdoc," said David. "I thought . . . I mean, everybody looks busy, you're still selling goods. Orders haven't stopped—"

"That's just it, you see, David," he put in quickly. "The thing is so bewildering because actually orders are up. We're even running behind in production. We just received a sizable order from Edinburgh Woolen Mills yesterday. I'm sending out invoices every day. I assume they're being paid. Our sales ledger has never looked better."

"What's the problem then?"

"It's just as our bookkeeper said. Since old Macgregor's death there have been no deposits into the account."

"Why is that?"

"She doesn't know. It's like the checks that should be coming in are being lost. Yet that can't be since everything is handled by direct deposit."

"Might that have changed since Uncle Macgregor's death? Maybe the payment checks *have* been lost."

"I can't imagine why. Orders from our customers

come to me. I prepare invoices when the orders are filled, then send copies to the MacNaughton firm in Lerwick. They should be receiving the payments as usual."

"Right, that makes sense. As our family's solicitors, MacNaughton administers the parent company for the estate's affairs and handles all accounting and tax reporting."

"The bookkeeper told me there's always been an ACH deposit to the account at the beginning of each month."

"What's an ACH?"

"A new term bookkeepers are using for automatic debits and credits into bank accounts. In this case it simply notes the money that comes in automatically from our accounts receivable."

"I see, passed on from the estate's parent account handled by the MacNaughton people. They are in charge of my parents' trust as well as Uncle Macgregor's finances."

"But no money has been going in. I've been sending out invoices as usual and as I said passing on copies to the MacNaughton firm for collection. But no deposits have gone into the operating account."

"Have you called the bank?"

Murdoc nodded. "They know nothing more than what I've told you. They said that the deposits stopped after the laird's death. They couldn't tell me more than that."

"To be honest, I never thought much about the Mill's cash flow," said David slowly. "My family's financial affairs have been overseen by the MacNaughton firm for years. I suppose I should have paid more attention. I've been so busy these past months . . . ah, well, we'll get on it now. I'm sure there's a glitch in the system. I'll give my uncle's solicitor a ring tomorrow."

"Thank you, David. That's a big relief." Murdoc let out a sigh. "It's been weighing on me."

23
REMINISCENCES

Above the Atlantic

Loni turned back several pages and read over bits and pieces of what she had written over the last two hours.

Planes make me pensive.

As I gaze out the window, endless billows of clouds stretch to the horizon. It is as if I am peering toward my own invisible past. I find myself squinting, almost as if hoping to catch a glimpse of something I have never seen before, some fragment of memory that will shed light on the mystery of belonging . . . the mystery of where I came from. But nothing is out there. At least that I've found yet.

No revelation . . . no visions. Only clouds.

I never travel without packing my journal in my carry-on, with its special pen tucked inside. You, dear journal, have come to symbolize my pensive side, that part of me that wonders who I am.

When I flip through the pages and read something I've written, or when I jot down a new memory, it feels like I am touching one of several "me's" competing for center stage of my life. Certainly the "journal me" is different from the person I left behind in Scotland. Although sometimes this past week I didn't know who I was in Scotland either—don't get me started on that place! Let's just say I don't plan on a return engagement anytime soon.

Loni turned and stared out the window across the empty seat next to her. She hadn't touched her journal on the flight over. With most of the trip behind her, all at once the memories were coming so rapidly she could hardly keep up with them.

Again she took pen in hand and began to write.

My most distant recollections are as hazy as the view from a 747's window. And tinged with vague sensations of sorrow.

My grandmother was always there— kind, gentle, consoling. Yet somehow I felt alone. I know she cared. More than cared—she loved me. But there was distance between us. Maybe it was only in my imagination. I know how much she loved me. Yet it could never be the same as snuggling into a mother's arms to hide from the world's hurts.

The earliest years of school were a blur. If she had friends, she no longer remembered them. Try as she might, she could not call up the face of a single playmate.

When she began to grow taller than her classmates, Loni couldn't remember exactly. By nine or ten it was obvious that she was different from the others. Everyone said girls grew more rapidly than boys. But she became *too* tall, taller than was natural. They'd called her names before. But when she was a head taller than anyone else in her class, the cruelty became worse than ever. Now they had something other than her unknown parentage to make fun of.

One horrible day stood out in Loni's memory.

———

The boys and girls were playing soccer on the school field. One of the girls stood out among the rest for she was as tall as her teacher. When she was able to keep her legs beneath her, even in a dress she could run like the wind. And she loved nothing more than showing up the boys at one of their own games.

Suddenly the ball flew out into the

middle of the field. The gangly eleven-year-old dashed for it! Two boys were after it too, but she was determined to beat them. Her little bonnet flew off, but this was her chance and so she didn't stop. She reached the ball and kicked it hard, shooting it straight toward the net. But she never saw the goal. Feet and knees tangled amongst themselves as she sprawled in a clumsy heap onto the grass, all skinny arms and spindly legs like an awkward newborn colt.

The whole field erupted in laughter. The two boys she had outrun to the ball now took their revenge, standing over her laughing and jeering.

"Look at the clumsy ninny!" taunted the boy named James. He was always the worst, a huge bully several years older. "Did you see her?" he laughed. "Like a giraffe trying to play soccer!"

Mrs. Schrock hurried over. "Get up! Get up, Alonnah!" she shouted. "Go get your bonnet this instant. This is disgraceful. You are not a boy. Now act like a girl."

She couldn't wait for school to get over. It was the first goal she had ever scored. But she hadn't been able to enjoy it. Under her dress her knee was skinned and bleeding. She knew Mrs. Schrock wouldn't care so she said nothing. Later, walking home alone, she couldn't help crying. Why were the others so mean? Was it because she was tall or because she had no parents? None of the others dared use the word *orphan* around Mrs. Schrock. She would have reprimanded anyone who said it openly. But they giggled and whispered the word when they could get by with it. And she knew that Mrs. Schrock, like the rest of the teachers, considered her too tall for a girl and a charity case. No matter how good her schoolwork, she never smiled at her. It was a terrible thing to know she wasn't liked.

Her grandmother came into her room that night and found her in tears. She sat down on the bed and took her thin granddaughter in her arms.

"What is it, dear?" asked the older woman in a comforting tone.

"Nothing, Grandma," she said, wiping her eyes. "They just made fun of me again today."

"I'm sorry," she said, stroking the long blond hair. "Was it that James McLeod again?"

"I'm afraid of him, Grandma," she

whimpered. "I'm afraid he'll hurt me when Mrs. Schrock isn't looking."

Her grandma drew her arms more tightly around her. "He's a bad one, I'm afraid. But try not to worry, dear. Bullies like him aren't as tough as they think they are. It's because he was held back a grade. He's got a chip on his shoulder like his father. There's a rumor that the family might be leaving the Fellowship."

"Why do they make fun of me, Grandma? Am I really so different?"

"You're tall, dear. Children make fun of anyone who's not the same as everyone else. But they will grow too and catch up with you."

"They'll never get as tall as me!" she said, starting to cry again. "And why does Mrs. Schrock look at me like I have some disease? I know she's thinking horrible thoughts. Where did I come from, Grandma?"

"Never mind about that, or about Mrs. Schrock," soothed the grandmother. "She never smiles at anyone. She is a lonely lady and needs our prayers."

"But she is sometimes meaner even than the other children."

"She doesn't like your grandfather."

"Why, Grandma?"

"It's not important, Alonnah. You are with us because God is taking special care of you. You are tall because that is how God made you—as a special person like no one else."

"Was my mother tall?" the girl asked.

Her grandmother did not reply. She looked away, an odd expression on her face.

"I don't know, Alonnah," she answered after a moment. Her voice was soft. "I did not know your mother."

The girl was so full of self-doubt and uncertainty that the significance of her grandmother's statement did not register immediately. Almost the moment the words were out of her mouth, the older woman regretted having said them.

She quickly went on. "Do you know what your grandfather told me today," she said enthusiastically. "He said he wants to start training you to work in the showroom. He said you are growing into such a smart young lady that this summer he wants you to greet the tourists who come in and show them about the store."

The girl stared. "He said that about me?"

"Yes, he did. He said it is time you learned the family business. He would rather have you in the showroom than in the workshop. He will keep making the furniture, he said, and you will sell it."

"Oh, I will!" the girl exclaimed. "Ask him when I can start, Grandma. Maybe I could work after school!"

Her grandma laughed. "We shall see, dear. You must keep up with your studies too."

"I will, Grandma! I can do both!"

"Then we will see what your grandfather says."

———

Loni smiled pensively. Thankfully her school experience grew less painful as the years went by.

Not everything in her journal was so serious and introspective. She started to close it, then could not help chuckling as her eyes fell on a penciled note she had taped to one of the back pages.

What had begun as a teenage whim had gained import in the years since. The original note in her youthful cursive read *Alonnah's Husband List*.

With several cross-outs it had been retitled several times. The entries on the list—with many additions, erasures, and new additions—had changed through the years too, from such expected characteristics as *Kind, Treats women with respect, Good-looking, Likes children and animals,* to more subtle qualities of character that her developing maturity had grown capable of recognizing as important.

What would her *Potential Husband Character Qualification List*—as it was currently labeled—look like if she were starting it fresh today, without the notations from when she was fifteen? Was *good-looking* really important in knowing whether you could enjoy a lifetime with a man?

Hugh was good-looking. He *could* be a little taller. But he was only half an inch shorter than she was. As long as she didn't wear heels when they were together, no one noticed. And they did make a striking couple. But did good-looking define his character? Of course not. It may have been his appearance that drew her attention a year ago. But since then, as she now rated Hugh against her list, she had to admit that he scored far beyond "acceptable" and well into the "high" range. Not off the charts, perhaps, but certainly suitable husband material. No woman could expect to find a perfect husband after all.

Maddy had laughed so hard she couldn't stop when Loni let slip about her list. To Maddy, of course, the whole thing was absurd. She had no intention of marrying *anyone!*

Loni closed the book and leaned back with a dreamy smile.

Within minutes her thoughts of childhood traumas and husband lists faded. Loni began to doze.

24

A Chief's Concern

Whales Reef, Shetland Islands

The two men walked down the stairs and out to David Tulloch's car.

Though he himself took little notice, every eye rested on Murdoc MacBean as he returned inside the Mill a moment later and made his way back upstairs to his office. The private and obviously serious conference between their chief and the factory manager seemed all but to confirm the rumor that something was very wrong.

How and with whom it began no one knew. But by the time the thing had multiplied and spread, there wasn't a single one of the Mill's workers who wasn't afraid for his or her job.

Why their beloved chief—maybe even laird by now—would shut down the Mill was a question fraught with even more surmises. But the longer the buzz persisted, the more characteristics of fact it took on. Before the week was out, not one of them doubted it was true.

But Shetlanders can be tight-lipped when they need to be. Not so much as a hint leaked out beyond the immediate factory-family. Thus two of the busiest tongues of the island—those of Coira MacNeill and Rinda Gunn—caught no wind of it.

David drove to the house he affectionately referred to as his "wee cottage" to distinguish it from *the* Cottage of the laird.

Notwithstanding what he had said to his aunt on the day of the funeral, David had not expected the legalities and protocols to take quite *this* long. He had continued advances to Saxe and his sister Isobel, as well as Dougal Erskine, from what he could afford out of his own pocket for their living expenses until the estate was settled. As much as possible the two Mathesons carried out their former duties, keeping up with their own and Dougal's meals, the upkeep of the house, and helping Dougal with the animals. In one sense, not a great deal had changed except that there was one less mouth to feed, and less laundry for Isobel. Saxe's so-called butlering had been so inconsequential as to make him less valet and more handyman, which might include everything from horse grooming and stall mucking to mending fences. But he always carried himself with the dignity of his position and continued to do so now. The needs of the three were so minimal that the strain on David's bank account had been negligible.

Keeping the Cottage and Auld Hoose functioning somewhat normally, however, was a far different matter than a factory of three dozen employees.

This news from Murdoc was troublesome. Obviously the missing funds from the accounts receivable must be due to the delay in resolving his uncle's estate. Like the rest of the island, the Mill property was owned by the laird. But why income from sales of the Mill's woolen products had stopped flowing was of serious concern.

David had always assumed the regular monthly stipend he received had been provided him in his parents' wills. Along with the grants he occasionally received for his work and research, and the income from lectures, tours, and conferences, he had never wanted for anything.

However, his stipend had also ceased with his uncle's death.

Curious indeed!

He had been so busy he had put off investigating it. He had enough income from other sources at this time of the year to hardly notice. Yet a disruption in both his and the Mill's bank accounts at exactly the same time could hardly be coincidental.

With winter coming, and no more lectures or tours on the horizon, and his present grant reaching the end of its funding, if the income from his parents' estate continued unpaid, his own cash flow would diminish sharply. He would not have enough cash coming in to supplement the Mill's expenses out of his own pocket, if it came to that. The Mill's expenses were *far* beyond his own personal means.

When he walked into his cold house, the skies over Shetland were dark, the thin line of pink at the horizon but a memory of the brief sunset. By then David had reached a decision. He would go into Lerwick tomorrow and see what he could learn.

Within the hour the Auld Hoose was warming under the influence of a blazing fire. David sat in his easy chair in front of it, boots off and stocking feet stretched toward the hearth atop a worn leather footstool. A favorite old book lay in his lap. In his hand he held a cup of tea. A plate of Coira's oatcakes sat on the low occasional table beside him.

He took a satisfying sip, adding the warmth of tea to the pleasure of the moment, then opened the well-worn nineteenth century volume and began to read.

25
REENTRY

Washington, D.C.

A sudden change in the drone of the engines ended Loni's nap. They had begun the descent into D.C. She tucked her journal away in her carry-on and hopefully with it the memories contained in its pages.

How happy she was to be returning to the United States. As she stepped into the plane for the homeward journey, she had vowed never to return to Scotland. The cold rain and wind had been incessant. She had ruined a pair of shoes from the wet grass and puddles, and she hadn't felt truly warm throughout the entire conference.

And the Scottish brogue! What became of the posh Queen's English north of the border?

Gazing out the window, she viewed a gorgeous day in the eastern U.S. The clouds had dissipated somewhere over the Atlantic. As the 747 banked toward Reagan International, the sky was clear for miles.

She couldn't help peering into the distance westward, trying to catch a glimpse of the farm country of southern Pennsylvania where she had grown up. One last fleeting glance back to a past she had left thirteen years ago . . . then a bumpy touchdown a few minutes later, and the frenetic pace of her life rushed back to engulf her like a tidal wave.

Fifteen minutes later, emerging from the jetway, she was surprised to see Hugh Norman standing there waiting for her.

"Hey, sweetie!" he said, coming toward her with a smile.

"Hugh!" exclaimed Loni. He took her in his arms and planted a kiss on her lips, then stepped back and handed her a bouquet of flowers.

"How thoughtful—thank you, Hugh," said Loni. "What a surprise to find you here! How did you get to the gate . . . past the security checkpoint?"

"The congressman made a call," replied Hugh. "Pulled a string or two at TSA, and here I am in my official governmental capacity to escort you through customs."

"Wow, lucky me!"

"So how was Scotland?"

"The conference was great," replied Loni. "The weather was awful, but I mostly kept indoors."

"Well it's great to have you back. I missed you!"

Loni laughed. "It's been less than a week!"

"What can I say? A hopeless romantic, that's me."

They made their way through the maze of lines at customs, expedited whenever Hugh flashed his ID. Soon they were on their way into the main terminal and chatting freely.

Suddenly a familiar voice broke into their conversation.

"Loni . . . Loni!"

"Ah, surprise, surprise," said Hugh. "The woman is *everywhere!*"

"Maddy!" called Loni, waving.

Maddy came hurrying toward them and, humorously given the difference in their height, embraced her affectionately.

"Did you come together?" asked Loni, stepping away and glancing back and forth between her boss and boyfriend.

"I had no idea she would be here," Hugh said. "I took an early lunch to meet your plane and take you home."

"And I appreciate it, Hugh—really, but—"

She turned toward Maddy with an expression that clearly shouted, *Help! What should I do?*

"I'm sorry, Hugh," said Maddy, "but I really need a few hours with Loni."

"It can't wait till morning? She just got back—"

"I'm afraid not."

"Come on, you two!" laughed Loni. "There's plenty of me to go around."

She turned toward Hugh with an apologetic expression. "Since I need to debrief Maddy," she said, "why don't I go back to the office with her? Then you and I can have dinner together— that is, if you're free."

"Sure . . . of course."

"Come by the office at five-thirty—"

"Make that her apartment," interposed Maddy. "You've had a long week, Loni," she added. "I promise not to keep you one minute past three. Go home, take a shower and unpack, and then you and Hugh can enjoy yourselves."

"It's all settled then," said Loni. "See you five-thirtyish, Hugh?"

"I suppose that will be all right. I'll make reservations at the Capital Grill."

Kissing Loni again, Hugh forced an obviously disappointed smile before turning for the nearest exit.

"The Capital Grill . . ." Loni repeated when the two women were alone, "I can hardly bear that place. Political types everywhere . . . egos and steaks!"

"Does Hugh know?" asked Maddy.

"I would never tell him."

"Why not?"

"It's his favorite place. He always sees someone he knows. It makes him feel good to mix with that crowd, so I don't mind. And I can find a decent salad anywhere."

"I don't think he was particular happy to see me," commented Maddy wryly.

"He knows the demands of my life," rejoined Loni. "Honestly, I had no idea I would see either of you here. What an honor—a congressional aide *and* the renowned Madison Swift! I could easily have taken a cab."

"No way—not when you're returning from a conference I sent you to. Though I did so for my own selfish reasons."

"How so?"

"To make you even *more* valuable to me. I just hope nobody else has their sights on your abilities."

Loni laughed. "If you say so."

She smiled as they walked toward the parking garage with a suitcase clattering behind each of them, struck again at what an unlikely duo they made. Loni was blond, five-foot-eleven and then some, easily over six feet in her heels. Her brunette boss, Madison Swift, might have measured five-foot-three in heels. Of course *she* never wore heels, or dresses either for that matter, but slacks and pantsuits only. Loni had filled out since her skinny school days. Powerful and athletic, she worked out in the gym five days a week—weights, stair-steppers, and various machines. She swam and ran regularly as well. Maddy was chunky and wouldn't have known what to do on an elliptical or rowing machine if her life depended on it. Her only concession to exercise was a recent vow to take the stairs instead of the elevator once a week up to her office on the seventh floor of Capital Towers. By any measure they were complete opposites.

"A good trip?" asked Maddy as they walked.

"Sure, I learned a lot," replied Loni. "Here, would you carry these?" she added, sneezing as she passed Maddy the bouquet.

"Chrysanthemums *again?*" said Maddy. "Didn't you tell Hugh you were allergic?"

"Yes, but he likes them, and it's the thought that counts."

"Tell him again."

"It's not worth hurting his feelings. Besides, I'm just glad to be home! Miss me?"

"Always!" said Maddy.

"Well, it's probably good you didn't come along—most of the women were wearing dresses." Maddy grinned.

"You think I'd have been out of place?"

"Just wondering what they'd think of you wearing a pantsuit."

"England's progressive too."

"But this was Scotland. And aren't you just a *little* concerned about what people might think?"

"I want them wondering," said Maddy.

"Why?"

"It keeps people off guard. They're not sure what to think. That gives me an advantage."

"That's weird!" Loni laughed.

"I never claimed otherwise!"

"Well, whatever else, you're a star in the investment world."

Maddy stuffed the bouquet into a garbage can they passed.

"Maddy, those were from Hugh!" Loni exclaimed.

"Yes, and he should have chosen something that wouldn't make you sneeze."

They reached Maddy's car. Maddy opened the trunk.

"Hugh's sweet, and he tries. I don't mind really," said Loni. They deposited her luggage and climbed inside the car. "By the way," added Loni as they inched out of the lot, "I have a bone to pick with you . . . what happened to that Indian summer you promised me?"

"I'm not sure I actually *promised*."

"Maybe not. But it was *freezing* over there."

"It's a nice balmy seventy-five here."

"Not in Scotland! And it was dark by five-thirty in the afternoon."

"You'll be back to normal in no time."

"Sixty-hour weeks, is that it?"

"I'll pump you full of strong coffee."

"Actually, I'd kill for a cup of *good* coffee!"

"Oh, look," said Maddy, glancing to the left where a mother and three girls in long dresses and white caps, their bearded father in a white shirt buttoned to the neck and round black hat, were getting into a car. "What an old-fashioned family. They must be Amish or something. I didn't think they drove cars."

"They're not Amish," said Loni, thinking how similar they looked to the family she'd seen on the Mall a few months ago.

"What are they then?"

"Probably Mennonite or maybe the Society of Friends. I'm not sure."

"Friends? What do you mean?"

"You know, Quakers. Surely you've heard of them. William Penn, the settling of Pennsylvania in the seventeenth and eighteenth centuries?"

"Sounds familiar, I guess. I've just never heard them called Friends. What are they?"

"The Pilgrims founded New England, and the Quakers founded the middle colonies—Pennsylvania, New Jersey, Maryland."

"If you say so. What are you, a professor of religious history or something?"

"Just interested," laughed Loni.

"So Quakers and Friends are old-fashioned . . . the long dresses and all?"

"Mostly not," replied Loni. "Ninety-nine percent of Quakers today are so modern and liberal they're more social and political than spiritual. But there are a few isolated Quaker communities that preserve their traditional ways and original Christian teachings."

"Like those back there?"

"Maybe. I can't really tell. But some of them

do wear what they call plain clothes and old-fashioned hats, keep to themselves, and operate their own schools and that kind of thing."

"Sounds pretty out of step."

The statement sent Loni's brain spinning. "I suppose in a way," she answered slowly. "But they're good people, dedicated to a way of life they treasure. It takes courage to live as they do." Even Loni was surprised by her words.

"How do you know so much about it?" asked Maddy.

"I just do, that's all."

As they drove away from the airport, Maddy began reeling off the list of agenda items she had been waiting for Loni to handle.

Every trip one of them took ended this way. "Reentry" they called it.

"Everyone's talking about the Fed meeting in two weeks," Maddy was saying. "They're wondering if they should move some of their assets into high-yield bonds. But I just can't get into the weeds with a long conversation with every one of them. You'll be able to plow through the list in a few days."

"Do they think you're clairvoyant . . . about the Fed, I mean?"

"Our clients think we know everything."

Loni laughed. "Do you think it's time we broke the bad news to them?"

"Actually," said Maddy thoughtfully, "I *do*

think the Fed will bump up the prime. We probably ought to email our clients—not with a prediction, but with several factors for them to consider."

"Any word on the New York expansion?" asked Loni.

"They've shoved a decision on that back until after the first of the year," Maddy answered. "It may not even happen till next spring or summer."

"Well, whenever it does, I'm sure your promotion will be part of it."

"Just make sure you don't say anything like that when we get back into the building. They might not pick me."

"Who else are they going to pick? Jones? He's been stuck in annuities forever. Not proactive enough. He's asked me out twice."

"And?"

"No way. And the point is, that to head up an entire new office I see no one in the company they would want other than you."

"They might look outside. Get a headhunter to find someone. There's word that some of Russell's top people want to make an upward move."

"It's you, Maddy," insisted Loni. "If you want my three cents' worth, I think the powers that be want to make *you* the face of the Capital Investments brand the moment they hit the Big Apple. Mark my words—they will have you in front of television cameras doing marketing infomercials by next summer. You'll be a VP one year from now."

"I'm glad you have such faith in my star!" said Maddy, chuckling. "And I haven't forgotten that I promised to take you to New York with me . . . *if* it happens. We'll do the Big Apple together!"

26

BEWILDERING ACCOUNTS

Lerwick, Shetland Islands

David Tulloch drove into the Shetland's chief city of Lerwick, *da toon* to Shetlanders. With a population of but seven thousand residents, many in the world would think themselves stretching a point even to call it a "toon" at all.

His conversation with Murdoc MacBean about the Mill's finances had worked on his subconscious throughout the night. In spite of his optimistic words to his cousin, David's sleep had been fitful. Along with what he considered a glitch with his own account, he was afraid that more might be involved than he had assumed.

Awake long before dawn, he took his usual morning walk about the island. Knowing bankers and solicitors kept different hours than sheep and their shepherds, he waited for the morning's third ferry and entered Lerwick a little before noon.

His first stop was the bank. There he succinctly laid out the problem with both accounts to the manager, a man he had not previously met by the name of Douglas Creighton.

After researching the matter on his computer, the manager looked up to where David sat waiting patiently. "It seems, Mr. Tulloch," he said, "that it is simply a matter of the automatic deposits normally made into both accounts having been suspended back in August."

"Right, I am aware of that," said David slowly, "no doubt because of my great-uncle's death. But what I am trying to understand is *why*. Why are funds from the accounts receivable not going into the Mill's account? And why would my uncle's death impact my personal trust account? I see no connection between the factory finances and the trust established by my parents."

"I really have no information on that. All I know is that single payments have been made on the first day of each month as regular as clockwork into both accounts, going back as far as the computer records them. They were suspended at the time of your uncle's death."

"And you can't tell me what the connection is?"

"I'm sorry," replied the manager. "All I have here are account numbers. Both accounts—yours and the Mill's—were funded monthly from a third source, another account, once monthly."

"From the estate . . . the parent company, I assume you mean," said David.

"I am afraid I am not at liberty to divulge that information, Mr. Tulloch. I'm sure you understand."

"Actually, I'm not sure I do completely. However, I respect your position. How then would you suggest I pursue this and get to the bottom of it? The Mill is in dire need of operating revenue for payroll and supplies."

Creighton thought a moment. "Perhaps you would excuse me," he said. "Let me make a telephone call."

David rose and left the office. Two minutes later the door reopened. The manager beckoned him inside.

"I have just spoken with Mr. Jason MacNaughton," he said. "He authorized me to tell you that the account in question is held by their firm, MacNaughton, Dalrymple, & MacNaughton."

David nodded. "Of course. They represent our family's legal interests. However, I still fail to see how the Mill's operating account would be connected to the trust of my parents."

"That I could not say, Mr. Tulloch. The bank handles the accounts per the instructions we are given, nothing more. I have only been in Shetland four years. I am sorry to say that I did not know either of your parents. I am unfamiliar with whatever arrangements they made. These are entirely legal matters. The bank, as I say, merely carries out predetermined instructions."

"I understand," said David, rising and reaching over to shake Creighton's hand. "I appreciate your help. It appears I have some further investigation ahead of me."

David reached the offices of MacNaughton, Dalrymple, & MacNaughton, Solicitors shortly before one o'clock. The small staff was just preparing to close up for lunch. Informed by his secretary that David Tulloch from Whales Reef was in the office, Jason MacNaughton, at forty-three the youngest member of the partnership, came out of his office to greet him. The two men had met occasionally over the past five years since the death of David's mother.

"Hello, David," said MacNaughton as the two shook hands. "Would you join me for lunch? I was just going out."

"Yes, thank you—I would enjoy that," replied David.

They left the building and walked along the sidewalk toward a nearby hotel.

"After the bank called, I was expecting you," said MacNaughton. "You have questions about the automatic deposits?"

"That's what brought me into the city. I knew there had been no deposits from the trust into my account recently. I was curious but not worried. I've had other income from my work through the summer and fall when I'm normally busiest. However, I had no idea the factory was in the same boat until yesterday when my cousin informed me of it. Just now at the bank I learned the automatic deposits into both accounts have been coming from the same source. So I am doubly confused. What does my parents' trust have to do with the operating account of the factory? And why have deposits into both accounts been discontinued, even though income is still being received for the Mill's sales?"

They reached the Kvelsdro House, went inside, and were soon seated at a table overlooking Bressay Sound. For the next hour, David's eyes were opened to the complexity of the circumstances facing him, and the reality of his own powerlessness to change them.

27
THE JOURNAL

Washington, D.C.

Loni had scarcely found a moment to herself since stepping off the plane on her return from Scotland. After a whirlwind afternoon catching up with Maddy, to the dinner date with Hugh yesterday evening, then nonstop again at the office today . . . she was beat.

She hadn't even unpacked yet!

Loni walked into her apartment at twenty past seven on her second day home. In her hand she carried an order of Chinese takeout. It was a relief to put the day behind her. Tired as she'd been, the time with Hugh had been comfortable, nice, a relaxing opportunity to catch up after the awkwardness at the airport, to tell him about her trip and hear what he'd been up to on Capitol Hill.

Tonight, however, she needed some downtime. She was glad for the chance to be alone.

She set the bag on the counter, opened the refrigerator, poured herself a glass of chilled mineral water, kicked off her heels, plopped into her favorite chair, and let out a long sigh.

What a day!

It wasn't the lingering jet lag from the trip so much as being instantly plunged back into the fast pace of her life as Madison Swift's assistant. She was suffering from emotional whiplash.

Loni sipped from the glass in her hand and glanced across the room. Her open suitcase and carry-on still lay on the couch from yesterday. Sight of them sent her mind drifting to her airplane reminiscences of the day before.

She almost never looked at her journal at home. The memories it stirred up were mostly reserved for travel. Yet she now found herself slowly climbing to her feet and walking across the room. She picked up the leather book where it lay with her things. She brought it back to the chair and slowly opened it.

As she flipped through the pages, her eyes fell on one memory after another. Were her past and present more intertwined than she realized?

She turned back to the opening lines of the first page. Those first words set the tone for all that had followed. Loni couldn't remember what had originally prompted them. Maddy had given her the handsome leather journal as a Christmas gift their first year working together. Shortly after-ward she had tucked it in her bag for a trip—she didn't remember why.

And then six miles above Kansas, without any specific plan, she had started writing.

I was six when my grandmother told me my mother's name, *she read.*

Alison.

How foreign the word was to my ears, even when I realized it sounded similar to my own, Alonnah. When I was alone I whispered it over to myself . . . Alison. It was the name of a stranger. How could a stranger be my mother?

There was never a time when I didn't know my parents were dead, that I was an orphan. My grandparents hadn't tried to hide the truth from me. They sometimes talked about my father, their son, Chad Ford. Though not often. My grandmother got misty-eyed on the few occasions when she told me stories of him as a boy. She never got over his death. How could she? He was her only son.

I somehow had the feeling that she blamed my mother. I don't know if that's true or why she would feel that way. When the subject of my mother happened to come up—which wasn't often—she didn't talk about her as a daughter-in-law, just as a shadowy woman with no story, no past. Just a woman who chanced to be her son's wife. There were even times I wondered if my parents had been married at all, if maybe I was illegitimate. . . .

Loni looked away from the page. The words in her own hand made her as sad as when she had first written them. Sometimes nostalgic melancholy felt good, cleansing in a way. At other times it hurt to remember.

What did other people feel when they thought of their parents? When an orphan who had never known them thought of her parents, it was with a painful longing so deep no words could describe it. It was a longing for something Loni knew she would never have. It was a deep and silent anguish, a hole in the middle of the soul that couldn't be filled.

She had it better than most, Loni thought. At least she knew her parents' names. And she knew her grandparents. But that wasn't enough to heal the ache.

During her college years she'd read several books about how others in similar circumstances came to terms with life and personhood differently than everyone else—like being adopted, the books said. Both brought unique heartaches. Yet adopted children had the possibility of searching for their birth parents. For orphans, that door was closed.

It probably was no surprise when, at eleven or twelve, Loni began wondering if her grandparents were *really* her grandparents. Morbid scenarios followed, with her at the center of them.

Mostly her gloomy fantasies took the form of

the age-old fairy tale theme: that Mr. and Mrs. Ford had found a baby wrapped in rags abandoned on their doorstep. To explain her unknown origins, the old couple had invented the story that her father was their son. But, she had wondered, maybe she wasn't really a *Ford* at all.

Her ambiguous origins remained buried in Loni's brain, the secret dread of her life. She was a foundling. A castoff. She had no name. No parents. No past. No roots.

Notwithstanding the nagging doubts, she dearly loved her grandparents. They were kind, truthful, and "honest as the day is long," as they would have described it. Yet she noticed odd expressions, heard whispered comments. She sensed her grandfather was mistrusted by some of the men. Their tiny religious community was dreadfully susceptible to rumors. She never knew the cause of whatever suspicions were harbored about him, but she imagined that she herself was the source of it. What else could it be but that her grandparents had brought an outsider, a black sheep, a heathen into the community?

Her classmates seemed to know the secret about her that she didn't even know herself. Her teachers seemed in on it too. She was different, strange, uncoordinated, and ugly. Her inner suffering gathered like a black cloud around the haunting reality that no one liked her, that she was an outcast.

Was her name even *Alonnah Ford?* Maybe her grandparents—if they *were* her grandparents—had simply given their family name to the waif they had taken in.

Loni looked again at the page before her.

> After I began to get taller than the other girls at school, that's when I was sure something was wrong, that I wasn't like the rest of them. The secret fear was that I didn't belong to the Fellowship at all. Once that thought entered my mind, I couldn't help thinking I didn't belong to my grandparents either. I was afraid—of what, I can't even remember. I would lie awake at night wondering if one day they would get tired of me and send me away, that I would be alone . . . just as I had come into the world. . . .

At eleven she began working in her grandfather's workshop. By twelve she'd graduated to the showroom where he displayed his handmade furniture. By degrees she was able to put the confusion, doubts, and fears of childhood behind her. The shop and showroom gave her a daily escape from the loneliness and humiliation of school.

Probably because of her height, she looked older than she was. The people who came in, tourists mostly and occasional dealers, were friendly and treated her like an adult.

Gradually she learned enough to converse knowledgeably about the various woods her grandfather used—oak mostly, but also birch, maple, mahogany—as well as about the different styles and designs and stains and varnishes. She became conversant in everything from pierced splats and cabriole legs to Pembroke tables and Victorian-era rosewood Davenports. She knew the difference between Chippendale, Adam, and Sheraton influences on English-period furniture and could point out her grandfather's use of the ideas and methods of the famous craftsmen of the past.

She loved it. She could hardly wait for school to end every day. The showroom became her life, a haven where she found purpose and acceptance, where she could be herself without secretly wondering what terrible things people were thinking when they looked in her direction. Her personality blossomed. Summers were best—not having to go to school at all.

Eventually her grandmother taught her about bookkeeping and bill paying. She took to the financial side of the work as naturally as a duck to water. She came to see how the whole business functioned together—the flow of money, products, inventory, wholesale suppliers, retail customers—all the details that fit into an intricately connected pattern, even for a small business. Then she began designing a few pieces of her own. Liking what he saw, her grandfather went to work on them. A few months later, several of her own designs turned up as finished pieces of beautiful furniture that appeared in the showroom.

The most exciting day of her life came when she sold a coffee table she had designed. She then knew she would never be happy spending the rest of her life in Pennsylvania farm country. Her future lay somewhere, somehow, in the business world. She had had a taste and she wanted more.

In her seventeenth year Loni realized she was ready to embark on an adventure of discovery into the wider world outside the confines of the Fellowship.

Disappointed at her decision, but ultimately giving their blessing, her grandparents allowed her to enroll in the junior college in Harrisburg.

Anticipating the change brought fears and uncertainties. The insular life of her grandparents' community was all she'd known. She had been brought up to think of the outside world as secular, foreign, unfriendly, and hostile.

How would she fare?

She had no idea. But she was excited to find out!

It would not be easy. She knew that her height

drew stares. Everyone in the community made jokes about it. Long ago she had learned to drop her eyes, look away, and try to ignore the whispers that came with the stares.

Arriving at junior college, however, reactions to the tall, slender newcomer turned out to be different from what Loni expected.

28

Unsettling Clouds on the Horizon

Whales Reef, Sheetland Islands

Though an early riser and usually in bed before nine o'clock, David's meeting with Jason MacNaughton in Lerwick had so preoccupied him ever since that he was unable to sleep. Well after midnight, he was alternating between pacing the house and sitting with a cup of warm milk and honey. He continued to replay the conversation over in his brain.

"You asked about your trust account," MacNaughton had said when they were seated in Kvelsdro's and had ordered. "You also asked why no deposits have been made in that and the Mill account. The answer to both questions is related. I must apologize for whatever inconvenience this has caused. As far as our part in the finances is concerned, we have always transferred funds into the factory account every month according to Mr. Tulloch's instructions. Those payments were suspended immediately last August. I merely assumed you understood the state of affairs since Macgregor Tulloch's death."

"I thought I did too," said David. "Perhaps I was wrong. What state of affairs?"

"The fact that his assets have been frozen pending the outcome of probate. Fortunately we have been successful in persuading the probate authorities not to touch your uncle's home or seize his physical assets. We thought it wise that you retained full access in order to keep the place up. Only the finances have been frozen at this point."

"Right," said David, nodding slowly. "I understand it takes time to finalize the details of an estate. But what does my uncle's estate have to do with the two bank accounts?"

"The accounts were both funded from *his* account."

David stared back at the attorney, trying to make sense of his words.

"There must be some mistake," he said. "What is deposited into my personal account comes from a trust my parents established for my sister and me. The other, the Mill's operating account as I understand it, handles the income and disbursements of the factory business. I assumed it was funded by the income from the Mill's orders, from receipts of accounts payable. How would my uncle's death affect either of those? My sister has been on the phone to me twice, wondering what's going on too. I told her it's just a temporary delay, which is what I assumed."

"It is a bit complicated," replied the lawyer. "Those complications are all the more tangled given that Macgregor Tulloch died without a will. That, of course, is the crux of the problem."

"What?" exclaimed David.

"He had no will. I assumed you knew."

"I had no idea!" said David, hardly able to mask his surprise.

"That has necessitated, as I say, the freezing of his financial accounts. It explains the suspension of payments into both accounts in question."

"I see," said David slowly. "Yes . . . obviously that would change things."

"My father had been speaking to him for years," said the younger MacNaughton. "Your uncle promised to rectify the situation. My father urged him to explain his affairs to you. While we knew there was still no will, and that fact concerned us, we thought he had at least spoken with you."

"Not a word."

"I suppose Mr. Tulloch thought there was no urgency, that he had plenty of time to take care of the necessary legalities. He knew you would be his heir and was not concerned about it. Apparently he and my father spoke on the phone not long before his death. Mr. Tulloch promised to write something up. My father urged him to come to Lerwick where he could dictate his wishes, sign it, and have it done. Mr. Tulloch promised he would see to it."

"And?"

"Nothing came of it. My father simply could not convey the complexities involved in modern probate proceedings, especially for an estate of this size, nor the idea that having no will would make things immeasurably more difficult for you. In many ways, I suppose, your uncle was a man of the past who had not entirely embraced the modern age. He was of an era when a handshake and word or two was as good as a legal document. I'm afraid those days are gone forever. Especially in matters of probate. Some of the laws are unbelievably complex."

"It would appear I am guilty of considerable naivety," said David. "I assumed his affairs were in sound order."

"His death was unexpected, I take it?"

"Completely. He seemed healthy as a horse. Well, in any event, now that I am acquainted with how things stand, what can I do to speed this process along? Especially for the employees at the Mill."

"I'm afraid at this point, David, very little. Unfortunately, you are in a powerless legal position. The inheritance and assumption of the informal title that goes with the property is not yet a legal fact."

"Isn't the matter of the inheritance a mere formality?"

"That is difficult to say."

"I'm not sure I understand."

"You are Macgregor Tulloch's closest relative and the presumptive heir. However, when the government gets involved in a sizable estate such as this, they leave no stone unturned before declaring probate settled and releasing the assets. The process could take a year."

"A year! Are you saying the accounts will be frozen all that time?"

"I'm afraid so."

"That will make the Mill's operations difficult. But what about the accounts receivable for the orders the Mill continues to fill and being paid for?"

"That is the unfortunate Catch-22," replied MacNaughton. "Since your uncle's estate owns the Mill, though money is coming into our offices for payment of the invoices your cousin sends out, which we deposit *into* the estate account as income, we are legally prohibited from authorizing expenditures to be made *out of* that account. It is unfair, I realize, that the income continues yet no expenses can be paid. Unfortunately, given the unique circumstances, that is the law. Money in your uncle's estate is actually piling up, but we are prohibited from disbursing so much as a penny of it. I am afraid the same awkward stipulation prohibits funds being deposited into your personal account as well."

"I still don't see the connection with my parents' trust," said David. "I did not know their finances were entwined with Uncle Macgregor's. I will find a way to manage. I'll get by on oats and potatoes if need be. My sister is feeling the change as well, though she is not so dependent on the trust for income. But a good portion of the island depends on the Mill in one way or another."

"I am truly sorry. Our hands are legally no less tied than yours. It is most unfortunate. Even the simplest of wills would have avoided all this." MacNaughton paused. "Actually . . . there is one other thing," he added, then hesitated again.

"What is it?" asked David.

"Those complications I spoke of may already have reared their heads."

"How do you mean? What complications?"

"It could get rather messy," replied MacNaughton. "When the government gets involved as I said, it is an extensive process. An heir hunter has been brought in to investigate. The complication I mentioned is that in addition to yourself, we already have another claimant to the inheritance."

"Oh?" said David, clearly surprised. "Who is that?"

"One Hardar Tulloch."

"Hardy!" exclaimed David, breaking into a laugh.

"You know the man, I take it?"

"Everyone in the Shetlands knows Hardy!"

"Is he a friend of yours?"

"We have known each other since we were boys. Hardy doesn't like me much. We were involved in more scrapes when we were young than I can count. He always got the better of it too," David added with a wry grin. "He is one tough bloke. There has long been a sort of division between the people of the island between those who value our Scottish and Celtic roots and those who revere the Scandinavian heritage of the Shetlands. Hardy champions the Viking cause. He loathes the kilt, pipes, and tartan. The mere sight of a kilt sets him off. He cannot stand the thought of our clan having emigrated from the mainland. He thinks of himself as a Norse God of Thunder and me as a wimpy Scotsman."

"He is a relative of yours?"

"My third cousin."

"According to my father, the other Mr. Tulloch's solicitor has presented documentation to show him as the rightful heir."

"Hardy has a solicitor?"

"He is represented by a firm headquartered in Edinburgh, a rather prestigious one actually."

David exhaled slowly. "Yes, that does complicate matters."

"I'm afraid so. We should set up an appointment for you to talk with my father," said MacNaughton. "He established the trust for you and your sister in the first place. He was intimately familiar with both estates—your parents' and your great-uncle's."

"I would like that very much."

"My father, as you know, is semi-retired. He and my mother left for Cornwall two weeks ago. The cold here has become increasingly burdensome, and they will be with relatives in the south until spring. When I speak with him on the telephone, though, I will explain the situation and see what light he can shed. Though we will hope that things may have resolved themselves long before he returns."

29
"LONI"

Washington, D.C.

Loni paused in her reminiscences, closing her leather journal and tracing the engraving on the cover with her fingers. She wasn't sleepy. Now that the memories had been unleashed, she couldn't stop them.

When she arrived on the Harrisburg campus, she knew she still turned heads as before. But when she summoned the courage to look up, she gradually realized that those heads were accompanied by smiles. If she gave them the chance, most people nodded or greeted her with a hello or a good morning.

They were *friendly* smiles! The teachers in her new classes treated her courteously too.

Gone were the suspicious glances and whispers. She was no longer a black sheep. She was simply one of several hundred other freshmen adjusting to the newness of college life.

Anonymity spelled freedom!

Freedom to become, to grow, to think, to explore life. Freedom to *be* whoever she wanted to be.

In the middle of an entirely new environment, learning new things, meeting new people, even the haven of her grandfather's showroom felt suddenly very far away. She was breathing deeply of the fresh air of her own newly discovered personhood.

The most dramatic outward change came after her grandparents had seen her safely settled and returned home. The very next day she went into town for some new clothes. By now Loni knew she was no mere foundling. Though her ancestry was still a mystery, that she at least had an ancestry was evidenced by the small inheritance left her after the death of her mother's father. Though she knew nothing about her grandfather on her mother's side, it was his will that made it possible for her to go to college. She was grateful that he had left enough for a few expenditures beyond the bare necessities of tuition, books, room and board, and a few nonessentials like *clothes*.

The prospect of going shopping filled Loni with both guilt and excitement. She had never been to a clothing store in her life!

In the midst of Pennsylvania Dutch country, the clerk assumed her nervous customer in the long drab dress to be Amish. She could not have been more kind and patient. She gently made suggestions that were not *too* dramatic. Loni walked out an hour later with two dresses, a skirt, two blouses, and a cardigan, her wardrobe for the coming year.

The next change would prove even greater, for it struck at the very core of her identity. If she did not know where the *Alonnah* originated, she could trace the beginnings of the *Loni* to an exact moment.

The first day of classes arrived. Full of anticipation and exhilaration, her first course of the morning was United States History. She sat as far in the back of the room as possible. After a few introductory remarks, the teacher instructed the students to write their names on the sheet being circulated.

She took the paper a few minutes later from the girl in front of her. Without planning what came next, she set her pen on the next line and wrote *Loni Ford*.

She walked out of the room at the end of the hour sensing a momentous change had come. Her life had taken a new turn.

Loni was born.

Her roommate that first year could not have had a more contrasting personality from her own. How such opposites could become friends was a mystery to her.

Kathy was thoroughly a young woman of the world—loud, brash, outspoken, confident. She swore nearly every time she opened her mouth. Loni heard words she never dreamed existed . . .

and wished she'd never heard. Kathy drank, smoked, and dated two or three times a week. Loni found herself in for a greater education than she'd bargained for. Yet in her own way, Kathy was kind to her goody-two-shoes roommate and, as the year progressed, made an effort to "behave" around Loni.

Kathy's ongoing project was to fix Loni up with one of her rowdy guy friends. She could not grasp how any girl on the planet could be so uninterested in dating. Yet Kathy also showed a tender, almost gentle side that came out around Loni—completely opposite from the face she presented to the world.

Another turning point came a month into the school year, which added its own dimension to her expanding self-image as Loni Ford. She was seated at the desk in their dorm room, homework spread out in front of her. Kathy plopped down on the opposite side of the desk and stared into her face, looking more serious than usual.

"What?" Loni laughed.

"I was just thinking how beautiful you are," she said. "Gosh—you are stunning!"

Loni stared back in bewilderment. "I don't . . ." she began. "I mean . . . you don't—do you really think so?"

Incredulity filled Kathy's face. "You're kidding, right!"

"No . . . about what?"

"You don't *know?*"

Loni shook her head, more perplexed than ever.

"Know how beautiful you are! Don't you know that every guy in this school wants to go out with you? You're gorgeous!"

Loni continued to stare back at her roommate. The words refused to register.

Then slowly Loni began to cry.

"Loni . . . gosh, I'm sorry," Kathy said quickly, "I didn't mean . . . I thought—"

"It's all right." Loni reached for a tissue, blew her nose, and struggled for a shaky breath. "I know it's probably hard to understand," she said after a minute, "but where I grew up, I was always an oddity, a tall, clumsy girl who didn't know her place. All my life I've felt *wrong* and that I didn't belong. What you just said . . . all of a sudden I was crying."

Kathy reached across the table and took Loni's hand. "I'm so sorry, Loni. I had no idea."

"I know. You're trying to make me feel good. And probably when I think about it later it *will* make me feel good," Loni added, trying to laugh. "The words just hit me funny, I guess. Whenever I look in a mirror, I still see the twelve-year-old giraffe everyone made fun of."

"I'd like to get my hands on whoever's made fun of you!" said Kathy. "I would—well, I won't say what. I know you hate it when I swear. All I can say is that they'd never make fun of you after I got through with them!"

Loni laughed again and grabbed another tissue. "You can always make me laugh, Kathy," she said, dabbing at her eyes.

"Sure better than making you cry!"

"I promise, nothing you say will ever make me cry again."

"Is that why . . . you know, not realizing you're pretty—is that why you don't date?"

"No, it's not that," Loni said. "I'm just not interested."

"But why not?"

"Because most of the guys I see, the ones around you—and I mean no offense to you, Kathy—but they are so superficial. They drink and talk endlessly about themselves and try to impress every girl they see. It's so shallow. If I met a young man of virtue and character, who had depth enough to talk about something real, maybe it might be different. But why should I waste my time with self-centered bores?"

"You do speak your mind!" Kathy laughed.

"Sorry," said Loni sheepishly.

"Hey, no problem. I guess I like having a good time. I never stop to think about virtue and character and all that. That would certainly change the dating game."

Thinking back, Loni recalled the day with a fond smile.

Kathy's words, even after so many years, went deep into her soul.

Does anyone, she wondered, see in a mirror the same image everyone else sees? Others are aware only of the outward shell of *appearance*. But when she looked at herself in a mirror, her self-perception illuminated something entirely different . . . what she was *inside*.

Until the moment those fateful words had tumbled out of Kathy's mouth, beauty was the last thing Loni had seen reflected back in a mirror. She knew she had changed since she was a girl. Yet when her eyes fell on her own face, it was just . . . her.

After that day she found herself paying more attention to the smiles coming her way. Were they because of what Kathy had said? Were people taking a second glance because they saw what Kathy saw? The idea was unnerving. But she could hardly deny that over the next months Kathy's words enabled her to carry herself with more confidence, walking tall even at nearly six feet.

At the same time, Kathy's words created a double-edged sword. Along with the newfound confidence, Loni also knew that the young men were often looking at her *face*. . . . not at *her*. She was just an object in their eyes, not a person.

All in all, though, Harrisburg's junior college represented two of the best years of her life. She received mostly A's and a few B's, confirming Kathy's good-natured observations that her beautiful roommate was more than a little weird.

She competed on the swim and track teams and became a standout in both venues. She shocked herself even more than her coaches when she began regularly winning the 100m freestyle in the pool, and the 800m and 1,500m on the track.

After two years, Loni's academic and athletic achievements resulted in a partial scholarship to the University of Pennsylvania. She majored in business, was lucky enough to meet Madison Swift at the fateful seminar that had changed her life, graduated from the university with honors, and, as the saying goes, never looked back.

She knew leaving the community and her eventual career path was hard on her grandparents. Nothing would have made them happier than for her to stay in the Fellowship, marry some nice young man from their Meeting, and one day inherit the business and continue the family tradition of Ford Handcrafted Furniture.

But she could never have been happy with such a life. She knew deep down that what her grandparents wanted for her most of all was the happiness of doing what fulfilled her most deeply.

After leaving for junior college at eighteen, Loni only returned to the community of her upbringing for a handful of birthdays, a half-dozen Christmases, and for her grandparents' fiftieth wedding anniversary. Even then she had done so cautiously. The last thing she wanted was to damage their reputation further. She had no intention of driving into town in her red Mustang convertible—her first major purchase after going to work for Madison Swift—weaving between tractors and wagons and pickups, and getting her poor grandparents subtly shunned as a result, if not being subject to an official *disownment* from the elders. On most such occasions she had crept in by taxi at night and left the same way. Very few in the community ever knew she was there.

Over the years most of her youthful anxieties gradually faded into the mists of the past. And now, at thirty-one, Loni knew that her mother and father, Chad and Alison Ford, had been killed in a traffic accident when she was less than a year old. She was still unsure of the details or how she had survived, and the Fords remained strangely tight-lipped.

But she had also accepted the fact that her grandparents knew little more than they were telling. That realization forced upon her the reality that her mother's life was a closed book.

She would never know more. There was no

denying, however, that all her life she would yearn to feel a mother's embrace and a father's love.

Loni drew in a deep breath and closed her journal. After a few more minutes she stood and returned it to the bookcase where she kept it between trips.

Turning away, she was arrested by the mirror on the adjacent wall.

She paused and gazed into her eyes. Her reflection stared back at her . . . and then seemed to speak.

You think you've moved on, it said as if silently reading her mind. *You think you've dealt with all that. You think you've got life figured out, with your past tidily closed up in that book you just put away. But don't be so sure. Alonnah is still alive and well. And you still don't know who she really is.*

30

CRAIGSMONT LOUNGE

Lerwick, Shetland Islands

The rough-edged Shetland fisherman had of course heard of the Craigsmont Lounge, but never in his life had he set foot past its threshold. It was in a part of town the likes of him did not frequent.

When the first summons came several months ago, at first he thought it a practical joke. But the invitation specifically warned him against breathing a word about it to a soul. And in light of the words *make it worth your while,* he had taken it seriously enough to follow the instructions, say nothing to anyone, and appear at the appointed place at the designated time.

His cautions had been well-founded. It had not been a joke. If the thing came off, it would be more than just worth his while, it would make him a very wealthy man. He might even become a regular at the Craigsmont in his own right.

When the second summons came two days ago, this time he harbored no doubts. He shaved, put on his best suit of clothes, and presented himself half an hour before the appointed time.

All his preparations were not sufficient to entirely remove from his person the characteristic aroma of his profession. He had come to the city on the *Hardy Fire*, alone. The worthy craft was so saturated with the smell of fish that it permeated everything that came aboard within minutes.

Even without that distinction following him through the door, he still would have drawn stares. Obviously he was no oil executive or businessman, notwithstanding clean clothes, combed hair, and shaven face. The man had *fisherman* written all over him. He lumbered in and glanced about uncertainly, looking every inch, to use a phrase appropriate to the circumstance, like a fish out of water. He shuffled to the bar and showed the man behind it the invitation in his hand.

Expressionless, the man nodded, walked out from behind the counter, and motioned for him to follow. He led him across the common room, halfway down a dim corridor, then opened a door. He gestured his guest inside the small private room and closed the door behind him.

Hardy glanced about. The luxuriously appointed room was empty. On his first meeting with the mysterious man who introduced himself as Smith, the interview in the pub had been brief. He'd been told little more than an overview of what Smith's people had in mind. Smith handed him an envelope that held a plane ticket to Edinburgh, a solicitor's card containing time, date, and address for a second meeting at which time more would be explained, and five hundred pounds in cash for his trouble. There was more where that came from, Smith had told him.

That was enough to get Hardy's attention. He had slipped out of Whales Reef without anyone knowing of it, had flown from Sumburgh to Edinburgh, met with Smith and the solicitor, signed a slew of papers—which he probably should have read more carefully, but he could scarcely understand a word of all the legal applesauce—and that was that. He returned home full of dreams and schemes. It was all he could do to keep his mouth shut and allow the slow-grinding wheels of the legal system to do their work. Word had leaked, of course. Smith told him to expect that and just to play it coy and cool, to exude complete confidence in the eventual outcome.

He'd heard nothing more from Smith or the solicitor's firm until two days ago.

Now he was in the Craigsmont again. A table in the middle of the room held a full pitcher of dark ale. Beside it sat a full bottle of Courvoisier. Glasses were provided. He was not a brandy man, but no one had to tell him what the pitcher and pints were for. He stepped forward and poured a tall glass full. He carried it to one of five easy chairs upholstered in rich blue leather and sat down to wait.

Hardy was halfway through his second pint when Smith entered. With him was a man Hardy did not recognize.

"Mr. Tulloch," said Smith, shaking Hardy's hand as he stood. The other man glanced about the room with an uncertain expression and sniffed a time or two. He did not offer his hand. No introductions were made.

Both men poured themselves glasses of brandy but remained standing.

"We have a few more papers for you to sign, Mr. Tulloch," said Smith, removing several folders from a leather satchel and spreading them on the table. "We brought them here for your convenience. There is no need for you to go to Edinburgh again. Our people are handling everything. You have filled out the application to have your birth certificate sent?"

Hardy nodded.

"It should be coming anytime then. There is also information on a new development we feel should help solidify your claim. We are very optimistic that this will, as we say, seal the deal."

"What information?" asked Hardy.

"It's all explained here," replied Smith, tapping the document. "So if you will just sign here"—he pointed and handed him a pen—"we can all be on our way."

PART 4

WINTER, 2005–2006

31
VILLAGE TALK

Whales Reef, Shetland Islands

In that mysterious, secretive, uncanny way in which news circulates in a church or village and becomes in time common currency without knowledge where the stories originated, Whales Reef was thus not long in learning that Hardy Tulloch may have held a closer legal relation to departed Macgregor Tulloch than Macgregor's favorite, the young chief himself.

Coira MacNeill, as always, was the first to know, as if the news had been borne on North Sea winds even before David returned from Lerwick after his meeting with Jason MacNaughton.

David had scarcely set foot back on the island before the whole village knew of Hardy Tulloch's claim to Macgregor Tulloch's inheritance.

Everyone was careful to mention no word of it in David's presence. Unsure which way the thing would go in the end, no one wanted to offend either of the present generation's scions of the ancient Tulloch name. It was best to keep one's own counsel. Even David's customarily garrulous aunt managed, with no small difficulty, to hold her tongue.

There was one, however, whose curiosity finally burst the bounds of reticence. David was taken completely off guard a week later when Coira MacNeill greeted him unexpectedly as he walked through the door of her bakery. She threw out the words of her question almost in the tone of challenge.

"Weel, young David," she said, "what are ye intendin' tae do aboot Hardy noo that he's likely tae be oor new laird?"

"What are you talking about, Coira?" replied David. His signature laugh echoed through the small shop and out into the street. In truth, David was stunned not only that she knew of Hardy's legal action, but that she apparently took it more seriously than he had upon hearing it from the younger MacNaughton. Coira may have been a gossip, but she usually knew one end of a walking stick from the other.

"Ye canna be ignorant o' the fact," she shot back. "A'body's talkin' o' naethin' else."

"They're not talking to me about it," said David noncommittally.

"Oh, aye! An' they wudna, ye ken. Why wud anybody speak tae yersel' o't? They wud be feart they might offend ye."

"Offend me!" David laughed again, now with genuine incredulity as he took up the speech of his boyhood. "Ye ken as weel as the naist that sich a thing's no aye likely, if no a'thegither impossible. Ye'll nae offend me wi' yer words, Coira MacNeill. Nor will Hardy Tulloch or onybody else. I dinna say I canna be offendet, but 'tis a sair difficult thing for a body tae du."

"Weel, yoong David, that's as well as may be," rejoined Coira, not to be outdone and ever eager to get the last word. "But whate'er's been said o' auld Macgregor an' the wayward ways o' his youth, aboot yersel' there's ne'er been a word—"

"No man ever brought a word of waywardness against my uncle," interrupted David in a tone of rebuke, returning again to the English of his education in order to enforce his words, "either in his youth or since."

"Oh, aye . . . no *man* perhaps. But a woman might."

"I know well enough that you and my aunt Rinda won't let your grudge against him die."

"I was thinkin' mair o' Odara Innes hersel'."

"And I've never heard a word of it from her," said David. "Nor do I think has anyone else. It's only you and my aunt and others like you who have kept it alive after fifty years. I'll grant you, Odara Innes may have been hurt—even treated badly for all I know. But there was never an accusation of anything untoward on my uncle's part. He married the woman, after all."

"Oh, aye, that he did. But what became o' the foreign cummer* is what I'm wantin' tae ken. Where is she noo, yoong David? Ye ken yersel' that naethin' good came o' her, an' that her blood's on his hands."

"Coira! That is a completely unfounded accusation. Not that I'm unaware of the evil whispers. But I thought you were of stiffer fiber than to believe such low tales. There's never been a shred of evidence pointing to all that foolishness that he killed her and hid the body. Now, you were about to say something about me. What was it?"

"Jist that ye've always been held in high respect on account o' yer bein' the chief," replied Coira, momentarily settling the feathers of argument. But David's rebuke made her all the more determined to get the better of him even if she had to get under a different part of his skin. "But whate'er's been said o' yer uncle, no word's been spoken against yersel'. I'm thinkin', though, that wi' rumors in the wind stainin' yer *ain* character, ye might nae take so kindly tae them that's spreadin' them. No that I wud do such a thing, mind ye. I'm jist sayin' that ye might be mair offendet than ye think."

"What would I have to be offended about?"

Cummer, Scots—A contemptuous designation for a woman, young or old, sometimes a supposed witch.

asked David seriously. "What rumors about me? I know of nothing blowing in the wind on my account."

"Naethin' concernin' yersel'," said Coira. "But the reputation o' yer grit-gran'father's may not fare sae weel—on yer father's side, ye ken, nor will ye fare sae weel when the ill news comes doon on yer ain head—yer grit-gran'dfather Tulloch . . . if he was a legitimate Tulloch."

"What are you implying, Coira?"

"Oh, naethin' mair nor what folks is sayin', that he mayna hae been a *true* Tulloch—o' the kind that can inherit I mean."

"Why would that be?"

"On account o' the man's mither nae bein' married tae the Auld Tulloch at all."

"That's preposterous. There's never been a word of such a thing against God-fearing old Ernest or Sally in a hundred years."

"Weel, there's word o' it noo."

"What word?"

"Jist what I asked ye when ye came in," replied Coira cryptically. "What ye intend tae du aboot Hardy's claim?"

"So that's it, is it? Hardy's behind this?" David laughed lightly, doing his best not to seem concerned. "What do *you* know about it, Coira?" he asked, more desirous of an answer than his casual tone let on.

"Oh, naethin' but what a'body kens. Jist that

Hardy's sayin' he's a closer relation to the auld blighter than yersel' on account o' yer grit-gran'father an' his mither."

"It's not necessary to disparage the dead by calling Uncle Macgregor an old blighter."

"Hae it yer own way, yoong David. Ye still haena answered my question—what ye intend tae do aboot Hardy."

"I intend to do nothing at all, and you can tell the other auld wives the same thing. If Hardy's the heir, then the courts will decide, and we shall all make the best of it. If he is named laird, I will be the first to offer him my hand and my service."

"Tish tosh, yoong David—ye'll du nae sich thing!"

"Then you don't know me as well as you think, Coira MacNeill, because that is precisely what I will do—and with an honest and sincere heart."

"But ye dinna think it's the trowth?"

"I will only say that I find it curious no one's made anything until now of whatever is behind all this, nor have I heard a word of this rumor about my great-grandfather and grandmother that seems suddenly to have sprouted. So I intend to ignore it until the matter is decided. Now, Coira, I'll have some oatcakes and butteries, if you're not opposed to doing a little honest trade other than trafficking in rumors."

32
WHALES FIN INN

David left the shop in the direction of the harbor and the center of town. A minute later he walked through the door of the Whales Fin Inn. At this hour the pub was occupied only by a handful of older men enjoying their morning coffee or tea, or for the early risers among them, their elevenses, perhaps with a scone on the side.

David walked into the kitchen where he found inn owner Keith Kerr and his wife, Evanna, busy preparing stew, soup, and haddock along with ingredients for a ploughman's lunch. They always assessed the day's weather before beginning food preparations. On this day a thick fog hung over the sea. Only about half the village's fishermen had gone out. Their clientele on this day could well be double the usual eight or ten regulars who came in at midday.

It was a well-established fact, and one of the island's most rigidly guarded secrets, that the prices on the inn's printed Bill of Fare and daily blackboard menu were outsider prices only. All island residents paid exactly half the printed amount. Knowledgeable women agreed that their prices were only marginally more than it would cost to make the Kerrs' soups, stews, sandwiches, fish-and-chips, and ploughman's lunches in their own kitchens. Notwithstanding that most of the potatoes, turnips, carrots, milk, beef, lamb, and of course fish were homegrown—raised and caught and purchased from the villagers—they wondered how Keith and Evanna could make sufficient profit to keep the place open. There were tourists and visitors from the mainland, but they hardly seemed numerous enough to make up the difference. Yet the islanders were enormously appreciative, the wives most of all. The unusual policy kept the Whales Fin Inn hopping nearly all year round.

Drinks were not included in the liberal pricing scheme, which was both a blessing and a curse. It was widely accepted as fact that the home brew of the Whales Fin Inn was, as the faded sign in front attested, *Shetland's Best Beer*. The secret recipe had passed through the generations since the time of Keith's great-great-grandfather Donal Kerr, who began importing the brew to stimulate business and counter the effects of the new luxury hotel built on the island during his time. Having to pay the going rate for a pint kept the men from consuming as much as they might have liked. That was the blessing. Yet its allure was enough that to limit oneself was sufficient to send a man into the doldrums. Hence the curse.

"Best of the morning to you, David!" said Keith. He stood at a wide counter chopping vegetables. Beside him Evanna was peeling potatoes with such a rapid motion that her hand was a mere blur.

"Hello, Keith . . . Evanna," said David. The tall chief found a spot on their sturdy wood work-table less cluttered with pans and plates than the rest, shoved a few things aside, and leapt onto it with his long legs dangling over the side.

"You were my father's best friend, Keith," he said, turning toward the inn's owner and lowering his voice. "If old Macgregor was like my grand-father, you're more like a father to me than any man in the world. If I can't trust you to speak as directly as my own daddy, there's no man I can trust. So tell me straight—are folks in the village talking about me?"

"They've always talked about you, laddie," replied Kerr. "They've been talking about you since the day you were born and they knew you'd be chief after your daddy."

"But are they talking about me *now* . . . since Macgregor's passing, I mean?"

"More than ever, laddie," said Keith, gathering up the vegetables from beneath his knife and sliding them into a pan. "There's no one folks'd rather see the chieftainship and lairdship come together again on his head than yourself after however many generations it's been since they was separated. The main thing they're wondering is what they're meant to call you now, chief or laird."

"The way I hear it, Keith," said David with a sigh, "the one title may not be coming down on my head at all."

"You'll be meaning Hardy, I'm thinking?"

David nodded.

"I wouldn't worry about him, laddie. His great-grandmum was the youngest of the Auld Tulloch's three, as everyone knows well enough, by his first wife, ye ken. And that was back in the day when lassies couldn't inherit. He hasn't hope of a brass farthing coming to him from that quarter. The inheritance is yours, no worry about that, and the chieftainship and lairdship both come to you along with it. Not that Hardy hasn't been strutting about with his chest puffed out like he's all at once the most important bloke in the Shetlands. Been bothering our Audney more than ever. But let him, I say, for pride goeth before a fall, as the Book says. Hardy's as big a blowhard as ever walked through the doors of our pub. And when he takes that fall, I'll be there thinking it serves the big lout right."

"Might not be a good idea to laugh in his face, Keith," laughed David, though seriously. "I've seen him lay a man out on the ground for less. What about you, Evanna?" said David, turning to Keith's wife. "What are the women saying?"

"Oh, naethin' more'n what Keith told ye," she replied, turning to stir the soup in the pot on the large stove. Her tone betrayed nervousness.

In truth, since news of Macgregor Tulloch's death she had felt unusually awed by David. The fact that David was now chief *and* laird—at least would be unless Hardy's claim turned out to be true—elevated the lad immeasurably in her estimation. Her superstitious Celtic blood could not help suddenly being more than a little afraid of him. She would have spoken freely in his hearing four months ago. Now she was reluctant to do so.

"Have you heard talk among the women, Evanna?" asked David more pointedly.

"'Tis naethin' but foolish talk."

"What is the gist of it?"

"Women are always more free wi' their tongues," she answered, still avoiding David's probing eyes.

"What are they saying?"

"Ye should ask your aunt."

"I intend to. Right now I'm asking you."

Evanna was rescued from the awkward moment by the appearance of her daughter. Audney Kerr walked into the kitchen with a basket of eggs she had gathered, bringing the fresh air inside along with her smile.

33

AUDNEY AND HER CHIEF

"I've eight fresh eggs for ye, Mum," called Audney as she bounded through the back door of the inn's kitchen. She stopped abruptly. "Oh, David," she said, "I didna ken ye was there. Best o' the mornin' tae ye," she added, giving his knee an affectionate slap with her free hand.

"And to you, Audney," replied David with a smile.

If Audney Kerr, younger than David by two years, occasionally addressed her chief in what an outsider might have considered a forward, almost flirtatious manner, nothing could have been further from her intent.

From before they could remember the close friendship of their fathers had thrust David Tulloch and Audney Kerr into the closest proximity. As children they had played together, gone to school together, bickered and laughed and argued together, and were as close as any brother and sister separated by two years. Both had younger siblings and thus also shared the common bond of being the oldest children of their families. Arna Tulloch had been a second mother to Audney, just as Evanna Kerr was to David.

After David's father went down in the terrible nor'easter that took the lives of several of the best men of Whales Reef, the prevailing view was that his widow was spoiling young David by keeping him from the sea. The rough and tumble life of a fisherman, notwithstanding its dangers, made men out of boys. Books and learning, then sending him off to university when he should have been earning his manhood on the deck of a fishing boat, was not for the likes of a strong-blooded Shetlander.

The girls of the island cared nothing for the opinion of their fishermen fathers. They found David all the more attractive that he spoke kindly to them, was well-schooled in literature and poetry and the world of ideas, that he loved the natural world of plants and animals. He was as athletic as any other boy, twice as handsome, and possessed a great joyful laugh that could be heard halfway across the island. He was polite *and* fun. What girl wouldn't be enchanted?

Had David turned out a weakling, the islanders might have thought differently of him. But he grew into the tallest young man on the island, a good inch taller than his huge cousin Hardy. Though he certainly possessed nothing like Hardy's girth, David was well-built, able-bodied, capable, and robust.

When the boy-chief, succeeding his drowned father, reached manhood, his allure was yet more captivating. That David showed every girl equal consideration while giving none indication that would betray the loss of his heart, made him all the more irritating a rival to the island's other boys. Every girl on Whales Reef, and not a few on the mainland, were smitten with young David Tulloch.

When he first left for Oxford at seventeen, most of the young men who had been unsuccessfully vying with him for the affections of the village girls were happy to see him go. When the ferry to Aberdeen sailed from Lerwick with David on it, every young man between fifteen and twenty-five on Whales Reef rejoiced.

Most of the islanders had little doubt, if David returned at all, it would be but briefly, in all likelihood with a degree in his hand, a wife on his arm, and his future secured in the great South. Like many Scots before him, King James VI the most noteworthy, he was certain to be seduced by the charms, fascinations, and temptations of England and rarely cast his glance northward toward his homeland again.

When David appeared the following summer, having added three more inches in height and probably two around his chest, there were some who did not even recognize him. The boy had grown into, if not altogether, certainly *almost* a man. The hearts of young women for miles swooned afresh, again to the annoyance of the village lads. But, they told themselves, he would soon be gone once more, perhaps *this* time for good.

For one maiden in Whales Reef, however, David's return from the university in the late spring following his first year proved life changing. That young lady was Audney Kerr.

By necessities of schooling and the differences in their ages, during the years of their early adolescence the two childhood friends had not seen as much of each other as previously. David graduated and departed for England, leaving Audney behind as a gangly fifteen-year-old, somewhat long in the face, still the rambunctious youngster he had romped and ridden and explored the island with years before, and not yet displaying the signs of dawning woman-hood.

The year of David's absence, however, wrought perhaps more changes on Audney than it did on the young squire. Overnight, it seemed, she had blossomed into a woman.

When David made his first appearance at the Whales Fin Inn after his return and beheld the young woman setting down two frothing pints in front of his cousin Murdoc and his uncle Fergus, he wondered where Keith and Evanna had discovered such a winsome new pub maid.

He approached the table and greeted his kins-men. Then suddenly recognition dawned.

"Audney!" he said in surprise. "Is it really *you?*"

"Aye, David," she said shyly. " 'Tis me."

"You've changed!"

"As ye hae yersel'."

"I suppose you're right!" laughed David, the sound of his cheery voice filling the pub. He pulled out a third wooden chair and sat down with the two men. "Bring me a pint as well."

The conversation was brief. Though the two exchanged but snatches of dialog throughout the summer, the few words that fell from David's lips that day were enough. Audney's heart smote her. David's increased stature, his muscular build, his wild mop of curly light-brown hair, the intoxicating flash of his teeth when he smiled, his musical laugh, the sheer poetry of his tongue speaking in such civilized southern tones . . . they were enough to stir the blood of any Scottish girl.

All summer Audney watched him with dark observant eyes. More often than was comfortable she found it necessary to glance quickly away to keep from betraying the tidal waves of emotion surging in her heart. When he went away again in the fall, alone in her room Audney wept. She knew she would never see him again.

Her fears were unfounded. The following May,

yet again David returned to his native Shetland isle. Those who assumed he would be ensnared, corrupted, and lost to the worldly pleasure grounds of England had misjudged their young chief. His southern sojourns only deepened his affection for his homeland. If possible, he considered himself more a Shetlander than ever.

David had become a polished, erudite, well-spoken, and traveled young man. The doubts about how he would turn out were put to rest. The islanders were proud of their young chief.

By his third summer home, now a strapping youth of twenty, his face maturing with the strong angular lines of manliness, at last David's eyes were opened to the flower of womanhood that had been unfolding during his absence. At eighteen, Audney Kerr had become the most beautiful young woman on the island. Her bashfulness of sixteen was gone. She had grown comfortable with the changes evolving upon her. She was full of spunk and fun, again the spirited and gregarious girl David had known in childhood, and was a favorite at the pub and inn. She was no less in love with David than she had been for two years. That secret, however, remained locked away in her heart.

The two friends of childhood were now young adults. Hope began to stir both in Audney's parents and in David's mother that they might in time become a good deal more. Such parental dreams, however, seemed unlikely. It was true that during the summer the two youths were often seen walking across the moors or along the sea together. Yet in spite of her obvious beauty, in David's eyes Audney remained the friend of former days, now the friend of his young adulthood, but little more.

34
RUMORS

David slid off the counter and stood to face Audney, though he had to look down several inches to meet her eyes.

"Keep yer seat, David!" she laughed. She handed the basket to her mother. "Ye dinna need tae be standin' up on account o' me walkin' into the room."

"You're a fine lass and woman, Audney. I can't well show you less respect than I would any other."

"Hae it yer way, David." Audney laughed again. "Ye always was a gentleman, e'en when I was a mere lassie. I'm nae aboot tae change ye noo."

"Would you change me if you could, Audney?" David asked with a mischievous grin.

"No a hair on yer bonny chieftain's head, David! Nae a hair. Ye're a true gentleman, a man whose heart any lassie cud hope tae win."

David turned thoughtful. "Audney," he said after a moment, "perhaps you will answer a question your mother sidestepped."

"What question wud that be?"

"I asked her what folk are saying about me— the womenfolk of the village."

"An' what should ye care what they're sayin', David? Ye ken weel enough that their gossip is o' no account."

"I need to know what's in the wind, Audney. I must know how to carry myself and if anything's needed from me. So, what are they saying?"

"Hae it yer way then!" laughed Audney. "They're worried, David."

"Worried?" repeated David. "About what?"

"Aboot what's tae become o' us if it's true aboot Hardy becomin' laird and inheritin' the haa* an' not yersel'."

"Nothing's going to come of it," David assured her. "Hardy has as much chance of becoming laird as you do."

"I'm nae related tae the Auld Tulloch like yersel' an' Hardy."

"I'll grant you that."

"They're also sayin' that ye shouldna be sittin' idly by an' let Hardy steal the lairdship fae ye."

David broke into laughter. "They think I'm sitting idly by!"

"Aye—though I only heard it frae Grizel Gordon palaverin' at the factory one day, an' ye ken what an unco unconvertet tongue she's got."

David sighed. "It's a wonder, with Grizel for a loose-tongued mother, that Rakel is endowed

---

*Haa—Shetlandic for the laird's house.

with such a sound head and common sense. Grizel causes more mischief than any six women on the island . . . well, except for Coira, who is her equal. Why would she say such a thing?"

"No one kens why ye dinna jist step into the lairdship yersel'," put in Evanna, breaking her silence. "Folk are sayin' it's ye ain fault for givin' Hardy the opportunity in the first place. Jist take it, they say, like ye ought tae do."

"What would they have me do?" said David. "You don't just *take* an inheritance. There are legalities to be observed. Uncle Macgregor died without a will. It is out of my hands. If Hardy inherits, there's nothing I can do about it. But that won't happen."

"He's older than ye, David," said Audney.

"That he is. But his only relation to old Ernest comes through the daughter who's not in line to inherit."

"Unless it's yer ain ancestor who isna in line," said Audney's mother cryptically.

"What do you mean, Evanna?" said David. "*None* of my ancestors are in line with Uncle Macgregor. It's only because he had no children that the line passes to me."

"But it mayna pass tae yersel' at a', if yer ain ancestors arena in line tae the Auld Tulloch."

"How could that be, when my daddy and his daddy before him, and his before him all came straight from him? In that regard, Hardy and I have an equal share of the Auld Tulloch's blood in our veins. We are both his great-great-grandsons. My blood comes through the youngest son, his through the daughter."

"Aye, but what if one o' the lines is legal blood an' no the ither?"

"I don't follow your meaning, Evanna," said David.

Again Evanna retreated into silence.

"What the auld wives are sayin', David," now said Keith, "is naethin' more'n what Hardy's been sayin' oot in the other room for the past week—that yer daddy's gran'father's no in line on account o' being illegitimate, born in sin, ye ken."

"What?" David turned to face his father's friend.

"That's what he's sayin', laddie, that the Auld Tulloch ne'er married yer grit-gran'father Leith's mither. She ne'er was Sally Tulloch at a', but remained Sally *Lipscomb* a' her days. So the evil rumor goes."

"And did Hardy spread it about?"

"I canna say where it came frae. Folks was jist talkin' aboot it one day. They say that the son born tae Sally and the Auld Tulloch—the man's youngest an' yer ain daddy's gran'father Leith, was naethin' but an illegitimate son. So the Auld Tulloch's rightful inheritance, they say, wi' auld Macgregor dead, noo passes doon through the daughter Delynn, an' straight tae Hardy, nae yersel'."

David was stunned. At last the gossip—and Hardy's legal claim—made sense. If the thing was indeed true, it would make Hardy both chief and laird of Whales Reef.

David left the inn a few minutes later with much on his mind.

35

Do You Believe in Christmas?

Washington, D.C.

Winter hit with a major storm in early December, dumping several inches of snow on D.C., a foot in New York, and nineteen inches in Boston. The storm passed into the Atlantic, leaving behind it a glittering white winter wonderland with blue skies and sunshine from Virginia to Maine. The chilly bright weather was predicted to hold through the holidays.

Loni Ford stood again at the window of her office and gazed down on the Capitol Mall blanketed by virgin snow. How beautiful it all was from high up where she stood. Though she hadn't spent a Christmas at home for five years, she was enough of a sentimentalist to decorate a tree while listening to Christmas music and do some baking with favorite recipes from her childhood. She loved the season, though occasional pangs of guilt inevitably nagged at her. Such feelings not-withstanding, she had wonderful childhood memories of sledding, maple syrup and cream mixed with fresh snow and eaten with a spoon, decorating the house with greens, caroling, the school play—the one time a year she could pretend to be a real actress—the services at Meeting, the handmade gifts, so many other traditions. Though she had not yet found a comfortable way to reconnect with that past, it was still a heritage she treasured.

These days she usually went somewhere else for Christmas. Skiing in the Poconos was one of her favorites.

But the holiday had come upon her without plans this year. Hugh had invited her—three times, actually, cajoling almost to the point of begging—to join him for Christmas with his family in Connecticut. She had managed to put him off, but if she didn't come up with an alternative soon, she would be left without an excuse.

She liked Hugh. As she had mentally checked off his favorable qualities on her Husband List, it was obvious the pros outweighed the cons by a good margin. He was, by any standards, a "great catch." She *might* even love him.

Until she knew for certain, however, meeting his parents signaled something premature. The fact she had no parents for reverse introductions somehow heightened the potential awkwardness. Until she had a clearer picture of their future together, she did not want to spend a holiday in the home of his parents. Such an encounter would carry too many subtle undercurrents.

An hour later, looking out the spacious windows of Maddy's office, Loni's mind wandered from the letter Maddy was dictating.

As she stared at the Washington Monument, with white covering the city, a much taller sky-scraping landmark came into Loni's mind's eye, one that equally defined its city's skyline 225 miles farther north.

Suddenly she realized that her fingers on her laptop had stilled.

"Oh, Maddy, I'm sorry!" she said. "Could you back up ten seconds—my mind just blanked out."

A few minutes later, when they were done, Loni began to leave the office, then hesitated. She turned back to face her boss.

"Maddy, do you have plans for Christmas?" she asked in a thoughtful tone.

"I never have plans for Christmas."

"You're not going home?"

Maddy shook her head. "My mom's taking a cruise. That's what she usually does when the holidays come around. It keeps her from having to deal with any religious implications. She always invites me along. But the Norway fjords in winter—no thanks!"

"How about coming with me to New York?"

"Christmas in the Big Apple . . . it sounds fun! But I thought you and Hugh—"

"Did he say something to you?"

"Not in so many words. But I ran into him in

the lobby a few days ago after he had been to see you. He implied that you and he were spending Christmas together."

Loni laughed lightly. "I'm afraid he is engaging in a little cart-before-the-horse gamesmanship. He wants me to meet his family."

"Ah," said Maddy, "a serious step."

"Exactly. And one I'm not quite ready for, especially at Christmas. Too many innuendos lurking around the edges. Anyway, I'm going to New York. I just decided."

"So the invitation is for real?"

"Absolutely!"

Maddy nodded. "Then count me in."

"And if you see Hugh, not a word," said Loni. "I'll tell him in my own way."

"Got it. What are you thinking of doing in New York?"

"I don't know yet!" laughed Loni. "I just thought of it. I'll look into what's playing on Broadway . . . concerts . . . I'll find out what's going on. I would like to go to a Christmas Eve service."

"Now that would be a first!" laughed Maddy. "For me, I mean."

Loni's expression asked the question she was thinking.

"I've never been to church in my life."

"Really?"

"Scout's honor."

251

"But you'll join me?"

"Sure, why not? It will be a new adventure for an atheist."

"Now I know you're joking!"

"No, really."

"You're an atheist?"

Maddy nodded.

"And you want to go to a Christmas Eve service?"

"Might as well. I'm curious."

"But . . . do you believe in Jesus?"

"I don't know. I never thought much about it."

"Then do you believe in Christmas?"

"How do you mean? Santa Claus with all the trimmings?"

"No!" Loni laughed. "I mean the *meaning* of Christmas. The birth of Jesus."

"Oh, yeah, baby in the manger and all that. No, I don't suppose I do. Just a myth like Adam and Eve and Noah's ark, isn't it? Why? Do you believe in the baby Jesus, come to save the world from sin and all that?"

"Yes . . . yes, I do."

"Well, I won't hold it against you!" laughed Maddy. "I guess everyone's got to have something to believe in."

"What do *you* believe in?" asked Loni.

"Everybody but me, I should have said."

"You continue to amaze me, Maddy. You are the most interesting person I know."

"You must lead a pretty boring life!"

"In any event, I will do some investigating and see which of the cathedrals are having a Christmas Eve service. Maybe they all do, I don't know. If you're game, I am."

"You really want to do the church thing?"

"I suppose I'm in the mood for a big-city Christmas service—choirs and organs and pageantry. We'll both have a new experience. And maybe an ice show? I'll see what I can find out."

"Can we go ice skating at Rockefeller Center?" asked Maddy excitedly.

"You're the boss, not me."

"Not for this trip, Loni. I'm just along for the ride."

36
BLEAK MID-WINTER

Whales Reef, Shetland Islands

As November gave way to December, the Shetland Islands were bound in the grip of sub-freezing temperatures during most of their fifteen hours of daily darkness.

The Christmas season on the small Shetland island of Whales Reef came sunless and gloomy. With but five or six hours of daylight in every twenty-four, and those hours often filled with stinging Arctic winds battering the islands, it was a time of year when many Shetlanders struggled to retain their optimism. Seasonal Affective Disorder could have been invented here.

Still, Shetlanders were a hearty breed. Their Norse and Celtic roots had been nurtured and strengthened in Europe's northern climes. Thus they made the best of it.

As if intensifying the cold, there was no denying that this year uncertainty was in the air. At the center of it was the question of the chieftainship and lairdship. Respect for David was high. But would that be enough to preserve the island's ancient heritage? Or would the idea of a clan chief, like a vanishing fragrance on the fading bloom of a romantic tradition, become one more abandoned relic of the past?

Winter presented its own unique challenges for the fishermen. Besides the weather, a sudden decline had set in. Whatever fish may have been in the ocean, it seemed they weren't running anywhere near Whales Reef this winter.

Only Hardy Tulloch with his inexplicable sixth sense seemed to know where to find them. He bought the boats of several local fishermen who were struggling financially and put the men to work for him. That he also could afford to engage one of Edinburgh's most prestigious law firms to prosecute his claim against Macgregor Tulloch's inheritance gave yet further evidence that finances were the least of Hardy's worries.

Meanwhile, he hauled one full load after another to the fish market in Lerwick and continued to receive top pound for his labors. How Hardy managed such catches when all the other boats were riding high in the water with empty holds, grumbled Rinda Gunn in the hearing of select ears only, he owed to closer acquaintance with the powers of darkness and the deep than was healthy for any human being who cared for the eternal destination of their souls. In truth, Hardy's success had more to do with state-of-the-art sonar equipment than the forces of darkness.

One thing was as clear as the gloom hanging over the island—Hardy was enjoying himself these days. He carried himself with such obvious gusto and with perfect confidence in the outcome of his claim to Macgregor Tulloch's money and property that by now most were forced to acknowledge the reality that it *might* in fact be true. No one doubted, as Hardy promised, that all the necessary documentation would be forth-coming in due course.

In the midst of the dismal fishing and the frigid weather, the idea of the island's fortunes winding up in the hands of one like Hardy Tulloch was enough to doom any hope for the future.

Everyone knew exactly what he would do the moment he became laird. He would instantly double everyone's rents. Those who couldn't pay, he would evict. No one had any doubt about that. He would probably shut down the wool factory as well.

37

CHRISTMAS IN THE BIG APPLE

New York City

Ten days after making their plans, the day before Christmas Eve, the two career women stepped off the train in New York's Grand Central Station, found a taxi, and checked into their hotel about three o'clock.

They relaxed, dressed, and went out to treat themselves to an evening at the fabled Chez Anatole where they had been lucky to get a table at all. Their dinner featured roast pheasant. The trimmings included hors d'oeuvres of escargot, new to Loni but she was game to try it, wine, a French Bordeaux, and dessert, a chocolate mousse laced with cream and crumbled shortbread. They topped it off with peppermint espresso from a small bistro on their way to a theater for one of the last Broadway showings of *Fiddler on the Roof.*

By the following afternoon, lugging several large bags, the sidewalks and stores on Fifth Avenue were so crowded the two could hardly move.

"I'm ready for a break!" said Loni. "These feet

of mine need a rest. I wonder if I'm going to make it to church tonight."

"We passed a tea shop a little way back," Maddy noted. "A sign in the window said Christmas Eve High Tea."

"Tea!" said Loni with a grimace. "Did I tell you about tea in Scotland? Let's just say it wasn't to my taste."

Maddy laughed. "High tea isn't about tea!"

"What then?"

"Everything that comes with it. It's fantastic. You can have coffee. You'll love it. Trust me."

"If you say so," laughed Loni. "Is this something you learned from your Scottish mother?"

"Yes. But high tea is as much English as Scottish. Let's go drop our things off at the hotel. Then I shall treat you to an experience you will not soon forget."

Thirty minutes later Maddy and Loni were seated, both with cups of coffee in front of them. Two trays of goodies were just being delivered to their table—a three-tiered glass tray filled with cakes and candies and cookies of every shape and color imaginable, and another with tiny sandwiches, fruits, and cheeses.

"So, this is your high tea," said Loni. "You were right, it looks promising."

"This is only the beginning. There will be more to come—we may need to save our next meal for tomorrow."

"If I'm going to make it past midnight," sighed Loni as they nibbled and sipped, "I think a nap may be in order."

"Midnight!" exclaimed Maddy. "How long does Christmas Eve service last?"

"It's a midnight service. Starts at eleven, probably ends at midnight or twelve-thirty."

"Then I may want to grab a few winks too."

Loni grew thoughtful. "Were you serious about what you told me back at the office," she said, "about being an atheist?"

"Yeah, I suppose," replied Maddy.

"You don't sound convinced."

"I'm not a card-carrying wacko about it if that's what you mean. I have religious clients. I don't want to offend them. I'm not going to protest Nativity scenes or put a Darwin bumper sticker on my car. I told you before, I don't think about all that. But if you pressed me . . . yeah, I would say I don't believe there is a God."

"Why do you celebrate Christmas then?" asked Loni.

"I don't know—tradition, just for fun . . . because it's a holiday. It's festive. I guess I like it."

"Did you celebrate Christmas growing up?"

"No. It was only my mom and my sister and me. My folks are divorced. My mom was nuts about her nonbelief. She hated religion. She constantly preached anti-religion. She *did* plaster her car with anti-Christian slogans. But we did presents at Christmas and had a tree and all that. She just made sure we knew the baby Jesus thing was imaginary and had nothing to do with the real origin of Christmas. By the time I was a teenager her vendetta against Christians began to annoy me. She protested *too* much."

"Yet you've seemed to follow in her footsteps."

"Maybe you're right. I suppose I adopted her general outlook, just not her passion about it."

"What about your dad?"

"He was never a factor in our lives. My mom hates him too. She made sure we saw him as little as possible."

"That's too bad."

"Yeah, it is. Now my dad's got Alzheimer's and it's too late for me to know him as an adult. It's my own fault—I waited too long. I allowed my mom's poison to keep me from contacting him once I was old enough. Then I got swept up in my career. It's one of a few guilts I carry around."

Loni sipped at her coffee.

"My mom wasn't a very happy person," Maddy added after a moment. "Still isn't. Her poisonous attitude toward my father actually did nothing but poison herself."

"Sounds like a little religion might do her some good."

"An interesting idea. Try telling her that! What about you?" asked Maddy. "What did you do for Christmas when you were young?"

"Oh, the usual Christmas-card kind of festivities," Loni said with a fond smile. "Church and music, visits with the relatives and people in the Fellowship, sleigh rides, and of course *food*. And lots of it."

"Sounds like my kind of Christmas—some of it, anyway. What do you mean, in the 'fellowship'?"

"It's what we call our church," replied Loni, "Where I grew up."

"Pennsylvania, right?"

Loni nodded. "Rural Pennsylvania."

"So what else did you do?" asked Maddy, reaching for the last triangle of sandwich.

"There are lots of old English traditions in our little community. Most of the families are English. That's where our Fellowship originated—in England. I used to love singing carols. It gave the season such an old-world feel."

Loni glanced away with a wistful smile. "And here we are in the middle of New York," she sighed. "No trees, no tinsel, no feast."

"What are you talking about!" said Maddy. "Every store has a Christmas tree. There are carols everywhere. We've been hearing them all day. You and I are going to open our gifts tomorrow in our hotel room. And we are going to have a feast too."

"You win. We *are* surrounded by Christmas. Still, don't you feel a little disconnected from it all? It's different from Christmas with family. I wonder . . . are we two old maids with no place to go for Christmas? Or are we two modern girls taking New York by storm?"

"Neither," said Maddy. "We're just trying to convince ourselves that we have something to live for besides our careers. And I may be an old maid before my time, but you need to stop talking like that! Hugh would marry you in an instant if you'd let him."

"You're probably right," laughed Loni. "Maybe a year from now he and I will be honeymooning here, though I'm not sure I am quite ready for *that!*"

"Nor am I," rejoined Maddy. "My life is complicated enough without men."

"You sound like me in college."

"No way!"

"Really. I didn't date once my whole two years in JC. It made my roommate crazy. She was constantly trying to fix me up. I told her I hated the superficiality of it."

"I can't believe you didn't date!"

"It's true."

"You had no excuse. But look at me—I'm hardly a woman who turns heads."

"Maddy, sometimes you are too much!"

"Too much what?"

"Never mind."

"So if you loved the holidays as a girl," asked

Maddy, growing serious again, "why didn't you go home for Christmas?"

Loni's thoughtful expression deepened. "You know my parents are dead?"

"You've mentioned it," replied Maddy. "I didn't want to pry."

"Being an orphan complicates everything. I had a dozen relatives among our community, but I was the only kid growing up with no mother or father. My grandparents were older by the time my parents were killed, and they were stuck with me. No, I mean to say they were wonderful, but . . . I don't know, I just had to get away from all that. It still feels strange when I go back."

"It's probably lonely for them now."

"You're right. But the longer you stay away, the harder it is. . . ." Loni's voice drifted away.

"That's so true. Why is that?"

"Nothing changes there, at least in my case. It's a huge conflict just knowing how to dress when I'm there. You either go back to your old ways and looks and act and talk like you were before, or if you are true to the new person you've become, you can't help disappointing them. They are very conservative, not politically but culturally. It's a hard situation to navigate. I think I've convinced myself that I'm actually doing them a favor by not going home."

"You mean by letting them think of you as you used to be?"

"Something like that. At least that's my rationalization. Though that cat was out of the bag years ago. They have a pretty good idea who I've become. In their own way they've accepted it. Besides, I like my new life. And anyway, this year I wanted to spend Christmas with you!"

"Thank you . . . thank you very much!" said Maddy, doing her best at an Elvis imitation. "But seriously, folks . . . I know what you mean. I wasn't particularly anxious to go home again either after last Thanksgiving with my mom and sister. The main topic of conversation was about me finding a husband. The magazines left in my room were a nice touch too, with the pages turned back where some great new diet had been circled with a Sharpie. In their eyes I'm an overweight single woman who, as the saying goes, isn't getting any younger. But maybe I like my life and my job and who I am. Even you were doing it this morning, Loni, without even realizing it."

"Doing what?"

"We were in that dress shop, and it was *Here, Maddy, try on this dress. It would be a nice break from your black tailored suits. Branch out, wear something pastel or burgundy.*"

"I'm sorry. That bright one I was looking at—

I thought it would bring out your beautiful eyes."

"But why? *Why* do you want to bring out my beautiful eyes?"

"I don't know. Because you have pretty eyes. Why hide them?"

"Loni . . ." said Maddy before pausing briefly. "You just don't get it, do you?"

"I guess not."

"I love you, Loni. But you have no clue what it's like not to be tall and athletic and beautiful."

Maddy's words hung in the air. Loni stared back almost as if she hadn't heard them. Her mind raced back to her childhood when she was awkward and gangly.

"I am who I am and I like it," Maddy went on. "Just don't try to fix me up with bright dresses that highlight my eyes."

"Okay. Agreed," Loni said with a nod. "I apologize."

"Good. Now that that's settled, we had better get back to the hotel for that nap before our night out—at church no less!"

38

RIVALS AND LOVERS

Whales Reef, Shetland Islands

A man identifying himself as Clement Ardmore appeared in Whales Reef during the first week of February, booked a room at the Whales Fin Inn, then proceeded to request appointments—not only with David and Hardy Tulloch, the two cousins at the center of the controversy, but also with every other Tulloch relative on the island.

On the second day after his arrival, Coira MacNeill announced that he was a private investigator, an "heir hunter" working for the probate court. How she came by the information she did not divulge.

Though David as titular chief might have been said to be the most important man on the island now that old Macgregor had been laid to rest, the title of most notorious and most feared surely went to his cousin Hardy.

Hardy Tulloch had grown up as the biggest and strongest boy on the island. By the time he was ten, no fourteen-year-old would dare tangle with him. At sixteen, still growing, filling out in all directions and actually not a bad-looking lad in a savage kind of way, he naturally assumed that any girl within five hundred miles would wilt in his presence.

What young women found attractive in such a one was a mystery. Yet there were girls who were drawn to danger as moths to a flame. Hardy strutted and boasted and engaged in all the games hot-blooded youths play to turn the heads of foolish maidens. It was hardly any wonder, by the time he was eighteen—a result of that curious feminine laxity of youth which causes teen girls to be swept off their feet by the least character-worthy young men—that he had left a string of hearts behind—not *broken* exactly, but certainly older and wiser.

All the while, Hardy's ego grew in corresponding measure to his size.

The small Whales Reef Tulloch clan was an anomaly in the Shetlands where Scandinavian tradition predominated. Though Norse blood intermingled freely with Celtic on their island, the clan traced its primary roots instead to the western Highlands of mainland Scotland. The lairds and chiefs of Whales Reef had always attempted to preserve that Highland clan tradition.

Hardy, however, despised the kilt, traditional Scottish dance, and Celtic music. He declared himself a Norseman through and through. He participated every year in Lerwick's spectacular annual Viking festival, *Up Helly-Aa*, marching through the streets in full Viking regalia behind the grand longship built for the occasion. With a thousand torch-bearing *guizers*, brandishing axe and shield, Hardy was in his element for the celebration, which culminated in the burning of the longship and a great fireworks display. His dream was one day to march at the head of the procession as the Guizer Jarl of the festival.

Through most of the years of their youth, Hardy dismissed his young cousin as a mere child, a weak one at that. When the two crossed paths, Hardy bullied young David mercilessly, whether from jealously or mere boyish cruelty, it hardly mattered. That his father and David's were both fishermen did nothing to draw together the two great-great-grandsons of the Auld Tulloch—the last laird and chief born in the nineteenth century, and the last upon whom both titles rested. Whatever had prompted Ernest Tulloch to split the titles seemed destined to taint his legacy to the third and fourth generation, the very generations represented by David and Hardy and their fathers.

From an early age Hardy hated hearing David referred to as "the young chief," a title Hardy coveted for himself. At the time of the accident that claimed David's father, Hardy was a menacing 190-pound seventeen-year-old with a temper, while David was a slender fourteen-year-old of a mere 120 pounds.

David mostly managed to stay out of his cousin's way. When the young chief left for Oxford, Hardy was a hulking twenty-year-old, by then shouldering an equal share of the workload of his father's business. He paid little attention to the changes taking place in David during the next three years. Though he visited the pub almost daily for two or three pints of ale with his friends, neither did he take much notice as Audney Kerr slowly turned into a woman.

All that changed, however, when David returned prior to his fourth and final year at the university. Suddenly Hardy was startled to see that David, like him, had become a man.

Most bitter of all for Hardy to swallow was the fact that every eligible girl on the island, and not a few on mainland Shetland, was in love with the young chief.

Hardy's eyes also began to see Audney Kerr in a new light. The change came one afternoon when David walked in and strode across the floor of the pub, greeting the patrons and being greeted in return.

Audney approached. Their eyes met. Audney's glistened briefly and she glanced shyly away.

Hardy saw it. Suddenly he beheld what Audney Kerr had become. Most important, he saw that she was in love with David. All the competitive spirit of his nature instantly rose up within him. His chief became a rival in love, that most perilous of rivalries.

From that moment on, Hardy's visits to the Whales Fin Inn took on new import. Henceforth, every afternoon when he walked through the door, he took it as a new opportunity to dazzle and impress.

Audney's rebuffs of his attentions, and the fact obvious to everyone in the village that she had eyes only for David, made Hardy all the more determined to possess her.

By the time David departed Shetland in the fall to begin his final year at Oxford, Hardy Tulloch vowed that before his cousin set foot on Whales Reef again, Audney Kerr would be his.

Like most vows, it was easier made than carried out. Hardy was shocked to find Audney not so willing to fall in with his designs. She spurned him with such wit, with a feminine bravado to match his own, that the very ring of her laughter became bitter in his ear. She dared laugh in his face at the suggestion that she accompany him to Lerwick for a weekend where they could "have some fun" together. And she did so in front of a pub full of Hardy's fellow fishermen.

Hardy seethed for days at the rebuke. But his anger at being made to look the fool by the village beauty, along with her obvious affection for his milksop of a cousin, only deepened Hardy's desire to have her.

No matter how long it took, Hardy swore that he would conquer Audney Kerr. In so doing he would prove himself twice the man of the so-called chief.

39
OVER DINNER

Washington, D.C.

Loni Ford and Hugh Norman had managed to see each other but a handful of times since Christmas. At last they both had the same night free and agreed to meet for dinner. Hugh suggested the Capital Grille, and Loni offered no complaint.

The moment they walked into the premier steak house on Pennsylvania Avenue, Hugh glanced about, assessing which movers and shakers might be present. As they were shown to their table, he paused to exchange a handshake and a few words with more than one acquaintance.

"Under Secretary of State . . . Assistant Attorney General," he whispered as they sat down, "There's a congressmen . . . one or two senators. And I think that's the vice-president's wife over there. A full house tonight!"

"Maybe I should leave!" quipped Loni. "You can schmooze to your heart's content."

"Don't you dare! Having you here is intrinsic to my public image." He smiled and winked. "You know, 'Who's that beautiful woman with Norman over there?' "

"Hmm . . . I'm not sure what to make of that."

"Nothing to make of it. In Washington you grab whatever attention you can. So, a couple of steaks?" said Hugh, glancing over the menu. Then he seemed to catch himself. "Oh, sorry," he added. "No meat, right?"

"Poultry and fish are okay, just not beef or pork."

"What will it be, then?"

"The Mediterranean spinach salad I had last time was good. I think I'll ask if they can add grilled salmon to it."

A few minutes later, the order placed, their waiter brought the bottle of Merlot Hugh had selected.

"So did you and Maddy paint the Big Apple red?" asked Hugh as the waiter poured the wine into their glasses.

"Hardly," replied Loni. "We shopped, went to a Broadway show, and Maddy treated me to a high tea. Actually I think the Christmas Eve church service may have been the highlight for me."

"The two of you went to church?" Hugh leaned back in his chair, sipping his wine.

"You're surprised?"

"I don't know. I just never thought of you as the religious type."

"I don't know that I am. I just wanted to go to church."

"And Maddy?"

"She's definitely *not* the religious type!" laughed Loni. "When I suggested it, she told me she was an atheist. But she was up for a new experience. So we went to the Cathedral of St. John the Divine, right in the heart of the city."

"I've heard of it," said Hugh. "Catholic?"

"Episcopal. The organ was wonderful. I've never heard Christmas carols sound so majestic."

"What did Maddy think?"

"She said she enjoyed it. I don't think she was just being polite either. What about you, Hugh? Are you an atheist?" Loni asked before she realized what she was saying.

"That's pretty direct!" he answered. "Actually . . . I don't know. Probably not. Though I rarely think about religion or God. I just take life as it comes. I suppose I believe there must be *some* meaning to it all. I don't know what I'd call it. But you believe in God, I take it?"

"I do."

"Were you raised that way?"

"I was."

"I suppose that's why you wanted to go to a Christmas Eve service. Meanwhile, I was confined with nothing to do except drink brandied eggnog with my parents the whole evening. I was in bed by eleven."

Loni smiled. "Just about the time Maddy and I were heading for church."

"My parents wondered why you didn't come."

"Sorry. I just wasn't ready for it. Maybe next Christmas."

"That's a long time from now, Loni. I still haven't figured out why you wanted to spend Christmas with Maddy instead of me. A guy could get the wrong idea. I realize she's your boss, but your whole life seems to revolve around work . . . and around her."

"She's also my friend, Hugh. There's nothing more to it."

"I know. But my parents are anxious to meet you. And I want you to meet them."

"What have you told them, Hugh? I hope you're not building me up too much. They're bound to be disappointed."

"Not a chance! Who could be disappointed in you, Loni? They'll love you. Why are you putting me off on this?"

"I'm not necessarily putting you off."

"That's how it seems."

"It's just . . . I don't know how to explain it, but having no parents to introduce you to . . . well, somehow it adds pressure, an awkwardness, to meeting *your* parents."

"I can be patient. Just don't wait too long. Oh, here's Senator McTavish. Let me introduce you. Hello, Senator," Hugh said, rising and shaking the man's hand. "Allow me to present Loni Ford."

"Charmed, Ms. Ford," said the senator, smiling

with an expression Loni wasn't sure she liked as he extended his hand across the table.

A moment later he was gone. Hugh resumed his seat.

"Well done, Loni," he said softly. "I've been trying to make inroads with him for months. This will definitely help. He has a bit of a reputation, if you know what I mean. He will *not* forget you! So what kind of a tea was that you said you went to?"

"A high tea. Actually it has very little to do with tea. They bring you trays of the most interesting cakes and meats and cheeses and crackers and scones to go with your tea or coffee. It's a Scottish thing . . . or British. Maddy knew about it. She's Scottish. I had no idea."

"Yet she sent *you* over to Scotland."

"I don't think she's particularly into her heritage, though she did say she might like to visit Scotland someday."

"What about you? Are you interested in your heritage?"

"I would if I knew how and where to find out more. My grandparents have told me very little about their side of the family, and my mother's side is a complete mystery. I've resigned myself to never knowing much beyond what I do now."

"Well, you know what they say—live in the present and all that. I suppose I've never cared much about my ancestry."

"You're right about the present, of course," said Loni a little wistfully. "Still, I would love to know more."

The waiter came with Hugh's steak platter and Loni's salad. When it resumed, their conversation veered into other channels.

"Do you have any hobbies, Hugh?" Loni asked.

"My, but we are being random this evening! High tea, religion, and now hobbies."

"Just curious," said Loni.

"Okay, I'll bite. What kind of hobbies?"

"Anything . . . you know, reading, model cars, cycling?"

"Who has time for any of that? You don't either, do you?"

"No, but I work sixty hours a week, not thirty-five like you."

"Ah yes, what can I say? The easy life of the congressional aide. So what do *you* do in your spare time?"

"I asked you first."

"And now I'm asking you second?"

Loni thought a moment.

"I read when I can," she said. "I love historical novels and the occasional mystery. Maybe that's what made me think of hobbies . . . a book I'm reading. And I would love to get back into woodworking."

"*Back* into it," repeated Hugh. "Did you used to be into it?"

"Not really. But I grew up surrounded by handmade furniture. I helped my grandfather design and make a few things. I suppose someday I would like to have my own woodshop where I could be creative. For me it's a form of art. I can't draw, but I am fairly good with a band saw and circular sander."

"I have no idea what those even are!"

"I was in an antique furniture shop a few months ago, not far from here, and it reminded me—"

"Oh, there's the vice-president himself!" interrupted Hugh.

"Do you know him?" asked Loni, following Hugh's gaze across the room.

"Nothing like that. I'm about twenty-seven levels lower on the food chain. But one never knows when an opportunity will arise."

The vice-president joined his wife, and slowly Hugh brought his gaze back across the table. He reached for Loni's hand. "Forgive me," he said apologetically. "What were you saying?"

"Nothing," Loni said and smiled. "Just reminiscing about my grandfather and family, about oils and stains on the hands . . . just random, as you say."

40
THE HEIR HUNTER

Whales Reef, Shetland Islands

The visitor to Whales Reef sat at the table in the corner of the Whales Fin Inn he had commandeered as his own since his arrival.

By late afternoon the pub would be filled with those fishermen who could afford its special draft beer. At this hour of the morning, however, it served as breakfast room to the inn's guests. On this day that guest list was a list of one. It consisted solely of Clement Ardmore, recently arrived from Edinburgh.

He had just filled his cup with tea when Audney Kerr came across the floor bearing a plate filled with eggs, sausage, tomato, haggis, mushrooms, and baked beans—standard fare for a Scottish cooked breakfast.

"Here ye be, Mr. Ardmore," she said.

"Thank you very much," he said. "It smells delicious."

Half an hour later, as Audney was clearing the table, their guest glanced up at her. "So, Miss Kerr, what can you tell me about these two men

279

I am to interview this morning—the Tulloch boys, Hardar and David, I believe are their names?" He studied the papers he had set on the table in front of him.

"Hardy and David, ye're meaning," replied Audney. "Ye make it sound like they're brithers, speakin' o' them as the Tulloch boys."

"They are cousins, correct?"

"Aye, but there couldna' be two more unlike men on the island."

"Unlike . . . in what way?"

"In *every* way. Ye'll ken weel enough what I mean when ye meet them."

Audney continued back to the kitchen with the tray. When she appeared with a fresh pot of tea, Ardmore spoke again.

"What can you tell me about the two?" he asked again.

"I'm the last one ye should ask!" laughed Audney.

"Why is that?"

She lowered her voice and smiled. "On account o' my fallin' head over heels for the one, an' the ither'd marry me next week if I'd let him."

"A proposal in waiting, so to speak."

"Ye might call it that. But it's no aboot tae happen."

"So you could be the next laird's wife, the Lady of Whales Reef, depending on which way this inheritance turns out."

"If I cared aboot bein' a lady, as ye say, what ye say may be true. But I dinna. An' the time for the one's done an' past."

"But you could marry the other, I take it."

"I'd sooner die a spinster!"

"Why didn't you marry the first of the two?"

"That's between me an' him, Mr. Ardmore, an' no one else."

"You probably wouldn't tell me which was which, if I were to ask?"

"I would not."

"I won't ask then."

"Why do ye need tae talk tae them at all, Mr. Ardmore?" asked Audney. "Whiche'er o' the two's auld Macgregor's rightful heir canna hae naethin' tae du wi' what either o' them might tell ye."

"That is true, Miss Kerr," replied Ardmore, nodding. "The probate courts are very thorough in these matters. In all truth I am here more for the purpose of taking stock of the deceased's holdings, do a preliminary evaluation of value, take photographs, and so on. My interview of the prospective heirs is purely routine. Mostly, I suppose, it is to satisfy my own curiosity. On the other hand, such interviews can be useful. Fraudulent claims are more common than you might think. So we assess the subjective data as well as the hard, cold facts."

Whatever further questions Clement Ardmore

might have had on his mind were to be answered soon enough on their own.

As if on cue, the door of the inn swung open. A gust of wintry air blew in, followed by a giant of a man. His thick mass of unkempt black hair was half covered by a tan wool cap. An unshaven face showed the month of black beard he grew annually for Up Helly-Aa. He had only been back from the celebration in Lerwick a few days and had not yet shaved. A brown-and-yellow wool plaid shirt was covered by an unbuttoned light-green mackintosh. He tossed the door shut behind him with a bang and strode across the room with a heavy-booted step. Hardy was obviously feeling the prowess of his Viking blood from the raucous festival just past. He was all the more puffed up from having been chosen to march in the front row of the procession behind the Guizer Jarl himself.

"There's Hardy noo," whispered Audney. She turned and hurried toward the kitchen.

With several quick steps, however, Hardy blocked her way.

"Where are ye off til in sich a hurry, Audney?" he said with a grin. "I came to see ye." He reached out and set a large hand on her shoulder.

"Ye came tae see Mr. Ardmore," retorted Audney. "Noo git oot 'o my way, Hardy."

She brushed past him and disappeared into the kitchen.

Hardy let out a great laugh and turned toward the corner table. "Ye're Ardmore, I take it," he said as he lumbered toward him.

"I am," said the heir hunter, rising.

A little tentatively he offered his hand, wondering if such a gesture was wise. He hoped the hulking fisherman did not crush it. "You are Mr. Tulloch . . . Mr. *Hardar* Tulloch."

"At yer service," replied Hardy, shaking the man's hand with surprising gentleness. Both men sat down on opposite sides of the table.

"Audney!" bawled Hardy over his shoulder. "Bring me a pint o' dark ale! Noo then, Mr. Ardmore, hoo can I be o' service to ye?"

Intimidated by the sheer physical presence and overpowering personality of Hardy Tulloch, Clement Ardmore did his best to gather his wits by shuffling the papers on the table. Mostly, as he had said to Audney, his purpose was to get a *sense* of those involved. Hunches carried no weight in probate court. He was, however, an investigator. Hunches sometimes led to facts. If someone was trying to pull a fast one, his nose usually picked up hints of it before the facts revealed it.

"You have, I believe," began Ardmore, "filed certain papers through your solicitors in Edinburgh in the matter of probate proceedings concerning the estate of Macgregor Tulloch, now deceased."

"If ye're meanin' that I'm auld Macgregor's rightful heir an' that we've got the papers tae prove it," said Hardy, "then ye'll be in the right."

Audney appeared and set a tall dark glass in front of Hardy. Again she made a quick retreat. Not that she wasn't curious about what gist the conversation would take. But Hardy's voice carried like a foghorn. She could listen just as well from behind the bar.

"Yes, well we shall see about that," rejoined Ardmore. "That is, of course, why I am here. And when you say *we* have the papers to prove it, you are referring to your solicitors?"

"Aye, *they've* got the papers tae prove it."

"And the basis for your . . . uh, your claim, as I understand it, since you are not in direct line of descent from Macgregor Tulloch—"

"Nae body's in *direct* line, Mr. Ardmore," interrupted Hardy. "Ye must ken that yersel'— auld Macgregor had nae children o' his own."

As if drawn by the desire to listen in on the interview in progress as much as by the approach of the luncheon hour, the pub quickly began to fill with the midday regulars, and a good number who were not. No one in the village had remained unaware of Ardmore's arrival. The moment Hardy was seen on his way from the harbor to the pub, as if by common design, cottages began to empty.

The pub was soon as full as it would be later in

the day. Among the curious was David's uncle Fergus Gunn, ensuring that whatever took place would be reported back to his wife, Rinda, and thence to every other woman in the village.

In the kitchen, Evanna and Keith scrambled to see what other offerings they could add to the lunch menu. Before another ten minutes had passed, Audney found herself scurrying behind the bar to keep up with the orders for coffee and beer.

"Yes, that is being investigated as well," Ardmore was saying. "The late Mr. Tulloch was, as I am sure you are aware, married many years before to a Norwegian woman."

"A' body kens it well enouch. But she disappeared, an' there were nae children tae come o' it. There was a rumor that when she left the island she was with child. It's jist naethin' but common gossip, ye ken. She was ne'er heard o' again."

"Yes, well nothing has been ascertained with any degree of certitude," said Ardmore. "It is of course being looked into, as are other avenues of inquiry including the attempt to trace the movements of a certain uncle of Macgregor Tulloch's by the name of Brogan, who left Whales Reef as a young man."

"There's naethin' in that vein to be found. A' body kens that fact weel enough."

"I'm afraid facts in a case such as this must be

substantiated with something more than village hearsay."

"He wasna heard o' again till he returned for his father's funeral, an' there were those that said by then it was too late tae make amends. Naethin' mair was kenned o' him after that."

"If that proves to be the case, and there was no progeny, then that perhaps strengthens your position, though I would want to give no indication one way or the other. Your claim, as I understand it, then extends back to the man's aunt, I believe."

"I'm in *direct* line, as ye say, to the Auld Tulloch himsel'," said Hardy forcefully. "Noo that auld Macgregor's deid, 'tis the direct line that matters, an' I'm the only one in that line. Ye can prove it weel enough by the birth certificates at Lerwick an' the papers wi' my solicitors in Edinburgh."

"We have those certificates on file, Mr. Tulloch. And when you refer to the 'auld Tulloch,' whom do you mean?"

"The *Auld Tulloch*—auld Ernest Tulloch, Macgregor's gran'father an' my ain grit-grit-granfather through his daughter Delynn."

"Ah yes, Ernest Tulloch." Ardmore nodded. "The last chief and laird, before his eldest son left Scotland."

In truth, Ardmore was a little surprised to find Hardar Tulloch, to all appearances a man whose bluster outran his intellectual prowess by several leagues, so knowledgeable and articulate in making his case.

"And that brings us to the other individual involved in the case," he went on slowly, "your, let me see here . . ." Again he glanced through his papers. "That would be your third cousin, one David Tulloch, the current chief."

Hardy laughed disdainfully. "He *calls* himsel' the chief," he said.

"You doubt the legitimacy of the title?"

"There's naethin' *legitimate* aboot it," said Hardy with obvious emphasis. "If ye're gettin' my meanin'."

"I don't think I do, Mr. Tulloch."

"The man's base born, that's a' there is tae say."

At the words *base born,* the conversations around the inn stilled.

Ardmore dropped his voice. "You don't dispute that he is Ernest Tulloch's great-great-grandson, just as you are?"

"Aye. But there's gran'sons an' there's gran'sons. 'Tis weel kent that the titled men o' times past didna always hae the morals tae ken the difference."

"However, you both could be said to possess equal claims. His lineage, however, comes through a son, yours through a daughter—before women were rightfully included in the inheritance laws."

"Aye. Except that my grit-grit-gran'mother was *married* tae the Auld Tulloch."

"What are you implying, Mr. Tulloch?"

"Only that David's wasna."

By now the only sounds came from the kitchen.

"Wasn't married . . . to Ernest?"

Hardy nodded, then took a great swallow from his glass as if to punctuate the veracity of his claim. He set the glass down on the table with deliberation and stared across the table.

"Folk has always believed," he said, speaking as if with the authority of a judge rendering a verdict, "that David an' his father an' gran'father came o' Ernest Tulloch's second wife after my ain grit-grit-gran'mother Elizabeth died. But she was ne'er his wife, the woman called Sally Lipscomb. David's name may be Tulloch on account o' the Auld Tulloch himself. But he's nae mair nor the bastard offspring o' a line o' illegitimate bastards comin' fae the auld man's mistress, nae his wife. The hussy Sally was ne'er Lady Tulloch."

The silence in the room was suddenly rent by a single voice. "Ye're a liar, Hardy Tulloch!" Audney cried from behind the bar. "Ye hae nae proof o' sich lies." She did not care that the eyes and ears of the whole village were on her.

"I'm afraid the young lady has a valid point, Mr. Tulloch," said Ardmore. "Even if what you say about the past may be true, it bears no reflection on subsequent generations. You would be advised not to use such inappropriate terms with reference to anyone in the present family."

Not relishing being put in his place by a stranger, Hardy ignored Ardmore's subtle rebuke. He glanced around the room, then back at Audney. "Has David said a word tae deny it?" he said with cunning smile

Audney did not reply. She knew, even if he could, that David would never deny an accusation.

"Ye ken as weel as I that he winna because he *canna*," Hardy went on triumphantly. "When the truth is kenned for a' tae see, I'll be chief *an'* laird. Where will David be then? An' ye'll be the lady o' the island yersel', Audney, an' the chief's wife besides," he added, glancing about the room with a smile and a few winks to the other men.

Audney was quick to recover her poise. "Ye think I will marry ye if ye become laird!" she retorted

"Laird *an'* chief," said Hardy. "Ye'll come tae yer senses soon enough, Audney Kerr. An' when ye do, ye'll be the wife o' Hardy Tulloch."

"In yer dreams, Hardy!" Audney shot back with a peel of laughter. "I wouldna marry ye if ye was the last man on Whales Reef!"

The laughter that now erupted through the pub, directed *at* Hardy rather than originating from him, was not so pleasant for him to swallow. He was accustomed to dishing it out, not being the butt of anyone else's joke.

But it quickly died down. The men of the island were wary of Hardy for many reasons, not the least of which was the very real fear that he might indeed be their future laird. He had never been one it was well to offend.

"Ye winna be laughin' once the inheritance is mine!" he said angrily. "None o' ye'll laugh at Hardy Tulloch then."

He shoved himself back from the table, rose and strode toward the door, casting dark looks at the tables where the laughter had been loudest.

Within thirty minutes everyone in the village knew every word that had been spoken between Hardy Tulloch and the island's high-profile visitor, as well as Audney Kerr's outspoken response.

41

A More Guarded Interview

By the time of David's scheduled interview with Clement Ardmore that afternoon, the pub was again empty.

Ardmore had had a light tea about two o'clock, then went for a walk around the village between rain squalls. He had been in Whales Reef just a little more than twenty-four hours and was already beginning to feel that no more desolate place on the face of the earth could be imagined. He was in his room upstairs resting when the second claimant walked in.

David and Audney chatted easily. David had been busy all morning with some repairs and modifications to his barns intended to increase the comfort of his livestock over the cold winter months. He had heard nothing of the morning's fireworks. Audney related the gist of what had taken place.

"News' o' it's likely all o'er the village by noo, David," said Audney. "What are ye goin' tae do aboot it?"

"There's nothing I can do, Audney. I've told you before that I'm not bothered by Hardy's talk.

Not that I don't want to see the thing settled. But my fretting about it won't change the outcome any more than Hardy's bluster."

"Ye dinna care what folk may think o' ye?"

David was silent several seconds "That is a good question, Audney," he finally said. "I don't know how to answer you."

"Jist tell me what ye think, then, David?"

"Who doesn't want people to think well of them?" David replied after a moment. "But I want them to think well of me as a man, not for something that happened in my ancestry several generations ago. What if Hardy is right? Maybe Ernest Tulloch didn't marry Sally Lipscomb, and so my great-grandfather Leith was an illegitimate son. We don't know. If it turns out to be true, does that make *me* illegitimate? Does that make me less the man I am, less worthy to be known as David Tulloch? Am I not still the same man I have always been?" He turned to face her directly. "Would you think differently of me, Audney?"

"Ye ken the answer weel enough, David. Ye ken the regard I hae for ye."

David looked deep into Audney's eyes and smiled tenderly. "I do know, Audney. You have *too* much regard for me."

"We've been a' o'er that a long time ago, David. Some day ye'll ken I was right tae say no when ye said ye'd marry me. 'Tis for the best. Ye'll see. Ye'll ken one day why I answered ye as I did."

"But I don't like Hardy still making his advances, Audney."

"I dinna mind so much. Weel, I do mind, but I can handle him."

"If it gets to be too much, you come to me."

"I dinna want ye getting' involved wi' him, David. Especially noo, wi' the future hangin' in the wind like. In his eyes, ye're his enemy. There's nae tellin' what he would do. Promise me ye winna speak tae him aboot me."

"I am still chief," said David. "I have to take care of my people. That includes you."

"He winna hurt me. My daddy'll see tae that. Promise me ye winna make a fuss wi' Hardy on my account?"

"I can't make that promise, Audney. If Hardy becomes laird, then we shall make the best of it, and I will serve him to the extent my conscience will allow. But if he threatens any woman's honor on this island—now or then—whether it's one of the old women or my aunt Rinda or Rakel Gordon . . . or you, he will have to answer to me for it."

Audney was spared further entreaties by the appearance of Clement Ardmore descending the stairs from the rooms above.

"Mr. Ardmore," said Audney, walking toward him, "here's the man ye came tae meet. David, this is Mr. Ardmore fae Edinburgh. Mr. Ardmore, I'm pleased tae hae ye make the acquaintance o' Chief David Tulloch."

"I am pleased to meet you, Mr. Ardmore," said David.

"And I you, Mr. Tulloch," replied the heir hunter, extending his hand.

"Your presence has caused quite a stir on our little island," said David. "You met my cousin earlier, I understand."

"A most enlightening interview, I must say. He is a confident young man."

David laughed. "That's Hardy."

Even as the two men retired to Ardmore's table to begin their conversation, a few villagers began to wander into the pub, hoping perhaps for a command performance, especially if Hardy happened to return.

Audney appeared a few minutes later with a tray, cups, and a pot of hot tea. For the next hour she did her best to busy herself cleaning tables and attending to the afternoon's influx of curious customers. But eavesdropping was not so easy as when Hardy had been one of the participants.

Two hours later neither Audney nor anyone else straining to listen knew anything of what had quietly passed between the two men.

42

CHIEF AND AUNT

David left the inn and made his way through the village, stopping in at most of the shops before paying a visit to the home of his mother's sister.

He walked through the side door into the kitchen with neither knock nor invitation. This house was a second home to him, and his aunt a second mother, and his *only* mother since the death of his own.

Rinda greeted him with her customary, "Noo then, yoong David, what hae ye tae say for yersel'?"

Most of the villagers who had watched him grow up were completely unaware of David's expanding reputation as an expert and spokesman—even advocate—for Shetland tourism, along with his ongoing scientific research. They knew he was gone frequently and traveled widely. They were also aware that he led tours and that visitors came to the island seeking him out. Word was that he was writing a book, but he had kept from the islanders that he had already published two. Least impressed of all at his rising stature was David's sharp-tongued aunt Rinda Gunn.

It was not her words that had earned Rinda Gunn a reputation for crabbiness, gossip, and irritability, but the tone in which she seemed to invest every syllable. Hers was a mode of expression colored by dissatisfaction, annoyance, and unspoken reproach. She might greet a friend on the street with "Fine day" yet convey the unmistakable impression that it would have been an even finer one had she not suffered the misfortune to run into the woman at all.

As she greeted David on this afternoon, her voice was anything but welcoming. Her tone, as well as her brow, indicated gathering thunderclouds.

David, however, made a habit of seeing the good in others, imbuing their words with the kindliest motive possible. More than anyone on the island, his aunt sorely tested this resolve. But his love for her was no less that he found her caustic tongue and grating manner trying in the extreme.

During the early years of his life, with his own parents still alive and busy with her own brood of seven sons and daughters, his aunt Rinda had exerted no special claim on the son of her elder sister. She would not have dared. Arna would not have stood for it. With Arna now gone, however, David had become the recipient of Rinda's middle-age irritability and sharped-tongued advice. Her own sons and daughters had endured all they cared to in their early years, and all but one had now put a safe distance between them-selves and their mother.

That her nephew was still unmarried at thirty-four was inexcusable, especially that he had let Audney Kerr slip through his fingers. The good Mrs. Gunn berated him for being more interested in birds and wildlife than in people. This alone gave ample fuel to her charge that he was failing in his responsibilities as chief, not living up to the proud tradition that now had come to rest, for good or ill, upon his shoulders. No chief, in her opinion, buried his nose in books, much less wrote them.

How Rinda's gentle-tempered husband, Fergus, put up with her incessant haranguing was a mystery. He not only put up with it, he loved his wife with a devoted affection marvelous to behold. Flowers and chocolates appeared on every birthday, anniversary, Christmas, and Valentine's Day. He had never been heard to utter a word of criticism toward his wife. If a negative word about her was spoken in his hearing, he invariably defended her, occasionally adding, as if in subtle recognition that he was aware of her occasional excesses, "She means weel an' that must count for somethin' in the end."

Perhaps she did mean well, though she had a rough way of showing it. Whatever it would count for in the end was hard to say. It was likely that her husband's good-natured spirit would count for more.

"Naethin' much, Auntie," replied David cheerfully to his aunt's greeting, hoping to deflect whatever darts she was getting ready to launch in his direction. "I've jist come fae the hotel speakin' wi' the fellow they call the heir hunter."

"Oh, aye, an' what was he askin' o' ye?"

"Jist aboot the family, aboot mama an' daddy an' daddy's kin. Hardy's set a rumor goin' that there was mischief afoot back in the auld times atween the Auld Tulloch an' his second wife."

"Oh, aye, a'body kens what's bein' said weel enough. So what are ye goin' tae do, yoong David?"

It was the second time David had heard that question today. "About what, Auntie?" he said.

"Everything, David. 'Tis a' o'er the village—ye're nae likely tae be the new laird. Are ye goin' tae meet the lie like a man? Are ye goin' tae fight back an' make yer mama and daddy prood?" As she spoke, she stood staring at him with hands on hips.

"I dinna ken yet if it is a lie, Auntie. I canna weel fight against it if it's the truth, can I noo? Ye wouldna hae me set my hand against the truth."

"Jist listen tae ye, laddie! What are ye sayin'?"

"Only that we've got tae ken the truth before we take up oor swords in the fight."

"If they're speakin' ill o' ye, then ye got tae fight against it, whate'er the truth."

"That is not a code I can live by, Auntie," said David, again assuming the higher tongue to enforce his words. He knew his speaking English angered his aunt. One thing his manhood had taught him, however, was that occasionally he must stand up to her. "Besides, I've heard no word against *me*. If the thing is true, the stain is on the character of the Auld Tulloch, not on me. On that score, we know nothing yet. I won't judge the man as it seems too many's willing to do. I've heard nothing in our family tradition but that he was the most godly man any on the island ever met. You know what they say about the room in the Cottage."

"Aye," she shot back, "that the bones o' auld Macgregor's wife's hidden in it where he killed her, an' then he locked the door an' none's been inside the room syne, nor kens where he hid the key, an' that he's taken his secrets an the key tae the grave wi' him!"

"That's all nonsense, Auntie!" David laughed with good humor. "It was the Auld Tulloch's prayer closet, not a burial crypt."

"Then why has the room been sealed up a' the years syne the woman disappeared?"

"As I hear it, the room was sealed up long

before his time by the Auld Tulloch's widow."

"Macgregor could hae opened it tae hide his evil deed."

"*If* he had the key, which he may not have—no one knows what became of it. Listen to yourself, Auntie—talking of murder and evil deeds. I won't dignify your insinuations with a reply. The Auld Tulloch was a God-fearing man, and I will believe nothing else until I am shown otherwise. Both his memory and that of my uncle Macgregor are deserving of my honor. And yours."

"I dinna ken aboot a' that. All I ken is that braggart Hardy Tulloch's likely tae become laird if ye dinna step in an' do somethin' aboot it."

"What would you have me do, Auntie, seize the title by force?"

"If ye hae tae du it, David, take up the sword o' yer clan! 'Tis what the auld Highlanders, yer ancestors, did, lad."

David could not help breaking out in laughter again. "This isn't the Middle Ages, Auntie. Disputes over property are not settled with swords. It's the twenty-first century and there are laws. Whatever happens will be decided by the law of the land."

"Aye, but ye're no speakin' like a chief, David. Ye soun' like a coward."

The word hit David with unexpected force. His aunt was as surprised as he. She had not expected to go quite *that* far.

Her tongue silenced by the power of its own

blunt force, she did not add to her momentary victory with another verbal thrust. She saw that she had hurt him.

But no apology followed. The words *I am sorry* did not exist in Rinda Gunn's vocabulary.

An uncomfortable silence filled the cottage.

At length David spoke. "*Do* you think I'm a coward, Auntie?" he asked softly.

"I dinna ken, David. I'm sayin' nae mair than that sometimes ye soun' a mite too acceptin' o' yer fate. I'd like it better if ye'd fight for what ye believe in."

"I hope I do, Auntie. I pray that I am willing and have the courage to fight for what I believe in. But a man has to choose when and where he fights. I believe in truth, and until I know the truth on a matter, I'll not take up the sword."

"All I'm askin', David, is what's tae become o' folk?"

"What do you mean?"

"The Mill's troubles—ye ken the rumors."

"What rumors?"

"Financial problems . . . that they'll be layin' folk off afore much longer."

"I know about the finances," David assured her. "It's nothing like you say. I hope you're not spreading such nonsense and worrying people."

"Maybe 'tis worse than ye ken yersel'," rejoined Rinda. "Ye're still the chief. An' there's nae reason ye winna be chief e'en after Hardy's named laird, if indeed things is as he says. Ye must do something for the island. Folks is lookin' tae ye, David."

"What would you have me do? I told you, I can't rush the probate process."

"A few o' the folk is desperate, David. Puir Noak Muir's in such straits he's had tae butcher one o' his family's cows."

"I didn't know that. Why?"

"He hasna a brass farthing tae his name. 'Tis been a dreadful season for the fish, ye surely ken that."

"It's been some hard months, yes. Why the Muirs in particular?"

"I dinna ken a' o' it. His boat's needed repairs an' a'body kens that the fish hanna been runnin' except oot past where the small boats can get til. An' his daughter had the trouble last summer wi' her kidneys, ye ken, an' it was a sore lot o' money."

"I was out of the country when it happened. Wasn't it covered by National Health?"

"They jist put the puir girl on a waitin' list an' said it wud be six weeks. Noak an' Meg was feart she wud die, so they went private. They had tae fly the girl tae Aberdeen. They're bad in debt as a result o' it."

"I didn't know—thank you for telling me, Auntie," said David, clearly concerned. "That *is* something I may be able to help with. I will certainly look into it."

43

SHEPHERD, HOUSEKEEPER, AND BUTLER

David Tulloch sat in his favorite chair, yellow legal pad in his lap, feet up before a warm fireplace full of glowing peats. He had arisen several hours before.

The burden of his heart was not for himself but for his people. If his cousin Hardy inherited possession of the island's property, the future for the island could hardly be anticipated with anything but foreboding. What mischief would his cousin undertake if he somehow managed to wrest away the mantle of the chieftainship along with the inheritance?

David desperately hoped it wouldn't come to that. He doubted the authority of the probate courts extended to the chieftainship at all. Yet it hardly mattered. The position carried no real power. If Hardy inherited he could do anything he wanted, with or without the chieftainship.

With Hardy as laird what would become of the island, the wool factory? Perhaps most important of all, what would become of the *spirit* of Whales Reef?

David stared at the sentence he had just written

about the migratory patterns and winter habitat of Shetland's puffin population. The words blurred on the page before his eyes. He had hoped to have a completed draft of his book roughed out before speaking commitments piled up in the summer. But anxiety over the future had robbed him of mental focus. He could not concentrate on his work.

David set his pen and pad aside, leaned back, closed his eyes and exhaled a long sigh. His mind was revolving many things. His conversation with his aunt several weeks before had upset him more than he realized. In her blunt way she had exposed the raw nerve of his own doubt.

"Ye're no speakin' like a chief" came the words yet again, which had been playing themselves over and over in his mind ever since. *"Ye soun' like a coward . . . I'd like it better if ye'd fight for what ye believe in."*

What *was* his responsibility?

In his own way, David was a sort of spiritual fatalist. He did not consider it his right or duty to interfere in the ordained order of things. Who was *he* to beseech God to change events on his own behalf? He would have described it as his responsibility to fall in with *God's* purpose, not pray for God to change circumstances for his convenience, and then to accept with grace what his good and loving Father and His creation had laid out for him.

Thus when the reality of his uncle Macgregor's estate came to light, David made peace with the situation. He would await the outcome and make the best of it. It did not fall to him to dictate events or even to pray for circumstances to be different from what they were. David's outlook represented a curious blend of traditional and modern thinking.

However, the nagging question plaguing him for weeks continued to poke and prod his brain: Were there times when one had to *fight,* when one had to lead, not follow, when, as the saying went, one had to take the bull by the horns? When did life require *action?*

One immovable reality remained, however. He could not change the law. His own actions could not alter the outcome. Nothing he did would determine whether he or Hardy was Macgregor Tulloch's true heir.

One thing he *could* do was get to the bottom of whatever was going on with the factory's finances. The Mill must remain viable. Even with Hardy as laird, David would do everything in his power to keep the widows and elderly women of the island provided with an income that did not depend on fish or oil. The lairdship notwithstanding, he would not relinquish the chieftainship without a fight. If Hardy tried to take it from him, as he had said to his aunt, at that point he *would* stand and fight.

As if punctuating his resolve, David set aside his writing, bundled up in several layers, pulled his thick cap over his ears, grabbed his favorite walking stick from the hall tree beside the door, and went out into the morning.

He struck out across the moor toward the center of the island. The landscape around him was covered in white frost. The last snow was gone now except for a few patches in the hollows.

With the frozen ground crunching beneath his feet, David crested a small rise. A great commotion greeted him as a small flock of twenty or thirty bleating sheep began scampering toward him. His uncle's three sheepdogs added their own enthusiasm to the morning symphony, rushing at him from across the moor.

Seconds later David was surrounded by a mass of white wool pressing close to his legs. Unable to get close to him for the sheep, the dogs flew about in a frenzy, barking and with tails wagging.

"Lads, lassies!" he laughed. " 'Tis only me! 'Tis naethin' tae ruffle yer wool aboot!"

Behind them David saw their shepherd ambling over the uneven terrain.

"Ho, Dougal!" he called, lifting his arm in greeting.

"Best o' the mornin' tae ye, Chief!" said the shepherd as the turbulence about David's legs thinned and the two shook hands.

Like David, the other was warmly clad in stout boots and a bright plaid wool coat with cap and gloves. A great beard of mingled black and gray shot out with wild abandon, as if he had sprouted a wool mane exactly like what grew on the backs of his four-legged charges. Hair of like shade protruded in equal abundance from beneath the wool cap on his head. With the tall crook-necked shepherd's staff in his hand, the man could have stepped straight off the pages of a nineteenth century Scottish tale.

"What brings ye oot on sich a cold day?" he asked.

"I had tae clear my head, Dougal," replied David. "The uncertainty o'er the future's weighin' on me mair nor I should let it."

"Aye, 'tis a difficult time for ye, I'm thinkin'."

Gradually the two made a wide arc in the general direction of the Cottage as they made their way slowly behind the flock.

"An' yersel', Dougal? Hoo are ye farin'?" David asked.

"I canna say I dinna miss the auld man," replied the shepherd. "He was both like a father tae me as weel's a frien'. Otherwise, I'm weel enough. The laird took good care o' me, as ye are yersel'. I'm wantin' for naethin'. I'm jist grateful tae hae the use o' my lodgin's."

"Ye'll git yer back wages when the thing's all settled—ye ken that?"

"Aye, laddie. I hae nae worries on that score. Ye dinna need concern yersel' wi' me."

"Ye been livin' at the Cottage for what . . . twenty-five years or more, Dougal? Naebody would think o' it bein' otherwise."

"There's one who might."

"I ken who ye mean. But Hardy's no laird yet."

"Aye, but puir Isobel's in a dither aboot what's tae become o' them when he is. She's certain he'll turn us a' oot wi' naethin'. Bless the woman, she takes good care o' me. But she's no what a body'd call an optimist. A more dour woman I haenna met."

David laughed. "I'll hae a word wi' her."

As they approached the large stone edifice that had served as the home of the lairds for more than a century, they saw a woman of middle age returning from the shed that was home to her family of hens, basket in hand. As the sheep scampered toward the barn, David walked toward her with a smile.

"Good morning, Isobel," he said. "A good supply of eggs today?"

"Middlin', Mr. David," she replied. "But weel enough for oor breakfast. Will ye join us?"

"I may at that, thank you."

"I'll put oot some fresh hay for the lads an' lassies," said Dougal as David and Isobel walked toward the kitchen door. "I'll join ye presently."

David followed the late laird's cook and housekeeper inside, where they were met by a man of stately appearance in his late fifties.

Saxe and Isobel Matheson, brother and sister, had lived at the Cottage for decades, serving Macgregor Tulloch as butler and manservant, housekeeper and cook. Neither ever married.

"Good morning, Saxe," said David, shaking the man's hand warmly.

"Mr. David," said Matheson. "Welcome back to the Cottage. We hope it will soon be your home."

"Time will tell, Saxe. We must await events. Until then, are you both comfortable?"

"Aye, we are, Mr. David. I only wish there was more for me to do. Are you sure there isn't anything we can do for you at the Auld Hoose?"

"It's a third the size of the Cottage, if that," replied David. "I must say I do enjoy Isobel's cooking. So I will continue to let you know when I need help."

Busying herself with tea preparations, Isobel set cups and saucers and a plate of oatcakes on the table. "Sit ye doon, Mr. David," she said. "The tea will be along directly."

They were soon joined by Dougal Erskine. The four continued to chat easily.

The three employees of David's great uncle had known David since he was a boy. Their respect for him, not only as nephew to the laird but as their chief, could not have been greater.

When David took his leave an hour later, he hoped he had succeeded somewhat in setting their minds at ease over the future's uncertainties.

44

BOOKS, ANTIQUES, AND SCONES

David struck out southward, reaching the ocean a few minutes later. He followed the shore path along the rocky uneven beach, then gradually turned westward, the pleasant sound of the sea on his left. Eventually he returned to the road, crossed it, and continued up a gentle rise inland.

Making a wide half circle around the back of the village, he arrived at length behind the small stone church and gated cemetery. To all appearances on this day, both church and graveyard were lifeless.

He skirted the church building, gazing upon the silent walls of stones, wondering whether much more life was to be found in it on Sunday than was apparent today. It was no secret that the present curate, Reverend Stirling Yates, had been sent to this remote parish, if not as a direct disciplinary action, then something very much like it. What exact trouble had arisen in his previous parish not even David's aunt nor Coira MacNeill knew.

Yates seemed a pleasant enough fellow. Whether he brought life to the church was another matter. How long he would be here, no one knew that either.

David continued around the church, down its entryway, and into town.

The Whales Reef Natural History Museum and Wildlife Shoppe, closed now for the winter, was one of David's favorite places. He paused and looked through the window. It was somewhat presumptuously named, he thought, as he peered into the darkened interior. But it brought a certain prestige to the village and benefited summer tourism. He had helped Wilma Welby, whose brainchild the shop was, to organize and set up the displays and advised her on which books and other items to carry. Binoculars, bird-watching guides, and small gifts of local interest comprised the majority of Wilma's inventory. He knew the place made no profit, but he managed to add a small stipend to one or two of his research grants every year to help subsidize it.

Few people were out on this bright, cold morning. Most hurried only to and from the market or Paper Shop or, as the day advanced, to the pub at the hotel.

A few doors farther on, David entered another small store, this one open. The small black lettering on the door read *Olde Worlde Antiques.*

"Hello, Harry," David greeted a man behind a cluttered desk. "I'm surprised to see you open."

"If I'm here I might as well keep the door unlocked," said the shopkeeper, Harry Menglad, a native of Lerwick.

"You don't sell much in the winter months, I suppose."

"Not to speak of. It's mostly Internet sales and sniffing out antique auctions on the mainland I might want to attend. I do most of my buying online these days. And with my specialty in walking sticks, fountain pens and such, I manage to do decently well."

"Well, when you are online, I am still looking for a set of Victorian bookends like I described to you. I saw them in a manor house on the mainland—a man seated on a stool surrounded by books. The artist or designer was G. S. Allen."

"I haven't forgotten."

"Thanks. I'd best be off. Happy sleuthing!"

David left the shop and continued on. He passed the small hair-styling salon—no matter what the weather or economic conditions, women *had* to have their hair done!—and the fishing shop, nearly always open, fair weather or foul. David stopped in to greet its owner, retired fisherman Hakon Osk, at one time a partner with his own father many years before.

"Hello, Mr. Osk. Please tell me you have some good news for our fishermen for the spring season."

"Sorry, laddie. Ye can ne'er predict when or

where the fish'll be runnin'. 'Tis nae different from when yer daddy an' me went oot—ye must jist trust yer instincts."

"These days it seems that Hardy's are the only instincts that can be relied on!" chuckled David.

"Aye," said Osk. "Mair that expensive new equipment o' his than instincts, I'm thinkin'. Hae ye heard that he jist bought Gunder Knut's boat?"

"I had not heard," replied David. "So now Gunder's working for Hardy too, along with Sandy and Iver?"

"If it keeps up, Hardy'll own half the boats in the harbor, wi' most o' the men workin' for him. If ye ask me, 'tis his design. It's mair siller for him, less in the pockets o' the men settin' oot the nets for him. He's a crafty one."

"I must say, I don't like the idea of him buying up the other men's boats," said David.

"The way I hear, he makes them a cash offer they canna weel refuse, promisin' they can buy their boats back once they're back on their feet."

"But will Sandy or Iver, and now Gunder—when will they ever have that kind of cash again? Hardy knows the chances of that are slim to zero. The fishing will rebound. It always does. I don't like the men giving up their boats because of a couple bad seasons."

"Aye, but cash money speaks in a loud voice, ye ken."

"I suppose you're right."

David bid farewell to his father's friend and left the shop.

He entered the Willows Tea Shop a minute or two later and sat down at one of its four empty tables.

"Good morning, Harriett," he said to the woman behind the half wall into the kitchen.

"An' tae yersel', Chief," replied the woman.

"How fresh are your scones, Harriett?"

"Jist yesterday, Chief."

"You have raspberry jam to go with them?"

"Oh, aye!"

"Then I'll have a scone, Harriett—warmed and with jam, if you please."

"Wi' tea?"

"I think perhaps I shall have a cup of coffee instead."

David continued to chat with Mrs. Gudrun as she warmed his scone and prepared his coffee. Though she mixed with the people of the village every day, she kept her own counsel. She was married to Hardy's first cousin on his mother's side. However, not a word about the disputed inheritance passed her lips, to David or to anyone else.

Leaving the Willows twenty minutes later, David walked past the post office, the seasonal gift shop Nibs and Nobs, and finally into the Paper Shop.

"Good morning, Garth," he said to a man with his back turned and busy with stacks of newspapers.

"Ah, David," said the shop's owner Garth Kennedy, turning around. "I was beginning to wonder if you would be coming in for your *Press and Journal* today. You're later than usual."

"I took the long way round," said David, "through the hills, you know. I visited for a while at the Cottage and had a scone at Harriett's."

" 'Tis a fine day for a stroll! They say another storm's due in a few days."

"It's that time of year." David set a pound coin on the counter and left the shop.

Seeing the light on and the Open sign visible, David walked toward what was arguably the most incongruous shop in Whales Reef. The gold leaf on the door read simply *Antiquarian Books, A. Lamont, Prop.* Located on the ground floor of a spacious stone house of two floors, the building's several ornate architectural touches spoke of more wealth than was indicated by any other in the village proper. Said to be of seventeenth century origin, it predated the immigration of Highlanders to the island and had long ago been home to its first lairds.

Armond Lamont, the shop's owner, was one of the town's recent residents, an incomer from four years earlier. The prim and proper Englishman was considered something of a strange bird. The village gossips belabored the point that he never went out without a walking stick or umbrella and was always impeccably attired from head to foot. They all wondered the same thing—what was such a dandy doing *here?*

Why had he chosen one of the most remote and inaccessible places in Britain to set up an antiquarian book trade? A cold, wet climate was the worst conceivable place for books, especially valuable ones. Nor could a remote island hundreds of miles from the mainland be considered a convenient location for a mail-order business, where every parcel began its journey on a ferry. Even in the summer at the height of the tourist season, no one came to Whales Reef for *books.*

Rumors abounded, ranging from speculation that he was running from the law or a former wife, to the more benign theory of a nervous breakdown from the pace of London's city life. The fact that no one ever saw customers in his shop, and that he had paid cash for the largest and finest house on the island save the Cottage and the Auld Hoose, contributed to the theory that he was independently wealthy. The most freely wagging tongues claimed he was worth millions.

Rumors did not merely circulate around Lamont himself. His house, too, came in for its share of speculation. Tradition had it that a tunnel ran from its cellars westward to the sea cliffs of the inlet situated halfway between the harbor and the ferry landing. This smuggler's tunnel was reportedly used to bring in a great variety of illegal goods from continental Europe between the seventeenth and nineteenth centuries. That Lamont was a history buff gave credibility to the notion that, if such a tunnel did exist, he would surely know of it.* After four years Lamont remained an enigma.

David walked inside and glanced about, but he did not see Lamont. By the time the shop's owner appeared, David was engrossed in perusing some enticing book spines in one of several alcoves.

"Ah, Mr. Tulloch," said Lamont, "I wondered who might be paying me a visit."

"The lure of books is always a temptation," said David with a smile. "Not that I don't already have more than I will read in ten lifetimes! How goes the business?"

"I continue to be surprised how much I sell over a year," replied Lamont. "As long as I keep my computer listings current, the orders come in."

---

*Exactly such a smuggler's tunnel was said to exist between the harbor of Symbister on the island of Whalsay in the Shetlands, stretching to the cellars of the laird's house or the *Auld Haa*.

"Do you have any buying trips planned?" asked David.

"I'm going to Edinburgh in a couple of weeks for a book fair. Afterward I will spend several days browsing through its wealth of used books in the many shops there."

"A delightful prospect!" David enthused.

"There are few things I enjoy more," rejoined Lamont.

"What are your personal interests, Armond?"

"Mostly first editions of your beloved Scots authors—Scott, Burns, Barrie, MacDonald, Maclaren. Anything whose content matches the antiquarian value is for me the rarest of finds—unusual in my business. Mostly people are looking at the edition and the condition, the boards and artwork—the book's externals. But when the content provides food for the soul as well, that is indeed what a book should be about."

"I couldn't agree more."

"Though I deal in books to make a living, what gives me the greatest pleasure is to sit down myself in the evening and read the *words* of an author I admire. If it happens to be an exquisite edition and binding as well, then is the entire essence of *book-ness* brought into harmony. The body and soul of the book are one. To be able to enjoy both simultaneously is a joy indeed."

"A poetic image. I shall remember that next

time I select a volume from my shelves and sit down in front of the fire."

By the time David completed his amble through the village, concluding with a stop at the inn and walk down to the harbor, then finally back to the Auld Hoose, he had resolved the question that had brought him outside three hours earlier.

He walked straight to the telephone and soon had Jason MacNaughton on the line in Lerwick.

"Hello, Jason," he said. "With the disposition of my uncle's estate still undecided, I think the time has come for more definite action on my part.

I need to speak with your father as you and I discussed earlier. I know he is in England, but I need to know more of what's going on."

"My father will be happy to see you," MacNaughton assured. "We remain hopeful that probate will be resolved soon. But pending that, I will telephone him directly. How soon do you plan to go?"

"I would like to fly to London as soon as possible—tomorrow if I can arrange it and if your father can see me on such short notice."

"I will organize a meeting for the day after tomorrow, or the day after that."

45
STUNNING REVELATION

London

That same afternoon, preparatory to his trip to London, David held a private conference at the Mill in the office of his cousin. David told him of his intended trip to visit the head of the solicitor's firm handling his uncle's estate.

"I am relieved to hear it," said Murdoc. "I was about to come talk to you myself."

"Has there been a change?" asked David.

"Only that the cushion in the Mill's account is nearly gone. I will be able to make only one more payroll."

"What!" exclaimed David. "Murdoc, why didn't you tell me it had become so serious?"

"I kept waiting, thinking everything would be settled."

David rose in agitation and paced the small room, thinking hard. "One more payroll," he said as if speaking to himself. He turned. "And then what?"

"I don't know, David. That's why I needed to talk to you. What do you want me to do? We cannot operate the Mill with no money."

"We will have to think about what is best," said David, shaking his head. "This is a blow. I suppose it had to come to this eventually the longer the thing dragged on." He thought a moment more. "Don't do anything yet," he said. "And tell *no one* what we've talked about. There are enough rumors circulating already. Let me see what I can learn from my uncle's solicitor. Then we will decide on a plan of action."

Three days later, in an environment whose contrast with the quiet, calm, cold, northern isolation of the moors of Whales Reef could scarcely have been greater, David Tulloch walked along a crowded and noisy sidewalk. Londoners around him were bundled in scarves and coats against the fifty-two degrees Fahrenheit of the late morning. For David it was twenty degrees warmer than what he'd left behind in the Shetlands—positively balmy!

He and the elder MacNaughton were to meet for lunch at the Shetland Club off Oxford Circus where the solicitor's firm maintained a membership. Walking into the dimly lit entry felt like entering the narthex of a cathedral. David felt as if he had left London's bustle behind and was again in the Shetlands.

MacNaughton was waiting for him and approached with outstretched hand. "Ah, David," he said. "How good to see you again."

"Thank you, and you," rejoined David with a smile as they shook hands.

"It has been a long time. I'm not sure I have actually spoken to you since your mother was alive."

"I came into Lerwick about four or five years ago with Uncle Macgregor," said David. "But your business was with him. I was in the office but briefly."

"Right . . . yes, I recall it now. But come, I have a table waiting for us."

He led David into the dining room where white tablecloths and carefully laid silver service caught the light from the tall windows.

"Something to drink?" said MacNaughton as they seated themselves and a waiter approached.

"Tea, I think," said David.

"Tea for my friend here, Fellowes," said MacNaughton. "I'll have my usual—a single malt Shetlander with a bottle of spring water."

"Very good, sir." The man nodded with old-school dignity, then evaporated away.

"Thank you for seeing me, Mr. MacNaughton," David began. "I know you are with family here in the south, and I apologize for the intrusion."

The gentleman waved away David's apology with his hand. "Not a problem at all. Actually, |it's rather a respite for me away from a houseful of grandchildren."

Both men laughed.

"I am happy if there is something I can do to help," the solicitor added.

"Thank you," said David. "Well then . . . my problem is relatively straightforward to state, though certainly not to resolve. As the probate process drags on, the situation on Whales Reef has become increasingly difficult. I simply need some answers."

"Yes, my son has filled me in on your . . . shall we say, your dilemma? You did not know that Macgregor had no will, I take it."

"That's right."

"That fact has complicated matters immensely. I did my best to urge him to make one—"

"I understand. Obviously his sudden death caught us all off guard. I am aware of the complexities of the probate process and the reality that I may not be Uncle Macgregor's closest heir after all."

"Right, I've been kept informed of that development . . . Hardar Tulloch, I believe."

David nodded.

"I know his father. An ornery one, the son?"

"You could say that," David replied. "However, even if I do not inherit, I am not so worried for my own future as for the island, for its people. Much of the island's welfare and livelihood, directly and indirectly, comes from the wool factory. Especially for many of those without other means of support, which was the purpose of the Mill from the beginning. It has now come to a point, however, when the Mill's bank account is nearly empty. After next month there will not be enough to meet payroll. The ongoing mystery is that there is plenty of business. Orders are coming in as always. I understand my uncle's accounts had to be frozen, but I am having difficulty getting a handle on why his death has so dramatically altered the finances of the factory."

The lawyer looked down, pondering how to begin. David waited.

"It is actually much simpler than you may realize," said MacNaughton after a few moments. "The correlation between your uncle's assets and the factory's operating account . . . actually, that would include your personal account as well—"

"The trust, you mean?"

MacNaughton nodded. "Your uncle wanted the relation between the accounts kept strictly quiet. We are, of course, bound by client confidentiality to honor that request, even in death, until his estate is settled and his heir named. I am, however, going to take the liberty of divulging your uncle's secret with you alone. As you are the presumptive heir and were always considered such by your uncle, I do not think I shall be disbarred for it. Our firm represents you as well as your uncle, and I see no serious breach of protocol involved."

He paused a moment, clearly deep in thought.

"Much of this, David," he went on, "goes back even to the time of your grandfather. And I must ask you to keep this conversation absolutely confidential. No one must know what I tell you until the estate is settled. I am bending the rules in your case. Nevertheless, we must still honor your uncle's wishes in the matter."

"Certainly. Agreed," said David. "What secret did my uncle hold concerning the factory?"

"Profitability, David."

"I'm not sure I follow you."

"There is none. No profit, and hasn't been for years. Accounts receivable is not able to cover expenses. Even if we were able to release the income from that account, which I believe my son explained we could not—but even if we could, the income generated from the factory's orders is only enough to generate about a third of the company's operating budget."

"But the factory has been operating smoothly for years, paying decent salaries, good benefits, with good working conditions. Anyone on the island in need of a job is given one, or at least that was the policy up until now."

"I understand, and that may partially, though not entirely, explain why a cash flow deficit exists every month. Simply put, the factory has been operating in the red, and substantially so, for as long as I can remember."

David stared across the table. He sat for a moment as one stunned. "I simply do not see how that can be," he said at length. "How has it survived, then?"

"The truth is, David, your uncle has been subsidizing the factory for decades. Our office had been under instructions from your uncle to make a deposit into the factory bank account each month in an amount necessary to keep six or eight months operating capital in the account as a cushion at all times. It was to keep his hand in the factory's finances invisible that he arranged for all income and accounts receivable to flow through our office. As far as anyone in Whales Reef knew, the monthly deposits in the factory's accounts came from income generated by the sale of its products. He wanted no one to know that the factory was being supported by his monthly subsidy."

David sat shaking his head. "That indeed explains everything," he said. "But did my uncle have the money to continue doing so indefinitely? What you describe must have been a serious drain on his resources. And the rents on the island are ridiculously low. He's never raised them that I am aware of. I must admit, this makes his finances yet more a puzzle. How could he afford to subsidize not only the wool factory but in a sense the whole island?"

"It was something he wanted to do," replied

MacNaughton. "His own expenses were modest at best."

"It is all the more remarkable when many on the island considered him a crotchety old hermit."

"He was not unaware of what was said of him. Still, he cared more for the people of the island than for his own reputation."

"So how could he afford to be so generous . . . benevolent, I suppose, is the better word?"

"Your uncle was a wealthy man," said the lawyer, "and a shrewd manager of his affairs, all appearance to the contrary. His estate is worth a great deal. Some of the land that came into his possession from the Auld Tulloch's estate was on mainland Shetland. There were several lucrative sales to oil interests back in the seventies and eighties. With the help of oil, your uncle's business acumen turned the Tulloch estate from a struggling, semi-feudal arrangement that could not have survived many more years into a very lucrative enterprise. The estate continues to receive income from certain oil leases that have proven profitable over the years. Believe me, you stand to inherit a small fortune, David. Sub-sidizing the Whales Reef wool factory made but a small dent in your uncle's assets."

"That no doubt explains why Hardy lost no time in stepping forward. It wouldn't surprise me if he knows more about my uncle's finances than he lets on . . . even more, apparently, than I did."

"You may be right. But he could know nothing about the factory. We have taken every precaution to keep that enterprise and the endowment invisible."

"You also mentioned my account and the trust my parents established for my sister and me. How did that come to be involved?"

"In the same way," replied MacNaughton. "The money for the trust went into your account every month from your uncle's account through our office, just as for the factory."

"He was subsidizing my parents' trust as well?" exclaimed David in surprise.

MacNaughton folded his hands together on the table, looked away for a moment, then back at David. "There never was a trust from your parents, David."

"What do you mean? Now I am really confused!"

"Your parents never had much money to speak of. There was the income from the legacy left by the Auld Tulloch to Leith and his descendants. As you know, your father raised sheep and had his fishing. The Auld Hoose with its hundred acres came down to your father unencumbered. So he possessed assets, but no cash. After your father's death, Macgregor saw the handwriting on the wall. He knew things would be hard for the three of you. He came to me requesting I set up a trust for your family to provide for you and your sister indefinitely. This included funding for your education."

"Yes, I was aware of that aspect. My mother never made any secret of where the money for university came from."

MacNaughton nodded. "He and your mother were not on the best of terms. But she knew of his arrangement. And when he went to her privately to lay out his scheme for an ongoing trust, she could hardly refuse. Even though it was entirely financed by your uncle, we established the trust in your parents' name as he directed. Neither you nor your sister were ever to know. But, again, because of there being no will, the payments into the two trust funds also had to be suspended pending probate."

David sighed and once more shook his head in disbelief.

"Your uncle took care of everyone else, watched over the villagers, provided for your future. He wanted you to be free to carry on your writing and research—he believed in the work you were doing—without having to worry about finances. Yet the one person for whom he did *not* make plans was himself. And now for lack of a few scribbled lines on a sheet of paper with his signature, the rest of his schemes are crumbling."

"All this will resolve itself once the estate is settled?"

"Of course. You will then control your uncle's assets and would be free to resume payments into the factory account. There could be sizable estate taxes. You may have to sell off some assets, but we can help with all of that. As for your trust, I suppose that will be unnecessary as the whole estate will be in your hands. The only decision would be to continue your sister's trust."

"Right . . . I see. And everything you say is based on the assumption that I indeed do inherit. If Hardy is named my uncle's heir, then all bets are off."

"In that eventuality, yes. All bets would, as you say, be off."

David returned to his hotel at the conclusion of his meeting and promptly telephoned Murdoc MacBean on Whales Reef.

"I see no alternative but for you to take steps for gradual cutbacks," he said. "Pending resolution of the estate, we need to stretch out what money remains in the Mill account for as long as possible."

"What do you want me to do, David?" asked Murdoc.

"Lay out plans for a reduced operating budget. You and I will go over it when I return. Think of ways to decrease costs, perhaps making gradual cutbacks in hours. If some workers would like time off, this is a good time to take it. We have to adopt a belt-tightening strategy while continuing to fill orders. But take no drastic steps that will arouse worry. We will do everything slowly. Assure your people that everything is fine."

David spent the next four days at the Kings College Library, researching for his current writing project. He also met with two prospective clients who were planning explorations to collect core samples of glacial ice, one to Greenland, the other to Alaska.

46

SUDDEN WORRIES

Whales Reef, Shetland Islands

David arrived back in Whales Reef after being gone the better part of a week. He did not even need Coira MacNeill's wagging tongue to tell him that a change had come during his absence.

As he drove from the ferry into the village, he saw aging Eldora Gordon making her way down the sidewalk. He pulled alongside, stopped, and jumped out of his car. "May I be privileged to give you a lift?" he said, offering the amazingly spry woman his arm.

"Oh, aye, laddie!" she said with a smile. "So ye're back fae the city, are ye?"

"And glad of it!" laughed David. "London is no place for the likes of me. You're not at the Mill today, Eldora?" he said as he helped her into the passenger seat.

"No, for several days noo, laddie."

"Why is that?"

"I thoucht ye kenned. I thoucht it came fae yersel'."

"You thought what came from me?" asked David.

"The changes up on the hill."

"What changes?"

"Mr. MacBean said he hasna the money tae pay us a'," Eldora answered. "Somethin' or ither aboot the laird's death, ye ken. He didna tell us much, only that hard times was upon us an' that we had tae work together till it was sorted oot. He said ye'd telephoned fae London aboot it."

David listened in angry silence.

"He asked for volunteers, frae those o' us who wouldna hae too grit a hardship if we had tae cut back oor hours. The first tae work must be the older women, ye ken, those that hae nae husbands or other income. Weel, I was thinkin' that I may be auld, but my brither Sandy takes good care o' me. An' I kenned some o' the others were mair sore o' needin' the work than me, so I said I'd stop workin' for a spell. I'm happy tae do it for the sake o' the others, ye ken."

"That is very understanding of you, Eldora," said David.

"Some folk is worried," Eldora persisted. "But not me. I ken that ye'll take care o' us. Ye winna let harm come tae yer folk, will ye, laddie?"

"No, Eldora, I certainly will not," replied David, doing his best to force a smile.

He was soon helping the elderly lady into the bakery. He jumped back behind the wheel, quickly turned around, and sped back out of town as fast as he dared and up the hill to the Mill.

When he entered the building, he immediately saw that fewer employees were on hand. He was even more conscious of the eyes turning toward him from every workstation. The fingers of the claques of women in their circles knitting seemed more lethargic. Every eye watched David as he went, though few faces wore smiles. He walked across the room and up the stairs to his cousin's office.

"I've just been talking to Eldora Gordon, Murdoc," said David. "She says you told the workers about the financial difficulties, that you needed to cut back their hours."

"I saw no reason to keep it from them," replied MacBean. "After your call from London, I assumed—"

"Murdoc," interrupted David, "I specifically told you not to worry them, to make changes quietly and discreetly."

"I'm sorry, David. I suppose I thought—"

"Thought what?"

"I don't know, that they needed to know why we had to cut hours."

"And now the whole island is agitated."

"I'm sorry, David."

David sighed and shook his head. "Well, it's done now. We'll have to make the best of it."

47

A Long Spring

Much to his dismay, David discovered that his cousin's premature revelation and subsequent actions had turned the island on its head. Even those whose fates were not directly connected to the wool factory felt the impact. The seeming inevitability of the Mill's demise spread a leaven of gloom throughout the community.

The Mill represented the lifeblood of Whales Reef. If the wool factory went under, how long would the market, pub, gift shop, and other small businesses be able to survive?

As peat was necessary for warmth, wool and fish were the twin foundation stones of the island's economy. Fishing and visitors and David's nature tours brought in their own share of revenue. But wool was the pride of Whales Reef. Could the village survive without the Mill?

A suddenly obvious fact came starkly into focus. They had taken the wool factory for granted. No one had given it much of a thought. Suddenly it became apparent just how greatly the island's well-being and commerce had depended on it.

Uncertainty was in the air.

If probate was not settled soon, both David and Murdoc MacBean knew they would be forced to shut the Mill's doors. If they stopped processing orders, customers would find other suppliers. Once those buyers jumped ship, MacBean was businessman enough to know it would be difficult to win them back. The future of the Mill could evaporate within months if they did not continue to fill orders.

MacBean paid half salaries in April. Those who chose not to keep working wouldn't lose their jobs. "When the finances are sorted and the Mill is operational, your jobs will be waiting for you," he assured them. Those who agreed to keep working at reduced pay would be reimbursed retroactively, with a ten-percent bonus added for all unpaid back hours . . . *if* the Mill survived.

Gradually orders piled up as April gave way to May and production decreased.

As David walked through the village these days, greeting the villagers as before, he sensed anxiety in the air. The looks they cast him as they returned his cheerful greetings told the tale. They were not optimistic about his chances against Hardy. He could tell many of them felt sorry for him. They knew nothing of Macgregor Tulloch's secret benevolence toward him and the rest of the island. Yet the dark rumor about David's ancestry had so taken root in their minds that they now looked upon him with pity, resigned that their new laird would be none other than Hardy Tulloch.

The common mind will invariably believe the bad over the good. With no evidence other than the man's blustering confidence, therefore, few by now doubted Hardy's tale about the illegitimacy of David's great-grandfather. Though silence is usually a more reliable indicator of innocence, as bravado is of guilt, the indiscriminating masses often draw exactly opposite conclusions from the two responses. The fact that David refused to assert himself and offered no word of defense against Hardy's charges seemed all the more to confirm the suspicion against his pedigree.

But the islanders accepted the approach of the inevitable with stoic resignation. If Hardy raised their rents, they would face that when the time came. They had endured hardships before. In these regions life *itself* was hard. They took it in stride with a fatalism that was not altogether a bad thing.

They still had no inkling of the extent to which their financial well-being had been essentially underwritten by Macgregor Tulloch. But they were astute enough to realize their rents were low by modern standards. They kept abreast of the outside world with newspapers and television. The more progressive-minded used email and the Internet. Though steeped in tradition, they were neither ignorant nor backward.

Some were quietly considering their options for relocating to the mainland. If such discussions around clotheslines and over fences and in shops and among the fishermen at their nets came within Hardy's hearing, he gave no indication of it. Nor did he let fall so much as a word what might be his intentions. If he tripled their rents and was suddenly faced with a mass exodus from the village, what good would it do him? So reasoned those who professed little anxiety over the future. If their rents were raised ten or even twenty percent, it wouldn't cripple them. Hardy would be foolish to raise them more. One thing no one had ever accused Hardy Tulloch of was being a fool.

If things changed dramatically, however, and they were forced to leave the island, they would sell their sheep and chickens and cows, take their few possessions with them, and start a new life elsewhere. But their values and traditions would remain no less deeply ingrained in their souls.

As summer approached, David divulged nothing of what he had learned from the elder MacNaughton. Besides the church building and attached cemetery, all of which comprised no more than three acres, the Auld Hoose was the only house on the island not owned by the laird.

At least he knew that ownership of his own home was secure, and that Hardy could not evict *him*.

As David went out early one morning, his responsibility as chief to the people of the island hung heavily upon him. The moment he had foreseen was at hand. It was time to stand and fight.

He knew his fight was not against Hardy, nor even for his uncle's inheritance. This was an invisible battle he must wage within himself.

Was he willing, for the well-being of his people, to lay down the one earthly possession he treasured more than anything in all the world, that asset which neither the probate courts nor his cousin nor anyone else could touch? Was he willing to give up the security of his own future?

Even as the question focused itself starkly in his mind, he knew the answer. It was a sacrifice he must make. One he would make without question. No true chief would do less.

Before the morning was out, David had gathered the papers and deeds and was on his way into Lerwick. There he arranged a confidential interview with Douglas Creighton. By the time he returned to Whales Reef later that afternoon, all the necessary documents had been prepared—an application for a massive mortgage against everything he owned in the world, pledging the Auld Hoose, all its property, and his future earnings as collateral against the loan and its repayment.

If he had waited too long to take some action—an accusation his aunt continued to harp on with importunity—the moment the funds came through, Murdoc would be able to pay all back salaries, resume the Mill's operations at full strength, and continue until his uncle's estate was settled once and for all.

PART 5

SUMMER, 2006

48

Whales Reef Solstice Fair

Whales Reef, Shetland Islands

As the Shetland days lengthened, the specter loomed of inevitable changes on the horizon. After the difficult winter and spring, few residents of Whales Reef felt they had much to celebrate as summer approached.

With the sun reaching its apex of the year, however, the annual solstice in June represented renewal and hope. The Whales Reef Solstice Fair was a long-standing tradition of both social and economic importance for the community. Perhaps, everyone hoped, the long sunlight hours would bring better times.

The women were scurrying to put finishing touches on sweaters, scarves, mittens, slippers, and all manner of handwoven and felted wool products for the village fair on the weekend prior to June 21. It would not be the only summer celebration or handcraft fair in Britain, but it was of ancient date and laden with tradition. Two ferries were enlisted for the weekend to bring visitors from throughout Shetland to the small island for the three days of the fair.

The island's sheep had been shorn of their winter coats earlier and now wandered the island looking uncharacteristically thin in the fuzz of their new coats. But several dozen of the laird's flock had been kept from their spring haircuts by Dougal Erskine for the purpose of the shearing contest, always one of the highlights of the festival.

The annual fair featured flowers, handcrafts, and spring produce—the latter including strawberries, new potatoes, carrots, turnips, some beans—as well as an abundance of homemade cheeses and jams.

The contest categories were so diverse as to give almost unlimited options to creativity, from food to art, from small to large, from creative design to presentation, from local paintings to the culinary delights produced in kitchens throughout the village. By midday Friday all the prizes would be posted beside their entries.

The eighteen rooms of the Whales Fin Inn had been booked months in advance, the one time of the year when every room was certain to be occupied. Pub and kitchen would work to capacity all weekend—Keith and Evanna in the kitchen, Audney at the bar and serving meals. During such busy seasons they also added Rakel Gordon to the staff. She would be especially busy this year, doing double duty when not engaged at the inn conducting a felting demonstration in the wool factory.

At last the long-awaited weekend came. By noon on Friday the 18th, the village was alive with activity. A variety of aromas from fires and kettles tempted the hungry to part with a few pence in exchange for their lunch. Booths and tables and amusements and every imaginable design of hand-knit wool products were spread out everywhere.

The tents were beehives of curiosity and excitement. Everyone was anxious to see the contest winners in every category from most perfectly shaped potato to most artful vase of sweet peas.

Even in the best of times there was never a great deal of money to be made at the island's annual celebration. Everyone grew their own potatoes and carrots and had a yard full of hens that delivered the family supply of eggs. Even so, eggs were on sale at every table, along with potatoes and carrots and home-canned preserves. Remarkably, though everyone had plenty in the larders of their homes, much produce indeed changed hands over the course of the weekend.

Indeed, describing the goods on offer for *trade* was the accurate term. Barter was more common than cash as the preferred medium of exchange. As hard as they prepared for it, few actually expected Monday to come and find a great deal more money to put in the family cashbox than they started out with. Nevertheless, they all saved up their pennies and 20p and 50p coins for the Solstice Fair. That was part of the fun. Spending was as greatly anticipated as selling. Money and produce might *circulate* between friends as a means of lubri-cating commerce in a village struggling to retain its optimism. It was not profitability that everyone looked forward to, but the social tradition of the community.

No Shetland gathering would be complete without fiddlers. By midafternoon on Friday the lively strains of violins could be heard. They would be joined by accordionists and dancers for Saturday evening's country dance—outside if the evening was warm, inside the factory building if not—which would last until the thin light of midnight began to give way to a new sunrise.

Neither would such a weekend attract sufficient men from the community without a suitable offering of animal flesh for sale or trade. Between the village and the Mill, in a large roped corral, were gathered an assortment of pigs, ponies, a few cattle, but mostly sheep to see what offers might be made. Gamekeeper Dougal Erskine, a man known for his genius with all animal flesh, was on hand to counsel, advise, and instruct. A handful of men were clustered about examining teeth and legs, hooves and flanks, discussing all things ovine, equine, bovine, canine, and porcine with as much animation as a claque of women around a knitting circle. Most had come for information, and a few hoping to purchase a ewe or ram of that special breed known as the Shetland Dunface, whose wool was earning a wider reputation with every passing year. The former laird's gamekeeper was recognized as the man whose efforts had almost single-handedly rescued the Dunface from extinction. Dougal Erskine was a household name in Scotland's sheep-breeding community, no less than was David Tulloch among those who studied the flora and fauna of the northern islands.*

Around the edges of the animal corrals could

---

*Along with the wind and seabirds, sheep are ubiquitous throughout the Shetlands, their total population on the islands standing roughly at 400,000. Approximately a quarter of those are native Shetland breeds, predominately a blend of Soah and Spaelsau brought from Norway by the Vikings. The fine wool of some of the native breeds sheds naturally in the spring. These fleeces are not sheared but "plucked" annually. The hardy sheep of the Shetlands are small and can survive in very hostile weather conditions and are able to manage on a meager diet. Not only do they eat whatever grass is available, they also eat seaweed. They are protected from the possible dangers of grazing on the seashore by a keen awareness of tidal flow. Not only are they able to sense when the tide has shifted, but they are also highly sensitive to weather patterns, often taking shelter well before a gale has begun to blow. Sheep supply the Shetlanders not only with wool, but with the mutton that, in many forms, is a dietary staple.

also be seen one of the oldest men on the island. He said little, though was spoken to by all who passed. He was short even for a Shetlander, standing a mere five-foot-four, wiry and unbowed in spite of his age. He carried a walking stick, not for lack of strength or balance but merely from force of habit. He and Dougal were more than friends. The older man—for fifty years the island's vet—was a mentor to Dougal Erskine in the full sense of the word. Erskine was the first to admit that eighty-nine-year-old Alexander Innes knew every creature that walked on four legs far better than he did. The two had worked together on the Dunface project from its inception. Innes's father had been gamekeeper years before. At his father's death the position had been offered him by then-laird Wallace Tulloch. But his own veterinary practice, and his reluctance to place himself at the behest of the mistress of the Cottage, made it impossible, he explained, for him to accept the laird's kind offer. The position was subsequently abandoned, and the laird's flocks declined until Macgregor's hiring of Dougal Erskine had reversed that trend.

With a Shetland Natural History Tour beginning on Monday—lectures, day trips, and one over-night excursion to the northernmost tip of Unst—and knowing the weekend would be hectic and full of distractions, David closeted himself at home Friday morning and into the early after-noon, going over his itinerary and putting the finishing touches on several of his planned lectures.

His need for solitude had a far more personal reason, however. The telephone call he had received an hour ago had been brief, but it had plunged him into the deepest despondency he had known since the death of his father. After the news he just received, it would not be easy to smile cheerfully through the festivities. Most difficult of all would be smiling through his aunt's jibes about his doing nothing to help the island's people, knowing that he had done all he knew to do . . . but that it had not proved to be enough.

Over and over, the call replayed itself in his mind, but he could not change its finality.

———

"Mr. Tulloch, hello—it is Douglas Creighton calling. I'm afraid I have some unfortunate news. I know you were hoping for the loan against your property to provide funds to underwrite operation of your island's wool factory. I am sorry to have to tell you that your application has been denied."

Stunned, for several seconds David said nothing.

"Mr. Tulloch . . . ?"

"Yes . . . yes, I am here," said David at length. "I don't know what to say. I had assumed that approval was a mere formality. The value of the house and land is far in excess of the amount I had requested."

"I understand your confusion. And you are right, of course—the asset value of the collateral would be sufficient even for a larger loan. Unfortunately, the underwriters examine not only collateral-to-loan ratio, but also cash flow and the income stream necessary to service the debt. In your case, though the asset value is unquestioned, your personal cash flow is not sufficient to guarantee the monthly payments. As you have told me yourself, your income fluctuates. And as incongruous as it may seem, the income from the Mill itself is outside your reach. The underwriters are reluctant to make a loan where even a remote contingency of foreclosure exists. This factor is based almost entirely on the long-term dependability of monthly income. I am very sorry. I understand your predicament. I sincerely wish the bank could help. However, I am afraid there is nothing I can do."

They chatted for a few moments more. It was clear, however, that this day would not bring the resolution David had hoped for.

———

David sat back in his chair and sighed deeply. He had never felt a greater sense of failure in his life. One thing was certain: he could divulge nothing of this to anyone. If only he hadn't hinted to Murdoc that a change would be coming soon. He should have kept his own counsel. He would not make that mistake today. He had so hoped to be able to alleviate the Mill's financial difficulties and to help Noak Muir get caught up on his medical bills. He would have to wear the mask, swallow his disappointment, put on a smiling face and happy disposition . . . and pretend that all was well.

A little after two he did his best to shove his doldrums to the back of his mind, dressed in his kilt and the other accoutrements of his family's traditional Scottish regalia, and set out for the village. The official opening of the annual festival was slated for three o'clock.

By the time he arrived, the expanse in front of the Mill was swarming with islanders and tourists. David ascended the steps of the factory and waited for quiet gradually to descend on the crowd.

"Welcome to you all!" David called out. "Especially to you who have come from throughout Shetland to join us, and also from mainland Scotland and England. As chief of our small but proud island clan, I extend hearty greetings on behalf of the people of Whales Reef. May you find the warmth of our hearts refreshing to your spirits, and may your parting be no longer as strangers but as friends."

A few cheers and shouts went up from the islanders to reinforce David's words.

"While some of our traditions," David continued, "reflect the customs of my family's forebears in the Highlands west of Inverness, we are also keenly aware of our Norse traditions as well. It is always our hope to synthesize *all* the good our heritage has to offer from its varied and historic bloodlines. Thus, I wear the kilt of my clan today in honor of my Celtic roots—a proud Scot *and* a proud Shetlander.

"We want to congratulate all the prize winners in the handcrafts, cooking, and art exhibits. We invite you to visit the tents to see the creativity of your friends and neighbors. And don't forget the sheep-shearing contest tomorrow afternoon, and tomorrow evening's *ceilidh* with Scottish music and dance.

"Now I conclude with a traditional toast, which I leave with you. *Here's ta dee and dy folk, fae me and my folk. An I hope it whin dee and dy folk meets me and my folk at dee and dy folk is a blyde ta see me an my folk as me an my folk is at seean dee and dy folk.*"

49
VISITORS AND MEMORIES

As the crowd disbursed, David wandered about, making an appearance in all the tents, shaking many hands and offering compliments for every display. This was one of the annual occasions where he took great pride in his role as chief—honorary as it might be.

About five o'clock he wandered into the Mill. He had hardly set foot inside when his cousin came hurrying toward him. The look on his face said clearly that he was hoping for good news. David did his best to let him down gently.

"No resolution yet, Murdoc," he told him. "You are managing things as well as can be expected under the circumstances. Keep things going as best you can a while longer."

MacBean left him, obviously crestfallen. David made his way amongst those drifting about the displays, greeting friends and many he had never seen before. At one side of the room his aunt Rinda sat at a spinning wheel. A small crowd clustered about, watching as she spun thin yarn out of a wad of wool roving at her feet.

"At yer spinnin', I see, Auntie!" he said, forcing

a broad smile. "Yer wheel spins sae fast it hums wi' music a' its own."

"An' what were ye an' Murdoc holdin' counsel aboot?" asked his aunt.

"You don't miss a thing, do you, Auntie!" laughed David. "Just mill business."

"Is somethin' in the wind, David?"

"Only that we are hoping for better times soon."

Before she could press him further, David heard a voice call his name. "Hello, Mr. Tulloch!" The accent was unmistakable. David turned to see two smiling middle-aged women hurrying toward him.

"Why if it isn't my two American friends!" exclaimed David. "Hello, Miss MacFarlane, and good day to you also, Miss MacFarlane."

"We simply must get you to call us Hazel and Freda, Mr. Tulloch," giggled the woman who had just spoken. "We Americans are not so proper as you."

"We're here for your next tour, you know," said Hazel, the older of the two spinsters.

"We made our reservations when we were here last fall!" added Frieda excitedly. "We always reserve ahead of time to make sure there is room for us!"

"We were *hoping* we would see you today," Frieda added in a mischievous tone.

Everyone in the village knew of the two American sisters. They came at least yearly for

David's tours and were the subject of much discussion. They followed David about, tittering like schoolgirls, making no attempt to hide their infatuation with the handsome young chief. That David was so gracious, handling every comment and question with aplomb and kindness, only encouraged them to consider themselves his special friends and confidantes.

"We thought perhaps we could treat you to dinner at the hotel tonight," suggested Hazel eagerly.

"I'm afraid Dougal Erskine and I are meeting with some sheep breeders this evening," replied David. "Tomorrow, of course, is the *ceilidh*."

"You *will* save a dance for each of us?" asked Freda.

"Do you know Scottish country dancing?"

"We are in a Scottish club back home."

"Then I shall definitely find you for the Dashing White Sergeant!" laughed David.

As they were talking, David had been slowly walking toward the opposite side of the hall where tables and chairs were set up for Rakel Gordon's felting workshops.

"Hello, Chief!" said twenty-nine-year-old Rakel as they approached.

"Hello, Rakel," said David, stooping to kiss her lightly on the cheek.

"Did you hear that, Hazel," giggled Frieda. "She called him *Chief!*"

David smiled good-naturedly. "Well, then, if you ladies will excuse me . . ." he said, then moved off through the crowd.

As he left the felting tables, David saw Armond Lamont walking toward him. The Englishman was attired as always in suit and matching waistcoat, topped to perfection with a black bowler hat. He looked as if he had stepped off a movie set.

"Hello, Armond," David greeted him as they shook hands and exchanged a few pleasantries. "I would think you might have a good many customers on a day like this," said David. "I'm surprised to see you here."

"I just locked the door for a few minutes," replied Lamont. "I, uh . . . I had a bit of business to tend to. I'll have my Open sign back in the window in no time." He glanced about the hall. He seemed uncharacteristically nervous.

"Do you manage some good business when visitors come to town?" asked David.

"A bit, but nothing much out of the ordinary," answered the bookseller. "I don't get many calls for a first-edition *Martin Chuzzlewit* or three-volume first of *Sir Gibbie* or an autographed *Salted With Fire* from those who attend country fairs. Still, one never knows. I set up a table of used paperbacks outside the door, and it attracts passersby."

"Well, best of luck to you. I hope some collector

comes in and takes that Dickens off your hands!"

Lamont nodded, then turned toward the felting table. David watched as he bent his head to speak to Rakel Gordon. In spite of the din, he was able to make out fragments of their conversation.

". . . tomorrow evening . . . perhaps attend the ceilidh . . ."

From the blush on Rakel's cheeks, David surmised the nature of the Englishman's inquiry.

". . . be working at the pub through teatime," she said shyly.

". . . come for you there . . . walk up together?" said Lamont.

David smiled to himself. So *that* was the business Armond Lamont considered important enough to close his shop! *Good for him!* thought David.

The object of the bookseller's interest was a girl who had been mercilessly treated in her younger years. The teacher of the younger grades in the school at the time was the same Miss Barton under whom David himself had suffered, a woman with eyes only for the prettiest of the girls. Rakel was smart enough, but to one with eyes only for appearances the poor girl was singularly uncomely. Miss Barton did nothing to protect an awkward black sheep like Rakel from the cruelty of her peers.

During her teen years, while every one of them fell for the island's young beauties, the boys of

Whales Reef shunned Rakel Gordon like a pariah. Sadly, so too did most of the girls. The one happy exception was Audney Kerr.

Now, at twenty-nine and thirty-one, the two were the best of friends. Remarkably Rakel Gordon had grown into a happy young woman. But she had never been on what would have been called a *date* in her life.

By the end of the weekend, however, it would be all over the village that Armond Lamont had taken a fancy to Rakel Gordon.

Still smiling, David continued toward the door. He was proud of Armond Lamont. There was obviously more to the man than met the eye.

As he left the factory, David saw ahead of him the parish minister for the Church of Scotland on Whales Reef, Reverend Stirling Yates. Sight of the man of the cloth, with the American accent of Hazel and Freda MacFarlane still ringing in his ears, sent David's thoughts back to that tumultuous time in the history of Whales Reef, and in his own life.

He had always sought the lonely moors and coastlines of the island during his seasons of pain as a boy, and as his sanctuary of thought and prayer as a man. In its own way, the loneliness of the island soothed his soul.

Unconsciously David glanced inland. In his mind's eye he saw himself racing across the open spaces from his home, hot tears in his eyes, on a day so very different from this. It turned out to be the day, it could be said, when his manhood had begun.

———

A fourteen-year-old boy sprinted across the moor.

If such were possible he would drive the anguish from his heart by sheer exhaustion. But there was no escape. The horror still echoing in his ears was too overwhelming. He could not exorcize the dreadful demon of truth.

His lungs heaved in bitter sobs. He ran and ran . . . a mile . . . two miles . . . and beyond. He ran for fifteen, perhaps twenty minutes, as hard as he could force himself. At last his legs could carry him no farther. He collapsed a hundred yards short of the northernmost extremity of the island.

He fell to the ground, sucking for air as if fighting for life. Indeed, he was fighting for life—fighting for the most basic human instinct—the will to live. At last he gave full vent to his grief. Wails of suffering poured out. They rose from his lips and were quickly lost amid the moans of stormy winds and the cries of gulls, lamenting a universe grown empty and desolate.

Word had come less than an hour before.

The single craft surviving the storm had struggled back to the harbor with the news. His father's boat, missing all night, was lost at sea.

His father was dead.

Dead! The hideous word sent shivers of terror through the boy's brain. He burst out sobbing afresh in great torment of heart.

How long he lay weeping, groaning, perspiring from his mad flight across the island, then sobbing again . . . time had no meaning in the midst of his anguish.

Ten minutes later . . . an hour . . . two hours . . . gradually he realized he was cold. An icy wind blew across the island out of the north. The boy climbed slowly to his feet. He was no longer crying. With effort he struggled to draw in a halting and unsteady breath of the frigid, unfriendly air.

Gradually he awoke to where he was. He was standing but a short distance from the treacherous cliffs on the island's north shore, near the Chief's cave three or four hundred yards farther west. This was arguably the most dangerous place on the island. Its overlook sat at the edge of a terrible cliff straight down to the jagged coastline below. He had come here with his father many times but had been forbidden to go near the cliffs alone.

Slowly he walked toward the bluff. Reaching what was known as the Great Cliff, he looked down. The sight was so terrifying his knees quivered. Wind whipped up the cliff face and blew him about unsteadily. The sheer drop of two hundred feet to the rocky shoals of the sea was fearsome, awe-inspiring. Yet on this day he did not fear it. Instead, it drew him with dark compulsion.

The gray sea below was wild and tumultuous. He gazed down, then out across the forbidding waters.

His father was out there . . . somewhere. The sea had been his life. Now it had taken his life.

A preternatural tranquility stole over the boy. It was the dispassion of resignation. Fate had brought him to this place. The island was full of stories of murders and suicides and lovers leaping from this exact spot into the abyss of death. Now it was his turn. Why should he not join his father?

If he leapt into the void, Miss Barton and Sister Grace would say he would fall straight into hell. But he would be with his father.

Who cared what they said. He hated them. He hated the Fountainites who were so religious they wouldn't speak to you if you weren't one of them. Reverend Aedon talked about God but was just as mean as the others. How could God be like them? People used to be kind to each other. That was before Sister Grace and Brother Wisdom poisoned their minds and told them they would go to hell if they did not acknowledge them as prophets.

He hated them all!

He hated prophets!

He hated churches!

He hated ministers!

He hated Americans!

Suddenly the tempest inside him poured out in a torrent.

"God," he yelled into the face of the wind, "why did you take my father? I hate you, God . . . I hate you!"

His voice was lost in the wind.

The words echoed back upon him and suddenly terrified him. Fearing he had spoken doom upon his own soul, blaspheming the Almighty and bringing the wrath of his punishment down upon him, he stepped closer to the edge of the cliff.

He took in a deep breath, summoning his courage, terrified at the thought of jumping, yet resolved to do so. It was the only escape from the pain, from people, from prophets and ministers and Americans . . . the only escape from God himself.

All at once the wind in his face abruptly ceased. A great calm descended.

His heart filled with awe. Some presence was near. A chill swept through his body. Paralyzed by terror of the unknown, he tried to turn to see if someone was creeping up behind him . . . but he could not.

His eyes still gazed out to sea. In the midst of the calm now spoke a gentle whisper, borne invisibly toward him from where his father lay sleeping the sleep of death.

"I am your Father," said the voice. "Find me . . . seek me . . . know me."

As suddenly as it had stopped, again the tempest rose in his face from the sea. Coming to himself, all at once he realized where he was and how great was his danger. Hurriedly he stepped away from the cliff, then turned around. He was alone.

The next moment he was walking, calmly now and full of strange sensations, back over the moor in the direction of the Auld Hoose.

His quest after the great Fatherhood of the universe had begun.

As he went, it had not yet occurred to the fatherless boy that he was now chief of the very island over which he walked. Nor did he think that a higher calling now rested upon him. It would take years, and the gradual maturing of his manhood, for him to recognize the scope of that calling.

In years to come he would think about such things on more profound levels than he was capable of thinking about them on this day. The chieftainship would come to matter to him more than his own life. When that time came, he vowed that never again would a foreigner steal the legacy of his people or work division among them. And never again would a chief remain silent when his people were threatened by evil or falsehood.

The bittersweet memory flitted by in a mere second or two. David's thoughts returned to the present. He summoned again the smile.

"Reverend Yates!" he said, falling in stride with the minister. "It is good to see you again. I was on my way to the sheep pens. Care to join me?"

"With pleasure. Tell me more about this

species of sheep that you brought back from the verge of extinction."

"I played but a minor role in it, believe me," said David. "The breed is called the Scottish Dunface. It is what is termed an unimproved breed. In other words, it is an original and ancient breed. That made its survival all the more important. Besides which is the fact that, along with that of some of the other native breeds, its wool is highly prized. Our own factory is the only place on the earth where the Dunface wool is converted from the backs of the sheep to finished product. It was mostly my uncle Macgregor and his gamekeeper Dougal Erskine, with the help of our esteemed Alexander Innes, who did the important work with the Dunface twenty or more years ago."

"I was very sorry to hear about your uncle," said Yates. "His death has apparently placed you in something of a predicament," he added carefully.

"Not really," said David.

"I understood that things were going against you in the matter of his inheritance," the minister said.

"My uncle left no will, if that's what you mean. That fact has complicated the inheritance, to be sure. His estate is in the hands of the courts. The fact that everyone expected me automatically to inherit has created a bit of a stir. But I am not worried about the outcome."

"A sizable inheritance plus the lairdship . . . they mean nothing to you?"

"A fair question," said David. He paused thoughtfully, then added, "I suppose all my life it has been assumed that one day I would become laird. It was one of those things one takes for granted. It turns out that such may not be the case. But it won't change who I am or what I want in life."

"An admirable attitude."

"Things happen for a reason. I never cared about being a man of means or property. Whatever comes, I will make the best of it. I hope I will meet it with a cheerful heart. My greatest concern is for the welfare of the people of the island. I take my chieftainship as a more sacred obligation than the lairdship. If not receiving the inheritance also renders me unable to do good for them as their chief, then I will be very sorry."

David and the minister arrived at the area that had been roped off for livestock. Twenty or thirty men were gathered inside the makeshift pens while a dozen or so sheep attached to their tethers nibbled at a scattering of hay at their feet.

Reverend Yates stood outside and continued to observe. David bent down, stepped through the rope, and walked inside. One by one the men turned, saw his approach, and greeted him. Handshakes went all around.

50
SHEEP AND FISHERMEN

Hardy Tulloch had been busy most of the day on his boat, having gone out with three of his men early and returning about noon. The weekend's affair was not the sort of spectacle for which he normally would give a brass farthing. He'd not attended the event in years, preferring to spend the time on the sea where fish could be caught and profits made.

But everything had changed now. He would soon be in possession of a sizable fortune. This would be *his* island. When that time came, he would reestablish the Norse tradition on Whales Reef, disposing of kilts and soppy dancing and folk music once and for all.

Wherever he went today, eyes would be following his every move. What ego could resist such attention? Certainly not Hardy's. What better than to make a grand entrance into the pub with a beauty from the mainland on each arm? He would show Audney Kerr she wasn't the only fish in the sea.

Hardy waited until late on Friday afternoon, then made his way toward the site of the day's festivities. He walked with head high and chest out, as if he already owned the land beneath his feet and every house he passed. Heads nodded with deference as he walked toward the animal pens.

Brushing past Reverend Yates and the elderly Innes without a word, he stepped inside the corral and strode brusquely into the center of the gathering.

"So, Erskine," he said loudly, "ye'll be *my* gamekeeper afore long. Hae ye sold any o' my ponies today?"

"Beggin' yer pardon, Hardy," replied Dougal, one of the few men on the island besides David not cowed by Hardy's swagger, "they're no yer ponies yet. If an' when ye do inherit—which I doobt—the ponies'll be stayin' wi me."

"Everything 'o the auld man's will be mine, Erskine," Hardy shot back, "including his livestock."

"I'd like tae see ye convince the ponies an' the sheep o' that," said Dougal with obvious contempt. "What ye ken aboot either wouldna fit on the head o' a pin! Nae, the lads an' lassies'll be stayin' wi' me."

"An' if I turn ye oot o' yer lodgin's at the Cottage that auld Macgregor let ye hae rent free—what then, Erskine? I'm a fisherman after a'. I dinna ken what I need a gamekeeper for. I may jist fire ye."

He glanced around with a grin, obviously trying to get a rise out of the older man.

"Ye canna fire me, ye big blowhard!" retorted Dougal. "An' if ye should try—"

Anxious to avoid a scene in front of their visiting guests, David stepped forward.

"If you no longer find need for his services," he said good-naturedly, "he shall come work for me! He'll take a room in the Auld Hoose and be *my* gamekeeper."

"I might sell all the livestock," snapped Hardy. "Where will the old fool be then?"

"Tut, tut, Hardy," interposed David quietly. "It doesn't do to speak ill of your elders. And whatever you may think, Dougal knows more about Shetland ponies and sheep in his little finger than you and I do combined. These men here have come all the way from Dumfries and Galloway to pick his brain. Our humble Dougal Erskine is considered quite an authority in some circles. Gentlemen," he added to the newcomers, anxious to hold the floor of conversation until the ruffled feathers had settled, "let me present to you my cousin Hardy Tulloch. Shake his hand and intro-duce yourselves. But keep on his good side—Hardy may shortly be the new laird of Whales Reef!"

Several of the visitors came forward enthusiastically. Having successfully deflated Hardy's anger by placing him at the center of attention,

David retreated into the background. Unobtrusively he pulled Dougal aside.

"Let Hardy be, Dougal," he said. "It accomplishes nothing to anger him. This will all be settled soon enough."

"The blackguard stirs my Celtic blude, David. I canna weel help mysel'."

"Please, Dougal . . . for my sake. Let us keep the peace a while longer."

"I'll try, David. Did ye mean what ye said, that if Hardy turns me oot, ye'd bring me tae the Auld Hoose wi' ye?"

"Of course, Dougal. You've been taking care of my flock along with Uncle Macgregor's all this time. Whatever Hardy may do or not do, I shall need you to see to my animals. You have nothing to worry about."

"An' the ponies?"

"Don't worry. We'll not let Hardy sell them. We have too much invested in both the wee horses and the sheep for him to undo our work. The breeds will be secure. Your chief isn't completely powerless yet."

The two had not noticed Macgregor's butler standing apart from the others, outside the pens yet close enough to hear most of their private conversation. Like the Englishman Lamont, he was bedecked in a full suit, though one of considerably older vintage. He likewise appeared out of place at a sheep pen beside farmers, shepherds, and fishermen in dungarees, boots, and work shirts.

Matheson now sought out the ear of the young nephew of his former employer. "If I might have a word, Mr. David," he said in a subdued tone.

"Of course, Saxe," replied David.

"My sister and I are appreciative that you've kept us on and allowed us to live in the Cottage since the laird's passing."

"You served my uncle faithfully," said David. "It is the least I can do. I only wish I had the means to keep paying you your full salaries."

"Don't you worry about that, Mr. David. Mr. Macgregor took good care of us, and we've been able to put some aside for a rainy day, as they say. As long as we've a roof over our heads, we're wanting for nothing."

"It is no more than you deserve. And our solicitors want you and your sister, along with Dougal and me, to look after the place during probate, even if it is for Hardy that we're doing so."

"That's just it, you see," Matheson went on. "I couldn't help overhearing you speaking with Dougal just now, and what Mr. Hardy said about no longer needing a gamekeeper. I'm thinking that if he's not needing a gamekeeper, he's not the kind who's likely to be needing my services either, or my sister's."

"We don't want to jump to conclusions yet, Saxe."

"But the handwriting's on the wall, isn't it, Mr. David? That's what folks are saying. What's to become of us if it's true and Mr. Hardy's becomes laird? He's sure to turn us out. We're too old to find positions in service. You know how it is, 'tis younger folk that are wanted these days."

"Who is saying these things that are worrying you, Saxe?" asked David.

"Mrs. MacNeill at the bakery, Mr. David. She asked me just yesterday what Isobel and I were planning to do."

David shook his head and tried to hide his annoyance. "She had no business asking such a question, Saxe," he said. "The estate is not settled yet. Don't you and Isobel worry about a thing. If need be, you'll move into the Auld Hoose too. The offer I made to Dougal goes for both of you as well."

"Thank you, Mr. David. I know that will ease poor Isobel's mind."

The two shook hands once more, and David left Saxe Matheson and walked toward the village.

As he went, David was unaware that the gaze of an expensively appointed stranger was following him down the hill. When he was out of sight, the man drifted away from potential eavesdroppers, then pulled out a mobile phone, punched in the first of its automatic numbers, and waited.

"Yes, I'm here, Mr. McLeod," he said quietly after several seconds. "A quaint and rather interesting place." A smile crept over his lips as he listened. "I understand," he replied. "As much as you might have enjoyed it, however, I think you might have drawn just a little too much attention—"

The laugh that sounded in his ear was too loud for comfort.

"That's right . . . yes, I believe high profile would exactly describe the situation had you come yourself . . . no, not at all . . . I am managing to blend in nicely . . . no one has the slightest idea who I am. What do you want me to do?"

"Keep your eyes on those two cousins," said the booming voice on the phone. "Learn what you can, keep your ear to the ground, listen to the locals jabber. You never know when you'll overhear a tidbit we can use."

"I understand, Mr. McLeod."

51

OF LAIRDS AND GOSSIPS

As David walked down the incline toward the village, he was accompanied by a steady stream making their way home for evening tea. Ahead of him he saw Odara Innes ambling down the road with a spry step.

"Good afternoon, Miss Innes," he said, falling in beside her. "You look like you could use a strong man beside you for the rest of the way down the hill."

"Bless ye, laddie!" she said. "Ye're looking right fine in yer kilt!" she added as she looked David up and down with a smile.

"I scarcely get half a dozen chances to wear it every year," laughed David. "On banquet nights of my tours, you know. Tourists love to see it. But since I rarely do so on the island, I have to make the most of these opportunities."

She took his arm, and they continued slowly along.

"I saw your father up with the sheep," said David.

"Ye ken my daddy—always wi' the animals."

"Is it true he speaks to them . . . and they to him?"

"I wouldna be one tae dispute it. I hae seen mair in my lifetime that canna be explained any ither way. The man's a marvel, e'en if it is his daughter sayin' it."

"How is his health these days?"

"Oh, jist fine. When he and I go walkin', 'tis me who can hardly keep up!"

It was silent a moment.

"Ye're no the only one who'll be missin' yer uncle, ye ken, laddie," said Odara at length. Her voice was soft and reflective.

"I do know that, Odara."

"I wish there hadna been sae many tales told o' him. Most of them werena true, ye ken. He was a good man."

"I know that well," said David. "If only more people of the village had known it like you do. But in a way, it was his own fault."

"Why say ye that, laddie?"

"My uncle kept to himself far too much. I think it hurt him deeply what people thought. He kept to himself because he didn't want to face their scorn."

"Aye," Odara said with a nod.

Neither spoke for a minute or two. It was David who next broke the silence.

"You caused quite a stir when you placed that rose on his coffin," he said, glancing over at her.

Odara smiled mischievously. "Give the auld wives somethin' tae gossip over, nae doobt."

A great laugh of delight sounded from David's lips. "You're right about that! Half of them say you did it out of spite. The others still don't know what to make of it."

"An' they ne'er will. But ye suspect the truth yersel', dinna ye, laddie?"

David smiled. "My uncle spoke most fondly of you, though he told me if I ever breathed a word of it, he would level me."

"He loved ye too much tae be sayin' sich things. But do ye think there's a will someplace, laddie, that's jist nae been found yet?"

"What makes you say that?"

"He told me he would leave me somethin' special in his will."

"Did he now?" said David thoughtfully.

"Aye he did. I told him it wouldna matter then what folks said o' us, an' that he needna bother on account o' the fact that he was boun' tae outlive me anyway. But he said I'd live tae be a hundred if I was a day, but that he wasna so sure o' himself."

"What do you think he meant by that?" asked David.

"Oh, naethin' tae speak o', jist that he was occasionally worried aboot them oilmen who kep' houndin' him, said they couldna be trusted an' that there was nae sayin' jist what they might do."

"What did he mean?"

"I dinna ken, laddie. But he was feared o' them, 'tis a' I ken."

"You don't think . . . was he actually afraid for his life?"

"I dinna ken, laddie."

They reached the village and made their way into the maze of streets, lanes, and alleyways that made up Whales Reef. David accompanied the daughter of the enigmatic Sandy Innes to her destination. She let go of his arm, then turned and looked up into the face of her young chief.

"If ye breathe a word o' what I told ye aboot yer uncle an' me tae another livin' soul, yoong David," she said, like most of the women of the village not above assuming the role of mother to the chief, "I'll deny every word o' it."

David laughed, bent down, and kissed her warmly on the cheek. She turned and went inside.

With much to think about, David returned to the main street and continued toward the center of town. A minute later he walked into the bakery.

Fortuitously, both women he wanted to speak with were present. They were engaged in low conversation over Coira MacNeill's counter. Their voices broke off the moment David entered.

"Hello, Coira . . . Auntie!" he said. "I didna see ye leave the Mill, Auntie."

"I'd been spinnin' since two. I was ready for tea. My Fergus'll be wantin' his as weel. I'll be at it all day on the morn's morn."

"Did ye hae a good day o' sellin' yer sweeties, Coira?" he asked the shopkeeper.

"Fair tae middlin'," she answered. "I'll hae a table up tae the fair tomorrow wi' young Rob Munro sellin' my biscuits, buns, an' pasties."

"I've just been speaking with old Saxe Matheson," David went on. "He tells me the two of you have been spreading a report that Hardy's as good as laird already. The poor man and his sister are beside themselves about what's to become of them."

"What tales hae that auld pigeon an' his goose o' a sister been spreadin'?" said Rinda irritably.

"Hold your tongue, Auntie. That's no way to speak about an honest man and woman. You should be ashamed."

In truth, Rinda Gunn had felt a pang of conscience the moment she saw David. The two had been discussing David's future and what was to become of *him* after Hardy inherited the estate. She now reproached herself for expressing her view that David had enjoyed too easy a life, berating her departed sister for turning him into an intellectual rather than a fisherman.

"I want the two of you to hold your tongues until the matter is settled properly," said David, looking back and forth between them. "If Hardy becomes laird, then that's as it will be. But there is no call to raise anxieties and fears. Honestly, sometimes the two of you spread more gossip about this village than any ten people should have to give account for when we are called to explain every idle word that has passed our lips. I want talk about the lairdship to stop."

"How dare ye speak tae us that way, David," said his aunt heatedly. The brief pang of conscience from a moment earlier was not strong enough to master her tongue. "I've said naethin' but what a'body kens for themsel's."

"What folks may be thinkin's one thing, Auntie," David replied in Scots as his own blood ran a little hotter than usual. "But ye needna add fuel tae the fires o' gossip yersel'. Gossip's a sin, ye ken."

"Says who?"

"If ye dinna ken that, it winna do nae good for me tae tell ye. What aboot yersel', Coira," said David. She no more relished being scolded by the young scamp, whatever people called him, than did his red-faced aunt. "Will ye promise tae haud yer tongue?"

"I'll haud naethin' for ye, yoong David, but the door as ye find yer way oot o' my shop if ye're goin' tae be insulting both me an' my customers!"

David laughed, refusing to be drawn into further argument with either of the two women.

"Have it your own way, Coira," he said. "I'll hold the door open for myself. But I might have thought better of you, Auntie," he added, not without a tone of kindly rebuke. "My request was an honest one and intended only for the good of the village. I'm thinking of poor Saxe and Isobel. If you can't respect my words more than to throw them back in my face, then I will wish a good day to you both."

The two women watched him leave, both still red-faced, though his aunt felt put in her place by his rebuke. She had spoken harshly to her nephew in front of another and already regretted it. In the privacy of her own kitchen she didn't mind treating David like one of her own children. But in her heart of hearts, though she considered him a bit of a pantywaist, she was proud of her nephew. She did not want him treated by anyone else with less than the respect the chief deserved. Coira's remarks rankled her as much as David's. She took her own leave on David's heels.

David walked on to the Whales Fin. While he had been seeing Odara Innes back to her cottage and was engaged with the two gossips at the bakery, Hardy had returned to the village. He now stood with several of his friends outside near the door of the inn with their cigarettes.

"Weel if it isna oor chief!" said Hardy as David approached along the walkway.

"And if it isn't our new laird too, eh, Hardy," rejoined David, "if all goes as you hope."

"There'll be nae *if* aboot it. So . . . what think

ye, lads, is the bloke a man or woman!" said Hardy, pointing to David's kilt with an insulting sneer.

David took the insult in stride. He had learned years before to laugh off his cousin's rudeness.

"You ought to try it sometime, Hardy," he said. "It's actually quite comfortable. I daresay you would look good in a kilt. What do the rest of you think?" he said, glancing around at the others. "Hardy in a kilt?"

They roared at the suggestion. A well-deserved ribbing at Hardy's expense followed as David made his way past them into the hotel.

Well after six o'clock now, the place was hopping. Every table was full, a buzz of conversation, laughter, and the clatter of dishes filled the large room. Audney and Rakel scurried about with trays of drinks, while Evanna came and went from the kitchen with platters loaded with fish suppers, kidney pies, vegetable plates, and steaks of fresh haddock, cod, and salmon. David walked up to the bar and joined his uncle Fergus, who was engaged with Noak Muir.

"I'm afraid I upset your wife just now, Uncle Fergus," he said, chuckling. "I saw her in the bakery with Coira."

"Wouldna take much tae rile the likes o' her!" said Fergus affectionately.

"Well, I apologize in advance if she takes it out on you when you get home."

"Wouldna be the first time!" laughed Fergus. "She may be the love o' my hert, but there's nae denyin' she's a sharp-tongued lassie when she's heated."

"What'll ye hae, David?" said Rakel, walking behind the bar and setting down a tray of empty glasses.

"A pint of Caffreys, if you please, Rakel."

She placed a clean glass beneath the Caffreys spout and pulled the handle, then handed him his pint and hurried off.

David lifted his glass of ale off the counter and made his way about the room, visiting the others at the bar and stopping to chat at several of the tables. After popping into the kitchen for a moment to say hello to Keith twenty minutes later, he set his empty glass on the bar and left the hotel, nodding as he again passed Hardy and his friends.

52
THREATS AND PROMISES

Hardy took several quick strides and quickly caught up with David. "I dinna like being laughed at, David," he said.

"What are you talking about?" said David.

"That remark about me in a kilt."

"It was nothing, Hardy!" laughed David as he continued on. "All in good fun. Don't take it so seriously. I laugh at your jibes. Surely you can laugh at mine. If you and I are going to be laird and chief, we'll have to get along."

"Speak for yourself. An' ye'd be advised tae tell that auld fool Erskine tae keep a civil tongue in his mouth. I *will* fire him if he speaks tae me in sich a tone again. I'll let the whole lot o' them go, the auld Mathesons wi' him."

"I take it, then, you are planning to move into the Cottage?"

"I haena decided yet. If I do, I'll git rid o' that auld man an' his sister."

"I would tread carefully, Hardy. If you become laird, you will need all the friends you can get."

"Ye're tellin' me what tae do?"

"I'm just giving you some good advice from a kinsman—it does no good to anger folks."

"It winna do for ye tae anger *me,*" retorted Hardy. "I want none o' yer advice. Nor yer interferin'. The next time ye speak tae me in front o' anyone as ye did up on the hill, it will gae the worse for ye. My business wi' Erskine was my ain, none o' yers. Ye had nae right tae speak so tae me."

"The island's people are my business, whoever else's it may be—and how they're treated as well."

"For noo. Once I am laird, there'll be nae mair chief."

"You plan to abolish the chieftainship? I doubt the islanders will like that."

"They will have nae say in it."

"Even if you become laird, you will have no power over the chieftainship."

"We shall see aboot that. I jist may hae mair power than ye ken. Nane o' it will matter if I evict the whole lot o' 'em."

"Who do you mean?"

"All o' 'em—the whole village."

"You could hardly do that, Hardy!" laughed David. "That would eliminate your income. What good would be a village of empty houses?"

"I might jist sell them an' make more'n twenty years o' rents."

"Who would buy them? Most of the village is a hundred or more years old. Its buildings would command little on the open market. You need these people as much as they need you."

"I need nobody, an' I need none o' yer advice. There's people who'll pay, an' good money, for the likes o' this land. I may sell the whole island, an' then where will yer chieftainship be? So stay oot o' my way, David!"

"Look, Hardy," said David, "I don't want to pick a fight with you." He tried to remain calm and spoke softly. "As I said, you and I need to get along."

Hardy's eyes glowed at the mere suggestion of mixing it up with David. Unconsciously his fingers began to twitch.

"Ye wouldn' actually think 'o fightin' me, David?" he said, his voice betraying his eagerness.

"I would fight no man for my own sake," replied David. "But for another, if it came to that, I would fight whoever it required. However, that is not my preferred method of resolving disputes."

"Dressed like that, I doobt ye're man enough tae fight anyone," said Hardy scornfully.

"What is it you think makes a man, Hardy?" asked David.

"Mair nor ye got yersel' aneath that kilt!" laughed Hardy. "Ye look like a milksop an' a woman in that dress! If ye fancy yersel' chief, ye bring disgrace upon the word. These are new times, David, an' no kilt will bring yer so-called Highland customs back. 'Tis the era of wealth an' big oil. Ye canna stop it. An' if ye git in my way when I'm laird, wearin' a dress or no, I'll lay ye oot on the groun'. So dinna anger me, David, an' stay oot o' my affairs, or it will go the worse for ye."

David turned toward his cousin and gazed into his eyes. "I will stay out of your way as far as my conscience allows, Hardy," he said. "And if you indeed become laird, I will give you my hand and my support. But if you hurt or are unjust to anyone on this island, be they man, woman, or child, you will have me to deal with."

David turned and left Hardy staring after him in mingled disbelief and fury.

53

A Sunday Drive

Eastern Pennsylvania

Loni Ford awoke on June 20 to a gorgeous, cloudless sunny day. Tomorrow was the first day of summer. A spirit of adventure suddenly seized her. In its wake came an equally surprising tinge of nostalgia. Her thoughts filled with fond thoughts of her grandmother and grandfather.

It took her no longer than a minute to make up her mind. She went quickly to the phone.

"Hugh . . . hi, it's me," she said when Hugh answered. "Would you like to go for a drive today?"

"Where?"

"The country . . . Pennsylvania. The mood just hit me to visit my grandparents."

"That's what, an hour or two? Sounds like a long drive!"

"More like two and a half, actually," Loni said. "So . . . you up for it?"

"I've had an invitation for golf with a couple congressmen today . . . can't pass up the opportunity."

"All right, but don't say I didn't give you the chance."

"Believe me," laughed Hugh, "I won't."

Loni hung up the phone and began planning the day. She would try to arrive an hour or so after her grandparents returned from church.

The expression on her grandmother's face when she opened the door several hours later nearly broke Loni's heart. In that moment she realized she had allowed too much time to pass, let too many precious years slip away.

"Alonnah!" exclaimed Mrs. Ford.

"Hello, Grandma," said Loni with a smile.

The older woman ran onto the porch and took Loni in her arms. She was three-quarters of a foot shorter than her granddaughter. That did not stop her from clasping Loni and holding her tight, weeping freely.

When grandmother and granddaughter finally parted, Loni's eyes, like her grandmother's, were wet. She couldn't remember the last time she had cried. She bent down and kissed her grandmother's wrinkled cheek.

"I'm sorry it's been so long, Grandma," she whispered.

Hearing the commotion on the porch, Mr. Ford came to the door.

"Alonnah, what a surprise!"

Loni embraced him affectionately.

"It is wonderful to see you! I can't believe you're actually here."

"It's me—in the flesh, Grandpa! You are looking well. And you too, Grandma."

"We are happy and healthy," replied Mrs. Ford. "Feeling our age, I suppose, but that's to be expected."

"What's the occasion, Alonnah?" asked Loni's grandfather. "You're not engaged?"

"Nothing as serious as that," laughed Loni. "It was a beautiful day, and tomorrow's the first day of summer. I felt like a drive in the country, a chance to see you both, so here I am."

"Well, we are delighted to have you. I hope you know you are always welcome—announced or unannounced."

"I do know, Grandpa, thank you. Actually," Loni went on, "speaking of . . . you know, I am dating a man. Hugh Norman is his name. I asked him if he wanted to come today, but he had other plans."

"What does he do?" asked her grandfather, leading the way inside.

"He works in politics, like half of Washington. He's an assistant to a congressman from Wisconsin."

"Is he a believer?" asked Mrs. Ford.

"I don't really know, Grandma," answered Loni. "He's pretty vague about spiritual things. I doubt he believes much of anything."

"We would like to meet him," put in Loni's grandfather, "before you get *too* serious."

"You won't put him through the third degree about his beliefs, will you, Grandpa?" said Loni, fun in her voice as she sat down on the aging couch.

"Not without your permission, Alonnah," he said. "You don't want to be marrying a man without knowing where he stands with God. But I promise I will say nothing without consulting with you."

"We'll cross that bridge when we come to it!" laughed Loni. "The subject of marriage has not come up. But we have been seeing each other for a year, so . . . well, you never know what the future holds."

"I suppose it's too much to think that you might stay for Meeting this evening?" her grandmother asked.

"That might be pushing things a bit," Loni said, keeping her tone light. "Besides, I suspect the two of you have already suffered enough grief over me. I don't want to stir all that up again at the Fellowship with my modern dress and—"

"Let us worry about that," interjected her grandfather. "You are beautiful, and any man who says otherwise, whether in our Fellowship or anywhere else, will have me to answer to!"

"My knight in shining armor!"

"And don't you forget it!"

Loni laughed.

"Anyway," she said, "I have to get back tonight for work tomorrow. It's a long drive."

"But you'll stay long enough to have dinner with us?" asked her grandmother. "We still have Sunday dinner at three."

"Absolutely. I'm not about to miss the chance to enjoy your cooking, Grandma!"

54
A DARING ATTEMPT

Whales Reef, Shetland Islands

The fair weather across the North Atlantic for the solstice proved to be the literal calm before the storm. By Friday of the following week, with David's Wildlife Tour behind him and Hazel and Frieda MacFarlane on their way back to the States, dark menacing clouds began gathering in the west. They portended high winds and evil seas.

When David left the village in midafternoon, the wind had risen to a frenzy. The sea was a cauldron of angry gray-green waves tipped with whitecaps. The horizon was a mass of black.

He hurried his cows into the barn, then did the same with the ponies. Dougal would see to the animals at the Cottage. Finally he carried several loads of peats into the house and was cozily shut inside by six o'clock.

The wind howled until daylight. David awoke to an island that had been drenched during the night. The wind had moderated somewhat and the rain abated, though the storm was far from past. After breakfast he dressed warmly and, with skies still threatening, went out into the tempestuous morning.

Waves roared along the sands and rocky bluffs, a mass of foaming white. The wind tore across every chimney of the island, blasting the white peat smoke horizontally with violence across the slates of the village roofs. Drawn to the roiling sea, David made his way along the shore and thirty minutes later approached the harbor. Twenty or thirty men were clustered in small groups along the top of the cement quay, gazing out across the turbulent waters. Those with binoculars were scanning the horizon. In the distance, sky and sea were virtually indistinguishable.

David walked toward them and stopped beside Noak Muir. "Surely you're not thinking of going out?" he said.

"I admit I was thinkin' o' it when I came doon," replied Muir.

"It would be foolhardy in that," said David, waving a hand toward the sea.

"I must gae when I can, David. Times is hard. Hardy's offered to buy my boat like he did Sandy's," he added, almost as an afterthought.

"Do you want to work for Hardy?"

"Nae for a minute, but Sandy's makin' a livin'. An' Iver too."

"Perhaps, in a way of speaking. But both have

lost their boats. They are now at Hardy's mercy."

"A man's got tae feed his family, David. Ah, weel, it winna matter noo anyway—Hardy's nae aboot tae be buyin' any mair boats noo."

"What do you mean?" asked David.

"Jist that," said Noak, pointing out across the water. " 'Tis the storm, like ye said yersel'."

"What's that to do with Hardy?"

"Haena ye heard, David?"

"Heard what?"

"Hardy went oot yesterday. He hasna been heard fae since."

"Hardy went out in *this?* Everyone knew this storm was going to pound the islands."

"Ye ken Hardy."

"He must have put in somewhere. He's probably riding it out in Lerwick."

"Folk hae been callin' aroun' everywhere, a' the small harbors an' coves, fae Fitful Head tae Lamba Ness. There's nae trace o' him. Aboot nine last night Keith at the hotel had a call fae the harbor master in Lerwick—picked up an SOS. They werena sure it was Hardy, but his was the only boat reported missin'."

"Did they get his coordinates?" asked David.

"I didna speak wi' Keith mysel'."

"Then I'll find out," David said, turning away. "We've got to go find him!"

"Oot in that! Look at it, David—ye said yersel' 'tis nae safe."

"Your boat can handle it, Noak. Get one or two men to go with us."

"Naebody's aboot tae gae oot in that! Not for Hardy."

"Whatever else he is, he is one of us."

"They'd gae for yersel' maybe, but nae for Hardy."

"Then it will have to be just you and me!" said David. He was thinking hard as he glanced about. "Get your engine under way. I'll run up to the hotel and see if Keith's heard anything new."

David sprinted off the quay and up the hill into the village.

Noak watched him go, his mind swirling with unpleasant memories. He had secretly prayed for an opportunity to redeem himself in the matter of the *Bountiful* from years before. The guilt he carried sometimes nearly overpowered him. To have watched as the boat of a friend went to the bottom still tore at his heart. How could he have been so foolish, he had asked himself a thousand times, to have believed all that Fountain of Light nonsense?

At last, it seemed, his prayer was being answered. Or, some might say, his sins were coming back on his own head. If he lost his life in the attempt to save a fellow Whales Reef fisherman, it was no more than he deserved. If only it were someone other than Hardy!

Yet Noak Muir, like his chief, had grown

spiritually as a result of the community's history with the dark influences of the cultish group. He had become sufficiently a man of prayer in recent years to recognize the great truth that he could not dictate those whom God would send into his life as the instruments and agents of answered prayer. He would not have chosen Hardy Tulloch for use in answer to his. Apparently God had.

David returned five minutes later and ran straight for the cluster of men watching as Noak hurriedly unfastened the ropes from his sturdy craft and made ready to cast off. Even in the harbor it was bobbing about like a cork with the other boats. What Noak had decided during David's brief absence told clearly enough by the smell of diesel smoke coming from the stack of his idling engine.

"You all heard by now that Hardy's in trouble," David called as he ran toward the others. "I need one or two men to go with us."

"Tae do what, David?" asked one.

"To find him!"

The small crowd shuffled uneasily. No one spoke.

"If it was anybody but Hardy, ye see, Chief," said Farlan Campbell at length. "Ye ken weel enough that he wouldna lift a finger tae help any one o' us."

"More's likely that he'd keep from helpin' us so he could git his clutches on another o' oor boats," added Stewart Scrymgour in a sour tone.

"He's right, Chief," added Les Balfour. "We got oor own families tae think o'. I'm no aboot tae risk my own neck for the likes o' him."

"Let Hardy's own men gae oot for him."

"Maist o' them's on Shetland," said Balfour. "He only went oot wi' half his crew."

"What Hardy would do is beside the point," said David. "It's what *we* are bound to do. It's time to be men and do what's right! Farlan, I know you're a shepherd like me. But you know your way around a boat as well as I do. Gordon, Iver, Gunder, Stewart, Douglas . . . Noak and I can't possibly make it out and back alone. I know the danger. We may all drown in the attempt. I realize I'm asking you to risk your lives. I'll think none the less of you for staying. Noak and I will go alone if we have to."

Ten minutes later, with a scant crew of five, the *Bonnie Muir* rocked out of the harbor. The three who joined Noak and David had also been there on that fateful day when the *Bountiful* was lost. They too had their own private reasons for heeding the chief's summons to courage.

Watching from shore, the rest of the men observed their sailing in silence. More than one felt guilty. Others wondered if they had seen the last of their foolhardy young chief and their friends. None, however, relished the idea of being aboard themselves.

Word had quickly spread through the village about the attempt. By the time of their departure, the harbor was lined with their friends and neighbors. Dire forebodings clutched at their hearts as they watched the brave little craft creep seaward.

Passing the outer harbor wall, they were soon being tossed about like a toy. Noak increased his speed. Bobbing up and down, the *Bonnie Muir* shrunk smaller and smaller, climbing one wave, then disappearing into the trough of the next. Half an hour later it was lost to the sight of the onlookers on a course bound for the last known coordinates from Hardy's distress call.

That signal was now more than fifteen hours old. By now he might be anywhere. All the men aboard knew the most likely possibility was that the *Hardy Fire* lay at the bottom. Still, if there was any chance the crew had made it safely onto a life raft, they might survive several days.

An hour out from Whales Reef, Noak was at the wheel doing his best to keep his boat from capsizing. David, Fergus Gunn, Gunder Knut, and Douglas Camden all stood on the dangerously swaying deck with binoculars to their eyes.

"We're comin' up on that GPS readin', David!" shouted Noak from the wheelhouse. "Ye see anythin'?"

"Not yet!" David yelled back.

"What do ye want me tae do? I canna cut the

engine. We'd capsize in these troughs. I've got tae stay movin'."

"Keep to a wide circle pattern within a mile or two of his last reading."

Struggling to keep their feet beneath them as waves pounded the hull and splashed high over the side, Noak's four crewmen were soaked to the skin. The slippery deck heightened the danger.

"We could be a quarter mile from them an' ne'er see them!" shouted Fergus.

"Sound your horn, Noak!"

He did so, but the blast was lost in the wind.

"'Tis nae use, David!" shouted Noak. "Even if they were near enough tae hear it, what good would it do? If they're on a raft, hoo would they signal us? An' we'd ne'er get sight o' them in these swells."

"Keep at the horn, Noak," shouted David. "If there's any chance the boat is still afloat, they might be able to signal us!"

With supreme effort, Noak manhandled his wheel to angle into each swell as close to forty-five degrees as possible, keeping his hull from being smashed to splinters by a direct hit. He also had to avoid the peril of getting caught in a trough parallel to two giant waves and capsizing straight over onto the side.

It was a treacherous game these hearty fishermen played every day with angry seas. A moment's lapse in concentration was enough to lose a boat and its crew. A wheel spinning out of control, a broken rudder, one mighty twenty foot wave . . . it could be over in seconds. Every time they set to sea they took their lives in their hands.

They struggled bravely for another two hours, sounding the horn, scanning the violent seas, and measuring a distance some two miles in every direction from the previous night's GPS signal. They knew well enough that Hardy and his men, whether aboard the *Hardy Fire* or a raft, could be halfway to Fair Isle by now, or run aground in the other direction on the shoals of Out Skerries . . . if they weren't already on the bottom.

"'Tis nae use, David!" called Noak at last through the open door of the wheelhouse. "We'll ne'er find them in sich a tumult! I'm afeart the wind's pickin' up again. We must think o' oor ain necks, man! 'Tis time tae turn back!"

"A few minutes more, Noak!" yelled David through the wind.

Again he pressed the binoculars to his eyes. The *Bonnie Muir* rose high, then crashed down violently. David lost his balance, sprawled to his back and across the slippery planking.

"Watch yersel', David!" cried Fergus.

But David was helpless to stop himself. Arms and legs flailing, he slid over the reeling deck toward the side. His feet shot beneath the lower guardrail. Grabbing wildly as he flew toward the sea, he managed with one hand to lay hold of the metal bar above him. He slung an elbow over the rail, then clutched the cable above it.

On treacherously unsteady legs, Fergus stumbled toward him.

"Hang on, man!" he called.

Steadying himself on the lurching deck with one arm around the top railing, Fergus bent down and stretched out his arm.

"Take a grip o' my hand, David!"

David released the cable and flailed at Fergus's hand.

With David's legs dangling over the side, suddenly the *Bonnie Muir* rocketed skyward. At the moment the hull reached its apex, Fergus pulled with all his might. Had the lurch of the boat gone against them, David and his uncle would have been lost.

But Noak's skill at the wheel averted disaster. He angled the rudder to lift the deck against the direction of the sea. Both men sprawled across the deck into a mass of rigging and nets. The instant they were away from the side, Noak spun the wheel back into the swell.

"Thank you, Fergus!" said David as they untangled arms and legs and got their feet beneath them. "You saved my life."

"We canna weel be losin' a second chief tae the squawls o' nature. I'd sooner hae gang ower the side mysel'!"

55

THE *HARDY FIRE*

After his brush with disaster, and knowing he had nearly cost his uncle his life, David was at last ready to admit defeat.

"Noak is right," he yelled into the wind. "It's too dangerous. It will do Hardy no good for us to follow him to the bottom."

"Haud on a minute—I think I saw somethin', David!" shouted Fergus

"Show me, Fergus! We'll ride the next wave up . . . point to where you saw it."

The two struggled across the heaving deck to the bow. The *Bonnie Muir* bottomed, then rose again on the swell.

"There, David . . . see ye off tae port!" cried Fergus.

Already they were diving again. Awaiting their next opportunity, Fergus stood with binoculars in place. David's pair of binoculars had long since gone overboard, but he squinted intently into the squall.

"I see't!" cried Fergus as they crested. " 'Tis the *Hardy Fire*! I'd ken it anywhere!"

"You're right! Noak!" called David, turning

and scrambling for the wheelhouse. "We've spotted Hardy's boat! Set a course ten o'clock to port."

"That's direct intil the teeth o' the swell, David."

"You'll have to tack!"

David hurried back onto the deck. Within ten minutes no doubt remained. They had miraculously found the *Hardy Fire.*

By slow degrees the vessel came into view. Clearly floundering, it had yet somehow managed to keep afloat through the long night's storm.

It took forty more minutes before they were close enough to see Hardy's men on board waving frantically.

David, Fergus, Gunder, and Douglas clustered with Noak in the wheelhouse. Not exactly keeping dry—it was too late for that—but at least they enjoyed a brief respite from the wind. Everyone's fate was in Noak's hands now as he guided his rescue craft steadily closer to the distressed vessel.

"What do ye want me tae do, David?" asked Noak. "I canna weel git too close in this swell— the two boats would crash intil kindlin'."

"Can you draw close enough to throw a rope between the two? We'll have to tow her back."

"I'll swing wide an' try tae come at her facin' the direction o' her prow."

"The wind's too strong for a rope," said Douglas.

"We cud try one o' my auld harpoon guns," suggested Noak. "Shoot high an' send a rope ower tae't."

"Jist so long as none o' the men git in the way!" laughed Gunder.

"They'll be nimble-footed enough, I'm thinkin'. I hanna used the thing in years. 'Tis naethin' but a spring—nae reason it wouldna work. Gunder, ye see it there?" said Noak, pointing outside across the desk. "See if the rope's still aroun' the tail o' the harpoon an' make sure the coil o' it's clear. When we're in place, I'll gae oot an cock the bonnie thing."

Gunder hurried outside while Noak continued to negotiate the waves and troughs in a circle around the *Hardy Fire*. Eventually the two vessels were pointing nearly in the same direction. No smoke came from the *Hardy Fire*'s stack. It had clearly lost power.

Coming as close as he dared, Noak turned the wheel over to Douglas and left the wheelhouse. Cranking the nose of the harpoon up to thirty degrees, he cocked the lever and then released the spring. The ancient mechanism snapped forward and launched the harpoon into the air. All eyes watched it fall into the water well short of its mark.

Noak rapidly reeled in the rope and recoiled

it for another try. The second was no more successful than the first. He reeled it in again, then ran for the wheelhouse.

"We'll hae tae git in line wi' the wind," he said. "An' git closer. Gie me the wheel."

Again Noak maneuvered his boat through the treacherous waves, this time coming alongside from the opposite direction and closing the gap to within a dangerous fifty feet.

Once more he turned the wheel over to Gunder, then ran onto the deck. He adjusted the harpoon to a steeper angle and aimed straight in the direction of the wind. Again he fired. The wind carried har-poon and rope high and straight. It flew over the deck of the *Hardy Fire*, clanking onto its far railing.

Great cheers rose from both vessels. Hardy scrambled to detach the rope from the harpoon's tail while Noak quickly let out all remaining slack so no sudden shift of either boat would snap the line.

Working hurriedly, Hardy tied the slender harpoon cord securely around the hook of a thick stout cable. At the same time, Noak resumed his own wheel and powered forward. He increased the gap to a safe distance and moved in line with Hardy's bow. At the rear of the *Bonnie Muir*, David, Fergus, Douglas, and Gunder wound in the harpoon line, considerably heavier now. Slowly they lugged the cable toward them. Ten minutes later, Hardy's cable was safely attached to a hook at the stern of the *Bonnie Muir.*

With a wave and a shout to Hardy, David ran inside.

"We're secure, Noak," he said. "Set a course for Whales Reef!"

Though the swell was as fierce as before, with the wind behind them and stabilized somewhat by the taut cable between the two vessels, the danger of capsizing was diminished. As the smaller *Bonnie Muir* chugged ahead with the *Hardy Fire*—more than double its displacement and tonnage—dragging heavily in its wake, progress was slow yet steady. No communication had been estab-lished between the boats. Whatever else had befallen the *Hardy Fire*, its radio was also out.

All day back on Whales Reef, the villagers had been coming and going. As dusk approached, they all knew if night fell upon the island they would never see their chief or his uncle or Noak Muir or Hardy Tulloch or any of the others again.

Shortly after three, with the gray skies begin-ning to darken, the tiny outline of two boats in the distance came into view. By then the harbor walls were lined with every man, woman, and child of the island. Great cheering and shouts rose into the blustery wind.

Inch by inch the *Bonnie Muir* came toward them, with the great *Hardy Fire* in tow.

Thirty or forty minutes later, the puffing rescue vessel rocked between the narrow cement walls of the harbor channel. The moment it was safely within the harbor's walls, every able-bodied man bolted across the quay. Fergus unhooked the trailing cable and dumped its iron hook overboard. One of Hardy's men cranked it in. Hardy and two others heaved ropes ashore. Dozens of eager hands leaned and grabbed to help pull the crippled craft the final few feet of its perilous journey. More joined in to secure it to the quay.

By the time David, Fergus, and the others stepped onto the cement a minute or two later, the *Bonnie Muir* was securely tied off and at rest. Another great cheer rose as Noak Muir emerged from the wheelhouse. He smiled sheepishly and followed the others ashore.

The harbor was filled with the sounds of backslapping and handshakes and congratulations from the men, and with tears and relieved laughter from wives, sisters, and mothers of those thought to be lost.

It would have been difficult for an observer to know which one was the day's greater hero, Noak Muir or Hardy Tulloch. Never one to shun the spotlight, Hardy made the most of the opportunity. The whole affair had suddenly become a great adventure. He denied absolutely that they had *really* been in any danger. They were simply riding out the weather.

"It'll take a mightier blow than a wee storm the likes o' that tae sink the *Hardy Fire*!" he laughed. "If we hadna lost oor rudder, we'd hae been in weel afore dark last night. Jist a bit o' ill-timed luck was a'. But she's a stout craft an' we would hae been up an' runnin' soon's the wind died awa'."

Along with the rest of the crowd, however, Hardy knew it had been a close one. Though he never would admit it to a soul, he had never been more frightened in his life, and he was man enough to set aside his pride and offer his hand to the one who had risked his life and his boat to find him in the storm.

As soon as his vessel was safely put to bed, he walked around the harbor wall. With obvious fanfare, and followed by a dozen or more of his fellow fishermen, young Ian Hay chattering away beside him, Hardy strode toward the *Bonnie Muir*.

A crowd was clustered about, peppering Noak and David and Fergus with questions. Seeing Hardy approach, they parted. Hardy walked into their midst.

"Gie me a grip o' yer hand, Noak," said Hardy, walking straight toward him. "Ye got my sincere thanks for what ye done, man. A real brave thing it was, in that wee craft o' yers. An' a right fine bit o' navigatin' it was as weel!"

"It was David that took charge o' the affair,"

said Noak. "He was captain o' the *Bonnie Muir* this day, no me."

"Then, David," said Hardy, turning toward his cousin, "I'm indebted tae ye as weel."

"Thank you, Hardy," replied David. The two shook hands.

"An' noo," Hardy added, turning to the crowd, "for as long as Keith's supply holds oot, the ale an' whiskey's on me!"

Another cheer went up. Hardy led the way from the harbor, followed by much of the village, to the Whales Fin Inn. After David and Noak and their crew, as well as most of Hardy's men, hurried home briefly for dry clothes, the celebrating went on most of the evening.

David was not a partying man. He preferred a small discussion between friends to a rollicking evening at the pub. Given the circumstances, however, he knew the importance of participating in the celebration. He hoped the day's events and the gaiety of the evening would have a calming effect on the islanders' uncertainty about the future.

He therefore remained at the inn longer than would have been his custom.

56

A DIFFERENCE

The storm subsided and blew away to the east. Those attempting to listen to whatever words of wisdom he had to impart found Reverend Yates's sermon the following morning punctuated by hammer blows from the harbor. Hardy had his rudder repaired by that afternoon. The *Hardy Fire* was on its way to Lerwick at dawn on Monday morning.

Hardy walked into the pub several days later, as was his custom when not at sea, about 5:15 in the afternoon. The room was full of the afternoon crowd. He saw Noak Muir at a table with several others. "Noak, my friend!" he called, stretching a burly forearm around Noak's shoulders. "Hey, lads," he announced, "this is the man who saved my life!"

"A'body kens aboot it weel enouch by noo!" rejoined one of them.

"Mind if I hae a word wi' ye, Noak?" said Hardy.

Noak glanced up at him, then slowly nodded and stood.

"What are ye drinkin', Noak?" said Hardy. "Bring yer glass wi' ye."

"Canna afford tae be wastin' my money on Keith's ale," replied Noak.

"Audney, bring us a couple o' pints!" Hardy called across the room. He led Noak to a table away from the others. Audney appeared a minute later and set two glasses down in front of them.

"Thank ye kindly, Hardy," said Noak, taking a long swallow. "I haena had a pint in two weeks!"

"Is it really so tough for ye?" asked Hardy.

"I canna seem tae bring in a hundred pound a week," replied Noak. "I canna weel survive on that. An' there's my daughter's doctor bills, ye ken."

"Hae ye thought mair aboot what I said afore, Noak?"

"Aboot sellin' ye the *Bonnie Muir*?"

Hardy nodded.

"I canna weel do that, Hardy. 'Twas my father's boatie, ye ken."

"Aye, an' 'tis a worthy craft, Noak. Ye proved that last week. But if ye need the money, why not sell it, an' buy it fae me again when ye're back on yer feet? I'll make ye the same offer I made the other lads. 'Tis a standin' offer—ye can buy back yer boat for what I paid ye."

"An' hoo much would ye be willin' tae gie me?"

"I'd pay ye twenty-four thousand."

"Twenty-four!" exclaimed Noak.

"I'd pay ye that today."

" 'Tis worth twice that."

413

"Maybe it is, maybe it isna. But 'tis that much less it will cost ye tae buy it back, ye see. 'Tis more cash than ye'll be needin', I'm thinkin', an' will make it that much easier for ye tae git back on yer feet an' make it yer own again later."

Hardy's reasoning seemed sound. Noak nodded thoughtfully.

"I'm no sayin' I dinna appreciate yer offer, Hardy," he said. "'Tis kind o' ye tae think tae help me oot."

"'Tis the least I can do for the man who saved me an' my crew."

"I'll hae tae think on it, ye ken."

Hardy nodded and rose. Noak returned to his friends.

Hardy sauntered toward the bar. The conversation that followed was reaching the point where it was becoming tiresome to the daughter of the inn's owners when the chief walked through the door.

David sat down with Noak Muir and his friends. They were discussing Hardy's offer to buy the *Bonnie Muir.* Behind them they could not help overhearing the heated exchange at the bar.

". . . no way for a lass tae be speakin' tae her laird," Hardy had just said.

"Ye'll no be *my* laird, Hardy Tulloch," said Audney.

"I'll be yer daddy's laird, an' it winna do tae

anger me, Audney, or I may find I'm boun' tae raise his rent."

"I ken weel enouch that ye canna wait tae raise everyone's rents!"

"Aye, I jist may hae tae do jist that on the buildings an' land I dinna sell for a nice profit. But the laird's wife may hae special privileges when it comes tae takin' care o' her parents."

"Ha! Ye think I'd marry the likes o' yersel,' Hardy Tulloch?" retorted Audney. "I told ye already—naethin', no if ye was the last man on earth, would make me think o' marryin' ye."

David's ears perked up at Hardy's mention of selling. It was the second time he'd heard him hint at such a thing, even implying that he had potential buyers. What did his cousin have up his sleeve?

David saw Hardy reach across the bar and take hold of Audney's arm.

"Let go o' me, Hardy!" she cried. "Ow! Let go, I tell ye!"

David stood and walked toward them.

"What do ye want, David!" Hardy growled. "This is none o' yer affair."

"If you're hurting one of my lassies, Hardy," said David calmly, "then I have no choice but to make it my business."

"She's no yer lassie. Ye had yer chance. Noo she's mine."

"I'm no yer lassie, ye big lout!" said Audney

angrily, trying to yank her arm away. "Noo let go o' me afore I whack ye in the face. An' dinna think I winna!"

Hardy roared with laughter but kept his fist tightly clutched around Audney's arm.

"Hardy," said David calmly. "She has asked you kindly. Now I am telling you to release Audney."

"An' who's goin' tae make me?"

David smiled. "I just heard Audney tell you that she would. Speaking for myself, I would tend to believe her. But if she doesn't, I will."

"Ye'll pay for it if ye try!" spat Hardy.

Thinking better of starting an all-out row in the pub, with a half dozen or more strong fishermen watching who would almost certainly side with their chief, Hardy gave Audney a rude shove backward. She fell against the counter opposite the bar and let out a cry.

David's face filled with indignation. Few things enraged him more than seeing a woman treated roughly. His fists clenched, and he took a step forward. But he too thought better of carrying the altercation further.

"If I see sich a thing again by yer hand, Hardy," he said, "I winna hold mysel' back fae givin' ye the thrashing sich a cowardly thing deserves. For noo I'll jist tell ye tae leave Audney in peace, an' gae yer way."

With the look on his face of an enraged bull,

quivering with fury to be spoken to in such manner by the younger cousin he despised, Hardy glared back at David. The fire in his eyes flamed with wrath. That he was strong enough and mean enough to kill, none doubted. Whether Hardy Tulloch *had* ever taken a life, no one knew. But in that moment there was no doubt what was on his mind.

A few chairs slid back on the wood floor. Six strong fishermen rose to their feet, ready to storm forward in defense of their chief.

With a movement amazingly swift for such a big man, Hardy spun around and strode with giant strides across the floor and disappeared into the night.

57
PLAN C

Houston

"Mr. McLeod . . . it is Bruce Thorburn."

"Hey, Thorburn," boomed the Texan's voice on the other end of the phone, "you got good news for me?"

"I fear not, Mr. McLeod," replied the Scotsman. "As I think your people say there in Houston, we may have a problem."

"What're you talking about? This is no time for jokes."

"I am afraid it is not a joke. It appears that we have encountered an unexpected setback."

"What in heck's gone wrong now?"

"Things were looking promising . . . I contacted you, as you recall, from the island during their summer fair. Everyone was prepared for our man to be installed as the heir. I managed to meet with the fellow in private as well—a great hulking oaf of a fisherman, as you may have heard. The man was as eager as we were to begin the process for sale of all the property the moment it is trans-ferred into his hands."

"Then what's the dang problem?"

"It seems that at the last minute the investigator hired by the court, the fellow Ardmore, unearthed a third potential heir to the property."

"How could that be! Where in the heck did he come from?"

"I have no idea, Mr. McLeod. The rumor is that it's an American."

"What in the Sam Hill's an American got to do with it?"

"I could not say, sir."

"Dad blame it—right when we had the big fella roped and corralled! So where does the thing stand now?"

"My sources and our solicitors are not optimistic about our chances at this point. It may be that whoever this individual is has a closer connection than either of the two Tulloch cousins."

The Texan exploded in an outburst of profanity.

"Yes, sir," rejoined Thorburn calmly, accustomed to his boss's temper. "It would seem," he added, "that perhaps we would be advised to regroup and consider Plan C."

The line was silent for several seconds.

"Find out who he is, Thorburn," said the Texan. "We've got to get to him before anyone else. If he's an American, then I'll pay him a visit personally. No more fooling around."

"Very good, sir."

"We gotta go straight after it and get this thing

done. Maybe this'll work out better after all. We'll be dealing with my kind, not these back-woodsmen of yours. Ain't no American likely to walk away when I put the dough on the table."

"I will find out what I can and get back to you, sir."

58
NEWS

Whales Reef, Shetland Islands

A week later, with a series of lectures in Edinburgh to the Natural History Society of Scotland behind him, David returned to Whales Reef looking forward to a few quiet days at home. There were no appointments on his docket for ten days.

He made himself a cup of tea, retrieved a stack of envelopes from the table, and settled into his easy chair to look through his accumulation of mail.

A letter from MacNaughton, Dalrymple, & MacNaughton caught his eye. Quickly he opened it.

Dear David,

Sudden unexpected developments in the investigation of potential heirs to Macgregor Tulloch's estate have just come to our attention through Mr. Clement Ardmore, acting in his capacity as investigator for the probate court. As your finances, and the future of the wool factory, may be seriously impacted, I want to explain these developments in person. Please call me at your earliest convenience.

I am,
Sincerely yours,
Jason MacNaughton.

59
THE LETTER

Washington, D.C.

Loni Ford was sitting in Madison Swift's office when the mail cart began its rounds on the seventh floor of Capital Towers.

Glancing in the open door as he passed, the young man who was in his first week on the job paused.

"Excuse me, Miss Ford, would you like Miss Swift's mail here or should I take it to your office?"

"Here is fine, Robert," answered Loni. She rose and walked to the door. "I'll take it."

"There's a registered one you have to sign for."

He handed Loni the postal slip. She signed it. He handed her the remaining stack and continued on his way.

Loni absently thumbed through the envelopes as she sat down.

"Anything interesting?" said Maddy.

"Doesn't look like it. I was expecting those papers on the Westminster acquisition and—"

She stopped abruptly. "Huh!" exclaimed Loni.

"What?"

"There's a letter for *me*. I never get mail here. It's the registered one!"

"Open it. Maybe you won the lottery."

"I don't play the lottery. Uh-oh . . . it's from a lawyer's office."

She passed the letter across the desk to Maddy. "You read it," she said with a serious expression. "It must be bad news. One of my grandparents must have died."

"Someone would have called you."

"But what else comes from a lawyer—a summons, a lawsuit . . . obviously it's bad news."

"Since when have you been using your middle name?" said Maddy, staring at the envelope. "I never even knew what your middle name was."

"What are you talking about?" replied Loni. "I *don't* use my middle name."

"Whoever this letter is from, they think you do. Alonnah Tulloch Ford."

"*Tulloch?*" repeated Loni. "I had a grandfather named Tulloch. But I never met him."

Maddy continued to peruse the envelope. "The name isn't the only unusual thing," she said.

"What else then?"

"This letter was mailed from Scotland."

"*Scotland!* Must be something to do with the November conference. Open it and see what it says."

"It's addressed to you," said Maddy.

"Just open it!" laughed Loni. "If it's bad news, I prefer to hear it secondhand."

Maddy slit the envelope and pulled out a single sheet of paper. Loni watched as her boss's eyes widened and her eyebrows arched. The next moment she let out a whispered *Whoa!*

"You look like you've seen a ghost," said Loni.

"You'd better sit down for this," rejoined Maddy.

"I *am* sitting down! Tell me what it says."

"Okay, but you're not going to believe it. According to this, some fellow in Scotland died. You've inherited his house."

"You've got to be kidding!"

"That's what it says—actually, this letter calls it a cottage."

Maddy handed back the letter."

Alonnah Tulloch Ford, Loni read.

Dear Miss Ford:

Last year in the small Scottish fishing village of Whales Reef in the Shetland Islands, Mr. Macgregor Tulloch passed away, leaving no will and no immediate family. After an exhaustive search in a difficult and controversial probate, we finally have been able to locate your whereabouts and establish contact with you as the closest living heir to Mr. Tulloch's estate. His holdings are sizable, and the estate includes the Cottage, Mr. Tulloch's lifetime home, as well as most of the acreage and properties of the island of Whales Reef. These will now pass to you.

Unfortunately, time is of the essence in this matter. As it has taken us so long to locate you and, working with attorneys in the U.S., to confirm your identity by certificates of birth and marriage, it is urgent that you sign documents and take possession of the property in person within two weeks. After that time it will pass to the next in line.

If you could email me of your receipt of this letter, and your plans, I would be honoured to establish a time when we could arrange for you to meet me in Lerwick and make plans for you to see the property.

I am,
Sincerely yours,
Jason MacNaughton,
MacNaughton, Dalrymple,
& MacNaughton,
Lerwick, Scotland
U.K.

60

IT'S YOUR DESTINY

Loni laid the paper aside, shaking her head in disbelief. "It must be a mistake," she said. "They've got me confused with someone else. I told you, my grandfather Tulloch died years ago."

"You're obviously connected to *somebody* with that name," said Maddy, pointing to the letter.

"Why have I heard nothing about it till now? My grandfather wasn't even from Scotland. He lived in Philadelphia."

"You should at least notify this man that you received the letter."

"I suppose you're right," said Loni thoughtfully.

Grabbing the letter and envelope, she walked slowly to her office.

She returned half an hour later.

"Thought you'd be interested," she said to Maddy. "I emailed the lawyer. I told him I received his letter but that there must be some mistake. He's already replied back."

"And?" asked Maddy.

"He says I am the one. He says Tulloch was my mother's maiden name, and after they traced her lineage to the U.S., they were led to me. He doesn't say how exactly. He assures me there is no mistake."

"Then congratulations!"

Loni drew in a long breath. "I wrote back a second time and said it was my intention to let the next in line have the inheritance, but that I would give him my final answer within a week." She paused. "What could I possibly want with a cottage in *Scotland?*" she added after a moment.

"Well, it's yours now," Maddy said. "You never told me you had relatives in Scotland."

"I had no idea myself! This is as big a shock to me as to you." Loni shook her head again. "I know virtually nothing about my mother's side of the family. When my grandfather died— my *other* grandfather, Grandfather Tulloch from Philadelphia—everything was secretive. My grandparents went to his house and packed up everything. I was his only relative, so his things came to me. He was in the furniture business too, just like my grandparents—those who raised me, I mean. Though they had had no contact with him, there was nobody else to see to his affairs. What-ever other relatives there might have been on my mother's side, I suppose he lost contact with them."

"What about his wife, your mother's mother?"

"I don't know," Loni answered. "I assume she died before that. I know nothing about her."

"Was anything left to you when he died?" asked Maddy.

"Yes—mostly from the sale of his house. That's how I was able to go to college, where I had the good fortune to meet a certain Madison Swift—"

"Then I am most grateful to him too!"

"—who plucked me out of obscurity at that jobs seminar and set me on the road to fame and fortune!"

"We hope!" laughed Maddy. "Just give me time—I'm working on it."

"You can leave out the fame part!" added Loni.

"So go on with the story about your grandfather . . . or *both* your grandfathers. I have to admit, it is confusing."

"It's confusing to me too," rejoined Loni. "That's why my past has been a mystery. I went through a stage when I even doubted I was a Ford at all. My grandparents' secretiveness didn't help."

"Why were they secretive?"

"I think it had to do with our community. It was very conservative . . . *ultra*-conservative. I suspect my mother may not have been of the same background. Maybe she wasn't a Christian at all, I don't know."

"By the way, does Hugh know you grew up as a Quaker?"

"No. Only you know that. It's not that big a

deal. But it's my own business, and I'd like to keep it that way."

"Fair enough. What about your real middle name . . . is that a secret too?"

"I don't know. I guess not. I just don't use it, that's all. It's Emily."

"Oh, that's nice—Alonnah Emily Ford. I like it."

Again Loni grew reflective.

"Whether it had to do with our community or not," she said, "for whatever reason, my father's marrying my mother must have caused a break between my father and my grandparents. Ninety-nine percent of Quakers are modern and liberal and 'worldly,' as they would say. We were part of the one percent, probably more like a tenth of a percent. If my father left the Fellowship to marry my mother, I suppose that would explain a lot. He would probably have been ostracized. Quakers call it *disownment.* It's basically the same thing as shunning. When my mother and father were killed, my grandparents took me in. The com-munity couldn't very well disown a baby. But this is mostly guesswork, what I've picked up through the years."

"So your grandfather died—your *other* grandfather—and you were able to attend the junior college from what he left you, before you got the university scholarship."

Loni nodded. "My grandparents sold off some

of his tools and furniture. There were a few things of Grandfather Tulloch's that remained shoved in the back of our storeroom that they said belonged to me. They were scrupulous about the money earned from his possessions. It was all saved for me."

"What kind of things were in storage? Maybe there are clues there to where he came from."

"I was young when he died," said Loni, "eleven or twelve, I think . . . maybe thirteen. I wasn't interested. I was plagued by my own issues at the time. It never really registered, *This is my grandfather who just died.* When you're young, you're not thinking about your heritage. I didn't think about the implications. Now I would give any-thing to know more about his side of the family—especially his daughter, my mother."

Loni paused, a faraway expression in her eyes.

"There was one interesting piece," she said, "now that I think about it. Probably two or three years later, my grandfather was talking to some customers. He asked me to go into his store-room and bring out a folding step stool and book ladder he had just finished but hadn't yet oiled and stained. I couldn't find it at first. I wandered deeper into the back of the storeroom. It was mostly full of junk and old lumber. Far at the back were the few things we still had from Grandfather Tulloch—a dresser and a table, boxes, some tools. Then a gorgeous roll-top desk caught my eye—English oak, stained dark. It wasn't tremendously old, probably mid-twentieth century. A small key was protruding from the keyhole. The top wasn't locked. I rolled it up, and a sense of mystery and antiquity swept over me."

"What was inside?" asked Maddy excitedly.

"It was strewn with papers, files, business things mostly, a few books . . . it all looked completely uninteresting to me."

"Did you look at any of it?"

"Not really. A minute later I closed the desk and continued my search for the step stool."

"There may have been clues in those papers. Imagine—old family records!"

"Maybe . . . I don't know."

"Is it still there?"

"I don't know that either," replied Loni. "My grandparents may have sold it by now. I'm sure it would have brought a good price."

"This letter you received could have something to do with all that."

"Maybe. Who knows?" shrugged Loni. "But remember, I hate Scotland. Whatever this so-called cottage is all about, I don't want it. Maddy, you said you were Scottish—I'll give it o you."

"You can't give it to me!"

"Why not?"

"It wouldn't be right."

"Okay then, you said you wanted to go to Scotland—your roots and all that—"

"After the way you described it," laughed Maddy, "I think I've changed my mind!"

"Maybe the weather will be better for you. Think of it as a vacation. You fly over there, sell the place for whatever you can get. What can a cottage out in the middle of nowhere be worth? If some old man lived in it all his life, it's probably falling apart. Whatever you can sell it for, we'll split the proceeds."

"I couldn't do that!" Maddy was laughing and shaking her head. "I'm too busy to take a vacation. And the letter said you have to claim the property *in person* within two weeks. Otherwise it goes to someone else."

"Then whoever they are can have it," said Loni. She crumpled the letter and tossed it into the can beside Maddy's desk. "Whoever's next in line is welcome to it."

Maddy did not reply. She grew thoughtful, then looked deep into Loni's eyes. "Do you remember when I first approached you at that seminar?" she asked. "Do you remember what I told you?"

"How could I forget?" replied Loni. "That day changed my life."

"What did I say?"

"That you felt you and I were to work together, that our meeting was destined, I think you said."

"I meant it. I've never doubted it since. You have become everything I knew you would. And looking back . . . I was just getting started myself. I wasn't much older than you!" Again Maddy paused. "So I am going to tell you something now, Loni, and I mean it as earnestly as I meant what I said back then. I don't think you can take this opportunity lightly. *This* is your destiny now, Loni. You have always said you have no roots. Well, maybe you do. Maybe this is the key to finding them. You have to see this through."

61
DECISION

The letter from Scotland worked on Loni for the rest of the day. So did Maddy's earnest admonition. She made several telephone calls to clients. She set up a meeting at three with a major investment group. She and Maddy were involved for the rest of the afternoon. Throughout it all, however, Loni was distracted.

As she was getting ready to leave for the day, her thoughts flitted to the wastebasket beside Maddy's desk. Maddy had remained behind in the conference room with their clients. Loni went across to Maddy's office and rummaged through the container. Hoping no one would see her, she clutched at the letter she had so unceremoniously wadded up earlier. Quickly she stood and walked out of the office.

She reached home by 7:30 p.m. By then she was obsessed with the letter. By ten o'clock she could think of nothing else. She read it over another four times, trying in vain to torture some meaning from between the lines she hadn't noticed before. But it was no more or less than what it appeared.

An old man in Scotland had died.

She had inherited his house . . . his "cottage."

All the doubts and fears and uncertainties of her childhood rushed back like a flood. She tried to read, tried to watch TV, then finally went to bed. She was still staring at the ceiling at two o'clock.

Maybe the little voice that had spoken from her mirror had been right. Maybe she *didn't* know who she really was.

After a night dozing but occasionally, by five o'clock Loni could stand it no longer.

Thirty minutes later, after a bracing cold shower to jar her senses back to life, and holding a double-shot espresso from her coffee machine, she sat down with a world atlas in her lap to find the Shetlands. There were the Orkney Islands just off the northern tip of Scotland. The west coast of Scotland was filled with dozens of islands of all sizes and shapes, but—

It couldn't be! There were the Shetlands in the middle of the ocean . . . hundreds of miles *farther* north!

"Goodness!" Loni whispered. It was worse than she imagined! The Shetland Islands were halfway to the North Pole!

That confirmed it!

Loni closed the atlas with a renewal of her resolve of the day before. All this fretting was a waste of energy. She had no intention of claiming ownership of a cottage *that* far in the middle of nowhere. Whales Reef, for heaven's sake. Even the name was desolate. It was probably surrounded by icebergs and populated with penguins. Or were penguins in the South Pole? It didn't matter—ice was ice!

It was time to put this cottage business out of her mind for good.

She went to her computer, opened her email, and set her fingers to the keyboard.

Dear Mr. MacNaughton, *she began.*

After a great deal of thought, I have decided—

Loni's hands stilled.

She waited a moment . . . then suddenly she was typing again. The next words that spilled out on her computer screen were not what she had planned.

—that I will make arrangements immediately to fly to Scotland. When I arrive I will decide what to do regarding the inheritance you speak of. I will let you know the details of my itinerary when I have it booked and make arrangements to meet you.

Yours sincerely,
Alonnah Tulloch Ford

Loni leaned back in her chair and read over the brief message again. She paused a few seconds longer before clicking Send.

PART 6

JULY 2006

62

REFLECTIONS ON
A CHERISHED HERITAGE

Whales Reef, Shetland Islands

Only the gravel crunching beneath his feet broke the silence as David Tulloch walked toward the black wrought-iron gate that led into the parish church cemetery of Whales Reef.

He had just returned from Lerwick where he had learned, at long last, the details for the resolution of his uncle's estate. The church was his first stop upon his return.

A crowd was gathered watching for the ferry. He smiled to himself, realizing that word must have leaked out about his errand. If they knew what had taken him into the city, the whole village was probably awaiting his report. He waved to those crowded around the dock. But they would have to wait a few minutes longer. He had to collect his thoughts first.

It was a small church that rose behind him. Constructed of gray stone blocks, it was more imposing vertically than horizontally. The austere Protestant structure had been laid out in the eighteenth century in a plain rectangle without attention to architectural flair. Its four walls gave way to steep slates, which in turn yielded to a narrowing pyramidal steeple that exploded skyward. A simpler yet more dramatically artistic representation of man's quest to reach the Almighty could scarcely be imagined.

In a location such as this, where sea mists, driving rains, and incessant winds were the norm, a steeple must be strongly anchored to keep from being battered to bits. This one was. It had survived, with repairs, for three centuries. Its topmost spire, however, was often shrouded in fog or slanting torrents, thus providing an even more fitting symbol of that unknowable and veiled Presence to whom it pointed. Its disappearance into the nebulous unseen heavens, even if only fifty feet above the ground, created a numinous aura of mystery in keeping with its avowed purpose.

The cemetery gate creaked on rusting hinges and swung open to David's touch. He passed into the ancient graveyard. The cemetery had been here longer than the present church building.

David made his way through the maze of stones and finally slowed in front of an irregular array of markers, headstones, and slabs representing the patrimony of the proud family name of Tulloch.

The shadow of the steeple tip fell fittingly

across a large marble stone, the centerpiece of the family plot. He looked down and read the name familiar to all islanders: *Ernest Tulloch, 1875–1953*. The man known as "the Auld Tulloch" was the last to claim possession of both titles, laird and chief.

David's eyes drifted to his right and left. Heedless of the significance of steeple and its shadow—pointing at once to the heavens above whence came life and to the ground where all earthly lives reached their final end—he took in the names upon each of a half-dozen moss-encrusted stone markers.

To the right of Ernest was buried his first wife, Elizabeth Clark, 1880–1904. Nearby, Wallace Tulloch, 1902–1976, the second son who had inherited the lairdship in place of his elder brother, had been laid to rest with his family to Elizabeth's right.

A short distance away rose a smaller stone for the younger sister, the Auld Tulloch's third born, Delynn Tulloch, 1904–1977, buried beside her husband, the daughter through whom her great-grandson Hardar Tulloch had based his recent legal claim as the rightful Tulloch heir.

David's reflections now wandered further and came to rest upon the marker of his own great-grandfather Leith Tulloch, 1909–1983, the Auld Tulloch's youngest and last born to whom the chieftainship had been bestowed, son of Ernest's second wife, Sally Lipscomb, 1885–1977, who rested to the old man's left.

Of the Auld Tulloch's four children, the name of his eldest, Brogan, was conspicuously missing from this final silent family gathering.

The newest grave behind the church belonged to Wallace's son, David's own great-uncle Macgregor Tulloch, gone from the earth less than a year.

Beside and around the stones that had first commanded his attention, spread out behind the church, David now glanced about the cemetery where the names of other Tullochs, and MacDonalds before them, were gathered as silent witnesses to a storied past with origins on the mainland of Scotland and on Shetland itself.

It was indeed a proud family history and tradition, though the fissure that had occurred in the family early in the last century remained an unresolved puzzle.

Already the sundial of the steeple moved on. Its shadow slowly rose in the sun's descending arc. It pointed now to no Tulloch. Time and destinies, fortunes and ancestries, moved on as inexorably as the sun crossing the heavens. The outline of the spire would continue to move throughout the afternoon and into the evening. In another hour it would cast its shadow upon the rock wall at the back of the churchyard. And still it would creep forward, lengthening like time itself, inching farther and farther, until suddenly in a moment it would leap the wall and be gone, the point of its silhouette disappearing into the great beyond.

Perhaps the shadow of the spire told the story of the Tulloch legacy on Whales Reef. Had the season of Tullochs come to an end? The sundial had pointed briefly to their names just as fortune had smiled on their lives.

But the dial moved on. It pointed now far away, to one yet unknown to the islanders of Whales Reef upon whom the birthright had now come to rest.

David drew in a sigh and glanced around him one last time. The dynasty of his branch of the family seemed about to end. Another era had dawned. The new laird of Whales Reef would be no Tulloch at all, nor a Shetlander.

Not even a Scot.

Not even British.

Ever since his boyhood encounter with the self-proclaimed prophetess Sister Grace, David had struggled to rid himself of antipathy toward Americans. All the youthful emotions stirred up by those days seemed determined to rise again. Was history destined to repeat itself? Was another outsider—yet another American who knew nothing of the island's history and heritage and cared nothing for its people—about to bring unwanted changes to this island?

What would the future bring to Whales Reef? And to him?

Only a moment more he stood. He had to come here first, to connect with his past, his roots, his forebears. He had needed to sense their presence as he readied to hand over their legacy to another.

But right now the villagers were waiting for him.

63

BRUSQUE INTERRUPTION

Washington, D.C.

Morning in the U.S. capital was just revving up to full speed. Though her own encouragement had tipped the scales toward Loni's decision to fly to Scotland, Madison Swift was already missing her assistant. And it was only Loni's first day out of the office! What would she do for the *next* five days? *Hire a temp,* Maddy wondered. But arranging for one would take time she could ill afford.

A loud voice in the outer offices interrupted Maddy's thoughts.

A few seconds later her door flew open, and heavy booted steps echoed across the floor. "Hey, little lady!" boomed a grating western drawl, "you the gal called Swift?"

Maddy looked up to see a giant of a man staring down at her. He was the perfect caricature of a bigger-than-life Texan. He looked more like oil than cows, with a huge white cowboy hat and string tie to go with the size thirteen boots.

"I am Madison Swift," said Maddy. "And you would be—?"

"McLeod, ma'am. Jimmy Joe McLeod."

"Do you have an appointment, Mr. McLeod? I don't seem to recall—"

"Nope, no appointment. Sorry for barging in like this, but I got business that can't wait. I'm looking for a filly goes by the name of Ford. Didn't catch the first name. But they told me you and she's tighter'n a couple—" He stopped abruptly and let his eyes drift over Maddy for a second. "Say, you and she ain't a couple of them *modern* city women, if you get my drift?"

Swallowing her indignation at the blustering lout's manner, Maddy struggled to preserve her calm. "I don't see that that is any of your business, Mr. McLeod," she said, rising and standing behind her desk.

"Ain't no never-mind to me. Heck, to each his own, I say. But I gotta find this gal Ford."

"Miss Ford is my assistant," said Maddy. "She is not here."

"Where is she then?"

"Out of town."

"Dang! I gotta find her. Just tell me how I can get in touch with her then."

"Look, Mr. McLeod—I don't know you. I've never seen you before. You come storming in here without the courtesy of a knock and interrupt my work. Then you expect me to divulge information—"

"Hey, whoa . . . back up a piece, little lady. Put that six-gun of yours in its holster."

Maddy's eyes flashed. "I'm not your little lady," she shot back. "Now I am going to ask you calmly to leave my office before I have to call building security."

"Whoa—you are a feisty one!" said McLeod, grinning as he looked down on Maddy's five-foot-two frame. "No need to get riled up. Just tell me where Ford has gone."

"Overseas," replied Maddy. "Her plane left an hour ago."

McLeod swore loudly. He thought a moment. "Where's she off to? You got the name of her hotel?" he added.

"You'll get nothing further from me. Now, do I have to call security?"

"Forget it, *Ms.* Swift," said McLeod, swinging off his hat and taking a low bow. "If she ain't here, I got no more reason to hang around. Much obliged."

Smoke coming out her ears, Maddy stared after the Texan while he departed as unceremoniously as he had come.

64
THE WAIT IS OVER

Whales Reef, Shetland Islands

David left the churchyard and walked downhill toward the village. As he went, he reflected on the day's events, thinking what he would say to the friends, relatives, and lifetime acquaintances awaiting him.

In their telephone conversation that followed Jason's brief letter of a week earlier, David had learned of the discovery of a third potential heir to Macgregor Tulloch's estate. The whole village had been shocked by the news he had relayed that neither himself *nor* Hardy Tulloch was rightful heir to Macgregor Tulloch's estate.

A closer descendent to the Auld Tulloch had been located . . . in America. Suddenly from out of the past rose renewed speculation and gossip. The oldest villagers had not forgotten old Ernest's eldest son who had gone to America. A multitude of stories erupted anew, not only about the long-lost son but bringing in their wake speculation about old Macgregor and his ill-fated Norwegian wife, whose body, the more sinister of the gossips insisted, still lay in the laird's sealed study—murdered by Macgregor himself.

The island had been in a tumult of expectation ever since. Much, however, still remained in doubt. David assured them that it was unknown whether the mysterious American would claim the inheritance in time. If not, the estate might yet go to the next heir in line. Who that next heir in line might be was not yet disclosed. The controversy erupted all over again: Would the next in line be David or Hardy?

At last definite word had come. Jason had telephoned David at the Auld Hoose yesterday evening. He had stopped at the Whales Fin Inn on his way to mainland Shetland earlier that same morning. He told Keith, Evanna, and Audney that the family solicitor in Lerwick had called and that he was on his way to the city, at long last, to learn the final disposition of the estate.

David had expected his day's plans to remain between himself and the three Kerrs. He scarcely took note of several fishermen at a table across the pub, or the interest with which their ears perked up as he had spoken with Keith.

As a result, Grizel Gordon got wind of it from her husband, Tevis, who heard from Noak Muir, who had himself overheard the conversation with Keith.

At this point everything was hearsay. That fact, however, did not stop Grizel from theorizing as fast as her tongue could wag.

Within five minutes she was talking Coira MacNeill's ear off in the bakery. The inevitable wind of news quickly spread to David's aunt Rinda Gunn. Within half an hour, as Grizel Gordon fairly flew about the village with her tongue on fire, *everyone* knew.

By all calculations—figuring David to be three hours ferrying both ways and driving to and from Lerwick, accounting for at least an hour in the city—the soonest, said Rinda, that he could return would be on the two o'clock ferry. Two or three dozen watchers were therefore on hand as the small diesel craft chugged toward shore a little before the hour.

But David was not to be seen.

By three o'clock the crowd awaiting the ferry had doubled.

Again they were disappointed.

At four o'clock, the entire village was out. Eager watchers lined the streets and lanes of Whales Reef. Even before the ferry docked, word raced from the crowd at the landing into the village that David's car was on board.

The chief had returned!

The watchers were quickly disappointed, however. David drove off the wooden dock, waved to the crowd, and continued up the hill to the church. Curious and anxious, they had no choice but to keep waiting.

Twenty minutes later they saw David, his car

still at the church, walking back down the hill. By then most of Whales Reef was congregated between the town square and the hotel.

David made his way into the village. The throng drifted along with him. For as many as were out, it remained surprisingly quiet.

David nodded to the villagers as he moved along the main street. The expression in his eyes, most said to themselves, did not bode well. Ever since the old laird's death they had worried about the consequences of a Hardy Tulloch lairdship. All at once an alternative loomed on the horizon that was entirely unpredictable.

Would an unknown American perhaps prove worse than Hardy? The truth in the old adage *Better the devil you know than the devil you don't* suddenly cast Hardy in a new light.

For Hardy's part, ever since news of the American began spreading through the village he had prowled around like a roaring lion vowing to fight the thing in court. He blamed David for ruining his chances. His exact reasoning remained uncertain, for if that were the case, in so doing David had apparently spoiled his own chances as well.

Whatever news David had for them, at least the wait was over. They would finally *know*. Would or would not the American accept the inheritance and become their new laird? That was the question on the minds of every man and woman in Whales Reef.

65

FIRST CLASS AND PRONTO

Washington, D.C.

"Hey, darlin', how you doing today?" boomed a loud voice in the line.

The ticket agent adjusted her earpiece.

"Just fine, sir. Where is it you're interested in flying?"

"Aberdeen."

"And flying from?"

"D.C., darlin' . . . Washington."

"And that would be Aberdeen, South Dakota?"

"I'm in oil, all right!" exclaimed her customer. "I know there's talk of drilling up north there, but take it from me, they ain't going to find nothing. No, I ain't headed to the Dakotas. My line of work is the real thing—Aberdeen, darlin' . . . *Scotland*."

"And when would you be traveling, sir?"

"Soon as I can. Right now. You gotta get me on something *today*. Got my own jet, but the engine's in for its million-mile checkup. You know, lube and oil, check the tires. The FAA boys are sticklers for that sort of thing. Came up to D.C. commercial. Wasn't planning nothin' overseas. But something's come up and I gotta get myself to Scotland."

"I don't know that we will have anything available on such short notice . . . I will check for you."

"And first class, darlin'. Gotta be first class. Don't care which airline, don't care if you gotta route me outta New York or Jersey or Atlanta or wherever. Don't care what it costs. I'm in D.C. now and I gotta get there any way I can. Like I say, first class and pronto!"

"I'll check all those possibilities. If you can just give me a minute . . ."

The line was silent for a couple of minutes.

"I don't find anything at all today, sir," said the agent at length.

"Dang! Pardon my French, darlin', I know you're doing your best. What do you got then?"

"There's a red-eye out of D.C. to Atlanta tonight. Then tomorrow British Airways has an afternoon flight into Heathrow with one seat left in first class. You would then connect to a flight arriving to Aberdeen early in the afternoon. That would be the day after tomorrow."

"That's the quickest you got?"

"Yes, sir."

"Then book it."

66

FLURRY OF NEW UNCERTAINTY

Whales Reef, Shetland Islands

David walked to the center of the square. Slowly the expectant and restless crowd closed in around him. Like a flock of geese descending onto an open field settling its feathers into silence, all murmuring ceased.

A stone bench sat at the base of the square's monument. David climbed up, stood on it, and glanced about. Every eye was upon him. He drew in a deep breath.

"Our new laird is on the way," he said.

A noisy rustling of feathers flitted through the gathered flock.

"On the way tae do what, David?" called out David's uncle Fergus Gunn from near the front.

More questions came firing at David in rapid succession.

"Is he or isna he goin' tae claim the inheritance?" asked David's cousin Murdoc MacBean.

"We heard he wasna keen on it," chimed in Noak Muir.

Gradually silence settled. "Our solicitor will

meet with the heir," David replied. "Papers must be signed before anything is official. But whatever happens we must make the best of it and prepare to welcome Macgregor Tulloch's rightful heir."

A great hubbub broke out.

"I'll no welcome him!" called out Tevis Gordon, whose wife beside him was more responsible than anyone for the size of the crowd.

More shouts, loud comments, and angry discussion drowned out whatever else David might have had to say. A dozen men voiced their vigorous assent to Tevis's sentiment.

Slowly a smile came to David's lips. He realized that he had neglected to reveal the most significant aspect of what he had learned in Lerwick. A few noticed his expression and quieted. David waited.

"There is one further piece of information you should know," he said. He paused and waited for complete silence. "Not only is our new laird an American, she is a woman."

"Oor new laird's a lassie!" cried Keith Kerr.

A furious protest exploded. If David had more to say, it was impossible now. Whether one or two of the women of the village might have been sufficiently modern in outlook to greet the news with rejoicing, their reaction could not have been discerned from the outcry against the news.

"A *woman* canna inherit," objected Tevis Gordon. "If they could, then wouldna Hardy's claim hae been first in line fae the start on account o' the Auld Tulloch's daughter?"

Voices all around chimed in their agreement. As traditionally minded as their husbands, women clamored just as loudly to be heard. The very idea of a *woman* inheriting the estate of Macgregor Tulloch was an outrage to the sensibilities of nearly everyone on the island.

"It's no mistake, Tevis," said David. "This is the twenty-first century—even on the Shetlands. Women are equal to men these days. Women are working on the oil rigs too."

The discontented murmurings continued. David stood patiently while the islanders gave vent to their aggrieved sense of injustice. The idea of calling a woman "laird" was inconceivable to them.

"Who is it, David?" shouted Rinda Gunn. "What right's she got tae be inheritin'?"

David waited until he could be heard.

"According to our solicitors," he replied, "I believe she is involved in investments."

"A banker!" said Rinda in a huff.

"I don't know."

"What will she do, David?"

"Our solicitor believes she may simply sell the laird's cottage and the rest of the property and return to America."

"What will become o' the lairdship then, David?" asked Fergus.

Gradually the seriousness of what was at stake began to dawn on David's listeners.

"That I cannot say," replied the man they looked to as their chief now more than ever. "It may be that the lairdship as we have known it will be a thing of the past," he added quietly.

David drew in a long breath. The crowd had at last been stunned into silence. This was not the response they wanted from the chief of their clan.

"It seems possible," David went on, "that the village and land, and perhaps your homes, could be sold. I will do all I can to persuade her to offer them to you first. Many of you have been worried that Hardy would do exactly that if he became laird. So things may turn out just as you expected. And look at the bright side," he added enthusi-astically, "it's possible the outcome may prove better than you thought."

"Hoo could that be, David?" chimed in a voice from the back. "It disna seem likely."

"It's no secret that there was considerable worry about what Hardy might do. I am only emphasizing it is pointless to worry until we know more for certain."

"What aboot the factory?" asked MacBean.

"It's too soon to say, Murdoc," replied David. "If she is not interested in continuing its opera-tion, the factory may be sold as well. But there is no reason we cannot buy it ourselves and continue as always. Community-owned businesses are very common these days. You would all have a share in the ownership of the Mill. You would be your own bosses, and I would contribute as well. Rest assured that whatever happens, I promise I will do all that lies in my power to preserve Whales Reef and our way of life."

David paused briefly. Every eye rested on him. "Truthfully," he continued, "I cannot keep the new laird from selling portions of the island. Hopefully that will not happen. However, if it should prove impossible to buy the factory building, with your help we will continue operations at the Auld Hoose. We can remodel my barns and transfer the wool factory there. As long as I have breath, and as long as the Auld Hoose and its property remain mine, not a one of you will lose your jobs. We will survive as we always have."

A great cheer went up for their chief. No matter what the future brought, in spite of Rinda Gunn's private grumblings to her nephew, most of the islanders knew that David would stand with them, even if it meant going down with them on a sinking ship.

"Is she a Tulloch?" asked Gordon's wife.

"She obviously has Tulloch blood in her veins, Grizel," said David. "But she is not a Tulloch in name."

"Then who *is* she?" repeated Rinda Gunn. "I'm askin' ye again, David! Hoo can she inherit if she's no Tulloch?"

"She is Macgregor Tulloch's legal heir," replied David, "the great-great-granddaughter of the Auld Tulloch through his eldest son, just as Hardy and I are his great-great-grandsons. She is a distant cousin that no one knew about. That's all I know."

"That canna be," objected Rinda's husband, as much of a local genealogist as the island possessed. "He was disinherited."

"That's only been a rumor all these years. But there's no evidence that it is actually true."

"Who's next in line after her then?" asked Rinda, "if she doesna take up the lairdship?"

"I don't know, Auntie. The court's full findings were not confided to me. If the woman claims the inheritance, it will not matter."

"Will ye meet her yersel', David?" Fergus put in. "Will ye offer her yer hand? I'm wantin' tae ken on account o' the rest o' us will want tae ken hoo ye'd hae us carry oorsel's."

"You all are to be no more nor less than you've always been to me—a friend and a neighbor. If she's your laird, then I would have you treat her with the respect due her position. She's got our blood, Tulloch blood, in her veins. She may be an American, but she's one of us."

David's last words were difficult for him to get

out and even more difficult for his listeners to hear. He had been thinking of exactly that quandary all the way back from Lerwick: Should he greet her upon her arrival and give her a royal welcome from the chief?

Whenever he thought about the American woman whom fate had appointed for him soon to meet, however, the face that rose in his mind's eye was that of the strange woman from America who had left their community in disarray so many years ago. He would sooner extend his hand to a rattlesnake than welcome Sister Grace back to Whales Reef! He had to keep reminding himself that Macgregor Tulloch's heir was *not* Sister Grace.

"Can ye fight it, David?" said Coira into the lull that had followed David's last words.

"I cannot speak for Hardy," replied David. "There's word that he's considering it. Speaking for myself, I have no desire to win an inheritance from a lawsuit. We must abide by the law."

"When's she comin', David?" asked Keith. "When will we ken mair o' what she intends?"

"A few days . . . possibly a week. I don't know exactly."

Though there was no more information to be had beyond what David had already furnished, the clamorous discussion went on for the rest of the afternoon. As teatime approached, the crowd gradually thinned. One, now another, then by twos and threes, they slowly drifted off in the direction of their homes.

By degrees the square emptied. Those disinclined to cease voicing their disgruntled complaints moved in the direction of the hotel.

David remained in the village, moving between square and pub, continuing to calm the people as best he could, allowing his smile and laughter and reassuring words to do their work.

By seven o'clock, Keith, Evanna, and Audney were doing a brisk trade in beer and ale. The pub remained crowded all evening. Dozens of separate and heated conversations continued until midnight.

The one man conspicuously missing from all of the hubbub in the town square and the pub was Hardy Tulloch.

67

UNSATISFYING DEPARTURE

Washington, D.C.

For the second time in less than a year, Alonnah Ford stared out the window of a 747 at the Atlantic, flying into an unknown as wide as the ocean below her.

She had hoped to tell Hugh everything, quietly and leisurely. But things had happened so fast. Their lunch two days ago hadn't exactly been the ideal environment.

"Hugh," she had said, "something's come up—I need to go back to Scotland."

"Scotland!" He laughed around his first bite. "I thought you hated it there."

"I thought I did too, but—"

"When are you going to stop letting Maddy run your life?" Hugh had interrupted. "If you don't want to go, just tell her."

Loni made a mental note: *Add to Husband List—Doesn't interrupt.*

"She's my boss, Hugh," she said. "You do what Congressman Finney tells you. Why shouldn't I do what Maddy wants me to do? Besides, this has nothing to do with Maddy. It's personal."

"What is it, then?"

"I told you, something's come up. I wasn't going to pursue it at first, but Maddy encouraged me to. She said it was my destiny."

"Your *destiny?* That sounds pretty mystical. What's going on, Loni?"

"Actually, I've come into an inheritance . . . in Scotland."

Hugh stared across the table. "An inheritance?" he repeated.

Loni smiled sheepishly.

"What kind of inheritance? Is it sizable? Is it something we can access quickly?"

Hugh's *we* did not go unnoticed. Loni tucked it away but offered no comment.

"I don't know . . . to all of the above," she said slowly. "Apparently it's a cottage and some land that goes with it. I know nothing more than that."

"What's it about—a long-lost relative or something?"

"More or less."

"Why did you never tell me about all this?"

"I knew nothing about it myself until a few days ago."

"How long will you be gone? I mean . . . you're not moving there!"

"Of course not," said Loni with a chuckle. "I just need to sign some papers and arrange for the place to be sold. A few days at the most."

"That's a relief! So . . . cheers and congratulations and all that, I suppose."

Even as he was speaking, the chime of his cell phone interrupted them. Hugh snatched it out of his pocket. "Oh, just a minute," he said to Loni. "It's the Speaker's chief of staff. I need a minute with her."

He jumped up from the table and hurried away.

Loni's gaze followed him across the room. *I really wanted to talk about this!* she thought to herself. However, the subject did not arise again when Hugh returned. She did not force it.

She had hoped for time at the airport to talk further. She wanted to show Hugh the letter from the solicitor, share her thoughts, maybe get his advice. If they had a future together, this sudden change in her personal fortune had implications for his life as well as hers. This was her *life,* not a mere distraction.

She hoped they might have a cup of coffee inside together and chat without interruption. She was taken off guard when Hugh dropped her off at the curb.

"Where will you be staying?" he asked as he pulled out her suitcase and set it on the sidewalk. "Hilton, Radisson, Marriott?"

"I doubt those chains exist where I'm going, Hugh," said Loni. "The letter called it a small fishing village."

"Sounds awful! The smell of fish everywhere! What's it called?"

"Whales Reef."

"Ah . . . quaint. Well, I have a lunch meeting in town. Have a great time. Hurry back. I'll miss you."

Hugh planted a kiss on her lips, then hurried back to his car and drove away. With mixed feelings Loni stood on the sidewalk outside Departures and watched Hugh's car disappear into the airport traffic. *Not much of a sendoff as I sail to meet my destiny,* she thought to herself.

When she turned to walk into the terminal, a sense of adventure gradually stole over her. She could not help being nervous, yet excited at the same time. It was exactly how she had felt when leaving for college. That opportunity had been provided by an inheritance from the mysterious Grandfather Tulloch.

Suddenly another inheritance from the same side of the family had landed in her lap, with shadows surrounding it of unknown family roots in Scotland.

She had grown since leaving home. She had launched out into the business world and was doing okay for herself. Yes, that previous adventure into the unknown had turned out well.

Perhaps this one would too.

68
HEALING TEARS

Eastern Pennsylvania

Loni's flight would take her to Amsterdam—
where she would set eyes on continental Europe
for the first time—then to Aberdeen, farther north
in Scotland than she had been the previous
November. She would spend the night in the
northern oil capital of Britain before flying two
hundred miles still farther over the North Sea to
the Shetland Islands. There, as Maddy had said,
her destiny awaited.

She had not written in her journal for months.
But on this occasion the book of personal reflections was no afterthought. It was the first item
she packed. Even as the plane banked upward
away from the eastern seaboard, she took it out
and set it in her lap.

Two hours later, however, she still had not
written a word.

On the day of her last entry, she had been
returning from Gleneagles, vowing never to set
foot in Scotland again. Now she was on her
way back, under the most different circumstances
imaginable. The confusion and uncertainty about

her past had suddenly been replaced by a new uncertainty about her future.

Now her past *was* her future. Maybe *that* summed up the adventure!

It was a future bound up in a mysterious past revolving around the name *Tulloch*. The classic movies about time travel were not entirely fanciful. It really was possible to go *back to the future.* She was doing so herself. That's exactly what this flight over the Atlantic was. To discover her future meant uncovering a past she never knew existed.

Thoughts of her past had always revolved around her childhood with her grandparents. Suddenly a great unknown world yawned behind those memories—a world stretching back in time to a distant heritage. Her genealogy was leading her across the sea to unfamiliar places with strange names and people she had never heard of. It was the lineage neither of Alonnah Ford nor Loni Ford, not even of Alonnah Emily Ford, but of the unknown Alonnah *Tulloch* Ford.

Who was this unfamiliar young woman with the strange name who had risen to dominate her life, this Alonnah Emily Tulloch Ford?

Who was "Loni" now?

She thought back to her visit to see her grandparents a few days earlier. The letter from Scotland had opened great reservoirs of love for them. All at once it came gushing into her heart. She truly *loved* them!

Whatever she might learn about her heritage, it was part of *their* story too. If her mother was indeed of Scottish descent, their son had married into the Tulloch clan. This was their destiny as well as hers.

It had been a good visit, thought Loni. She was seeing her grandparents through different eyes. Loni smiled. Maybe she was finally growing up.

At last she set her pen to the next page of her journal and entered the date.

Who are you, girl? she found herself writing. *Are you Alonnah . . . or Loni . . . or someone you don't even know . . . someone you are about to meet?*

Her pen stilled as thoughts, emotions, images, faces, and memories flooded into her mind. Her grandmother's face had brightened when she opened the door four days ago just as it had in June.

"Goodness gracious!" Mrs. Ford had exclaimed. "Two visits in less than a month!"

"Hello, Grandma," Loni said with a smile. "Yes, I know. Surprise again!"

Hearing Loni's car drive up, her grandfather hurried toward the porch from his workshop. He embraced Loni in a great hug. "What is the occasion, Alonnah?" A serious expression spread across his face. "Nothing wrong, I hope?"

"No, I'm fine. Actually . . . I have some news, something I wanted to tell you personally."

"Come inside!" said her grandfather.

"Have you come to tell us you are engaged to that young man of yours?" asked Mrs. Ford as they made their way into the living room. "What was his name again?"

"Hugh," laughed Loni. "No, Hugh and I are not engaged." She took a chair opposite her grandparents on the sofa and pulled out the folded letter from Jason MacNaughton. "Something's come up. Something that will probably change my life." She paused, still holding the letter. "I received this a few days ago. It concerns my mother—well, indirectly I suppose you would say—and therefore, though even more indirectly, my father . . . your son, Chad."

Mr. and Mrs. Ford glanced back and forth at each other as Loni stood and handed the letter to her grandfather. She resumed her seat while her grandparents read it together.

After a few moments they both looked up with expressions of astonishment.

"What a shock!" said Mr. Ford. "I hardly know what to say."

"Do you know anything about it?" asked Loni.

"What do you mean?" he asked.

"Were you aware of these family connections to Scotland . . . my mother . . . have you ever heard of this man Macgregor Tulloch? Did you have an inkling of any such possibility?"

"No, nothing," answered Mr. Ford. "Only that this is the name of your grandfather Tulloch who died in Philadelphia when you were thirteen—Alison's father. We never knew anything about his past, or hers. Chad told us nothing about Alison."

He paused and blinked a few times. A grief-stricken expression came over his face. Loni had never seen such emotion on his face.

"We didn't give him the chance," her grandfather went on. "We regret that now of course. We regret many things. We were so caught up with the Fellowship having to remain pure, not mixing with worldly Christians, odd as it seems now, especially not with liberal Quakers. Our exclusivity blinded us to more important things." He looked away, dabbing at his eyes.

"That isn't all of the story, William," said Mrs. Ford. "Chad cut off communication with us when he met Alison. He didn't give *us* the chance to see how we might have been able to work through it. We didn't hear from him for four years."

"I know," said her husband. "There was blame on both sides. There always is. But had we been more open, perhaps he would not have felt the need to cut off contact with us. But I take much of the responsibility on my shoulders. It is a grief I have to bear."

Loni listened in silence, embarrassed to hear such a personal outpouring from the grandfather who had always seemed so stoic in her eyes.

A lengthy silence filled the room.

"I suppose I have been guilty of the same thing," said Loni, "distancing myself from the two of you, turning away from the Quaker heritage you raised me in. I am sorry for that."

Loni's honesty was unexpected. It caught her grandparents off guard.

"I am so grateful for the training you gave me," Loni went on. "I am appreciative that you took me in and cared for me, and for all the ways you loved me. You were the best grandparents a girl could have. I love you both so much."

She rose and went to them. They made room for her between them on the worn and familiar couch. She embraced both in turn.

"I love you, Grandpa," she said, leaning against his chest. "I am sorry for the pain I've caused you."

He stroked her hair but could say nothing. His eyes were full.

A minute later Loni turned and stretched her arm around her grandmother. "I'm sorry, Grandma . . . I love you."

"Oh, sweetheart!" began Mrs. Ford. She could say no more for her quiet weeping.

69

THE LETTER BOX

When the emotion had passed, all three wiping at their eyes, Loni resumed her place across the room.

"Do you still have any of Grandfather Tulloch's things?" she asked after a minute. "I remember some of them in the storeroom in the old barn, Grandpa. Is it possible something of my mother's could be there too?"

"I doubt it, dear," replied Mr. Ford. "But whatever we have is still there just as you remember it. I've not looked at it in years. You are welcome to whatever you can find."

"Is that roll-top desk still there?" asked Loni. "I remember it having some papers and things."

Mr. Ford nodded. "It's there. All the way in back along with decades of junk and leftover bits from the business."

"Would you mind if I had a look?"

"Of course not. It's yours," said Mr. Ford. "Your grandfather Tulloch's things belong to you, and anything of ours you would like as well."

"There is still some money in the account too, which we set up for the sale of your grandfather's things," added Loni's grandmother. "It's only a few hundred dollars. Most of it, of course, went to your college. We should get the last of it transferred into your name once and for all."

"I'm not worried about that," said Loni. "But I would like to look through the desk."

She and her grandfather rose.

"I'll put out some tea and a plate of cookies," said Mrs. Ford as the two headed for the door. "Hot chocolate for you, Alonnah?"

"Sounds great—with a dollop of whipped cream like you used to make it for me. I don't ever want to be skinny again!" she added with a laugh.

"I have some in the fridge. You'll stay for supper and the night?"

"Thank you, Grandma," replied Loni, turning back with a smile. "I would like that."

Mr. Ford and Loni made their way to the huge barn that had long ago been converted into his woodworking shop and storage warehouse. Sights and smells assaulted Loni's senses with delicious nostalgia: wood, dirt, tools, oil, sawdust, varnish, diesel, the ancient broken-down John Deere tractor, even faint reminders of straw and hay from a time long past when the barn had housed cows rather than furniture. Every inch filled her with memories of her years growing up here. Her grandfather's hands dark with stain and oil as he restored a vintage antique, the happy summers working together in the showroom—these were some of the fondest memories of her youth.

She followed her grandfather deep into the recesses of the barn as he pulled one chain after another dangling from bulbs high overhead. Each new burst of light revealed open beams and rafters from which hung a century's accumulation of dusty cobwebs. Winding through boxes and stacks of boards and plywood and wood scraps, they reached the farthest end of the building. In the corner Loni saw the old desk exactly as she remembered it.

There was the key still protruding from the lock at the base of the roll-top.

"Here it is," said her grandfather. "Wherever it came from—I place it as American, not very old judging from the brass fittings—probably 1950s. It is yours, Alonnah. I've never even looked inside it since the day we brought it here. Frankly, I had all but forgotten it."

Loni slowly turned the key and rolled up the top. It slid as effortlessly as if it had been constructed the day before. *What craftsmanship!* she thought with a smile.

"I'm sure you want to be alone with your thoughts," said her grandfather, turning back the way they had come. "I will leave you to see what you can discover."

Loni stood for a long moment gazing down at the desk. It was cluttered with papers, files, a few books, odds and ends of assorted junk. It mostly appeared uninteresting and valueless—receipts, invoices, orders for furniture, small bills. Cubby-holes and drawers were stuffed with pencils, pens, half-used rolls of masking tape, nails and screws, containers of dried glue and ink, fasteners, old batteries, reading glasses, a few coins, a magnifying glass, small tools, pocket knives, rulers, tape measures, sketches of furniture, scissors, and decades of accumulated miscellany. A small can of marbles was shoved to the back of one drawer. Loni ran her fingers through them with a smile. Were these from her grandfather's boyhood?

One by one she opened the small drawers of the upper desk, then the large lower drawers to the right and left. Nothing attracted her eye that seemed likely to shed light on her mother's family or her grandfather Tulloch other than a myriad details of his business. The most interesting discovery was a box of business cards that read *Tulloch Fine Furnishings and Antiques—Old World Craftsmanship with Modern Functionality: Grant Tulloch, Philadelphia, Pennsylvania.*

How interesting that both her grandfathers spent their lives in the same business. She took one from the box and placed it in her pocket.

Loni continued to explore the cubbyholes and drawers for anything she might have missed, taking care to pull the large drawers all the way out so that she could probe to the back of each one.

In the middle drawer of the left side she discovered a sheaf of tax filings and legal-size letters and envelopes. That might be interesting, she thought, to learn more about her grandfather's business.

She continued to rummage about, moving again to the drawers on the right. Reaching the bottom drawer a second time, she pulled it completely out. Behind more piles of folders and business invoices, she caught a glimpse of a partially buried black wooden box with papers strewn over the top of it. She reached in, removed a handful of papers, then took out the box. It measured about eight-by-ten inches and some three inches high. A tiny key was inserted into the lock on the front of the lid.

A tingle surged through her. Whatever was inside this box, she sensed she had discovered something important.

Hurriedly, she cleared away the desktop, set the box on it, then slowly turned the key. A tiny click sounded as the lock gave way. She lifted the lid.

An audible gasp of astonishment escaped her lips.

The box was full of letters! Beside them lay an unusual necklace with small stones hanging from one another and a locket beneath them, all suspended from a gold chain. The stones were clearly valuable. She reached in and lifted it out, examining each of the delicate fittings. With her fingernails she carefully unclasped the locket.

She gasped again as her eyes fell on the tiniest photograph possible, faded with time, of a young woman's face. Her heart was pounding. She stared at it for several long seconds as if being drawn back in time . . . through years, through decades, perhaps even more. Was she imagining it or did the features of the unknown face bear a faint resemblance to her own?

Fingers trembling, she closed the locket, held the necklace of intricate design in the palm of her hand a few seconds longer, then turned again to the open box in front of her.

The letters now drew her attention.

The envelopes were obviously old, the paper yellow and faded.

Setting the necklace aside, with a reverent hand quivering again with anticipation, she lifted the top letter from the stack. The name on the front of the envelope, in faded black ink, penned by an unmistakably masculine hand, read *Emily Hanson.*

She caught her breath at the words.

Emily . . . her own name! The envelope was postmarked from Scotland.

But Emily *Hanson* . . . who could it be?

Loni opened the envelope and withdrew two sheets from inside. On the top was written the date 1924.

Dear Emily, she read.

It has now been a month—

Loni stopped. Still holding the sheets of the letter, she closed her eyes and took a deep breath.

She could not read further. This private and intimate correspondence had not been meant for her eyes. If a time came when she felt it appropriate to read them, she would do so . . . but not today.

She folded the letter and replaced it in the envelope.

A book lay beneath the stack of letters. She could see the edge of its brown cover. Something else was underneath that too. She had heard it jostling about at the bottom. Whatever else besides letters this box contained, however, and whatever secrets they possessed, they would have to wait. She set the stack of letters back inside.

Keeping out only the necklace for now, she closed and locked the box, then removed the tiny key from the lid.

Carrying several books and the locked letter box, with the necklace safely tucked inside a handkerchief in her pocket, she had left the barn and returned to her grandparents.

A flight attendant brought Loni's thoughts back to the present.

"Miss Ford, is it?" she said.

Loni nodded.

"I have your vegetarian meal."

"Oh . . . thank you." Loni glanced down at her

journal, put her pen away, and closed the book.

The letter box from the roll-top desk was in her carry-on. The few books she had brought from the desk were packed in her suitcase. She had looked at neither since leaving her grandparents. For now, books and box remained veiled treasures whose secrets awaited discovery.

Unconsciously her fingers went to the tiny key she had slipped onto a chain that now hung from her neck.

She was waiting for the right time to turn that key again in the tiny brass lock. When that day came, then she would delve more deeply into the secrets of the letter box. If the letters indeed held answers, she needed to read them in peace and quiet. If her heritage led to Scotland, then in Scotland she would explore what further revelations the box had to disclose.

The rest of the flight went quickly. The transfer in Amsterdam proved much easier than flying through Heathrow. Before Loni knew it, she was touching down in Aberdeen.

She had booked a room at one of the airport hotels. The sun was shining, the air crisp and bracing. She arrived shortly after noon. After checking into the hotel, Loni took a taxi into the city.

She found herself unexpectedly enchanted with Aberdeen's energy, antiquity, architecture, and bustling modernity. She wandered about for hours, poking in and out of dozens of shops. She found a lovely light sea-green wool shawl, so soft and finely knit she had not been able to resist. The label read *Whales Weave, Shetland.*

Might as well get into the spirit of the Shetlands! she thought as she took it to the cashier.

Carrying her bag, she made her way to the end of Union Street, then down along Market Street, gazing at the variety of boats and ships large and small. She began to wonder if she had misjudged Scotland. Aberdeen—at least when the sun was shining—was magical!

70

SHETLAND AT LAST

Lerwick, Shetland Islands

Loni was scheduled to meet solicitor Jason MacNaughton at his Lerwick office as soon as she arrived. Having unexpectedly enjoyed Aberdeen, she could not prevent a pang of anxiety to be leaving the mainland behind—with nothing but ocean and icebergs between her and the North Pole!

Wanting to appear professional yet suitably traditional for her appointment with the lawyer, she put on her favorite rose-colored dress. Finally, she slipped the mysterious necklace from the letter box that she had saved for this day around her neck, added the tiny key on its chain under the neckline of her dress, and with the shawl she had found yesterday around her shoulders, she set out for the Aberdeen airport.

Within minutes of taking off, the plane banked up over the North Sea. Scattered white clouds extended in all directions. The skies remained calm, the sea below a deep blue. After an evening at the hotel, a morning in the airport, and surrounded by it in the small plane, far from sounding boorish, the Scottish tongue began to get under her skin. The accent was rhythmic and musical. Suddenly the Queen's English of London seemed stuffy, drab, and boring!

After a flight of about an hour in the fifty-seater, Loni found herself touching down at the Sumburgh airport on the southern tip of what they called mainland Shetland.

It wasn't the wasteland Loni had expected. The airport was modern. Evidence of big oil was everywhere. Texas accents mingled dissonantly with whatever it was Shetlanders spoke. She judged the temperature perhaps in the mid-fifties. Mr. MacNaughton had arranged for her to be taken into the city.

The driver who met her at the gate, holding a paper neatly printed with *Miss Ford,* was all she could have imagined—short, stocky, red-faced, and with a three-day stubble of beard. She saw his sign, approached, and smiled.

"Hello, I am Loni Ford," she said.

"Aye—pleased tae make yer acquaintance, Miss Ford," he said eagerly. He removed his wool cap briefly as he stared up at her tall form, then replaced the cap on his head and took her suitcase. "Gien ye'll jist follow me, Miss Ford."

He led the way out of the terminal while speaking amiably in what, to Loni's ears, might as well have been Greek, Norwegian, or ancient Gaelic. Until she managed to convey that she needed him to speak more slowly, she understood not a syllable.

The man chatted away as if they were old friends. Loni punctuated his monologue with nods and smiles and an occasional "Uh-huh." He was giving her what she gradually gathered to be some of the history and lore of the Shetlands. All she understood for certain was that the discovery of oil had changed everything for these remote islands.

The man continued to talk during the twenty-mile drive into the city. As they came into Lerwick, with ships and tankers and huge warehouses and refineries wherever she looked, the influence of North Sea Oil was inescapable. Her driver then embarked on the twenty-five-cent guided tour of Shetland's largest city. Loni was surprised at how modern and bustling it was.

They pulled to a stop alongside one of the city's tallest buildings.

"Here ye be, Miss Ford," announced her driver.

He jumped out, retrieved her suitcase, and opened her door. Loni stepped onto the sidewalk and began to open her purse.

"Nae, nae, Miss Ford—none o' that," he said. " 'Tis a' taken care o', ye ken. Ye'll be owin' me nae so much as a farthing. Jist go in. Mr. MacNaughton's on the third floor."

"Thank you very much," said Loni with a smile.

"Nae bother, Miss Ford. Ye jist gae on yer way an' enjoy Shetland."

Pulling her suitcase behind her, Loni walked inside and found the elevator. A few minutes later, she found herself face-to-face with the author of the fateful letter that had turned her life topsy-turvy.

Jason MacNaughton greeted her warmly. "I cannot believe my eyes, Miss Ford, to actually see you at last. I apologize," he quickly added. "I call you *Miss* . . . but perhaps you are married."

"No, I am unmarried," Loni replied.

"I see . . . well, I must say, you have been a mystery lady. No one even knew you existed until a short time ago."

"I still don't quite understand all this," said Loni as he led her into his office and offered her a chair. "I am uncertain how you found me. I knew nothing about my family connections to Scotland. I also was surprised that you addressed me with a middle name, one that actually is *not* my middle name."

"Right. Once we were able to confirm your identity from the birth records, we became aware of that," said Mr. MacNaughton, "We only used the *Tulloch* because it was your mother's maiden name and the thread leading to you."

"It is not a name I know much about."

"Yes, I understand your parents were killed not long after you were born. I am sorry. I suppose that has been the nub of the difficulty in locating you—that the family lines had been hidden and needed to be searched out."

Loni nodded.

"But you are here at last . . . so tell me, what do you know about the name Tulloch?"

"Only that I had a grandfather of that name whom I never met. He died when I was thirteen. My Ford grandparents were notified and saw to his effects."

"Well then you should know that if you took all the Smiths and Joneses in America and put them together, you would get some idea of the name Tulloch in the Shetlands. There are dozens of septs and clans and families by the name of Tulloch."

"I'm sorry—what is a sept?"

"A smaller branch of a clan. Sort of a clan within a clan, you might say. And the point is that unraveling a complex inheritance where there is no will can be truly a mess. Another thing you may not know is the strong ties of many Shetlanders to Scandinavia. The Shetlands were once part of Norway, not Britain. You will notice linguistic similarities to the old Norse tongue, and a unique form of English that is part Norse, part Germanic, as well as hints of ancient Anglo-Saxon. Throw in some Doric and it can be quite daunting."

"I've noticed. I have enough trouble understanding mainland Scots!" laughed Loni. "The man who drove me from the airport—I hardly understood a word he said."

"Yes," said MacNaughton, "Dickie Sinclair—a colorful man indeed. Not much to look at, I'm afraid, but he has a heart of gold. He's a good friend. He and I grew up together, and I would trust him with my life. Believe it or not, in addition to his taxi and limousine business, he is a part-time minister."

"I would never have guessed that!"

"In some circles he is known as Dr. Richard Sinclair. I fall back on the privilege of boyhood, but I doubt many others would call him *Dickie*."

"Does he shave before taking the pulpit?"

MacNaughton laughed. "Honestly I couldn't say. I've never heard him preach. Though come to think of it, I did attend a funeral he officiated, and he was very nicely turned out—clean-shaven and impeccably attired in suit and ministerial collar."

71

THE COMPLEX ESTATE OF MACGREGOR TULLOCH

"Who is this Macgregor Tulloch whose death is the reason for my being here?" asked Loni.

"He was the cousin of your grandfather, Grant Tulloch," answered the lawyer.

"So the inheritance, if I am indeed the legal heir, is a distant one? He would be . . . what, my great-uncle or something?"

"More distant even than that," MacNaughton replied. "As I have plotted out your genealogy, you would be Macgregor Tulloch's first cousin, twice removed. In other words, you are two generations down the line from your grandfather Grant Tulloch, who was his first cousin."

"Your letter alluded to other potential heirs. What is their connection to Mr. Tulloch?"

"Exactly the same as yours—first cousins, twice removed. There are two men on the island—third cousins to one another, and to you as well—who stand in the same relation to Macgregor Tulloch as yourself. They called him 'uncle,' but he was also their distant cousin."

"Then why me rather than one of them?"

"Because you are descended from the Auld Tulloch's eldest son."

"What is an *Auld* Tulloch?"

"Auld is *old,*" said MacNaughton. "That is simply the term by which Ernest Tulloch is known. He was the last Tulloch who was both laird and chief on the island. He would have been your great-great-grandfather. He is the common ancestor to all three of you."

"When did he live?" asked Loni.

"He was born in the nineteenth century. He died in 1953. By then your great-grandparents were already in the States."

"Was there a family split or something?" Even as the question left Loni's lips, she recalled her own father's breach with her grandparents.

"I don't really know," answered the lawyer. "All we know is that, for reasons not passed down, your great-grandfather Brogan Tulloch, Ernest's firstborn, left Scotland for the United States. Subsequent to that, Ernest divided the lairdship and chieftainship between his two younger sons, though it remains a mystery why he did so. That was a long time ago. The Great Depression, the Second World War—those were times when people moved about a good deal and lost track of each other. I know no details, and apparently neither does anyone else in the family."

Loni took in the information thoughtfully. "It sounds like either of the others you mentioned—

my, uh, cousins—would have a claim to the inheritance equal to mine. I cannot imagine anyone being thrilled about an American showing up at the last minute. It doesn't seem right. I suppose everything you've said confirms what I have been thinking of doing since hearing of this."

"What is that?"

"To sell the property or turn it over to the next rightful heir. You would know how to handle it legally. I really have no interest in a property in the Shetlands."

"I took it from your decision to come to Shetland that you intended to take possession."

"You were under the impression that I planned to *move* here, take up residence?" asked Loni.

"It's not every day one inherits a significant property. I suppose I merely assumed you would."

"Good heavens, no!" said Loni with a laugh.

Quickly she recovered herself. "I'm sorry," she said. "I don't mean to make light of it. I know there is a great deal at stake and that it is a serious decision. Perhaps you could explain what you mean by a significant property? In your letter you called it a cottage."

"Perhaps you are under a misapprehension about the term *cottage*," said MacNaughton. "The word is not always a designation of size. Some of Scotland's great manor houses were called cottages. In this case, the reality is not so grandiose as that. The late Macgregor Tulloch's Cottage, as it is known, is a modest dwelling of two floors, approximately six thousand square feet, nine bedrooms, five bathrooms, if I'm not mistaken, several sitting rooms of varying sizes, a great room, and a large stone fireplace that is quite wonderful."

"It sounds enormous!"

"By the standards of the rest of the island, it is a very large dwelling indeed."

"And one man lived in it . . . alone?"

"In a manner of speaking. He had a butler and housekeeper, as well as a gamekeeper who had an apartment attached to the barn."

"A butler!" Loni shook her head in disbelief. "Remarkable."

"There is one additional room that is something of a mystery—a locked study. No one has been inside the room for years."

"Why is that?"

"Apparently the key disappeared years ago. It seems the late Mr. Tulloch refused to have it opened. The story got around that the door would not again be opened until the key reappeared on the island."

"So where is the key?"

"No one knows. There are other stories too, considerably more sinister. Old wives' tales, no doubt."

"What sinister stories?" asked Loni.

"I don't know that it is my place to spread—"

"Please, Mr. MacNaughton, I want to get any unwelcome news out on the table. The place isn't haunted, is it?"

"No, nothing like that."

"Then what is the sinister secret about the locked room?"

"Only a rumor that it contains the dead body of Macgregor Tulloch's wife, a Norwegian woman whom he married as a young man but who disappeared and was never seen on the island again."

Loni shuddered. "Maybe I will *leave* it locked!"

"It is all nonsense, I assure you," said MacNaughton. "Villagers are great for strange stories and gossip. Gives them something to talk about. All in all, however, it is a marvelous home, the locked room notwithstanding. I think you will be quite taken with it. It's not a castle by any means, but more than adequate for any humble aristocrat of the previous century. It was originally the residence of the laird and chief when the two titles rested with the same man— the last of whom, as I said, was your great-great-grandfather Ernest Tulloch."

"When you say *chief*, what exactly is that . . . like an Indian chief?"

MacNaughton smiled. "Not exactly." If he was offended by Loni's ignorance concerning all things Scottish, he gave no sign of it. "It is a term designating head of the clan. Times have changed, of course, and things are much different now. The two titles laird and chief are now separate. This sort of feudal system, for lack of a better term, is not really part of Shetland life. But Whales Reef has deep ties to the Highlands of the Scottish mainland. Their lairds have preserved that tradition to a large degree. Whales Reef, you might say, marches to a different drum than most of Shetland. Anachronistic, perhaps. But its people have been well provided for by their lairds for generations. The chief, whose role is more that of a spiritual figurehead, lives in the other large dwelling on the island, the Old House it is called. You, as the heir, will be the new laird."

"I'm sorry again . . . what exactly is it you mean by *laird,* if I am saying it correctly?"

"The traditional Scottish term for *Lord.* Landlord, if you will. You will basically own the majority of the island. You will be landlord of most of its houses and buildings. Their tenants pay you rent. The only properties excluded from that are the church and the chief's residence and land."

Loni shook her head in bewilderment. "As I told you, Mr. MacNaughton," she said after a moment, "it is probably a moot point anyway. It is not my intention to take possession."

"I suppose that is your prerogative, though I must say it is most unusual."

"Why? If it is mine, would it not be mine to do with as I please?"

"Technically. But that is a very modern and, if you will forgive me, also a selfish way of looking at it."

"How would it be selfish for me to offer to let someone else have it?"

"What about your duty, Miss Ford?"

"My *duty* . . . to what, to whom?"

"To the people, to the island, to your heritage, to the family, to your ancestors and their legacy. Inheritances are accompanied with duties and obligations to those who have gone before. Don't they teach you these things in the United States?"

Loni did not reply. She was reminded of her grandparents and the heritage of their Quaker past. They had so badly wanted her to embrace that heritage and carry it on. Would they too have considered it her *duty* to do so?

She had already turned her back on one legacy. Was she now going to do so with another?

"Of course, I will do whatever you instruct me to do," MacNaughton went on. "But I strongly urge you not to act rashly, Miss Ford, or to make a hasty decision. Please at least give the matter serious thought for a few days."

"I plan to be on a flight back to Washington the day after tomorrow."

"I hope you will change your mind. I would

at the least implore you to visit the island and see the Cottage and property before making a final decision."

"How far is it?"

"A drive of thirty or forty minutes, then a ferry ride across the isthmus to the island."

"A ferry ride! I thought I was already on the island."

"The Shetlands comprise many islands. Whales Reef is one of its medium-sized ones, though it is only some four miles from top to bottom—north to south, as it were. The ride across is short, ten or fifteen minutes. In addition to the Cottage, there is the land to consider as well. It is not agri-cultural but mostly used for grazing sheep. There are also some oil leases here on Shetland included in the estate."

"It sounds as though I underestimated everything about this," said Loni, letting out a long sigh. "It is more complicated and extensive than I imagined. Still, it remains my intention to see to the legalities, sell or transfer the property, and return to the States as quickly as possible."

"Again I implore you not to make a hasty decision. Having said that, however, the final documents must be signed in a timely manner. I hope you will at least see the property?"

"Yes, of course."

"Good. I took the liberty of arranging for Dickie to deliver you there this afternoon. You can spend the night and stay as long as you wish. I have arranged everything for your comfort. The housekeeper will have fresh linens on the beds. The kitchen will be well-stocked. I have also arranged for a rental car to be delivered to you at the Cottage early tomorrow morning."

"Thank you. I'm not sure all that is necessary for such a brief stay."

"Nevertheless, all will be ready for you . . . for however long you do stay. But now," he said, glancing at his watch, "it is nearly one. I hope you will join me for lunch. Then perhaps I can show you a little of our fair city. I arranged for Dickie to be back at 3:30."

"Before we go," said Loni, "I would like to know who is next in line for the inheritance. I would like to meet him."

"Actually . . ." began MacNaughton slowly, "I'm afraid that is somewhat ambiguous."

"In what way?"

"There is some question of the legitimacy of a marriage back in the family line, which could disqualify one of the young men I mentioned. That is one of the reasons probate has dragged on so long. I am merely a private solicitor and am not privy to the complete findings of the probate court. I have not been told definitely who would inherit if you do not sign the inheritance documents."

"You must have some idea."

"I only know which direction their decision was leaning before your identity was discovered."

"Then may I ask toward whom is it leaning?"

"It would be premature of me to—"

"Please, Mr. MacNaughton. I would like to meet him. It is probable that I will want either to decline the inheritance or else follow whatever legalities are necessary to sell or transfer the property to him. What is his name?"

"He is a Tulloch," said MacNaughton with obvious reluctance. "A fisherman by the name of Hardar Tulloch, though of a different branch of Tullochs. He would, as I said, be your third cousin."

"How may I contact him?"

"That will not be a problem. Everyone on the island knows Hardy Tulloch."

72
ON THE TRAIL

Atlanta

"Hey, Thorburn . . . Jimmy Joe here. Got just a minute—in Atlanta about to board a flight to London. I'll be up in your neck of the woods tomorrow afternoon. You get the email with my itinerary?"

"I did, Mr. McLeod."

"Good, good! Then you meet me at the airport when I land in Aberdeen. Book us both on the first flight you can up to the islands. I'm fixin' to stay on that filly's trail before the scent goes cold, know what I mean?"

"I seriously recommend that you reconsider, Mr. McLeod. The last thing we want to do is—"

"You leave all that to me, Thorburn. She's an American, isn't she? Know anything about her?"

"Nothing."

"Well, whoever she is, she's gotta be able to use the dough—just a flunky to some ornery gal who thinks she's big stuff in D.C. Money talks, Thorburn, you mark my words. I know how to deal with her kind—seen 'em a million times. Gotta head this thing off at the pass."

"Nevertheless," said the Scotsman, "we have to play it out without causing waves. It may be that the big fellow can win her over. We'll get her to sell to him, and we'll advance him the money, then buy from him as per the previous arrange-ment. It could all still work as we planned. But I strongly recommend that we not push too hard."

"That's all okay, but I got my own way of doing things. So I'll see you tomorrow, Thorburn. You just get me to the Shetlands, you hear? I'm going to rope in this gal before anybody puts contrary notions in her head."

73
Into the Country

Shetland

The taxi sat in front of the office building as Jason MacNaughton and Loni Ford walked back from lunch through Lerwick's downtown district. The colorful figure of the unshaven minister-chauffeur stood on the sidewalk beside it.

"Good afternoon tae ye again, Miss Ford," he said, again removing his cap.

"And to you, Mr. Sinclair," rejoined Loni with a smile.

"So ye ken my name noo, do ye? Has this bounder o' a solicitor been spreadin' tales aboot me?"

"He has indeed, Mr. Sinclair. I know all your secrets!"

MacNaughton laughed. "Not to worry, Dickie," he said. "I told her none of the juicy stuff. I'm saving that for when I need to blackmail you!"

"An' ye call yersel' a lawyer!"

"Miss Ford's luggage is still up in my office," MacNaughton said. "If you could bring it down, then take her to Whales Reef and see her safely to the Cottage."

The man disappeared inside the building. Loni and MacNaughton exchanged a few final words.

"If there is anything you need or that I have neglected, Miss Ford," said the solicitor, "telephone me immediately. You have my card."

"Thank you, Mr. MacNaughton," replied Loni. "I'm sure I will be fine. I will be in touch."

Sinclair returned with her bags, and they were on their way.

"Mr. MacNaughton tells me you are also a minister," said Loni.

"Aye, that's me—a jack o' many trades."

"If you don't mind my asking, why two professions . . . and such diverse occupations?"

"I pastor a wee kirk o' nae mair nor forty or fifty folk," answered Sinclair. "Isna a parish kirk, ye ken, an' the folk canna afford tae pay me. Nor would I take it if they could. I haud what some would call unorthodox views, Miss Ford. One o' those is that I dinna think the Word teaches that ministers are tae be paid. So I earn my ain livin', an' give o' my time as a pastor wi'oot obligation. 'Tis hoo I think it ought tae be in God's Kirk. I hae my taxi an' limousine service as what they call my day job."

"That is very interesting," said Loni. "That is also the custom in the Fellowship where I grew up."

"Aye, so ye're a believer yersel', then?"

The question took Loni off guard.

"I, uh . . . uh, yes," she answered, though her tone betrayed an obvious lack of conviction.

"What was the Fellowship ye spoke o'," said Sinclair, "if ye dinna mind *my* askin'?"

"Quaker. I grew up in a small conservative sect of the Society of Friends."

"Oh, aye—a Quaker, are ye?—George Fox an' John Woolman an' the like. Ye come o' a long line o' righteous folk. 'Tis a rich an' worthy heritage."

They settled into the drive, and Loni grew pensive. The long talk with Jason MacNaughton replayed itself in her brain, working deeper and deeper into her consciousness.

As they bounced along the two-lane road, though occasionally distracted as they whizzed along on the wrong side of the road, Loni found herself caught up in the mystery of what she had become involved in. How often, she thought, does someone find themselves heir to a property from the "old country," from a long-lost relative they've never heard of? The whole thing was straight out of a Victorian novel. MacNaughton's description of the Cottage as the former residence of the laird and chief added yet more romance to it all.

Quickly the city was behind them and they were driving along through open country. The scenery became more and more desolate. At last they crested a small hill. Coming down the other side, the road ended abruptly.

In front of them lay the ocean. Sinclair braked to a stop and turned off the engine.

"What now?" asked Loni.

"We wait for the ferry. Shouldna be more'n half an oor."

74

THE FERRY

Loni's intrepid driver got out of the car and strolled toward the landing. Loni followed.

The scent of the sea, suddenly so close, assaulted her with wonderfully evocative sensations she could not have described had she tried. Whereas the predominant smell she would always associate with her childhood was wood, she could already tell that the predominant fragrance of the Shetlands was the sea.

She walked onto the thick wooden planks of the landing. It was precarious in her heels. She had to be careful for cracks between the boards. A bank of fog was drifting toward them. Nothing beyond two hundred yards was visible.

"Whales Reef's oot there across the water, Miss Ford," said Sinclair as she came alongside him.

"And there is no way on or off the island except by ferry?"

"Aye."

American and Shetlander stood side by side for several minutes in silence, mesmerized by the gentle lapping of the waves along the shore.

"Do you mind if I ask you something, Mr. Sinclair?" said Loni at length.

"Of course not, mum."

"You are a minister."

"Aye."

"Would you mind . . . that is, I've never asked anyone this before, but would you pray for me?"

"Aye. I hae been doin' that already, Miss Ford."

"You have!"

"Aye."

"Why?"

"I could see ye was uncertain o' what's tae come tae ye, an' that ye was feelin' a mite lonely."

"How could you have known? That is exactly what I am feeling. I'm nervous. I don't know if I will know what to do."

"Then I'll be prayin' that the Lord'll speak tae ye, an' that ye'd hear Him, an' that ye'd ken what He's sayin' tae ye. An' I'm honored that ye'd ask, Miss Ford. There's nae greater measure o' friendship than tae haud a brither or sister up intil the Father's care."

"Thank you, Mr. Sinclair."

The unlikely man of God wandered off the dock and some paces along the shoreline. Loni knew he was praying for her.

Eventually the muffled drone of an engine was heard faintly through the mist. Five or ten minutes later, a small rusting ferry came into view through the fog.

Loni returned to the car as the boat docked. The

minister-cabman was already at the wheel. One lone car drove off. Sinclair turned on his engine and eased forward onto the deck.

Minutes later they were off across the water. Loni got out of the car again and made her way to the front of the little craft.

Soon they were in the midst of dense fog. Loni could see nothing but frothing water below the hull. With the fog came a chill. She pulled her new shawl up more tightly around her neck and shoulders.

Loni drew in the aroma of salt spray, delighting in the splashing sound of waves against the prow as it ploughed through the calm summer's sea. No one else stood about on the deck. For Shetlanders, ferrying the many waters of its inlets and lochs and sounds was nothing out of the ordinary. For Loni, however, even this brief voyage was new and magical.

She felt more alone than ever. She had nearly reached her journey's end, though she could see nothing of what lay ahead.

The very fog surrounding her was symbolic of that reality, concealing many things from view that perhaps she was about to discover. She was alone and yet . . . was she at last drawing near the very roots she had always longed for?

All the religious training of her childhood stole upon her out of the past—the quiet meetings, the Quaker tradition of silence, prayer and Bible time with her grandparents, her grandmother's comfort amid the suffering she endured at school, the humble way her grandparents had deepened spiritual truth into her. Their influence had worked into her as if by osmosis.

She realized then how deeply she treasured that past. It now seemed so far away.

All at once she desperately wanted to touch that life again. Even after leaving home, that past had been an unseen anchor to her existence. But she hadn't recognized it. She had let the tether to that anchor slip from her grasp. She didn't even know how to pray. She had to ask someone else to pray for her.

Maybe it was time she learned how to pray from her *own* heart.

Loni closed her eyes. She let the chilly mist wash over her like a microscopic cleansing rain. As she stood, a calm slowly filled her.

At last she opened her eyes. Staring into the dense cloud of white as if looking toward a future she could not see, Loni began to pray:

God, I know I've let you slip out of my mind these last few years. I hope I haven't let you slip out of my heart. But I don't want to forget the foundations that were built for me, that made me who I am.

I am grateful for the recent visits with my grandparents, reminded of so many good things in my years with them, and that I don't want to forget you. I want you to be part of my life.

Whatever is about to meet me on the other side, beyond the thick fog on this strange island called Whales Reef, I want you to be part of it. Help me know what I am supposed to do. Do I have a duty, like the lawyer said?

I feel more alone than I have ever felt in my life. Yet there is something exciting about it too. I realize I need your quiet voice speaking to me now more than ever. So please speak to me and guide me. I realize how much I need you . . . and want you inside me.

Help me, Lord—help me know what to do.

75

STRANGER ON WHALES REEF

Whales Reef, Shetland Islands

The ferry began to slow. Loni could still see nothing. Her hair was dripping from the fog. She felt no different. Yet her prayer was a beginning. She was ready to discover what lay beyond the mist.

She returned shivering to the taxi. Sinclair smiled as she climbed inside. It was one of the most tender smiles Loni had ever seen.

"Ye'll be at yer destination, Miss Ford," he said. "We're aboot tae dock at Whales Reef. Noo I'm nae one given tae the prophetic, but I'll just tell ye this—ye hae a great adventure ahead o' ye. I canna say where that adventure will take ye. But I'll say this tae ye, lassie—embrace the adventure because yer Father's wi' ye. He loves ye, an' He's got yer wee heart in the palm o' His great hand."

"Thank you, Mr. Sinclair," she said softly. "Thank you so much. I will not forget your words. I promise."

A dull thud beneath them signaled their arrival.

"Then let's take ye ontil Whales Reef," said Sinclair, starting his engine. He eased off the ferry, across the dock, and onto the island.

Almost immediately the fog began to lift. A few of their surroundings gradually came into focus.

"There's the kirk on yer left," said Sinclair as they drove past a road leading inland from the sea. " 'Tis up on the hill, though ye canna see it jist noo on account o' the fog. An' there's the wool factory," he continued. "Ye can jist see a bit o' the building."

Small cottages with attached barns and gardens and surrounded by low stone walls spread out from the road in both directions. They gradually gave way to larger buildings, and long rows of two-story stone homes appeared on either side of the single street, their doors and windows just beyond the narrow sidewalks, so close that Loni could almost have reached out and touched them.

Who lives behind these doors and windows in these long blocks of stone? Loni wondered. If she decided to accept it, would they hate her for taking the inheritance away from one of their own, the fisherman whose name she had already forgotten?

As they reached the center of the village, the buildings now began to display shop signs painted on doors and windows or on signs hanging from above. She felt like she had been transported to a scene in a Dickens novel.

The variety of shops whose signs she read as they passed was remarkable: Nibs and Nobs Gifts and Misc., Gretta's Hair Salon, Olde Worlde Antiques, Willows Tea Shop, the Whales Reef Natural History Museum and Wildlife Shoppe. And there was a bakery, a small bookstore . . .

What people were out turned to stare as the taxi passed. Their expressions did not appear welcoming. Did they know it was *her* who was invading their town?

Glancing back and forth on both sides, Loni now beheld a large building called the Whales Fin Inn. Its sign boasted the best beer and fish and chips in the Shetlands.

The door of the place stood open. Several men and two women stood near the entrance in animated conversation. A great laugh sounded from one of the men. It was followed by an unintelligible outpouring from one of the women that sounded anything but friendly toward the tall, good-natured man in front of her. The man laughed again, though the small enclave quieted as the taxi slowly drove by.

"There's the village square," said Sinclair as they passed the hotel. "The harbor's doon tae the right, jist there, where the fishermen keep their boats."

Soon in the country again, Loni caught an occasional glimpse of the sea to their right, and hints of open fields to their left. Occasionally she noticed what she thought were grazing sheep, though it was difficult to tell through the fog.

Several minutes later they slowed as they came to a long driveway leading off the road to the left.

A short man with walking stick in hand, ancient by the look of it, stood at the side of the road. He stared straight into the car window as they turned into the drive. Loni had the uncomfortable feeling that he knew who she was, perhaps even that he was waiting for her.

Their eyes met through the glass. Loni glanced away as they drove by.

"Who was *that?*" she asked.

"I dinna ken, Miss Ford," replied Sinclair. "He looked a rum one."

"He was staring right at me."

"I'll make sure he isna there when I leave. I dinna want anyone botherin' ye."

"Thank you. I would appreciate that."

After another minute the car slowed and came to a stop in front of an imposing structure of granite. At first appearance it looked as though it had been transplanted from the heart of one of Aberdeen's more exclusive districts.

"Weel, here ye be at yer new place, Miss

Ford," said Sinclair, stepping out to open her door. " 'Tis what they call the Cottage."

He retrieved Loni's bags, and she followed toward the front door of the massive, two-story, gray stone house of three wings.

Loni slowed her step to take it all in. In the fog she could make out little more than the outline of the building. It rose out of its surroundings in what to all appearances was the middle of nowhere. From the distance behind them, muted by the fog, came the unmistakable sound of waves breaking on the shore.

The doors were unlocked. Sinclair disappeared inside with her bags. He returned and approached Loni where she stood in the enormous entryway.

" 'Tis time for me tae return til the city," he said. "Dinna forgit, lassie—embrace the adventure. God is wi' ye. He winna let naethin' but good come tae ye."

Loni smiled, stepped forward, and bent to give the short man a warm hug. "Thank you, Mr. Sinclair," she said. "You don't know how much this time has meant to me. You were a stranger when we first met. Now you are a friend."

76
THE COTTAGE

Loni walked through the large double doors of solid oak at the front of the Cottage, which Sinclair had left open. She found herself standing in the middle of an expansive entryway with a high vaulted ceiling. Into its midst swept a wide flowing staircase of well-worn light oak. It made a picturesque half circle down from a landing above that rounded the entry and from which corridors led off in opposite directions into the two main wings of the house.

Loni gazed about for several seconds in wonder, then continued through two more double doors into what was obviously the great room the lawyer had mentioned.

Notwithstanding the lawyer's modest description, to Loni's eyes this might as well have been a castle! She could only stare awestruck at what surrounded her. She had stepped into another world, and back in time a hundred years. Several tall cases displayed an array of books with leather spines that were doubtless older than the house. Antique tables, writing desks, couches, chairs, sideboards, and lamps were arranged throughout. On the walls hung colorful tapestries, several works of Renaissance art, as well as numerous oil paintings of men and women of past generations. It still had not registered in Loni's brain . . . everything she was looking at was *hers!*

A fire blazed away in an enormous fireplace surrounded by a stone hearth. The interior of the house was warm and pleasant. Mr. MacNaughton had thought of everything, right down to having someone light a fire for her arrival.

Adjacent to the great room, Loni wandered into the kitchen. Just as MacNaughton had said, it was well-stocked. A note taped to the refrigerator read *Supper inside.* On the counter sat a coffee maker, beside which lay three unopened bags of coffee, including one of Starbucks Yukon Blend. Whoever was responsible for the preparations, they were doing their best to keep the American happy! Next to them sat a box of Scottish Blend tea and a second of Nambarrie. Beside the coffee and tea sat three boxes labeled OATCAKES.

What are oatcakes? Loni wondered. She had not encountered them at the conference the previous November.

Returning to the entry, her bags still in the middle of the floor, Loni ascended the magnificent stairway. Halfway up to the first floor, her legs nearly gave way.

She stopped, took hold of the bannister, and caught her breath. She was so tired she was about to drop. Jet lag and fatigue had suddenly kicked in.

Continuing to the top, she plopped into one of several chairs about the wide landing that was surrounded by a waist-high balustrade and overlooked the entry below.

It was already past five o'clock British time. She couldn't go to bed yet. And she certainly couldn't take a nap this late in the day. It wasn't too soon, however, to check out her sleeping accommodations.

She pulled herself back to her feet and walked through the two wings of the upper floor. Everything was clean and tidy. Locating what was clearly the master bedroom, she returned downstairs. With flagging energy she lugged her suitcase and carry-on back upstairs and deposited them in the room.

She left the room and wandered back along the corridor. As she came to the landing at the head of the main staircase, situated between the two corridors leading east and south, an ornately crafted oak door caught her eye. Curious, she walked over to it and tried the handle. The door was locked. No other door in the place had been locked.

Then Loni remembered.

She jerked her hand from the door handle. This was one room she did *not* need to explore . . . at least not yet. For the present she intended to stay as far away from the locked study—or burial crypt!—as possible.

She hurried back downstairs and returned to the kitchen. Surveying the supper options in the refrigerator, she found enough food for three people. All the containers were marked: quiche, steamed vegetables, two slabs of breaded fish, something called Cullen Skink. She certainly was not about to try that! She decided on half a slice of fish and a small portion of vegetables.

By the time she was finished with her modest meal it was approaching seven, the sun still high in the sky. She pulled all the drapes in the room of her chosen accommodations, but was only partially successful in darkening the room.

She was in bed by seven-thirty.

77

FIRST GUEST

If it was possible both to sleep soundly and fitfully at the same time, Loni did so. She dozed in and out of consciousness all night, ever aware of the faint sound of the sea. The subtle sensation was mesmerizing. Yet the peacefulness came with a sense of lonely isolation.

She awoke to the cry of gulls. Feeling wonderfully rested, she stretched and sighed contentedly.

Was she *really* in the Shetland Islands . . . at the edge of the world? Surging like a slow incoming tide into her mind came the astonishing, unbeliev-able thought. Did all this—the huge house, the fields surrounding it, the village she'd driven through—did it all really belong to her?

She couldn't wrap her mind around it. It was too overwhelming to think about. Relieved to put the idea of the inheritance aside, she remembered what Mr. MacNaughton had said about the view of the sea. She rose from bed, walked to the window, and pulled back the drapes.

The view under a thick cloudy sky was not exactly stunning. Visibility extended perhaps half a mile. There was the ocean, but the gray water and gray sky were not particularly spectacular. Inland, in the opposite direction, only bare fields were visible. Not a tree in sight. She saw sheep in the distance. Did the sheep belong to her too?

Loni showered, dressed, and descended to the main floor. The fire that had greeted her upon her arrival had gone out in the night, so she set about building a new one. Thinking fondly of her grandfather's morning ritual in front of the fireplace at home, she tried to remember how he stacked paper and kindling into a sort of teepee before lighting them. It took her some time, but the box beside the fireplace was well supplied with old newspapers, matches, kindling, and firewood. Before long she had three or four good-sized logs blazing away. Where the supply of wood had come from she couldn't imagine. From the little of it she had seen, the island seemed devoid of trees. And what were those peculiar black chunks of dried dirt in a box next to the firewood? While she was waiting for the fire to do its work, she happily discovered a modern thermostat on the wall. Soon she felt evidence that the central heating was in good working order and up to the task of heating such a large house.

She brewed an enjoyable cup of coffee and made herself a light breakfast with her first exposure to Scottish oatcakes. They were certainly too dry and plain to be called *cakes*. But with jam she discovered them a surprisingly tasty alternative to toast. Afterward she bundled up and went outside.

The air was thick with moisture. Drops hung from every blade of grass and fence post. A car sat in front of the house. How and when and by whom it was delivered, she didn't know.

She could now see far enough inland to make out green hilly fields, amply dotted with rocks and small boulders, with a high hill across the fields in the distance. Two large barns and a few small outbuildings stood behind the house. Evidence of animal life came from that direction as well. On the fourth side, directly east, was the sea.

A path angled northward away from the house. After a short walk on the path, she found herself standing on a bluff, gazing out over the ocean. Gentle waves splashed on a gravelly shoreline twenty or thirty feet below. Some distance along the uneven shore to her left stretched a sandy expanse of beach.

She returned the way she had come. After another cup of coffee, she set out to explore the house more thoroughly than her fatigue had allowed the previous evening. An hour later, she went outside again. From the front doors she started along the drive toward the main road. She had gone about halfway when ahead of her she saw the same man standing at the end of the drive exactly as he had been the day before. Again he seemed to be waiting.

Loni paused a moment, then summoned her courage and continued toward him. He watched her as she came. He did not seem surprised. Again came the distinct impression that he was expecting her.

As she approached a slow smile spread over his face.

Loni could see that he was a gentleman. She judged him to be in his late eighties or early nineties and maybe eight or nine inches shorter than her. His smile was knowing, tender, sensitive. She knew she had no reason to be apprehensive.

"Hello," she said. "Is there something . . . are you waiting for someone?"

"Aye, miss," replied the man. "I've been waitin' for yersel'."

"For *me?* You knew I was coming?"

"Oh, aye. I knew ye would come."

"How long have you been waiting?"

"Nigh on fifty years an' mair." He still wore the hint of a smile. "Though ye're a mite taller than I expected."

Loni wasn't sure if she had heard him correctly. "I've never been here before," she said.

"Not yersel', lassie. But her spirit's been here all these many years. I see her in your eyes."

"Whose spirit?" said Loni.

"Yer grit-gran'mither, as near as I can make it oot," said the old man.

A tingle went through Loni's frame. "I remind you of someone," she said, "someone you knew?"

"Aye." His eyes probed her face, still with an expression that said he knew more than he was saying.

"That must have been a long time ago. Fifty years, you say?"

"Aye, a long time. Over eighty years syne I *first* laid eyes on her."

"Eighty years! But how could you . . . ? I mean—"

"I'm an auld man, lassie," chuckled the man "An' I was but a wee tyke back then. But I mind the day weel. She came an' sat doon wi' the two o' us. A puir wee birdie was dyin', ye see, an' we were helpin' it gae back til its Maker in peace."

"That is the lady I remind you of?"

"Aye—yer grit-gran'mither."

Again Loni felt strange sensations welling up inside her.

"Dinna ye worry, lassie," he added, smiling more broadly this time. "I hae my wits aboot me. Some folk dinna think so. I'm in the way o' sayin' odd things noo an' then. Folk dinna ken what tae make o' me. But the auld laird understood me, as did my own daddy, an' as do the creatures. I see the look o' question in yer face. But I'm nae talkin' nonsense. I ken weel enouch who ye are."

"You said she sat down with the two of you," said Loni. "You and who?"

"The laird. My daddy was his gamekeeper. The laird an' I were fast friends after that day, though as I said I was jist a wee laddie." He reached into his pocket and pulled out a tiny thin coin. He handed it to Loni.

She turned it over in her hand. "It's nearly worn smooth," she said. "What is it?"

"A farthing, lassie. They're nae used noo."

"I've heard of them, but have never seen one. How much were they worth?"

"A fourth o' a penny—the smallest coin in Britain. 'Tis made o' brass—a worthless bit o' metal, except for the trowth it has tae tell. I've carried it wi' me for a' the years syne. He gae it tae me that day sae that I wouldna forget. He wanted me tae learn the lesson o' the dyin' wee birdie."

Loni smiled and handed back the coin, satisfied he was not as loony as some might take him for. Completely enchanted, Loni realized she had made her first acquaintance on Whales Reef. She was curious to hear more of what he had to tell her.

"Would you like to come inside for a cup of coffee or tea?" she asked.

"Aye, miss, that I would."

"If you want tea, you may have to make it

yourself," said Loni as she led the way toward the house. "I'm afraid I'm not much of a tea drinker. I'm Loni, by the way. Loni Ford."

"I'm mair pleased than I can tell ye tae make yer acquaintance, lassie. An' naethin' could make me happier than tae tell ye aboot yer gran'daddy, the Auld Tulloch . . . an' his Sally an' the lad Brogan. If ye came tae Whales Reef seekin' yer past an' yer inheritance, as folk is sayin', 'tis those gone before that are the true inheritance. I didna ken the auld laird's first wife, God bless her. She died yoong, ye ken. Ye're descended fae her, no fae Sally as is oor chief."

"Your . . . *chief?*" repeated Loni. The seeming anachronism was as unexpected as the first time she had heard it in the solicitor's office.

"Aye, ye'll meet him soon enouch, I'm thinkin'," he replied. "He'll be yer half cousin, or the like, many generations back, near as I ken. He's descended fae Sally's son Leith. But though I didna ken yer ain grit-grit-gran'mother, Elizabeth was her name, I knew the Auld Tulloch's Sally weel, an' a fine woman she was. This was their hoose the auld laird's, Ernest by name, an' his Sally's, though I'm sure they told ye that. If ye're goin' to bide in their hoose, ye need to ken the man an' woman they was."

"So the man called Ernest is the one you call the old laird?"

"Aye, yer gran'daddy the Auld Tulloch."

"I don't believe he is my grandfather," corrected Loni.

"Oh, aye. But there's too many grits tae keep track o' so I called him yer gran'daddy. I call a' those who gave us life fae the auld days, the cloud o' witnesses, ye ken, oor gran'daddys and gran'mithers."

"And Sally was his wife?"

"Aye, his second wife, after the death o' yer grit-grit-gran'mother Elizabeth. Brogan was their firstborn son—yer grit-gran'father who went to America."

Loni smiled and shook her head. Even though she had heard substantially the same outline of her ancestry the previous day in Jason MacNaughton's office, she could not help being confused all over again.

"Do you mind if I ask your name?" she asked as their steps crunched along the gravel toward the Cottage.

The old man smiled. "The laird sometimes called me Wee Mannie," he said, "but my name is Alexander Innes. Folk call me Sandy. I'd be privileged for ye tae use the Sandy yersel'."

78

A Mysterious Old Man with a Story to Tell

"Ye wouldna ken it," said the man called Sandy Innes as they walked into the Cottage. "Ye see me wi' naethin' but snow on top. But my hair was as orange as a ripe carrot on the day the laird gae me the farthing I showed ye."

Loni led the way inside and straight through toward the kitchen. Turning, she realized her guest was no longer beside her. He was standing in the middle of the entryway. He had taken his cap off, revealing the mass of snowy-white hair he had just spoken of. Deep emotion spread over his face. She detected a tear stealing from one eye.

He glanced toward her with a poignant smile.

"Right here was the last time I laid eyes on the dear man's face," he said. "They set him oot here—jist here where I'm standin'—for the payin' o' oor last respects the day before the buryin'. He couldna see me then, o' course, except through the eyes o' his heart, which is the best kind o' seein' o' a'. But I'll ne'er forget his peaceful, sleepin' face."

He breathed in deeply, smiled again, then

rejoined Loni and followed her into the kitchen.

At Loni's behest, Sandy took upon himself the task of preparing tea. As he did, he urged Loni to try a cup. It was the first time she had tasted tea with milk. *Not half bad,* she thought.

Two hours later, Loni Ford and Sandy Innes still sat in the great room of the Cottage of the late laird Macgregor Tulloch. Thoroughly engrossed, Loni had been listening to stories of Whales Reef and its history and people, from times long past to the present. Though almost six decades separated them, they were talking together like old friends.

She found Sandy engaging, humorous, energetic, and sharp as a tack. He reminded her of her grandfather back home. She found herself strangely warmed by his presence in the Cottage with her.

Loni had heard all the details of the unlikely trio who had come together to care for a dying bird. She learned much about Ernest Tulloch and the family of her ancestors. She would have liked to know more about Elizabeth Clark Tulloch, her own great-great-grandmother. But she had come to know Sally—who was something like Loni's *step*-great-great-grandmother— through Sandy's warm recollections.

She had also learned about the peculiar blocks next to the firewood, which weren't dried dirt at all. A nice fire of dried chunks of peat now blazed in the hearth, though Sandy confessed himself bewildered where the wood could have come from, for no one on the island burned anything but peat. Loni had even begun to understand the Shetland dialect more easily.

As they enjoyed a second pot of tea with oatcakes and fruit, she found that the amber brew, softened with white, was growing on her.

"You may succeed in making a convert of me yet, Sandy!" laughed Loni. "I never thought I would drink three cups of tea in the same day. And I am definitely hooked on the oatcakes! As for the peat, it gives the fire a character all its own."

Sandy smiled. "I like tae imagine that there'll be peat fires in heaven."

Silence fell. Both sat with cups in hand, staring into the fire, their minds dwelling on earlier days.

"You mentioned the last time you saw Mr. Tulloch," said Loni, "the auld laird—is that how you say it?"

"Jist fine, lassie."

"When was that? He's been gone now, what is it—about fifty years?"

"Aye. That was the day o' the viewin' here at the Cottage. He was laid tae rest two days later. Everyone came tae pay their respects tae the man, though not a' kenned him for the man o' God he was. 'Twas the last time yer whole family was t'gither. Yer grit-gran'mother had returned too. I hadna seen her in twenty-five or thirty years. She didna ken me at first, till I told her who I was. But I could ne'er forget her eyes . . . yer eyes, ye ken."

Loni nodded. "I would love to hear about it."

"Aye," said Sandy. "I remember the day as if it were yesterday. He was aye one who kenned what it meant tae give his care intil the hand o' the Father o' sparrows an' men."

Though soft, his voice at times scarcely more than a whisper, Sandy began to tell Loni about the day of her great-great grandfather's funeral. As she listened, the conviction stole upon Loni, exactly as Sandy had said, that *this* was the inheritance she had come to Scotland to discover. It was not the Cottage at all. The true inheritance was the people who had come before, and the legacy they had left.

"It was a day o' tears an' rejoicin'" Sandy went on. "Tears for us who kenned him here, but I hae nae doobt a day o' rejoicin' for the angels in the land o' his new home. The whole village was on hand tae bid him farewell. I walked along oot fae the village, behind the carriage that bore him, alongside my wife an' oor daughter. Twas a drizzly cauld day, wi' rain in the air, an' a solomn hush spread oor the island."

PART 7

OCTOBER
1953

79

THE COFFIN

Whales Reef, Shetland Islands

It is said that dead men tell no tales.

The man resting in a plain coffin—plainer than some might say was appropriate for a man of his station—had hoped that in his case exactly the opposite would prove true.

His heart's desire was that his earthly days, like his Master's, might signify as much, and in some cases perhaps *more* in death to those he loved than it had in life. It would be many years before the results of that prayer would be revealed.

But on this particular day, the most that could be said was that the dignified repose of his temporary tabernacle meant many things to those who had known him. His death had caused a tumult of controversy, conjecture, not to mention one outburst of scarcely concealed wrath, among those family members who had gathered in the great room of the Cottage two days before. Three had prior inkling of what was coming when Lerwick solicitor Arthur MacNaughton stood to read the will of the family patriarch.

What followed was as unprecedented as it was

unexpected. The terms of the document would change the fortunes of this island and its people, as well as the dead man's descendants, for generations to come.

Over the next forty-eight hours, word of the will's contents circulated through the village like a brushfire. How the villagers learned of it was a mystery. No one from the extended family had breathed a word of it.

The rampant speculation fueling the island's rumor mills no doubt doubled the number making today's pilgrimage to view the body. Not that they expected to learn anything from mourners bearing the Tulloch name. But when news of *this* magnitude was in the wind, every woman in the village would be nowhere else but in the middle of it. If dead men told no tales, one of the living might inadvertently let some tidbit slip, which, if overheard, could send out a juicy new branch on the ever-widening gossip tree.

The man at the center of everyone's thoughts was himself far removed from the commotion surrounding today's final display of his earthly temple. Its purpose had been fulfilled. He had no more use of it.

That his prayers were heard, he had had no doubt when he prayed them, and certainly had none now. How and when those heaven-launched arrows would descend back to earth—perfected, elevated, and glorified into oneness with God's eternal purpose—as answering shafts of light into the hearts of those to whom they were aimed, was known only to the Father of Lights, the Hearer and Answerer and Glorifier of Prayers.

Like many who followed the Master, the life of Ernest Tulloch was misunderstood by many. Few in a village who esteemed him could be said to have truly known him. The quiet passions of such men of stature in the heavenly realms are most often invisible to those whose vision is earthbound.

Happily death does not close the door to the impact of a man's life. The parting of the curtain between temporal and eternal is often required to unlock the hearts of those left behind to depths of virtue obscured by earthly reality. To what extent, therefore, this man's life would signify more in the generations to follow would depend on the men and women whose lives, both physically and spiritually, would descend from his to the third and fourth generation.

Ernest Tulloch had three sons and one daughter, all of whom loved him. They would continue to discover more and deeper aspects of his influence in their lives for the rest of their days. Two of the sons and the daughter now stood on one side of the open casket, gazing down at their father's ghostly white face. Their eldest brother, Brogan, was expected later.

Ernest's widow and second wife, Sally, draped

in black from head to foot, stood opposite the three. She was from northern Shetland and a traditionalist. Some may have objected, but she knew that a conventional open-casket viewing was appropriate. Most would not feel they had dutifully paid their final respects unless they saw her husband's face.

Sally smiled at Wallace and Delynn, her husband's son and daughter by his first marriage, then at her own son, Leith. She then lifted the black veil over her face, walked across the entryway, and opened the two large oak doors.

The four flanked the entry. A somber line already gathered outside. Behind them a steady stream was coming toward the house from the village.

Sally and Leith on one side, Wallace and Delynn on the other, nodded in welcome as one by one the villagers began walking slowly into the wide foyer. The interior doors into the rest of the Cottage were all closed.

In silent single file the mourners approached, each pausing a second or two before the open casket with their dead laird lying peacefully inside it. A few murmured soft words of final farewell. Most of the women shed abundant tears as if a king had died. Then they slowly circled around behind the coffin and made their way through the opposite side of the double doorway and back outside.

Many men along with the women wept, and without shame. They were descendants from Celts and Vikings. Among people with such blood in their veins, it was honorable to weep for their chiefs, kings, and great men.

"I was one o' the mourners that day," said Sandy as Loni sat listening. "I was but a yoong man o' thirty-seven years. I paused beside the still form o' the auld laird longer than the rest. Though many on the island bore traces o' Celtic blood, ye ken, along wi' the Norse, my papa always told me I had Celtic temperament tae the core. I couldna help the tears risin' in my eyes at the sight o' him. An' I let them stream down my face. As a wee laddie I had learned tae love the man, an' I loved him yet more as a man."

80
THE PROCESSION

A storm blew in that night. It still blustered about the Shetlands on the day of the funeral.

Perhaps bereavement fares best under gray skies. Chilly winds, with now and then a burst of rain, contributed their share of comforting gloom to the mood of mourning.

The string of walkers making their way out of the village two days following the viewing at the Cottage, clustered mostly in family groups, were bundled against the day's weather with overcoats and scarves over black suits and dresses. Every head was covered. A few carried umbrellas.

Leading the procession, drawn by two Shetland ponies, a carriage bore the body of the leading man of the small clan that made its home on Whales Reef.

The iron-rimmed wheels clattered rhythmically over cobbles in cadence with the musical *clip-clop* of the ponies' hooves. Behind the hearse walked the chief's widow, sons and daughter with wives and husband and grandchildren, followed by numerous nieces, nephews, cousins, and in-laws.

After the family, keeping a respectful distance

in a long slow-moving train, came the village.

Conversations were muted and cautious. Even in this modern era, most of these island descendants of Celtic and Viking ancestry were more than a little superstitious about death. It didn't do to say too much. *Someone* might be listening.

Not that anyone was worried about celestial eavesdropping on the part of the man whose body this community of witnesses would soon commit to the ground from whence came all humanity—earth to earth, ashes to ashes, dust to dust. None on the island harbored a word, nor so much as a thought, against the "lord of the island." In a time-worn phrase, he was universally beloved by all who knew him—tenants, friends, wife, sons, daughter, as well as those who had chanced to make his acquaintance during the course of his seventy-seven years. All but one—the eldest of his two daughters-in-law.

The laird himself would have considered it more important that a few present on this day had not only loved him, but also *knew* him. Among those privileged to both love him and know him were two who had traveled five thousand miles to be here on this day.

The village undertaker, suitably attired in black tails and top hat, led the carriage off the road and to the right. The faithful ponies followed without need of word or rein, drawing the black-shrouded carriage up the incline toward the church. Reaching their destination, the six men among the family cortege designated for the honor came forward, unloaded the casket, and carried it inside, where the vicar waited solemnly to receive it.

A brief rupture in the clouds shot a momentary explosion of sunlight from the heavens into the dreary afternoon. For a few seconds the church stood bathed in the glow of eternity.

Sally Tulloch turned toward it, lifted the black veil from her face, and closed her eyes with a melancholy smile. The sun's warmth on her cheeks felt like a kiss from the next world.

As quickly as it had come, the crack in the sky closed. The stones of the church returned to the dull gray of the sky and the sea. Still the rain held off, though the mist hovering in the air grew thick and heavy.

As of one accord, three generations of Tullochs made their way inside the seventeenth century kirk.

81

THE INHERITANCE

The passing of Ernest Tulloch marked the end of an era. The Auld Laird, as he had endearingly been called, represented one of a shrinking number of links on Whales Reef to the 1800s. He was the last of his bloodline to remember the Victorian decades now imbued with an aura of nostalgia and veneration. Wallace, his second son and inheritor of the title, in spite of his fifty years, was of the new century. He would always be thought of as the *Yoong Laird* to those who had known his father most of their lives.

The appellation suggested no lack of esteem for Wallace, who now sat beside his elder brother in the front row of the church. The island's affection for the new laird might well in time match that for his father. None had complaint about Wallace, other than the occasionally whispered observation that he had married unwisely, that his wife ruled the home rather more than any man should have to endure.

If a few of the village women harbored skepticism about the future, their doubts generally gathered like a nebulous cloud about the new Lady Priscilla Tulloch who would soon be mistress of the Cottage. The Auld Laird's widow, however, Lady Sally, ten years younger than her husband and equally beloved, still a handsome and forceful woman of sixty-eight, was certain to keep the shadowy figure of her husband's daughter-in-law from causing undue mischief in the seat of influence she was rumored to have coveted for decades.

If Ernest Tulloch's death raised questions, they could be reduced to the single conundrum on everyone's lips since news of the will's content had been announced: *Why did Ernest Tulloch split his inheritance?*

The lairdship and the chieftainship had resided on the head of the same man from the first days the island sept had been formed out of the larger Clan Donald in the final decade of the eighteenth century. Driven from the Highlands by the infamous clearances, Ranald MacDonald, second son of the chief of the small Highland sept west of Inverness, had immigrated with a portion of the clan to the Shetlands. There, the new and smaller Whales Reef sept had prospered. By the time Ranald's son Duncan was chief, he owned most of the island. The clan was by then well-established with a feudal tradition more in keeping with its Highland past than was found on the rest of the Shetlands. Having no sons himself, and to preserve the lairdship and chieftainship on the head of a single male,

Duncan willed both property and title to his son-in-law Frederick Tulloch, a native Shetlander. His son, William Tulloch, known as the Great Tulloch, had renamed the clan "Tulloch." This William was Ernest Tulloch's father.

Splitting the titles between Ernest's two younger sons had created a firestorm of conjecture. The island was talking about nothing else. It was enough that Wallace was not Ernest's eldest son. That fact alone distinguished the inheritance as unusual. For a second son to inherit, however, was not *altogether* unheard of. It was a long-established fact that his brother Brogan's inheritance would be in doubt when he sailed for America twenty-eight years before. Unless he returned, everyone was certain that Wallace would, in Brogan's stead, inherit the lairdship.

But for the youngest son, Leith, seven years younger than Wallace at forty-four, to be named chief, the shock waves rocked the island like an earthquake. Once it was public, news of the laird's will made the front page of Lerwick's newspaper, and was written up in the mainland's *Northern Scot* as well. Did Brogan's return for the funeral signify more than was apparent on the surface? Might he have come to wrest the inheritance from his brother?

The only individuals untroubled by the whirlwinds of gossip were the three Tulloch sons.

Brogan's younger brothers, Wallace and Leith, both admitted that they had known of their father's intentions but had been sworn to strict secrecy. Wallace possessed no ounce of ambition. He was delighted with the prospect of sharing the duties and responsibilities of the family legacy with his younger brother. Lady Sally had probably known of her husband's plans as well, but she was saying nothing.

There was one, however, who had definitely *not* foreseen the startling development. Wallace's wife, Priscilla, made no attempt to conceal her chagrin. It was no secret that Ernest had not approved of the marriage in the first place. But Priscilla had cast her spell over Wallace and persuaded him to ignore his father's objections. Father-in-law and daughter-in-law had endured a precarious relationship of distance ever since.

Priscilla judged the decision to bestow the two titles separately as a personal slap in her face. Having the stature of her future station so peremptorily undercut from beyond the grave sent her into more than one tirade of fury. She had no intention of sharing the rank of first woman on the island with Leith's wife. Her disdain for the soft-spoken local lass was sharpened by the knowledge that most on the island loved Moira dearly and had not stopped rejoicing since learning she was the wife of the new chief.

It was not merely in the matter of the two titles

that Ernest's will enraged his daughter-in-law. His modern sense of fairness would spell the ruin of all she had counted on. Modest legacies in the form of income-producing investments to Brogan, Delynn, and Leith ensured it would be more difficult for her and Wallace to make ends meet from the meager village rents. And his deeding of the Auld Hoose and its adjoining property of one hundred acres to the chief and his posterity shrunk yet further an inheritance that should have belonged to Wallace in its entirety. She had married for money and prestige. Now Ernest had robbed her of both. Rumors were afoot that Priscilla planned to contest Ernest's will in the courts. There was little she could hope to accomplish, however. Ernest had seen to every legality. The thing was ironclad.

And now, as the villagers walked quietly up toward the church, more than a handful were looking forward with inward anticipation to see how Lady Priscilla would conduct herself. Would she show respect for the memory of the father-in-law who, in her view, had insulted her and her husband? Would she allow her antagonism to exhibit itself in full public display?

It was well known that Leith, still in his teens at the time, had been more outspoken than his father in opposition to his brother's marriage to the young widow from mainland Shetland. But their disagreement over the marriage never came between Ernest and Wallace, nor between the laird's two sons.

Priscilla never forgave either Ernest or Leith. And though Ernest had done his best to forge what modicum of relationship was possible with Wallace's wife, on Leith's part the years since had only strengthened his mistrust of his sister-in-law.

82

THE GRAVESIDE

The rain held off. The venerable and historic stone church gradually filled.

Once inside, no more words were spoken. Beside Sally sat Brogan, eldest of the next generation at fifty-two, noticeably graying although tall and stately. With him was his diminutive American wife whose brief sojourns to Shetland were remembered fondly by many in the village. Next to her sat Wallace and Priscilla, beside them Ernest's only daughter, Delynn, her husband, Jock, and finally the youngest, who occupied the locus of the speculative maelstrom, Leith with his wife, Moira.

Every man, woman, and child who called the island home was present, not to mention a good number from mainland Shetland, even a few dignitaries from London. The two doors and all the windows remained opened so that when pews and aisles and foyer were crowded to capacity, those gathered in the open air around the church could also hear.

The first portion of the service did not last long. The vicar moved quickly through the expected remarks and prayer-book formalities. Indicating for the assembly to stand, he then led family and pallbearers carrying the casket outside. He would deliver his eulogy at the graveside.

The silent shuffling mass left the church and crunched its way across the gravel surrounding the building as the coffin was slowly borne aloft in front of them, then across the wet grass to the iron-enclosed cemetery of ancient date. Through the irregular conglomeration of stones and markers, the vicar and family led the way to the Tulloch family plot. There an open grave lay ready to embrace the newest member of the proud family to be received into his final resting place.

The casket was set in place beside the dark hole that yawned ominously out of the earth. The family gathered close. The rest of the village spread out around them on all sides, gradually filling most of the cemetery.

Children clung to their parents, afraid to let their eyes drift toward either casket or grave. Death was too fearsome to look upon. Even a momentary glance sent shivers of dread up every spine of less than ten years, and up not a few spines much older than that. Ernest's two grandsons, Macgregor and Alexander Tulloch, both in their twenties, cousins and sons of Wallace and Leith, stood together. The younger cousins—Delynn's three, Leith and Moira's two daughters, and Wallace and Priscilla's three younger teens—all stood silently behind their parents.

The vicar took his place and resumed his remarks. Opening his Bible with suitable solemnity, he read several of Ernest's favorite passages. He then presented a brief summary of the laird's life with dates, accomplishments, contributions to the war effort, and improvements brought to the island under his tenure. In closing he mentioned by name all the family left behind, including the ten grandchildren who stood listening and, with the aid of a scribbled addition to his notes from a brief interview with Brogan before the service, Ernest's eleventh, a grandson, not present, and his single great-granddaughter. He ended the service in formal prayer.

Led by Lady Sally Tulloch, weeping gently, the family members now filed in a circle around the casket. Some set hands tenderly for a second or two on the shiny wood. Others followed Sally's example and stooped briefly to kiss the coffin. Most held flowers, which they reverently laid on top of it.

When they were done, the sexton, aided by Ernest's three sons, carefully lowered the casket into the ground. What flowers remained were tossed in after it. Sally took several steps back. The rest of the family did likewise.

Gradually the villagers came slowly forward to pay their own private respects to the dead. A few eyes drifted in Priscilla's direction, wondering if any fireworks from that quarter might still be in the offing.

Sandy Innis looked over at Loni, who was listening with rapt attention. "I dinna mind tellin' ye, lassie," he said, pausing to wipe his eyes, then smiling at the memory, "there were again tears in my eyes as I came forward. I paused at the open grave an' said another prayer for the dear man. Then I stretched oot my hand that I'd kept clasped a' the time inside the kirk an' turned over my palm an' opened my fingers. I can still see the wee sparrow's feather fall fae my hand an' drift tae rest on top o' the coffin wi' the flowers that had been tossed on it.

"I ken what the farthing means, laird," I whispered. "I winna forget."

When the silent parade had completed its processional past the graveside, Ernest's three sons and daughter stepped forward. A little uncertain as to protocol, the undertaker glanced awkwardly at Brogan, but then handed the spade to Wallace as new laird. With all eyes upon him, the laird's second son filled it with earth from the pile heaped beside the grave and gently tossed it into the hole.

A muted *thud* echoed from below. A stifled cry escaped Sally's lips at the awful finality of the sound.

Wallace handed the spade to Leith. A second clump of earth followed the first. Delynn came next, with Brogan, the eldest, completing the ritual.

Macgregor, the nephew he had met for the first time the day before, now stepped forward. Brogan handed him the spade. As the eldest of the next generation present, Macgregor did his duty with spade and earth, then handed the spade to Leith's son. Alexander did the same, followed in turn by a few of the younger male cousins, then a line of more distant relatives. As a good number of the village men moved forward to participate in the time-honored rite, the undertaker provided two more shovels. Presently the plops of earth came rapidly. Not a soul left the churchyard until a mound of sheltering earth was heaped high over the dead.

Sally and her son and two stepsons and step-daughter made their way through the iron gate out of the cemetery and back toward the church. There they spread out and were slowly engulfed by visitors and well-wishers pouring out of the cemetery behind them. Conversations throughout the churchyard gradually resumed. Many now gave voice to their surprise to see Brogan among the family.

83
THE VILLAGE

A yet thicker gray settled over the churchyard. Almost instantly rain began to fall.

A few black umbrellas sprang up. Rain, however, was in the nature of life here, so no one was especially bothered. As long as there were coats, boots, and hats, let it rain.

Slowly the human tide moved out of the cemetery, with innumerable ebbs and flows and eddies of its movements. Most of the islanders sought Lady Sally and the laird's four grown children for a handshake and few final words of condolence. The rain and size of the crowd made the would-be receiving line more cumbersome than otherwise. The home of the departed would be open for the rest of the day. Rather than stand waiting, a good number said to themselves that they would pay their respects to Lady Sally later in the afternoon.

As the throng drifted back toward the village, now that the dead had been put to rest, the mood of mourning gave way to an occasion for visiting, small talk, renewal of acquaintance, and that all-important sustaining ingredient to any small community—circulation of the latest gossip.

For the remainder of the day, Brogan found himself more the center of attention even than the widow or new laird or new chief. His presence presented Whales Reef with a delicious entrée of rumor possibilities. Half of those present had woken that morning without an idea that Brogan was back on the island. Eyes widened to the size of saucers at the apparition seated in the church with his two brothers and sister. Reports and stories and all manner of what the Scots called *clishmaclaver* had abounded concerning the disappearance of the laird's eldest son back in the twenties. Suddenly here he was again! Though they had been forced to postpone speculation— like dozens of unspoken dams ready to burst— the appearance of the long-lost elder brother now set tongues to wagging.

Had he returned to take back the lairdship that had just been passed to his brother?

And what of the chieftainship? If Brogan had come back to claim his inheritance, where did the youngest son, Leith, now stand?

It was actually a visitor from London who raised the question, though indirectly, to Ernest Tulloch's eldest son as the funeral train slowly walked through the village.

"I say, Mr. Tulloch," said a voice from behind. Its owner came up and fell into stride. "I don't know if you remember me, but we met some years ago—up there on the hill," he added, motioning behind and to his left, "at the hotel."

Brogan turned to eye the man, taking in his London accent and silvery hair as he quickly scanned his face. "I believe I do remember," he replied slowly. "An investigator of some kind . . . a reporter, now that I think of it."

"Very good!"

"Just give me a moment . . . it's coming . . . if I am not mistaken, let me see . . . it would be Mr. Glendenning, I believe."

"I congratulate you on your memory," rejoined the journalist. "You are exactly right. Robert Glendenning, from London."

The two men shook hands warmly.

"I must say, it is most unexpected to see you again," said Brogan, "especially on such a day."

"And may I introduce my son." The Londoner indicated a boy beside him. "Alexander, this is Mr. Brogan Tulloch, onetime heir of the man whose funeral we have just attended."

Brogan smiled and extended his hand to the lad.

"Ever since I was here," Glendenning went on, "I have been fascinated with the Shetlands. I confess, your islands became something of an obsession for me."

"I am intrigued."

"It is as much your fault as anyone's."

"*Mine* . . . how so?"

"You were the first native Shetlander, so to speak, I had met. You spoke with me candidly and . . . who can say why, the place began to exert a spell over me. I've been back a number of times. I became well-acquainted with your father, wrote a couple pieces about him, actually—during the war, you know."

"Really. I would like to read them."

"I hope we shall have an opportunity to talk further. But are you . . . are you here to *stay?*" Glendenning's eyebrows arched significantly as he emphasized the word.

"Have I changed my mind about the titles and all that?" asked Brogan.

"I would not want to put it *quite* so bluntly on the day of your father's funeral," replied Glendenning with a coy smile. His tone, however, carried no doubt about the intent of his question.

"You need have no worries about offending me," said Brogan, chuckling lightly. "But no, I made my decision years ago. I remain content. I still believe it was for the best, as was my father's decision to pass on the lairdship and the chieftainship separately to my brothers."

"Yes, I heard about that. Besides paying my respects to a man I considered a dear friend, I admit hoping I might learn the inside story about his will. Perhaps obtain Lady Sally's permission to write a story about it."

"As for the inside story, I don't know who you will get that from," said Brogan, thoughtfully. "My father is dead. The only person who might have that information is Sally. I think I know her well enough to be assured she will reveal nothing."

"I am certain you are right."

"But though I am not privy to his thoughts, my father's decision seems nothing less than a stroke of genius. What better way to move our small island clan toward the modern era than with a devolution of power—a decentralization that is voluntarily given, not forced upon an unwilling monarch."

"The benevolent king?"

"Something like it, perhaps."

"Your father may indeed have been a genius," agreed Glendenning. "Far-seeing, certainly. Though his kind of genius, if I may call it that, is not usually perceived by those who look for greatness as the world judges it."

"Spiritual realms, you mean?" asked Brogan.

Glendenning nodded. "His impact upon my life lay in those regions more profoundly than any other."

"That is a story I am eager to hear!"

"So how long will you be staying?" asked Glendenning.

"Unfortunately, only a week. Then my wife and I will return to the States."

"Is this your first time back since you left— when was it, in the twenties?"

"Actually, I returned for a visit after the war. I

had a wonderful reunion with the whole family, especially with my father. We had the good fortune to be assigned together for a time during the war as well."

"Anything dangerous and exciting?"

"Parts of it, yes. Do I detect another story brewing in your head?"

"Always! Did you and he ever talk about his legacy and the inheritance?"

Brogan smiled. "Perhaps. But those conversations will remain between myself and my father."

Glendenning nodded. "I respect that. Do you have family in the States?"

"Yes—one son, Grant. He and his wife gave us a granddaughter three years ago."

"Congratulations. And her name?"

"Alison."

"You are staying at the ancestral home, I take it?"

Brogan nodded. "Many memories," he said. "The place is as full of life and energy as ever, though obviously that will change now with my father gone."

Sally and Brogan's wife walked up to join the two men and the younger Glendenning. Greetings and introductions followed.

"Welcome again to Whales Reef, Mr. Glendenning," said Sally. "Thank you so much for coming."

"My condolences, Lady Tulloch. Your husband was a great man."

"Thank you. He was indeed. But the funeral is past. This is no time for formality—you have always called me Sally. I see no reason to change that. Will you join us at the Cottage? The villagers will be coming and going all afternoon."

"With pleasure."

"If you are staying over, it would be a privilege to extend our hospitality for as long as you are in the Shetlands. We would love to have you stay with us. Indeed, I insist on it."

"Even in grief, you are the perfect hostess."

"Nonsense. You are as good as family. Besides," Sally added, "I will not be mistress of the place much longer." A hint of irony crept into her tone. "I may not have many more opportunities to freely extend invitations to my *own* guests."

"You're not leaving the island?"

"Nothing like that."

"What then?"

"I only meant that Wallace and Priscilla will be moving over from the Auld Hoose and taking up residence in the Cottage. He has succeeded to the lairdship, you know."

"Yes, I heard. And you anticipate . . . some awkwardness?" probed Glendenning, the investigative reporter subtly surfacing.

Sally glanced toward him with a wry smile, but was silent.

"What my stepmother is reluctant to say," put in Brogan, "is that she will soon be relegated to the role of *dowager* Lady Tulloch, while the new laird's wife, shall we say, makes herself at home."

"Surely the house will remain yours? Your position will be honored no less than before."

"Not exactly," said Sally, replying with cautious candor. "Wallace will be laird now. The house therefore goes to him. Times have changed. I will have to adapt, even if it means moving to an apartment in the south wing. Priscilla has had her eye on our quarters on the east side for years."

"And you are in accord with such changes?"

"I will be a dutiful and cooperative mother and mother-in-law. It is time for me to be a grand-mother and not a laird's wife."

"What about Leith, Sally?" asked Brogan.

"Leith and Moira and their family will move over to the Auld Hoose when Wallace and Priscilla come to the Cottage. It will be a great chaotic shift of residences!" she added, laughing. "Two families moving in opposite directions across the island, each to take up residence in the other's home."

"When do you expect all this to take place?"

"No doubt as soon as Priscilla can manage it," said Sally. "At the moment she is none too pleased with me. It would not surprise me if they begin tomorrow."

84
THE REUNION

"From the looks of it, we already have a full house," said Sally as they walked up the driveway toward the Cottage.

They walked inside. No hint remained of the somber viewing in the entry hall of two days earlier. Light and life had returned.

Most of the family had already arrived. Sally's daughter-in-law Moira, hostess for the day, was scurrying about in the kitchen with her two daughters, housekeeper, and cook, pouring tea and setting out platters of sandwiches and sweets. Already the villagers had begun to trickle in. Every woman who arrived carried something edible to contribute, whether casserole or oatcakes or plate of turnips. By day's end the Cottage would be filled with enough food to feed the island for a week.

Two notables who were not present were Wallace and Priscilla. They had taken the western road home from the church in their car to the Auld Hoose. With the titles now split, it would become the chief's new residence.

A young man in his mid-twenties, tall, ruggedly built, and handsome, came forward to greet Brogan and his wife.

"Hello again, Uncle Brogan," he said with a smile.

"Macgregor," said Brogan, shaking hands with the son of his brother Wallace.

"My father wanted me to tell you that he will be over later. He very much wants to talk to you."

"And I him! I must say, seeing you walk up just now," Brogan added with a light laugh, "if I didn't know better I would think I was talking to him! Your resemblance at the same age is striking."

"I will take that as a compliment!" laughed Macgregor. "I would add that it is an honor to meet you . . . again. I was too young when you were here after the war. I had been hearing about you all my life and was probably a little awed to see you in the flesh. It is different now to see you and talk to you as—"

"Man to man," suggested Brogan.

"Something like that," Macgregor said and smiled. "Anyway, I hope to have the chance to visit with you further."

"So then," Brogan said, "what were all those things you heard about me?"

"About yours and my father's exploits all over the island," replied his nephew, "replete with Vikings and caves and all manner of legends."

"Don't believe everything your father tells you!"

"Perhaps I shall have to get your version of events while you are here."

Their conversation was interrupted by the appearance of a striking girl in her mid-teens. Unlike most others on this day, she had little interest in the elder Tulloch. Her eyes were reserved for Wallace's son.

"Hello, Macgregor," she said.

"Oh . . . hello, Odara," replied Macgregor. "This is my uncle, Brogan Tulloch. He's an American. Uncle Brogan, this is Odara Innes, daughter of our veterinarian."

"Good afternoon, Miss Innes," said Brogan. "I'm not really an American, though I do live there. I will always be a Shetlander."

Only moderately intrigued, the girl briefly took in the features of Brogan's face. Her interest, however, lasted only a moment. She quickly turned and flashed her eyes again on Macgregor.

"Go have something to eat, Odara," he said. "Uncle Brogan and I have things to talk about."

Obviously disappointed, the girl wandered off.

"Now there is a lassie with serious interest in you," whispered Brogan.

"She's only seventeen," rejoined Macgregor.

"She is a beauty."

"I'll give her that. But young."

"She'll grow."

"Then ask me what I think five years from now. Ah, here's Alexander."

Leith's twenty-three-year-old son now joined them.

"Hi, Uncle Brogan," he said, giving his uncle a friendly handshake. "Don't let this chap sell you any peat bricks and tell you they're gold!"

"Does he make a habit of such things?" laughed Brogan.

"He's always looking for an angle with the tourists," quipped Alexander, "especially foreign women."

"Is he now—?" said Brogan.

"A complete fabrication!" rejoined Macgregor.

"Come now, cousin," chided Alexander, "you cannot deny that a foreign accent turns your head."

"That sounds like me!" said Brogan. "I was terrible that way when I was young. You had better be careful, Macgregor," he added, turning back to the older of the two. "One never knows where one's antics will lead. That's how I met my wife!"

If their two fathers were not bothered by the island scuttlebutt about the laird's will, the friendship of the two cousins was equally unscathed by the controversy. The best of friends, Macgregor and Alexander were likewise delighted by the fact that they would one day, like their fathers, share in leading their clan, one as laird and the other as chief.

As uncle and two nephews chatted amiably, Brogan's wife was approached by a redheaded young man in his late thirties.

●　●　●

I could tell she didna ken who I was at first, said Sandy with a smile. So I hung back. I was jist waitin' tae attract her attention wi'out fanfare. My wife an' my sister were at my side, an' I couldna help smiling, wonderin' if she'd remember the day on the moor wi' the Auld Laird. I felt a mite sheepish standin' there amid all the family, greetin' one anither.

Then at last she saw me waitin' tae speak tae her, an' she glanced toward me wi' an expression of question, then took a step toward me.

"Hello . . ." she said uncertainly.

"Hello, Miss Hanson . . . or Mrs. Tulloch, I mean," I said. I could feel the smile widening on my face. But still she didna ken me.

"I'm sorry," she began, "but I . . . I don't seem—"

"I see ye dinna remember me," I said. "'Tis been a long time. I was but a wee urchin. We met one day oot on the moor w' the laird. We were helpin' a wee sparrow die in peace. Then we met again in Annabella's cottage."

She drew in a gasp as recognition dawned.

"Of course! Sandy Innes! Oh, I can't believe it. Sandy, how absolutely wonderful to see you again!"

She stepped forward an' embraced me like a son. As short as the other men o' the island considered me, I stood at least three inches above the dear lady. She was a tiny one, she was!

"I would like ye tae meet my wife, Daracha," I said.

"Daracha . . . what a beautiful name. I've never heard it before."

My wife smiled an' curtsied shyly.

"An' here's my sister, Eldora," I said. "She wanted tae meet ye as weel. Ye see, they've both heard the story o' the wee sparrow many times."

"I am happy to meet you both . . . Eldora, Daracha. Your Sandy will always be a dear friend in my memory. Sandy," she said, turning again to me an' shakin' her head kinda like she still wasna altogether sure it was me, "you cannot know how many times I have thought of you through the years. And now here you are with two lovely women at your side!"

"An' oor daughter Odara is aroun' somewhere," I said, glancin' aboot. "I'm afraid she has eyes for the new laird's son."

The dear lady laughed, an' the sound o' her voice is wi' me still.

Meanwhile, Brogan, Macgregor, and Alexander had now been joined by several of the younger cousins, all of whom stared up at Brogan with wide eyes and expressions of mingled curiosity and awe. Like the two older boys, all their lives they had been hearing about this mythical man who had gone to America. Now here he was in front of them—full of life, good-looking, pleasant, on happy terms with everyone, to all appearances the apple of Sally's eye, or at least one of several, for she made much over her family.

By now groups from the village were arriving rapidly. Brogan found himself facing a steady stream of former acquaintances anxious to exchange greetings. They were older, grayer, sporting less hair, and carrying more pounds. Brogan had to have his wits about him to pull up the dozens of names from his memory to attach to the faces surrounding him.

"I say!" he exclaimed as two men approached, "if it isn't Donal Kerr . . . and Kyle MacNeill! The two men who keep Whales Reef supplied with beer and bread!"

"Yer memory's as sharp as yer eye is keen, laddie," said Kerr with a laugh. "Fan ye went tae America, I lost ane o' my best customers!"

Brogan roared with laughter.

"Hoo's the brew in America, Brogan lad?"

"Canna haud a candle tae yer's, Donal," replied Brogan, briefly taking up the dialect of his youth. "'Tis enough tae turn a man into a teetotaler! Hoo's Nyssa?"

"She's aboot somewye, an' anxious tae see ye!"

"An' I her. Hoo aboot yersel', MacNeill? Hoo gaes the trade in butteries, breads, an' fancies?"

"Middlin', Brogan," said the baker. "My son'll be takin' o'or from me naist year, ye ken."

"Yoong Tavish! Weel, good for him. I wish the lad weel. An' dis my e'en deceive me?" said Brogan. "Is that Laren Gordon ahin ye . . . an' Dinky Munro?" he added as another group of men from the village joined them. "An' if it isn't Cousin MacBean an' Uncle Peter!" he continued to exclaim, going around the expanding group and shaking each man's hand in turn.

"How du ye keep in mind o' us a'?" asked Peter Gunn.

"I never forgot a soul on Whales Reef," said Brogan to his great-uncle. "Most of you I saw seven years ago. You haven't changed so much. And who's this laddie beside you, Uncle Peter?"

"My son, Fergus."

"Hello, laddie. I'm Brogan. You and me are family somehow or another, but to tell you the truth I'm not sure of all the connections between the Tullochs an' MacBeans and Gunns and Cauleys. Can you blame me for being confused!"

85
THE STUDY

When evening came, every Tulloch from the Cottage and the Auld Hoose—by blood and marriage—was exhausted.

At ten o'clock, every bed and pillow was occupied, every light off, and sounds of slumber filled the two ancestral homes, as well as that of Delynn's family in the village.

By seven the next morning, an enormous fire blazed away in the huge stone fireplace of the Cottage. Sally's housekeeper had tea and coffee ready for the earliest of the risers, with fresh pots added as family and guests wandered down the stairs.

Brogan entered the familiar breakfast room about nine and saw Sally, her grandson Alexander, and Robert Glendenning and his son engaged in animated conversation.

"Hello, all," he said. "Whew—I had no idea how tired I was! I must have slept ten or eleven hours!"

"Airplanes do that to you," said Glendenning. "I had to fly over to New York and back a few years ago in the space of four days. I didn't recover for two weeks. Get several cups of Mrs.

Graves's strong coffee into you is my advice."

"Nothing could sound better," said Brogan, dropping into a chair. "Good morning, Sally."

"And to you, Brogan," rejoined Sally, rising and walking to one of the sideboards laden with food and drink.

"Where's Leith?" asked Brogan.

"Out with the sheep," answered Alexander.

"Good for him. A chief's first duty is to his herds and flocks, the Bible says . . . loosely translated, that is! I've been meaning to ask," Brogan added. "I didn't see Annabella Raoghnailt yesterday. Is she still living?"

"She passed away since you were here last," replied Sally as she poured out a cup of coffee.

"That's a shame. We had hoped to see her."

Sally set a cup and saucer in front of her stepson. "Cream, as I recall?"

"Sally, you are a dear—thank you!" said Brogan. "And yes, cream if you have it."

"We have *everything,* thanks to the villagers' generosity!" said Sally, walking over to the pantry. "Jugs of fresh cream from the island's cows, and anything else you could want."

"The only thing missing right now is Dad," said Brogan as he sipped from his cup a minute later. "The last time I was here, he and I were enjoying coffee together, just like this. But you never stop to think, *Hmm, this may be the last time I see this person.* It's easy to take the best things in life for granted. I wish I hadn't waited so long to rekindle that most precious of human relationships . . . between father and son."

"Your father understood, Brogan," said Sally. "You had your own life to live. There was the Depression, then the war, financial difficulties, travel was expensive. The island's finances slumped badly too, as you know. We really couldn't afford to help."

"Of course, I've told myself all the reasons," said Brogan. "Still, I should have found a way to come sooner."

"Don't forget that you and your father both *tried* to correspond, and your efforts were subverted."

"Believe me, I will never forget that! I only hope someday I will find a way to forgive it."

"Fortunately, even such duplicity could not prevent love finding a way. Your time together during the war, and then your return here when it was over, were highlights of his life. He spoke of it ever after, and of the bond he felt with you."

Later that afternoon, as predicted, Priscilla appeared at the Cottage with a loaded truck and two hired villagers. Wallace followed as she marched through the door with an apologetic expression on his face at the obvious importunity of his wife.

Sally used the opportunity to take Brogan and his wife aside for a private talk.

• • •

"Strange tae say," said Sandy as a thoughtful expression came over his face, "I happened tae be in the Cottage at that moment. I saw the three o' them holdin' counsel together as they walked toward the staircase."

"I thought only the family was at the Cottage on the day after the funeral," said Loni.

Sandy nodded. " 'Tis true . . . mostly true, that is. But ye see, there'd been a problem wi' one o' the laird's ponies, givin' birth she was, an' I was at the Cottage till the wee hours. So I came back that next afternoon tae see tae the bit wee coltie an' that all was weel wi' both mother an' the tiny animal, no bigger than a doggie."

"And was all well?" asked Loni.

"Oh, aye—the newborn was healthy an' hungry an' already scamperin' aboot on his wee leggies. An' what I was sayin' is that Sally was oot wi' me in the barn—that was her way, ye ken . . . she loved the animals, an' her hert was as full o' them as it was for the folk on the island. When I had done in the barn, she told me tae come into the hoose an' see the folk again an' hae a bite tae eat, an' when I left tae take a platter or two back home tae Daracha. That was her way, ye ken—everyone on the island was welcome in the Cottage.

"I went inside wi' Lady Sally an' sat doon with Brogan an' yoong Macgregor. Wallace's wife eyed me sternly as I came in—that's the Lady Priscilla, ye ken—an' I knew what she was sayin' wi'oot her sayin' it, that I'd nae mair see the inside o' the Cottage once she was mistress o' the place—which was true enough. She was a rum one.

"Then Lady Sally took Brogan an' his wife aside an' said she wanted tae talk tae them, in private, ye ken. It was time for me tae be goin' by then, an' as I was leavin' they were jist disappearin' up the stairway. O' course I ne'er heard a word o' what passed a'tween them. 'Twas family business, ye ken, an' none o' mine. But I knew the laird an' Lady Sally weel enough tae ken what it was likely aboot. Whate'er passed between them nae doobt concerned the heritage that's come tae ye, an' the laird's legacy, an' the inheritance ye came tae Whales Reef tae discover."

Sally led Brogan and his wife upstairs into her husband's study off the landing at the top of the stairs. Once there, she closed the door behind them. She inserted a large key, ancient and iron-brown, into the lock and turned it. A dull metallic *clank* signified that the three were cloistered inside the private chamber of learning, study, and reflection, the sanctuary and prayer closet of Ernest Tulloch. Sally removed the key.

Brogan sensed the import of the moment. On every side the antiquity and venerable effluence of the room's contents emanated an aura of wisdom and, for Brogan, bittersweet nostalgia.

Occasional tables contained piles of books and random keepsakes and memorabilia, every one of which had a story. Paintings and a few tapestries and tartans hung from what space on the walls was not covered with books. Faded and worn colorful Persian rugs lay underfoot. Most striking of all, however, were the floor-to-ceiling bookcases lined with hundreds of volumes spanning the centuries. Pervading the room floated the distinctive intermingling perfumes of old oak, varnish, leather, wool, paper, ink, and dust.

"Oh, look—there's the roll-top desk I brought him," said Brogan, indicating an oak desk that sat against the far wall of the room. "And open, as if still in use."

"It was never closed," said Sally. "He sat at it every day. This other desk in the middle of the room he used for business. Your roll-top was his spiritual retreat in the sanctuary of his study. It is where he kept his writings and most prized devotional books."

"It makes me happy to hear that," said Brogan. "I can visualize him sitting there."

He stood staring down at several stacks of books, papers, two bound journals, and at least half a dozen Bibles. Two Bibles lay open. His father had obviously been using this place almost until the day of his death.

"He treasured this desk," said Sally. "All the more knowing that you made it with your own hands. He continually raved about the craftsman-ship. He marveled as well that you were able to transport it safely all this distance."

"That was somewhat difficult," Brogan said with a smile. "But it was something I wanted to do, something of myself that I could give him."

"It meant the world to him." Sally paused briefly. "How fitting," she went on as her eyes flitted about. "Here is his favorite Bible, open to the fourth chapter of Philippians. And this Moffatt Testament, almost equally marked, open to second Timothy, chapter four. He knew his time was short. And here are the Scotsman's four volumes of sermons in a place of honor between Ernest's favorite bookends, along with Drummond, Kempis, Kierkegaard, Woolman . . . and his new friend Kelly, which was never far from him."

"Seeing this desk again," said Brogan at length, "I think I will make some drawings when I am here, to compare with the originals in my files. Grant and I will make another at home—an exact duplicate. It will be a tangible reminder of my father."

"You could ship this one home," said Sally. "Nothing would please me more than for you to have it."

"Thank you, Sally. But this desk needs to remain just where it is. It is part of my father's legacy."

Sally's deportment became solemn and reveren-tial. The dignified stature of her years enfolded her countenance as she sat down in the faded green leather chair behind her husband's business table. She lay the key down she had taken from the door. Scattered over the surface in front of her were an assortment of papers, files, folders, and documents mostly in his own hand, several fountain pens, and an inkwell.

Sally's two guests eased themselves into the two chairs opposite her.

"What a wonderful place this is," said Brogan softly. "It looks so different to my eyes now than when my father brought me here for our annual birthday talks before we struck out over the island. I was oblivious then to the spiritual currents running within him. Suddenly everything is imbued with . . . I don't know what to call it other than holiness."

He grew yet more pensive.

"The last time I saw him, he and I sat here together for hours," he went on. "The years of separation seemingly gushed out. Depths were opened in both of us. He told me about his favorite books and authors. It was a side of my father I hadn't known as a boy. Though I am now over fifty myself, I realize how much I still have to learn about him."

Brogan took in a deep breath and exhaled slowly. "Every inch, every book, every memento, speaks volumes about the man he was."

"You cannot imagine the joy it gives me to

hear you say those words," said Sally. "I needed to know if you had eyes to see what is here. I suspected it after your last visit. When I saw you and your father walking out on the island together, heads close in conversation, and when you disappeared in here for hours at a time, I sensed that deep waters were flowing. Hearing you say what you just did, I know more than ever how true that was. You are seeing into who your father truly was . . . and *is*."

"I am *beginning* to see," said Brogan. "It makes me all the more regret those years of my youth—even my prodigality, in a sense—when I did not value the wisdom he had built into my life. I know it grieved him that I misspent some of my best years keeping him at arm's length." He paused and smiled sadly. "Yet the memory of that makes me all the more appreciative of the constancy of his love for me."

"Did you and he ever talk about that time?" asked Sally.

Brogan nodded. "Yes, we did. We shed a few tears together. Though that time with him was precious, the years apart could not be recaptured. We were grateful for the reunion, but it was not enough. I know we both wanted more."

Brogan heard his wife crying softly. He reached for her hand.

"I believe that the secret to that more," said Sally at length, "even the secret to regaining those years, may lie in this room. In what way, I cannot say. Something is here that will be revealed, whether to one of us or one who comes after, I have no idea. Your father's vision of what life with God truly means, his life's prayer, will live on. It will bear a hundredfold fruit . . . somehow, God only knows. I sincerely hope and pray that that fruit will live on as the inheritance of this family is passed to others, extending into future generations through men and women of Ernest's posterity who are not yet born, even in the lives of your own grandchildren and great-grandchildren, who may one day sit in this very office again."

As she spoke, Brogan continued to gaze about, sensing the eternal import of all that surrounded him.

"This room, this study, these books, his Bibles, your father's writings," Sally went on, "everything here is his earthly legacy. His character, of course, is the true legacy. Yet this room will always be a reflection of the character of the man we knew and loved. It was the greatest privilege of my life to share your father's spiritual journey. Whenever he and I sat here together, to talk, to pray, even if it was just on occasion to enjoy our morning coffee here, I always had the sense that I was entering the inner sanctum of Ernest's deepest humanity. I'm sure you felt that when you shared this room with him seven years ago. This was the prayer closet of his soul."

86
THE BARD

"All this explains why I asked the two of you to join me here," said Sally, breaking the silence. "With Wallace and Priscilla moving into the Cottage—I can hear them unloading furniture below us even as we speak!—much is certain to change. Even before Ernest told me of his plans, I knew Wallace would one day take up residence in the Cottage. But I vowed that no one would touch this room. Ernest tried diligently to make peace with Priscilla, yet I could see in her eyes that she considered him a doddering, pious old fool rather than a man to be honored."

Sally grew pensive.

"Having been subject to her influence for so long," she went on, "I honestly have no idea what Wallace now thinks about your father's spirituality. Every man and woman has to decide how much of their early influence they will carry into their adult years. Wallace and I don't really talk. I am firmly convinced, however, that if she has the chance, Priscilla will dismantle this office, sell off the books, and dispose of Ernest's possessions and writings into the rubbish bin."

"She wouldn't!" exclaimed Brogan's wife.

"Don't be too sure, dear. Remember the confiscation of the letters," said Sally. "But as I say, I determined that it would never happen. I have taken steps to make sure of it. Ernest didn't think about his legacy. He assumed his four children would split up his books and whatever else you wanted and take the rest to a charity shop. I knew it was up to me to preserve his books and personal things. I am willing, as I said, to be a dutiful ex-laird's wife. But Priscilla will *not* touch this office."

"Couldn't you simply tell Wallace and Leith and Delynn to preserve it as is?" asked Brogan. "And then . . . I don't know, everyone could make use of it as a study and library."

Sally's smile was full of sorrow. "I would have no confidence that Priscilla might not eventually persuade Wallace to go against my wishes. They will be living here. As possession is nine-tenths of the law, Leith and Delynn would be powerless to do anything about it, especially after I am gone. Even if she were prevented from actually disposing of Ernest's possessions, Priscilla could crate them up and put them in storage and turn the room into her own private salon."

Brogan shuddered at the thought.

"So, as I said, I have taken steps," continued Sally. "Over his initial objections, I finally prevailed upon Ernest to stipulate this office and its possessions as mine throughout my lifetime, as a separate part of my flat within the main house, and mine to pass on the use of as I think best. He said it was unnecessary, that Wallace would know how best to accomplish my wishes. But I persuaded him, and it was written up as a codicil to the will, which I asked Mr. MacNaughton not to divulge. No one knows of it except you two."

She breathed out a long sigh. "Priscilla will hit the roof when she finds out. I intend to tell her while the two of you are here. That may blunt the force of it somewhat. With you and Wallace and Leith backing me, I don't think Priscilla will dare oppose me. Even if she does, the arrangement will be legally binding. I will tell her that I will do all she asks of me to the extent my conscience allows. But I will also tell her 'You will *not* go into the study.' As angry as she will be, I think Priscilla is superstitious enough to be wary of intruding on the domain of the dead."

"Just what does the codicil provide?" asked Brogan. "What other steps have you taken?"

Sally did not reply immediately.

"You know your father split the titles between Wallace and Leith," she said at length. "I always held out hope that you might return and become laird after all. Your father knew you were content with your decision to give up the inheritance. Before you met again during the war, he told me he intended to offer it to you once more."

"Which he did," Brogan said. "We talked and

prayed together. I reaffirmed that I was at peace with it."

Sally nodded. "He had to struggle with it a while longer, but he came to be at peace with it as well. That being the case, I intend to add a third component to the inheritance so that all three of Ernest's sons will share equally in his legacy."

"If you're talking about finances and money, Sally . . . honestly there is no need. With Grant taking a greater interest in our furniture business, we are back on our feet and—"

"It's not that, Brogan," said Sally. "There is precious little of actual cash to spread around, especially with a separate provision now being made to support a chief as well as a laird. Wallace and Leith will have their hands full simply making ends meet. Rents have not kept pace with expenses, I'm afraid. However, I am speaking of your father's entire legacy. The final third of that legacy—in addition to the lairdship and chieftainship—is symbolized by what this room represents."

Again Sally paused thoughtfully. "Your father considered himself a Highland Scot as much as a Shetlander," she continued. "He was deeply proud of his MacDonald roots and their traditions. Therefore, along with the lairdship and chieftainship of our small clan, I am taking it upon myself as the chief's wife and widow to add a third title."

"Another title besides laird and chief?" asked Brogan.

"Yes, I am appointing a bard to our small clan," Sally answered.

"A *bard,*" repeated Brogan. "I thought they went out in the eighteenth century. Harps, poets, holy men and all that?"

"I prefer to think of a bard as a spiritual seer, a visionary, one who sees into God's eternal purposes."

"Ah . . . I see what you mean. That describes my father to perfection!"

"Perhaps it is old-fashioned. It's certainly more Celtic than Shetlandic. But maybe it's time to reclaim some of the old ways. And I believe the bardship can be a powerful symbol. I believe it represents your father, and that matters more to me than anything."

"Acknowledging my father posthumously as honorary bard—I love the idea!" exclaimed Brogan. "You shall have my full support as well."

Sally's lips parted in an enigmatic smile. Slowly she nodded.

"You have apprehended my meaning perfectly," she said, "as I was sure you would. You indeed understand the spiritual legacy your father left behind. Therefore, I am certain you will also understand the importance of protecting this room. Though the bardship may be honorary, my rights over this room will be legal and binding.

Ernest's will also gives me power to transfer those rights. I intend to do so by naming a Keeper of the Key to act as caretaker—curator, if you will—of the former laird's private sanctum. This room will henceforth be the Bard's Chamber. As I said, I have instituted legal steps to ensure that it remains as it is, outside the jurisdiction of either laird or chief . . . or spouse. The Keeper of the Key will have sole right of possession, transmission, and occupation of this room and all its contents. If he becomes unable to act in that capacity, or fails to pass it down, the title will devolve to the chief."

Sally gazed deeply across the desk into Brogan's eyes. When she spoke again, it was in a voice of authority.

"Brogan Tulloch," she said, "I am naming you Keeper of the Key to the Bard's Chamber."

87
THE KEY

In spite of the solemnity of the moment, Brogan's mind was spinning with practicalities.

"But, Sally," he said, "we will be leaving soon. I understand about preserving the room. And I appreciate the confidence you have in me. But shouldn't *you* keep the key so you can continue using the study? I will be in no position—"

"I can't risk it, Brogan," rejoined Sally. "What if my own time comes suddenly? I don't want to trust matters to happenstance if the key remained in the house. I must secure the intent of the document I have drawn up well beyond any possibility of mischief."

As Sally's resolute tone sank in, a deep solemnity settled upon her stepson once again.

"What few books and other things I would like to keep," Sally went on, "I will take to my new rooms. Beyond that, when you leave Whales Reef and lock this door behind you, your father's legacy as contained in this room will remain sealed until your return, or until you pass on the responsibility I am entrusting to you."

"But . . . shouldn't possession of the key and

the preservation of Dad's legacy rest with one who is actually here on the island?"

"Just the opposite. It will be more safely protected for posterity by one who is *not* here. Not even Priscilla, or another of like ambition, will dare break the door down to gain access. As much as she despises what this room stands for, she will be sufficiently cautious of gossip and tradition, not to mention the wrath of the gods, to prevent her bringing in workmen with axes and sledge-hammers. The key must remain safely out of reach.

"I am hale and hearty," Sally continued. "I hope to live many more years and entertain you for many more visits. I have to meet that grand-daughter of yours! Ernest was so thrilled when your letter came three years ago! However . . . one never knows the future. Therefore, I intend to conclude these arrangements while you are here, so that when you leave, everything this room represents will be protected and preserved."

Sally paused, stood, picked up the key from the desk, and walked out from behind it and took her place in front of her stepson.

"Rise, Brogan," she said.

Brogan did so.

Sally held out her two hands in which lay the key.

"Brogan Tulloch, son of Ernest Tulloch, Keeper of the Key to the Bard's Chamber, this key and the contents of this room are now yours."

Brogan bent forward and kissed Sally on both cheeks. "You do me a great honor," he said in a husky voice. "I pray I will be worthy of your trust."

"I have one additional bequest," she said after a moment. She took up two slender volumes from the desktop. "Your father wanted you to have these two books. His affection for the perspectives of certain Quaker writers was deep and lifelong. These two volumes were rooted in his own spiritual pilgrimage and were among his most prized possessions. Because of your own Quaker affiliations, he knew the two of you would value them as he did."

"Thank you, Sally," said Brogan. "We will treasure them."

He extended his arms around his stepmother and wife. The three stood silently in affectionate embrace, reflecting on the import of what had been established on this day. All three felt the presence in this room, as they had the day before in the cemetery, of a cloud of witnesses—historical, literary, and spiritual—that had gone before.

Most of all they were keenly aware of the man who had gathered the wisdom of so many other witnesses about him. This room had been his home. They would miss him. But his spirit would live on in their hearts.

88

The Legacy

The following afternoon, Sally Tulloch walked slowly about the private sitting room and adjoining bedroom and lounge that she and Ernest had shared throughout most of the first half of the century.

They had lived through both world wars and the Great Depression together. It was time to say good-bye to these rooms. The changing of the guard had come. Priscilla had given her three days to transfer her belongings to the south wing.

Sally moved to the sitting room's large window that looked out upon the eastern shoreline and northern quadrant of the island. In the distance, walking across the moor, their backs to her, she saw Ernest's three sons. They were close together, Brogan in the middle, eldest and tallest, his arms slung in filial camaraderie around the shoulders of his two brothers. The three were obviously engaged in deep conversation.

Sally smiled. A wave of peace swept through her. She closed her eyes and exhaled a contented sigh.

Ernest's sons were *together*. Whatever their differences of outlook, spiritual direction, and personality, whatever years and miles and even wives had separated them and may separate them again, the three Tulloch men loved, honored, and respected one another.

Ernest had done his job well.

His legacy would continue. The generations lived on. All three, each in their own way in the years to come, would send down their own roots into an ever-expanding family posterity.

Thus the proud heritage of their family name would spread in widening circles into the lives of sons and daughters, grandsons and grand-daughters, and all who came after them.

PART 8

JULY 2006

89

ARE NOT TWO SPARROWS SOLD FOR A FARTHING?

Whales Reef, Shetland Islands

The great room of the Cottage fell silent as Alexander Innis concluded his narrative.

"Thank you, Sandy," said Loni at length. "You have filled in so many pieces of the puzzle. I had no idea I had such a rich heritage."

"Lady Sally an' I visited many a time," said Sandy with a pensive tone. "An' through the years she told me a good many bits o' the story beyond what I saw an' heard wi' my own eyes an' ears."

"I have one more question," said Loni. "It seems I have already asked five hundred today—I hope you don't mind."

"Nae a bit o' it, lassie."

"You told me earlier about the farthing the laird gave you, and that at the funeral you whispered that you knew what it meant. What did it mean?"

Sandy smiled. "The laird kenned the day would come when I would read the passage aboot sparrows dyin' an' two bein' sold for a farthing. He knew I would realize what the Lord meant aboot the Father's care for His creatures, large

591

an' small. It was his way o' telling a wee laddie that his life was valued by God, that I had worth, jist like that puir birdie was precious tae me as a wee boy."

He took the farthing from his pocket and again handed it to Loni. "Did ye notice the engravin' on it?"

Loni held it close, then turned it over. "It's a sparrow!"

"Aye. 'Tis the symbol o' the Father's care for His creation."

Sandy rose slowly to his feet. The afternoon had grown late. They had been talking for hours. He ambled to the fire, knelt down, and added a fresh handful of peat chunks to the flames.

"That should keep it goin' through the gloamin'," he said. "I'll come by tomorrow in the afternoon an' show ye whaur the laird keeps his peats an' help ye bring a fresh supply into the peat box here by the hearth."

"That is very kind of you, Sandy," said Loni.

"Noo, lassie," he said, standing again, "ye'll be wantin' tae acquaint yersel' wi' this hoose an' the folk that hae come afore ye. I'm thinkin' by noo ye hae many things on yer mind ye need tae reflect on. 'Tis time I left ye on your own."

Loni walked with Sandy to the front door and bid him good-bye.

Again she was alone in the Cottage. Yet she no

longer felt alone. The heritage of the generations surrounded her.

She returned to the great room and sat a long while thinking about Sandy's recounting of the funeral fifty years before, and all the people who had been present. Already she had forgotten most of the names!

Her reverie was interrupted by the sound of an automobile engine on the gravel outside. She rose and went to open the front door. A white-clad young man was approaching the house from a delivery van. He was carrying an enormous bouquet of flowers—red, white, and blue, with three American flags protruding above them on slender flagpoles amid the flowers.

Loni burst out laughing at the sight. It was so thoroughly *American,* so completely incongruous to the entire mood of the place!

Was this someone's idea of a joke?

There appeared to be at least three dozen carnations and—oh no!—chrysanthemums! They were set in a tacky white vase whose shape was intended as a replica of the Statue of Liberty.

"Are ye Miss Ford?" said the man in thick Shetlandic.

"I am," replied Loni.

"American, by the look and sound o' it?"

"I'm afraid so," answered Loni. In light of the garish floral display, she felt oddly embarrassed to admit the fact.

"These are for yersel' then, mum." The young man handed her the bouquet. " 'Tis a letter for ye in the envelope. Good day tae ye, mum."

Loni lugged the vase inside and set it on the kitchen table. She sat down and opened the envelope. A typed, faxed letter was enclosed:

I hope you arrived safe and sound, she read. I also hope these flowers find you, along with this faxed note. I had to search high and low in Lerwick, wherever that is, to find a florist who would deliver them to your island. They had a special American bouquet for the 4th two weeks ago—I guess there are lots of Americans over there. They said they had plenty of the flags left, and I thought it would make you feel right at home—

A sudden sneeze interrupted her reading. Loni reached for a tissue, then continued.

I had no idea what directions to give them other than that you were at some "cottage" on Whales Reef. Great news— Congressman Finney's chief of staff will be on maternity leave from now through the end of the year. He wants me to fill in for her! It's temporary but an opportunity to take the next step up the ladder. That means I will be in the thick of his reelection campaign. Hurry back. Can't wait to tell you all about it!

Love, Hugh

Loni set the letter on the table with a smile. She appreciated the thought, but she had better put the flowers outside before a serious allergic reaction set in.

She filled the vase with water and carried it back out to the front of the house. There she set them to one side of the door. She would enjoy them, but outside.

Hugh's words reminded her that she had not yet finalized her plans to return to the States. One thing was certain—the idea of leaving the following morning was out of the question. She would call and postpone her return flight.

She still had not even been into the village. All she knew of it was through the window of Dickie Sinclair's taxi. She had much more to learn about her ancestry and this place her Tulloch relatives called home.

She would walk into town tomorrow.

90

THE KEY AND AN OLD JOURNAL

Beginning to grow sleepy, Loni went out for a walk to the shore. The sea air would wake her up and also clear out any remaining effect on her sinuses from the chrysanthemums.

When she returned to the house, she took out her journal and pen and began the overwhelming task of describing the memorable visit she had had with Sandy Innes.

She had scarcely begun recording the story of Ernest Tulloch's funeral when her thoughts were interrupted by a distant peal of laughter from inland across the moor. It was faint, coming from a great way off, yet was full of life. She knew it as the same laughter she had heard when the taxi drove past the hotel the previous afternoon.

As the melodic sound died away, Loni flipped to the back pages of her journal. A quizzical smile came to her lips as she scanned her Husband List. How could she have omitted something so obvious?

To the bottom of it she now added the single word *Laughter*. She looked at what she had written, then added: *Laughs easily and often, though not too much, and knows how to make others laugh.*

She turned back to the page she had left a moment earlier. Writing further about her conversation with Sandy, however, was too daunting. She had to let it settle a little more first.

It was at last time to explore the letter box she had brought from the desk in her grandfather's storeroom. She was ready to learn whatever secrets it had to reveal.

Laying pen and journal aside, she walked to the hearth. The box sat where she had placed it on the thick, white marble mantel above the fireplace.

She took it down and returned to what had already become her favorite chair in the house. Carefully she removed the tiny key from the chain around her neck.

For a second time she unlocked the box and slowly lifted back the lid.

There inside were the letters exactly as she remembered them.

She removed the entire stack. Beneath them lay the brown leather book she had glimpsed earlier. Older and with an ornate design embossed on the cover, it was remarkably similar to her own journal.

She lifted the book out of its resting place where it had lain for so many years. As she did, her eyes fell on an object that made her suddenly forget the letters and book altogether.

In the bottom of the box was a large, nearly

black, and partially rusted iron key some four or five inches long. It was the biggest key she had ever seen in her life. She reached in and took hold of it. The feel of the cold metal sent a tingle up her arm. Was this the key to the mystery room upstairs, the locked study of Ernest Tulloch?

There was only one way to find out!

Loni leapt to her feet, ran from the room, and, with the key clutched in her hand, bounded up the oak stairs two at a time. Reaching the landing, she slowed as she turned to approach the locked door.

What would she discover behind it?

If Macgregor Tulloch had killed his Norwegian wife and left the body inside, she might as well find out and get it over with.

With trembling hand, Loni inserted the key into the keyhole in the middle of an ornate brass faceplate. It slid in effortlessly.

She turned the key.

A metallic clank echoed through the house as the dead bolt slid back. A second revolution of the key released the latch.

With the key protruding from the door, Loni tried the handle. It gave way to the pressure of her hand.

The door swung open.

Heart pounding, Loni stepped tentatively inside. The sight before her took her breath away.

As she walked into the room, locked for so

long, sensations filled her much like being in her grandfather's workshop. She found herself surrounded by tradition, craftsmanship, and learning. One thing that had definitely not been hidden away in this room was a dead body!

Everywhere she looked were books. The room was filled with furniture whose styles she knew well—a sideboard, chairs, and a roll-top desk that appeared to be an exact duplicate of the one back in Pennsylvania—faded Persian rugs on the floor, tapestries, and paintings on the wall. And the rich aroma of antiquity.

She had stepped fifty years back in time, yet she also felt strangely as if at long last she had come home.

Twenty minutes later, Loni slowly descended the stairs and returned to the great room. Her spirit was calm. The quietness of the ages had stolen over her.

She sat down again. The letter box and brown leather book lay on the low table beside the chair. She took the book in hand and opened it. *The Journal of Emily Hanson* was printed inside the cover.

According to Sandy's tale, this was the journal of her great-grandmother!

Loni turned back the leaves to the first page. It was dated 1924.

I am so excited, she read in a compact and precise feminine hand. *I have just learned of an opportunity to travel as a lady's companion to the Shetland Islands in Scotland . . .*

Loni could hardly believe her eyes. This was an account of her great-grandmother's coming to Scotland eighty-two years before!

Trembling with the thrill of anticipation, Loni began to read. Within minutes she was completely engrossed in her great-grandmother's story.

She read late into the night.

91
Sleepless in Scotland

Aberdeen, Scotland

A groan of mingled frustration sounded in a dark hotel room. A great paw of a hand reached for the bedside light. Its owner rolled over.

The clock on the table read 2:18 a.m.

An expletive echoed off the walls. The Texan sat up, reached for the bottle on the nightstand, and poured the crystal glass beside it half full of single malt, then swallowed it in a single gulp.

"Whiskey'll cure anything that ails you . . . everything except jet lag!" he muttered.

Jimmy Joe McLeod flipped on the TV and did his best to sit up in bed with two undersized pillows stuffed behind him. He remote-controlled his way through the paltry offering of channels. He finally settled on world weather, which circled back around to the floods in Texas every six or eight minutes and thus held some moderate interest for him. But the sleep-inducing power of continuous weather reports was negligible. He could probably watch Japan's stock report, in full swing by now, but he was a confirmed Dow Jones man. The Nikkei held no interest for him.

After thirty minutes he gave up the attempt. He rose, taking bottle and glass with him, and walked across the room to where his briefcase sat open on the couch. He pulled from it the file on Whales Reef. This was not the file—compiled by his own people—that had first come to his attention five years ago, showing oil reserves, land ownership, proposed sites for a refinery, and all the details that made this particular island such a potential gold mine.

This new file had been faxed to the hotel yesterday. He sat down, poured himself a full glass of Scotland's fabled *aqua vitae*, the "water of life," and began perusing the sheaf of papers. He found a list of the ownership and tenancies of the entire island's property, along with a complete dossier on the four principal players in the protracted probate investigation that had recently been concluded.

> Macgregor Tulloch . . . grandson of Ernest Tulloch . . . prior to his death, owner of all island property except church and a house with acreage known as the Old House . . . deceased 2005.

He knew all about the old Tulloch coot. Blamed fool must have been living in the past century not to care about being rich! Hardly mattered now. Who could have known the old geezer was going to drop dead? If he'd known that, he'd have gone after the heirs a long time ago.

> David Tulloch . . . owner of Old House and its attachments and land . . . son of Angus Tulloch, fisherman, deceased . . . great-great-grandson of Ernest Tulloch through fourth child and third son, Leith . . . age thirty-five . . . initially assumed inheritor of island property and chieftainship of clan . . .

"Chief! What is that all about?" said Jimmy Joe to himself. And who was this old fellow Ernest, and why did everything trace back to him?

> Hardar Tulloch . . . leading fisherman of island . . . great-great-grandson of Ernest Tulloch through daughter, Delynn . . . age thirty-eight . . . claimant to Macgregor Tulloch's estate with legal proceedings pending contesting recent court findings and advancing his claim as rightful heir . . .

His people had apparently taken this Hardar fisher fellow under their wing and were engaged with their solicitors in validating his claim. If things went his way and probate was reversed, they would have him in their pocket.

Alonnah Emily "Tulloch" Ford . . . at present named by probate court as Macgregor Tulloch's heir . . . great-great-granddaughter of Ernest Tulloch through eldest son, Brogan . . . age thirty-two . . . executive assistant employed by Washington, D.C. firm Capital Investments . . . no known connection to Shetland Islands . . . unknown red herring in the mix only recently come to light . . . in all likelihood can be induced to sell . . .

Red herring was right!

How had she come into the picture at the eleventh hour when no one had known of her existence? If only they'd been able to get to the old codger before he kicked the bucket! Though who could tell? he mused—might turn out for the best. He'd never met a woman he couldn't sweet-talk out of the gold fillings in her teeth!

McLeod took a long, slow swallow of whiskey as his eyes continued to scan the sheet in his hand.

An uncommon name, Alonnah. Seemed he'd heard it before . . .

Nope, couldn't quite place it. Something was struggling to rise from his subconscious of a past he had all but forgotten.

That name . . . *Alonnah* . . . why did it strike a familiar chord in his memory?

Ah well, he thought, *probably nothing.*

92
ANOTHER VISITOR

Loni Ford awoke to her third day in the Shetlands with the peaceful sound of the sea once again in her ears.

She rolled over in bed with a contented sigh. She was enjoying herself far more than she had anticipated. Thoughts of the previous day slowly flooded her with pleasure: the visit with Sandy, his wonderful reminiscences of her great-great-grandfather's funeral, her opening the locked study and discovering the priceless treasures contained within, then ending the day reading her great-grandmother's journal until she could stay awake no longer.

She had already delayed her planned departure back to the States. Maybe tomorrow she would think about how long to stay. But not today.

Twenty minutes later, Loni descended the large oak stairway, her great-grandmother's journal in hand, and followed her new morning routine—building a fire, putting water on for coffee—she might even try the tea again—and setting out oatcakes, butter, and jam.

Soon she was enjoying what Sandy Innes would call a feast.

An hour later she was seated with her feet up in front of a wonderfully glowing fire of peat, again reading her great-grandmother's journal. On the low table beside her sat a large mug of tea, properly flavored with milk. She read for perhaps another hour when she was startled out of her reverie by musical chimes. No clock in the house made a sound like that. It must be the doorbell.

Loni rose and walked to the entryway. She opened the door. There stood a man she had never seen before, about her own age, perhaps a year or two older. He was even taller than her, with unruly curly brown hair falling over his ears and forehead.

"Good morning!" he said with a smile. "You are, I take it, Miss Ford?"

"Yes, that's right," said Loni, returning his smile. Her eyes flitted to the vase of carnations and chrysanthemums she had set outside next to the door.

"I noticed them too," said the man. "Quite a lavish bouquet, I must say . . . and very American." Then he added with a hearty laugh, "My trifling little offering certainly pales alongside *that!*"

It was the same infectious laugh Loni had heard on the island twice already.

Her visitor handed her a small sprig of purple heather tied with a tartan ribbon.

"I picked this for you," he said. "It seems a rather paltry gift now, but it is all I have to offer. I am David Tulloch. I came by to welcome you to Whales Reef."

ABOUT THE AUTHOR

Michael Phillips is a bestselling author of a number of beloved novels, including such well-known series as *Shenandoah Sisters*, *Carolina Cousins*, *Caledonia*, and *The Journals of Corrie Belle Hollister*. He has also served as editor of many more titles, adapting the classic works of Victorian author George MacDonald (1824–1905) for today's reader, and his efforts have since generated a renewed interest in MacDonald. Phillips's love of MacDonald's Scotland has continued throughout his writing life.

In addition to his fifty published editions of MacDonald's work, Phillips has authored and coauthored over ninety books of fiction and nonfiction, ranging from historical novels to contemporary whodunits, from fantasy to biblical commentary.

Michael and his wife, Judy, spend time each year in Scotland but make their home in California. To learn more about the author and his books, visit fatheroftheinklings.com. He can be found on Facebook at facebook.com/michael phillipschristianauthor/. To contact the Phillipses or join their email family, please write to: macdonaldphillips@sbcglobal.net.

Center Point Large Print
600 Brooks Road / PO Box 1
Thorndike, ME 04986-0001 USA

(207) 568-3717

US & Canada:
1 800 929-9108
www.centerpointlargeprint.com